The AGAPE
It (AH-gah-peh)
Journey

Eleanor Tremayne

Scotoma Books Publishing

Copyright © 2021 Eleanor Tremayne

All rights reserved. No part of this book may be reproduced or transmitted in any form or by any means, electronic or mechanical, including photocopying, recording, or by any information storage and retrieval system without permission in writing from the publisher.

Scotoma Books Publishing—Hamilton, OH
ISBN: 978-1-7323245-4-1
Title: *The Agape*
Author: Eleanor Tremayne
Digital distribution | 2021
Paperback | 2021

This is a work of fiction. The characters, names, incidents, places, and dialogue are products of the author's imagination and are not construed as accurate.

Dedication

My personal *Agape Journey* was inspired several years ago when I met Lowell Michelson, Pastor at Lord of Life Lutheran Church in West Chester, Ohio.

Several years later, when we were fortunate to move to St. Augustine, Florida, Pastor Richard Dow of Memorial Lutheran Church of the Martyrs added the final touches needed to complete this novel.

My sincere gratitude and thanks to Pastor Lowell and Pastor Dow for encouraging my imagination, providing spiritual guidance, and the Biblical research needed to complete my vision of *The Agape Journey.*

Acknowledgments

The Agape Journey would never have been completed without the assistance of two very dedicated ladies that spent hours editing my manuscript.

First, my sincere thanks to Dr. Mary Sisney, a retired English Professor from California State Polytechnic University, Pomona, my graduate advisor and the author of *A Redlight Woman Who Knows How to Sing the Blues*. Working with Dr. Sisney was indeed a joy.

My second editor is a remarkable woman that I became friends with at *Lord of Life Lutheran Church* several years ago when we studied together at the Stephen Ministries. Without the many hours Cynthia Wilson Campbell spent editing grammar and offering creative suggestions, this novel would still be a work in progress. I am so fortunate that our paths crossed, leading you, Cyndi, to my *Agape Journey*.

Chapter One

Imagination is the actual magic carpet.
                                    Norman Vincent Peale

Cairo, Egypt
July 1992

Nobody in their right mind travels to Cairo, Egypt, in July. But then again, there has never been anything normal in my life. By the time I was thirteen years old, my passport had more stamps than an international pilot's passport, and it was my third one.

Although most of the time I was nothing more than a footnote in my mother's life, she did insist on taking me with her on many of her exotic travels. Cairo was only one of these. Dubai, Reykjavik, Seljalandsfoss, and Bagan are a few other places that most people have not even heard of. Well, maybe Dubai.

But, it was my visit to Cairo that began this entire obsession with the *Agape*. One afternoon my mother was exploring the Al-Azhar Mosque with her Egyptian guide Cheops. He was, of course, named after a pharaoh; quite a common practice among Egyptians. I decided that this was the perfect time to begin my adventure wandering around the Cairo Marriott Hotel. At one time, this building was initially constructed as a royal palace. Probably the reason why there are so many fascinating rooms around the lobby. But my immediate attention was on the Omar Khayyam Casino. Perhaps it was the exotic name that piqued my interest, or maybe the very fact that it was forbidden for children to enter the casino, that made me determined to somehow find my way past the security guards. They were permanently stationed outside the two front French doors leading anxious visitors into the "den of iniquity." It was explicitly those elaborate crystal panels creating a chasm of rainbow colors that beckoned me to enter each time I passed by.

Although these officers, who looked more like military guards than security guards, were always busy verifying passports, I was still pretty sure that it would be impossible to slip past them or even the well-dressed guests crowding the entrance.

It was fascinating to watch the many pretentious women wearing chinchilla stoles, mink capes, diamond tiaras, eager to begin their evening charades. Even from a distance, I could recognize the Channel aroma. It was the same scent my mother always wore.

Then, of course, there were the gentlemen dressed in black tuxedos. Some were even wearing head turbans. Anxiously they were looking at their gold Rolex watches, eager to make their bets at the gaming tables and other games of chance that were beckoning them from afar.

Nevertheless, even with all of this excitement and confusion, I just instinctively sensed that once I tried to move past the front desk, someone would immediately apprehend me. Just the thought of hearing my mother's rage was a detriment enough to stop me from being careless. Managing my way inside would have to be through another portal.

Suddenly, from nowhere, I noticed there was a door just a few feet away marked **NO ENTRANCE.**

Could it be this easy? Could I walk through that door as Alice does through the Looking Glass into another world? What do I have to lose? If I am caught there, I can easily explain how I was lost simply trying to get back to the lobby.

Very calmly, I reached for the doorknob, turned it, genuinely expecting it to be locked, when to my pleasant surprise, it opened. Within seconds I was in the casino behind some heavy black velvet curtains. They reminded me of those seen in a Broadway theatre. The slight opening allowed me to look through to the other side. What I witnessed was a room filled with sparkling chandeliers hanging majestically throughout a predominantly dim-lit arena.

It was when my eyes started to adjust to this darkness that I recognized some of the ladies, and gentleman that was in front of me in the casino lobby earlier. They were now at tables with cards, roulette wheels, drinking, laughing, and smoking.

Nobody seemed even to notice me now. That is until I felt my shoulder being yanked. When I turned around, it appeared to be some odd boy about my size. Before I could object, he was leading me into a dark cave that appeared from nowhere.

"And who may I ask are you? How did you get here, and why?"

I heard this mysterious voice ask, but I wasn't sure how to answer.

When he lit a candle on what appeared to be an altar, I realized that this person was not a boy at all. He was a little person with very wrinkled eyes and a small twisted mouth. But, It was his white Nero jacket that caught my attention. I recalled my mother had one of these jackets when they were a fashion statement during the 1970s. They were modeled after the Indian Achkan or Sherwani style with a mandarin collar. It was worn by Jawaharlal Nehru, the Prime Minister of India. Later both the Beatles and The Monkees wore these jackets. I saw them on several of my mom's old LP albums.

After a few more minutes of uncomfortable silence, I decided to answer the dwarf's questions. After all, he actually might be able to provide me with some answers about this Omar Khayyam.

"My name is Imani Lewis. I am an American citizen visiting Egypt with my mother, researching tourist locations for a very prominent international travel organization. You may want to consider being more hospitable if you ever expect people from other countries to visit Cairo," I said,

sounding quite convincing, if I might say so myself.

"What type of name is Imani? It certainly doesn't sound American to me. And, why are you in this casino? Surely you must realize that children are not permitted in any gambling venue."

The little person sounded quite annoyed at this conversation.

"Well, if you really must know, my name is Arabic. Of course, you already know this. It means faith or belief. I suppose my mother hoped that by giving me such an inspiring name, my personality would evolve likewise. I don't think that has happened yet. It may never happen. And, I am not a child. I am thirteen years old. A few days ago, in Athens, I menstruated for the first time. That makes me a woman. In some African tribes, I would be ready for marriage. But, thankfully, that isn't an option. I never plan to marry. Marriage and especially children make life just too complicated. Anyway, I am here because I want to know who Omar Khayyam is and why this casino is named after him," I said, finding a lounge settee with inviting cushions in the corner.

The dwarf listened carefully but never responded. That made me somewhat nervous. I wasn't sure what might happen next. If he couldn't help me with some answers, the least he could do was let me leave without causing an incident.

After what seemed like a long pause, the little person handed me a small bronze vessel with a warm beverage inside. I was not sure if I dared taste it, but when I did, the flavor was quite refreshing. Not what I expected at all. It was pomegranate, rosemary, and cinnamon blended with a hint of chocolate. When I finished, I felt pretty relaxed, even sleepy. Without any encouragement, I stretched out on the sofa with my head on the satin pillow. Soon everything just disappeared.

When I finally woke, I was back in my hotel room, sleeping quite naturally on my bed.

Was I drugged? Did I enter the forbidden casino? How could there be a cave inside a luxurious casino where a little person lives? Too many questions with no answers.

The following day when I awoke, my mother was already having tea on the veranda, watching the lively scene of street peddlers on the Nile River.

"Good morning, munchkin. Whatever you found to do yesterday must have been exhausting. I was back by 6:00 pm, and you were already in bed for the night," my mom said.

I wasn't going to share with her what happened. I wasn't sure myself what was going on. When I returned to my room, I found on my nightstand *The Rubaiyat of Omar Khayyam*. When I opened it to the first page, there was a note:

To Imani Lewis on her journey to finding The Agape.
 Omar Khayyam

It was many years later, after my mother passed away, that I seriously read *The Rubaiyat*. By that time, I knew that Omar Khayyam was a philosopher, mathematician, astronomer, and poet who lived in Persia (now known as Iran) from 1048 to 1131. His family was well known for tent making and perhaps even carpets. But, it was his poetry and philosophy that intrigued me the most.

I never learned who it was that gave me *The Rubaiyat,* that time in Cairo. If there was a little person, I never saw him again during my stay at the Marriott. The signature in my book was a mystery. Where it came from, also a mystery. But, it was the reference to *Agape* that perplexed me the most. I had no idea what that inscription meant until years later when I read a concise article about *The Agape Carpet.*

According to the writer, there is a carpet or tapestry that has passed through the centuries. Numerous historical events are significantly attributed directly to a carpet known as *The Agape.* Once the events have been adjusted accordingly, the carpet disappears again only to appear unexpectedly somewhere else without any forewarning.

Apparently, for the past hundred years, there have been writers, historians, scientists, and scholars throughout the world who follow the *Agape* trail just waiting for it to return. Unfortunately, no one has admitted to ever seeing this carpet in our lifetime.

What is even more intriguing to me than the actual *Agape Carpet* is the mystery surrounding it. Indeed, whoever discovers *The Agape* will make a fortune. With all of this ambiguity, it does make me reflect on how close I may have been once to some of those answers years ago at that Marriott Cairo Hotel.

Was it merely an odd consequence, or perhaps fate, that I have now been provided the opportunity to write an article about the King Tut Exhibition? Since this is a historical event involving a world tour with ancient relics, I am immediately interested. My last visit to Cairo was twenty-five years ago.

Although I am going on a writing assignment, I insisted that the travel coordinator book my stay at the Cairo Marriott. This time I will visit the casino and maybe even reconnect with that odd dwarf.

"Are you certain that you want me to book the Marriott, Imani? The Westin Cairo is considered phenomenal. It is where all the executives stay. Much more modern, and it is authorized, so I can use it if you want it?" Priscilla asked.

"I am sure that the Westin is far superior to the Marriott, but I have personal reasons why I want to stay at the Marriott. Besides, corporate should be thrilled that they are saving money," I said, without wanting to explain any further information.

"Alright. It's your call. But, can I assume that the First Class or Business Airline tickets are acceptable?" Pricilla asked.

"Absolutely! I intend to be as comfortable as possible traveling internationally. I haven't lost my mind completely," I said.

Priscilla was laughing on the other end of the phone.

This assignment would require that I remain in Cairo for one week. However, if I needed to stay longer, I knew that my editor would extend my stay. First, I planned on researching all that is known about the *Agape* before leaving for Egypt. Which I soon learned was not much. There was very little reliable information specifically addressing any *Agape Carpet*. What was becoming apparent is that much of the information that I found was not supported by any traditional documented research. There have, however, been stories handed down by past generations. Folklore, perhaps? Maybe. But, the fact that so many of these stories are the same around the world supports the theory that *Agape* is much more than an urban legend.

First, I discovered that shepherds many centuries ago were the first people attributed to rug making. At that time, it was a practical necessity to prepare people for the harsh elements of weather. Some have traced the origins of rugs to the Far East, while others claim that it was the Siberian weavers who first created these carpets. There did, however, come a time when the purpose of rugs changed from a craft to a statement of fine art.

Artisans began to use their ingenuity to create unique designs, explore various dyeing techniques and offer patterns with diverse symbolic imagery. This established an entirely new clientele who began seeking these new rugs as works of art.

The trade routes from China began to initiate personal prayer rugs for the Islam community. When the spread of this religion continued into Spain and Eastern Europe, so also did the necessity of rug making.

Eventually, the Oriental rug became a luxury statement in palaces and formal residential living areas. But now, these carpets were not for keeping walls and floors warm; they were to illustrate a family history, a great accomplishment, or even to request a gift from the gods.

Carpet makers were commissioned for many special events, and their rugs demonstrated an artistic masterpiece weaved forever on a wool canvas. Each was unique, with various symbols telling their own stories.

Carpet makers weave the dreams that change the lives of those who buy their art. These dreams are shared with others. Some choose to ignore the power of those dreams; others introduce their own imagination preserved in the threads of the carpet.

The *Agape Carpet* originated in Siberia during the same time as *The Pazyryk Carpet,* although they were not found in the exact location. In 1949 *The Pazyryk* was discovered in the grave of a Scythian nobleman in the Bolshoy Ulagan, a dry valley in Kazakhstan, and is now hanging in the Hermitage Museum at Saint Petersburg, Russia.

Although the ice preserved *The Pazyryk*, it did not possess the same powers as *The Agape*, which traveled sixteen centuries to continents that *The Pazyryk* never even knew existed.

The Agape also has a definite purpose. To fully understand what that purpose is, there must be a clear understanding of what *Agape* represents. This is not easy since *Agape* has been interpreted differently by many scholars. Nevertheless, everyone does agree that the word, *Agape,* originated from Greek philosophy in the 6th century BC.

It was a time in Greece when many people were struggling to survive invasions that continued through the Hellenistic Period. Philosophy arose from this need to make sense out of a very troubling world. Out of this desire to discover peace came various explanations for love. *Agape* is defined as pure love. An emotion that accentuates an unselfish love.

Agape has also been used to define love feasts or a communal meal. In every sense, *Agape* is now accepted in Christianity to express the unconditional love of God for his children.

Knowing all of this makes the *Agape* journey to its current resting place crucial. Like all journeys, the stories that accompany the travel are as thrilling as the destination.

Ardabil is a town northwest of Iran. When Shaykh, an ancestor of the Safavid Dynasty (1501-1722), passed away, the court commissioned Dana Bashir, the most prominent rug maker in the village, to prepare a holy carpet in his burial shrine. This may be the same *Agape* carpet that contains the threads of hair from Jesus and his Apostles. However, when archeologists discovered the shrine, there was no carpet inside. Instead, there was a handwritten blueprint of what the rug may have looked like. Those images are similar to other descriptions of the *Agape*.

I hope to consult with some of the leading authorities that I will meet here in Cairo. They might be able to move me closer to understanding what those symbols on the *Agape* have in common with the other carpets. Even more so, will these clues lead me to where *The Agape* will appear next?

Chapter Two

I found a door with no key; there was the Veil through which I might not see.
Omar Khayyam
The Rubaiyat of Omar Khayyam

Imani Lewis
Cairo, Egypt 2017

The Nile River is a captivating image to view at any time of the day. It is possible to stay fixated, watching for hours the variety of people from many walks of life. They are all drawn to wherever the water flows. Some with a specific purpose, many others with no agenda appearing randomly. I watch all of this from the balcony of my hotel room vicariously at any time of the day. I imagine that each of them has a story. All more entertaining than mine. For who could not. They all live in this historical time capsule surrounded by the archives of antiquity.

The father of all African Rivers, the Nile, is also noted as the longest river in the world. Unfortunately, I am not being paid to enjoy these sights. My appointment at The Grand Egyptian Museum with the lead curator of The King Tut artifacts is scheduled for early tomorrow morning. I plan on spending several days examining the artifacts, interviewing the curators, and capturing some rare photos of this most extraordinary traveling exhibit. Once this has been accomplished, there will be a few extra days to proceed with my research on the *Agape*.

After resting from my long intercontinental travel and time change last night, I finally headed downstairs to The Omar Khayyam Casino. The same one that fascinated me so many years ago. It was not at all how I imagined it would be. First, there was no line waiting to enter. Nor were there any men or women dressed in elegant attire. The black, floor-length, strapless evening gown that I purchased from Calvin Klein, especially for this event, was the most impressive garment anywhere in this casino. Most women wore comfortable slacks with maybe satin blouses or even a traditional loose kaftan. Men wore polo shirts. Some were accented with a sports jacket over a pair of designer jeans.

There was still a security guard checking passports since Egyptian citizens are not allowed to gamble. I thought this quite ironic. They are encouraged to work here, gladly taking money from others, but are forbidden to risk their own hard-earned money.

Once I was inside, there were still many people at the various gaming tables, slot machines, and cocktail bars. What I was not able to recognize was anything that appeared like a room leading to a cave. Perhaps I could ask one of the card dealers who is not busy. There are always those few dealers who are just waiting patiently for someone to sit at their table.

I walk the entire perimeter of the casino, getting a feel for this setting. This is when it occurs to me how similar a casino is to a carnival. Just as the familiar amusement booths lure people into taking a chance at winning a giant stuffed animal or perhaps a fish swimming in a glass bowl, the dealers tempt their customers for a chance to fulfill their dream. The only missing link is the carnival cronies. Those who entice you with their promises that "everyone is a winner." Here, instead, the pit boss offers anyone who takes a seat complimentary cocktails. That is, of course, only while they are playing their choice of various card games.

After I circle the gaming arena twice, I finally strategically select an empty blackjack table. It is located in the corner. The dealer smiles. He is relieved that, at last, he has a "victim." The name on his badge is Abanoub. Most likely not his God-given name.

"Good evening, and welcome to the Omar Casino," Abanoub says pleasantly but rehearsed.

"Thank you," I reply, watching him shuffle the eight packs of cards expertly.

"That doesn't look easy, Abanoub. You must have been doing this for a very long time. You aren't going to take all my money quickly, are you? If so, I will have to leave, and then you will be by yourself once again," I said, hoping to start a conversation.

"Unfortunately, my lovely lady, I am not in control of who wins or who loses at my table. It is up to the gods of fate that determine that," Abanoub says, moving the cards toward me to cut.

I know enough Arabic to recognize that Abanoub means father or king of gold. So, when I point this out to him, he is somewhat surprised.

"Are you Arabic?" Abanoub asked," almost whispering so that nobody can hear him.

"I may have some Arabic blood flowing through these veins but not enough for you to worry about. I am an American citizen," I answer, cutting the cards directly in the middle, keeping my eyes on Abanoub the entire time.

"I am curious if you know of any secret passages into this casino? I understand that it was once a castle," I ask, feeling quite confident while holding in my hand a queen of heart and a queen of diamonds.

Abanoub turns over a king of spades and a six of hearts, requiring him to take another card. As I expected, it is a ten of clubs. I win my twenty-five-dollar bet.

Neither of us shows any emotion. But, when Abanoub finishes dealing the next hand before continuing, he motions the cocktail waitress to come to the table.

"There are many secret passages known only by a few people who work in this hotel. Some are used as places of refuge in the event of hostile attacks. But how would an American tourist know anything about this?" Abanoub asks, surprised.

I ignore his question, instead I turn toward the cocktail waitress

"I would like a Perrier with a fresh lime, please," I say, handing her a chip equivalent to a five-dollar bill.

Turning my attention back to the table, I double my bet to fifty and wait for Abanoub to deal my two cards before responding to his question. This time I have a BlackJack. One Ace of Hearts, with a Jack of Clubs. Just as I predicted. But, before I turn it over,

I say,"I am an American journalist, not a tourist. Perhaps that makes a difference?"

When I turn over my cards, I can tell by the look in Abanoub's eyes that he is not happy about losing two hands in a row to an intelligent, smart mouth American.

Nevertheless, he pays me my winnings without saying a word. I am about to get up from the table when another man sits down across from me. This requires Abanoub to shuffle the cards once again.

"Forgive me for listening to your conversation, but I am a curator at the National Museum, and I might be able to answer your question about the secret caves. Let me introduce myself. I am Alexander Drakos. And, you must be, Imani Lewis, from the United States."

I was immediately taken back that this stranger knew who I was, but at the moment, I was more interested in the hand Abanoub was dealing me than in answering Mr. Drakos.

Blackjack was more than a card game to me. It was a competition that I did not enjoy losing. And, most of the time, I did not. But, this time, the dealer was showing a King of clubs, and I only had a sixteen. The odds say that regardless of what I do, my chances of winning are not good.

Nevertheless, I ask for another card. It is a three of hearts. Not bad, but probably not good enough.

Mr. Drakos also takes a card and loses his hand. When Abanoub turns his card over, he shows a total of seventeen. I am relieved to have won again. So, when Alexander Drakos offers to buy me a drink at the bar, I collect my winnings and leave the table quite satisfied.

"Are you a professional card player," Alexander asks once we are far enough away from the table that no one can hear him.

"Oh, no, of course not. But I do enjoy playing. Only if I win, I must admit I am a bad loser," I said, taking a seat at the cocktail lounge bar.

"And, you Alexander, what attracts you to the gaming world? It is my understanding that Egyptian citizens are not allowed to gamble in the casino?" I ask, pursuing the exotic cocktail menu.

"Oh, I am not an Egyptian citizen. My native land in Athens, Greece. Like you, I am here to learn more about the Tut artifacts that will be touring worldwide."

"Are you a reporter?" I ask inquisitively.

"Oh, no... I am an anthropologist on assignment to determine if we can benefit from any of the work already completed by our Egyptian allies," Alexander says.

Although it never occurred to me that Egypt and Greece are allied, it didn't seem necessary to bring that up. What I did want to hear is what Alexander might know about these mysterious caves located in this casino.

When the waitress takes our beverage order, I choose to be safe and have another Perrier. It is now that I have decided to bring up my initial question about secret passages.

"You mentioned at the Blackjack table that you know something about the secluded caves inside the castle?"

"Yes, being an anthropologist and visiting Cairo, as well as many other ancient cities, I have heard about some passages hidden throughout this structure. What I have learned is that previous to the reconstruction, there were a few transient holy men that found places inside the castle where they were safe from any outside threats. These were used primarily to keep them hidden from any potential enemies," Alexander said, handing his credit card to the waitress. She soon returned to the table with our drinks.

"But, who exactly were these holy men, and why were they hiding?" I asked directly.

"Nobody knows who they are or were. There is always some religious uprasing here, and religious persecution is part of the historical fiber of this country," Alexander added.

Sharing too much more with this stranger made me slightly nervous. I might need to interview Mr. Drakos shortly. My childhood story with the little person who lived in the casino cave was more information than I wanted to reveal. But perhaps Alexander could give me some general insight. I am anxious to know that what happened years ago was not just the imagination of a very creative child.

"Has anyone else collaborated this story about these mysterious caves? Or is it what we in America call an Urban legend?" I asked, sipping on my drink.

"Well, if you mean has there been any photographs, or any other official documentation, unfortunately, no. I have a colleague, who years ago, was allowed to explore the underground mazes of this castle. He claims that the caves still exist. Although he was not allowed to take any photographs, he did sketch some extraordinary drawings of altars surrounded by plush sofas. It appeared like something one might find in a secret rendezvous dwelling," Alexander said.

"That is quite fascinating. I wonder what all this mystery is about. I mean, someone must be aware of what is happening here. This hotel is considered one of the most impressive hotels in Cairo," I said, offering more bait.

"Exactly why nobody wants any publicity. As long as there has been no real collaboration to prove any of these '*Urban Legends*', then everything remains safe," Alexander said, obviously knowing nothing more.

I wanted to add that I was a witness to this mystery. Not only did I see firsthand some hobbit-like little person, but he also drugged me and somehow carried me to my hotel room when I was only thirteen years old. But, I knew better than to open that basket of cobras.

Since my meeting at the Cairo Museum is tomorrow at 9:00 am it I have decided to end my evening early.

Alexander Drakos at least verified for me that there were caves in this building. I now know that I am not the only person to have seen one. Whatever, or whoever, was living in this underground citadel when I visited as a child felt the need to share with me part of their secret. Somehow that also included the *Agape*. If not, why leave me the *Rubaiyat of Omar Khayyam* with a personalized note?

After a very restless evening awakening several times, it was the ringing of my phone that alerted me to rise and shine. All I wanted to do this morning was hide and sleep. With or without my consent, the day was officially starting.

A basket of fresh croissants, sweet rolls, orange juice, as well as a large pot of coffee was delivered to my room promptly by room service. For some reason, my head felt like I had been drinking all night. Hangovers from Perrier is the worst, I thought, laughing.

Thankfully, the coffee made everything right once again. Within an hour, I was downstairs in the lobby waiting for my private car to take me to the original Egyptian museum in Tahir Square. Once everyone arrives, we will be taken to the Grand Egyptian Museum. Although the museum is still not open to the worldwide public, reporters are invited to be the first ones to experience all the new additions.

Cairo traffic can only be compared to downtown New York. It is always busy, night and day. But, the most frightening experience is when these drivers merge in and out of traffic like threading a needle. I am always thankful when I arrive at my destination alive.

Today I am greeted by what appears to be at least fifty museum ambassadors, as well as a crowd of news reporters with their photographers. Since I am a freelance journalist, the magazine I represent always sends its photographers independently to the assigned location. Although typically we meet before our first shoot, I was notified yesterday that there was a connection problem with my photographer's flight resulting in a serious delay. This means that I will need to do all of the preliminary footwork creating a backtrack map for him whenever he does arrive. Fortunately, this problem does not happen often, but when it does, it creates extra work for everyone.

"Welcome to Cairo! My name is Alberto Mohammad. I have been assigned to assist you with photography until your assistant arrives," the young gentleman politely said.

"That is a very kind gesture; but, how old are you? Are you even out of prep school?" I asked, confused.

"No worries, Ma'am, I am much older than I look. And, my equipment is all first-class," he assured me, proudly showing off his camera and VIP Badge.

"You do seem to be legitimate and. It will save me hours of additional work. Do you have any idea where we are going to start on this adventure?" I asked.

The chaos surrounding us at this moment reminded me more of a marketplace downtown where everyone tries to push their wares in front of the tourist crowds rather than a press conference.. These reporters were all fighting each other for a prime location.

"Well, if you trust me, I suggest that we bypass all of the introductions here and go directly to the Grand New Egyptian Museum. We will be able to get unobstructed photos, and you won't have to wait in line to talk to the curators," Alberto suggested leading the way.

"I like how you operate, Alberto, but are you certain that we will be able to get into the ground floor museum. It isn't even completed yet," I said, hesitant.

"No worries. I have friends that work there. We will be inside before this crowd is even finished with their formalities. Trust me!"

"Okay then, let's make this happen. By the way, my name is Imani Lewis," I said, extending my hand.

"I know. I volunteered to be your guide when I learned about the delay and that you needed a photographer. My grandfather knew your mother many years ago," Alberto said, rushing me out of the reception room before I could ask him any further questions.

Chapter Three

The moving finger writes and having written moves on. Nor all thy piety, nor all thy wit, can cancel half a line of it.

Omar Khayyam

Imani Lewis
Summer 1999

MY mother died on July 18, 1995, during a hiking expedition to Mt. Kilimanjaro with her latest lover. Knowing her fear of heights, the decision to go there was one I never understood completely. Perhaps it was precisely that fear of heights that tempted her to prove that she could accomplish anything, regardless of her anxiety.

And, like everything else that Sarah attempted, it was a well-organized plan. Maybe that is why when my grandmother told me the news, I was more shocked than saddened.

One year before the fateful journey, my mother and Laura, her latest love interest, decided to dedicate themselves to a rigorous training regimen. They were told by many friends, all of whom had accomplished this trek, that the climb was not only a physical endurance test but also a mental challenge.

Laura was the one who convinced my mother to stretch herself beyond her limitations. I recall one afternoon before the training started that my mother seemed to be tentative, even reluctant.

"You must have complete confidence in yourself, Sarah. How will you ever know what you can accomplish if you don't look beyond what your fears are," Laura said confidently.

"I truly admire your grit Laura, but I am not sure if I have the same dedication as you do. Besides, I also have to consider Imani. She is my responsibility, and if anything should happen…well, you know what I mean," my mother said, trying to justify why she was now thinking about changing her mind.

Listening from the nearby kitchen, I found that statement quite astounding, coming from a woman who only wanted kittens and never accepted the responsibility to care for them once they matured. Once they began to grow, she abandoned all of them. Sarah knew nothing about nurturing kittens or children.

"Imani is fifteen years old, Sarah. Soon she will be moving on with her own life. What you do with your life from this point on should not be determined by your daughter," Laura said convincingly.

I wanted to object at this point. I wanted to remind Sarah and Laura, for that matter, that a mother-daughter relationship is not determined by age, or at least it should not be. And, ours was much more complicated than what Laura was suggesting.

Since my mother's job required that she travel most of the time, I lived with my grandparents in Noetzie, South Africa. However, there were also stretches of months when my mother and I spent time alone together in a small but quite comfortable loft in TriBeCa, New York.

During those months, we would visit art galleries, music concerts in Central Park, eat sushi at Hirohisa in Soho, buy tickets to Broadway shows sporadically, and drink frozen hot chocolate at Serendipity. This was, of course, before Laura moved in permanently. Then it wasn't quite as comfortable. I found myself traveling alone to South Africa more often.

Before Laura, my mother and I were pretty content. We seemed to understand both of our places. I was pretty obedient, as long as the rules were equitable, and mom enjoyed sharing with me all of her adventures. She also would take me as often as possible around the world with her.

Sometimes I thought that Sarah's occasional resentment toward me was somehow related to my absent father, Bran Hughes. For years I was convinced that this was because I reminded her of Bran. But, later, I realized that however Sarah felt about me, it was genuinely sincere.

I was really just a hiccup in her perfect life. Before me, Sarah lived life as a free spirit. This commitment to nobody allowed her to make choices that only affected her. That all changed when she met my Dad.

Bran Hughes was an airline pilot for the British Royal Air force when Sarah met him. She was on an assignment at St. Davids, a city in Wales. It is the resting place of the patron Saint David. Although it is the smallest city in the United Kingdom in population and urban area, Sarah decided to add it to her travel itinerary. The sightseeing company she represented was promoting castle trips to less recognized historic sites. That small-town fit the criterion.

Sarah, with her camera crew, began traveling throughout Great Britain, locating many exciting castles. The team started at Hermitage Castle in Scotland. It is a valley well known for much bloodshed during the Middle Ages.

What made this site particularly interesting is that it was also the dramatic scene of a perilous journey by Mary Queen of Scots. When the Queen heard that her trusted nobleman James Hepburn, the fourth Earl of Bothwell, was wounded by some cattle thieves, she decided to ride across the twenty-five-mile rugged terrain to find Hepburn.

Many thought that this was a secret lovers' tryst since a year later, he became her third husband. Regardless of the truth, this would make an exciting caption to promote a romantic castle trip.

Next was the lovely Fa'side Castle in East Lothian, Scotland. It was a historical fortification during the Anglo-Saxon conflicts that has now been converted to bed and breakfast. Perhaps a fascinating addition that many people would not know is that in 1616, Robert Fawside, the twenty-year-old heir to this dynasty, was murdered by his servant, Robert Robertson. Robertson was later beheaded on Castlehill at Edinburgh for the crime.

Sarah always selected locations that included more than just well-known historical facts. That is what made her an essential asset to the firms she represented. For me, it was always fascinating to be in the locations that my mother wrote about.

Next on my mother's itinerary was a short visit to Ballynahinch Castle, located in Connemara, County Galway, Ireland. It was built in 1546 by Donal O'Flaherty, husband of Grace O' Malley (Grainneuaile). Once Donal died, Grace became the head of the clan. Her life as a Pirate Queen is steeped in legendary history.

Grace O'Malley was much more than a nobleman's wife; she was a fearsome leader of her clan. She spent her life dedicated to fighting the opposition to keep King Henry the VIII's armies from invading her homeland of Ireland. Despite being told that the battlefield is no place for a woman, Grace led her followers.

Ambitiously independent, Grace refused to allow her life to be airbrushed through history. She was often referred to as Grainne Mhaol, meaning bald or having cropped hair. This name was given to Grace after her long hair would catch in the ship's ropes, resulting in her father refusing to take her on trading expositions. When her father understood that she had shaved her head to avoid this problem, he was embarrassed at his attitude toward her. Once again, Grace was allowed to join him on his voyages.

In 1593, when Grace met Queen Elizabeth at Greenwich Palace, she refused to bow, asserting that she was not the Queen's subject.

But, one of my favorite stories about Grace, who soon became one of my favorite heroines, is the one when she attempted to visit Howth Castle and was told that the family was at dinner and that all the gates were closed forbidding her to enter.

Grace would not accept such an insult and retaliated by kidnapping Christopher St. Lawrence, the Earl's grandson, and heir. Her terms included a demand that the gates always remain open to unexpected visitors and an extra plate be set at the table every evening.

Not only were those terms met, but a ring was also given to Grace by Earl Howth as a pledge to the agreement. That ring remains in possession of an O'Malley descendent to this day, as does the original arrangement remains at Howth Castle. Furthermore, In addition, there is also a street in Howth named after Grace O'Malley.

The land where Ballynahinch Castle was built in the early fourteenth century is now a splendid luxurious hotel. It was during my mother's stay there that a Welch photographer traveling with her suggested visiting St. David's.

All of this information was never revealed to me until after my mother's passing by someone claiming to be a "close" friend who attended her *Celebration of Life* ceremony. My grandparents hosted this event in New York.

Since I never recalled my mother having any close friends, this story did not sound credible. Nevertheless, my grandmother did reconfirm much of this information, which is why I eventually accepted that some of it must have been accurate.

When I started to research St. Davids, I learned that it is a cathedral city located on the River Alun. Although the actual resting place is known as Pembrokeshire, it is St. Davids that everyone refers to when citing where the Patron Saint was born. To understand why the people of Wales so revere this tiny village, one must know why David is a Saint.

Personally, it was essential to understand why my mother chose this particular place with a stranger to conceive a child. Then I learned something quite fascinating. St. David was born on a cliff on the southwest coast of Wales during a ravaging storm. Both his parents were royalty. His father was the Prince of Powys, and his mother, Non, was the daughter of a Menevia Chieftain. Many also believe that David was King Arthur's nephew. More so, Saint Patrick, of Ireland, was also born at St. Davids.

I suppose my mother must have thought that somehow all of this historical inertia would be an ideal place to become pregnant. There is no other answer. After all, Sarah had many different opportunities to become a mother if that was ever really what she wanted to achieve. I was also often reminded by Sarah that I was NOT an accident, which made all of this even more mysterious and confusing. Regardless of these nuances, it is St. David's story that isfascinating.

Being educated in the monastery of Hen Fynyw, David was a student of St. Paulinus. Legend has it that David performed several miracles, including restoring Paulinus' sight when he went blind.

During the battle against the Saxons, David also advised the troops to wear leeks in their hats, distinguishing them from the enemy. The leeks later became one of the symbols of Wales.

By the time David died, at over one hundred years old, he had traveled as a missionary throughout Wales, and Britain, founded twelve monasteries, including Glastonbury, and became an Archbishop of Wales, at the Synod of Brevi, Cardiganshire, in 550AD.

After David's death on March 1, 589AD at Minevia, his influence spread throughout Britain and Ireland in the Roman Empire.

But, what was it precisely that attracted my mother to this unknown Bran Hughes? Indeed, it had to be more than all the ancient religious relics that surrounded them.

What I have surmised, with very little evidence and after many years of reflection, is that Bran must have been a prolific storyteller. His talent overwhelmed my mother's rational being, sending her into another universe. Sarah had finally met her match. That kindred spirit, I was confident, must also flow through my veins.

What I am still trying to understand is how this inherited storytelling talent beckons me to follow *The Agape*. Learning about my father, I am convinced, is an essential missing link that will help resolve this question.

For many years, Bran Hughes was a mystery that I needed to solve. All that I knew was that his name was Bran and that his name means, "Blessed Giant," a king in British and Welch folklore.

Bran is also frequently translated to crow, or raven, the son of the god Llyr. In later legends, Bran was a king of Britain who was slain while attacking Ireland.

The few pictures that I was able to find in an old album of my father certainly confirm that he looks like a god. His bronze hair, verdant green eyes, muscular body, and radiant smile could be that of a famous international actor posing for a publicity shot.

When he is pictured with my mother, Bran appears to be a giant, overshadowing Sarah's small stature. But, what I immediately noticed was the intense, poignant, and even piercing, deeply embedded expressions on my mother's face. It was a look that I never saw on her face again while she was alive.

For many years, I was banned from mentioning my father's name. Even asking questions about him was forbidden. Finally, I was once told that when I could completely understand the circumstance, I would concede that there is no need for a father. I am still waiting for that revelation.

It wasn't that my mother disliked men. She knew many. It was just that she would never permit any man ever to invade her private space again. That space included me.

What Sarah could never deny is that my father's genes are dominant. My auburn red hair and green eyes reminded her constantly of those months she spent at St. Davids. I am the everlasting permanent image that she could never ignore.

But, it would not be my mother to share any of her memories with me. That only happened years after her death. One afternoon, when my grandparents moved us to Cape Town, a mahogany wooden box appeared in my room. The first thing that I noticed was the large lock on the outside. It was nothing that I had ever seen before.

At first, I thought that the movers mistakenly or by negligence, left this chest in the wrong place. Once I found my grandmother, she assured me that the box was in the correct room.

"Your mother, Imani, was a highly complex woman with many extraordinary virtues. Being a mother was not one of them. Since her tragic death five years ago, I have wanted to share this treasure with you, but with this movie, and now that you are at Columbia University so many miles away, there never seemed to be the right time. Today, I decided, it was finally the right time for you to meet your father. He is someone that you should have known much earlier," Nani, my grandmother, said, handing me the key that was hanging from a chain resembling a rosary.

"But, what is inside this locked box, that is so mysterious? Indeed not my father," I asked, not quite sure if I wanted to know.

Whatever this box held inside for these many years was going to change my life. At twenty years old, I was pretty content with my status quo. I had moved on from questioning my heritage, learning to accept my positive qualities and negative inhibitions. I only had one more year at Columbia University. After that, hopefully, I could find an internship with a major broadcasting company or newspaper. Did I want to complicate all of this with what resembles a Pandora's Box?

Unfortunately, I also knew that ignoring the ominous contents would only continue to be more daunting. It was my instinct that finally led me to place the key in the keyhole. I turned it, waiting to hear the inviting click...

Chapter Four

If I touched the earth, it would crumble; it is so sad and beautiful. So tremendously like a dream.

Dylan Thomas
Clown in the Moon

Imani Lewis
Cape Town Africa

Cape Town, South Africa, is an entirely different world from New York. Even the tiny seaside community of Noetzie, South Africa, where I grew up with my grandparents, while my mother was on travel assignments, seemed isolated.

But, Cape Town is the second-largest city in South Africa after Johannesburg. Nevertheless, a significant change from Manhattan. Someone, I recall once told me that if the Western Cape were a woman, it would make the entire world jealous. This may be true. However, the decision to move here was quite unexpected.

When I received the phone call that my grandparents were relocating, It immediately changed my plans for a summer trip to London. I felt obligated to assist in any way that I could. They were all that remained of my family, and I knew that my grandparents would not be with me for very much longer. It was my responsibility to care for them with the same love they had always shown to me.

It was primarily because of my grandparents that I never felt lonely. When I was with them, they provided me with so many other exciting experiences encompassing my life that there was no time for sorrow.

I also had a mother who traveled to some of the most exotic places on earth. She would often include me on those expeditions. Being bored was never an option. Even when spending time with my grandparents in South Africa, I never really considered my life unusual. It was always a comfortable lifestyle.

Before retiring, both my grandparents worked for the American embassy in Boston, Massachusetts. When the embassy was offered them to relocate to South Africa, they both agreed that it would be an excellent opportunity to expand their horizons.

Years later, when my mother arrived in South Africa, after spending a year in Wales, she brought with her a one-year-old daughter. That is when my grandparents decided to retire and settle down quite comfortably at a remote seaside community known as Noetzie Beach. To reach our home, it was necessary to take a dirt road leading to a secluded beach encircled by castles. Maybe even more interesting (although not to me as a child) is that close by exists one of the last remaining homes of the very rare African Black Oystercatchers.

These prominent charismatic wader residents used to flock near the conservative marina where I resided. Gathering nearby, with their glossy black plumage, pink legs, and feet, I moved as close as possible to watch them hunt for mussels, limpets, and worms. Whenever I heard their distinct high pitch piping sound, I would attempt to mimic them. Occasionally one would turn its curious head at me. Those red ring eyes would stare fearlessly as if I was the intruder.

My life was always simple, uneventful, and predictable, at least while in South Africa. Traveling with my mother that was another story. Then, it was like opening a new adventure book and writing my chapter on blank pages. It was the antithesis of normality.

One day, when I was about ten years old, and my mother was on an assignment without me, I recall asking my grandmother if all mothers left their daughters for months with their grandparents.

All the children that I knew lived with their mothers and fathers. For a while, this difference in lifestyle wasn't noticeable to me.

Then my grandfather explained that I was like those Oystercatchers that enjoyed freedom on the beach.

"If you want to have a free spirit, Imani, you must learn now how to spread your wings. Here you live independently in a controlled environment. Your grandmother and I are all you need to fulfill this. Having too many odd birds flocking around only prevents chicks from learning how to fly on their own," he said, kissing me on the top of my head. He was pretty satisfied that he had answered my question.

He had. I never really asked again. That is why this mahogany box, now unlocked, was agitating me. If I ignored it, then how would my life change? It wouldn't. Everything would remain the same. But is that what I want?

No. Obviously, No! Life will change whether I open this box or not. But, once I do make that decision, I have some control over the following choices. After all, I can decide to stop exploring the contents inside at any time.

What I never expected was to find so many letters addressed to me that were never opened. They all appeared to have Welch postmarks. Thankfully, someone, I presume my grandmother, organized each letter chronologically.

The first letter I opened was dated May 8, 1980. It was written on my first birthday.

My dearest Imani,

How I long to cradle you in my arms just once more. The smell of your hair reminds me of an ocean breeze gently mixed with lavender and honeysuckle. You are the most beautiful child that I have ever seen. When I speak to you, I can see your eyes sparkle like fireflies dancing jubilantly.

Oh, my darling, I will never allow you to forget how much love I still have in my heart for you. One day, many years from now, when I am no longer here on this earth, you will finally understand all that has happened.

Your father, now and forever,
Bran Hughes

Every letter that followed, and there were 180 letters, were dated on the 8th of each month. At first, this didn't seem pertinent. I was more anxious to read what was written than to notice when it was written. But, finally, I understood the significance. My father chose the day I was born each month to write me a new letter. It was as if he wanted me to realize that the day I was born was meaningful to him.

What was still ambiguous was why all of these letters were kept from me. If my mother didn't want me to know anything about my father, why didn't she simply throw all these letters away? I still don't know the answer to that question.

My grandmother was also at a loss. She said that once Sarah realized that the letters were arriving monthly, she asked her to keep them in this safe chest and never show them to her again. There was no further explanation.

The Bran letters, as I now referred to them, were not all read in one sitting. I spaced the times and places where I would read this collection over several years. Now that I reflect on that decision, I think it was my way to assure there would never be an ending. You know, like a favorite movie or novel that you want to keep going forever?

There were months when I almost forgot about the letters. But, then when I returned once again to my trove, it was as if I was rekindling a new friendship. You see, Bran wrote about so many different topics that he became more than a father; he was also my tutor and my mentor. One letter might be a history lesson on the Welch culture, whereas another letter would be a collection of poems that he composed. There were even sketches of the countryside and portraits of people in the community. Sometimes Bran would include a page of music that he had written, with lyrics. I would close my eyes and imagine him singing only to me.

The final letter that my father wrote to me is still unopened. It may never be opened. Throughout the many years that followed, I would return to these as *Letters of Wisdom.* That was how I would now refer to them. Each time I reread a letter, I would try to discover something new. Remarkably this always worked.

However, what is still a mystery is why my mother returned to South Africa after spending the first year of my life with Bran? How could she walk out of his life with me and never explain why?

After my mother's death, I, of course, remained with my grandparents. But, we never spoke of my father's letters or even my mother's life for that matter. I was immediately encouraged to focus only on my education and future as if nothing in the past was significant. Of course, I followed those instructions. And, life did seem relatively easy.

When I applied at Columbia University, it was my first and only choice. Returning to New York seemed like the natural next step in my life. South Africa was another world, one that I was ready to leave. Then that mahogany box appeared from nowhere.

After graduation from Columbia University, I was accepted at a small independent newspaper as a freelance journalist. Before even my first day, I received a phone call that my grandparents, who were now in an assisted living home in Cape Town, had become increasingly ill. Without hesitation, I was on the next flight home, electing to postpone my new job.

By the time that I arrived in Cape Town, only my grandmother was still barely alive. I sat down next to her, stroking her white hair, holding her tiny hand, whispering to her, "It is me, Imani. I have come home to be with you, Nani."

A few minutes passed before my Nani opened her eyes. I could tell that she was waiting for this moment.

"Imani, my love. I am so proud of you. Always remember that whatever happens from this time forward, you have been the most incredible journey of my life," Nani said quietly.

"It is now another journey Nani that will bring you peace. Rest, and always know that my love for you will be forever," I said, feeling the tears on my cheek.

"It is the *Agape Journey* that will give you peace, my Imani. Don't turn away as your mother did. Never forget this."

Those were my grandmother's final words and the second time I heard about this *Agape Journey. Why was this so important to my Nani?*

First, the little person in the Cairo casino left me the message of *The Agape,* and now Nani on her deathbed. But, it was not until I returned to Cairo for the King Tut assignment, many years later, that everything began to start making sense.

Chapter Five

Love is our most unifying and empowering common spiritual dominator. The more we ignore its potential to bring more excellent balance and deeper meaning to human existence, the more likely we will continue defining history as one long inglorious record of man's inhumanity to man.

Aberjhani
Encyclopedia of the Harlem Renaissance

Imani Lewis
Cairo, Egypt 2017

"Albert, you mentioned earlier that your grandfather knew my mother? I never knew that Sarah returned to Egypt after that one time that I accompanied her. How did they know each other?" I asked after the photoshoot had finished.

"Let me take you to Club 88. It is a spectacular new restaurant that opened a few months ago located directly on the Nile River. We can celebrate the successful conclusion to the end of our project and the beginning of a new friendship," Alberto said, extending his hand to lead me outside.

It sounded like an obvious deflection to my question.

"I thought that Egyptians were forbidden to drink alcohol," I said, following Alberto outside.

"It is estimated that 90% of all Egyptians are Muslims, and only 10% are Christians. What this means is that alcohol is considered haram or forbidden. But, let me assure you, Imani, we Islamics have found many other ways to celebrate." Alberto said this in a charming tone.

I hope that there was nothing said to suggest that I was romantically interested. During the entire course of our week together I made certain that our relationship was exclusively professional. Never did I mean to suggest anything but friendship. The very last thing on my mind was to pursue an international affair, especially in Egypt with someone who looked like a youngster. As mysteriously and tempting as Cairo is, with all of its romantic charms, there is also a very intimidating sense. A surreal power that can be both intimidating and controlling.

This uncomfortable, atmosphere that lingers around me is something that I never share with others. Nevertheless, it is enough to keep me very cautious about becoming too friendly with anyone from this ancient country.

"Now that you are finished with your King Tut story, will you be returning home to New York immediately?" Alberto asked, weaving in and out of traffic.

"I am extending my stay by a few days. That is if I am still alive after this crazy car ride," I said, truly frightened by all the drivers nearly colliding with us during the entire trip downtown.

"Ah, Imani! Certainly, my driving isn't any worse than those taxi drivers in Manhattan?" Alberto rebutted.

"If what you say is true, most of them are probably originally from Cairo," I said, relieved that we were finally parking.

"Safe and sound. Nothing to ever worry about when you are with me, Imani," Alberto said, opening the massive glass door leading to the front of the restaurant.

The first thing that I noticed was plenty of marble, surrounded by mirrors and crystalline light fixtures everywhere. This was contrasted with the wood floors and lush greenery. It was quite a distinction considering that everything outside is so dry.

A tall gentleman, dressed in a formal black suit, greeted Alberto with a friendly embrace. After a few words in Arabic that I could not understand, I was introduced formally.

"This is my good friend, Imani Lewis from America. She is a very distinguished journalist writing a story about our famous King Tut," Alberto said.

Before I could correct him about my "distinguished" title, Alberto added that the gentleman was his cousin, Renaldo, part-owner of *Club 88*.

"It is a pleasure meeting you, Miss Lewis. I have reserved for you and your guest, Alberto, the finest seating on the terrace with unobstructed views of our beautiful Nile," Renaldo said proudly.

"We appreciate your kindness, dear cousin. This is truly a spectacular venue! Already it is being talked about throughout the city. You should be very proud, Renaldo," Alberto said, politely pulling the chair out for me.

"We have plenty of competition, but I am happy with the reception thus far. Enjoy!" he said, leaving us alone to savor the sights.

"Now tell me, Imani, what is it that will keep you here the next few days? Have you booked some sightseeing? You must plan a visit to Luxor. It is famously known for its ancient Egyptian sites. It is the most excellent open-air museum in the world. This is where The Temples of Karnak are found. At one time, the intellectual center of Egypt. There you will see Chapels, Pylons, Obelisks, and more than 900 acres of space. Every known Pharaoh has built, destroyed, or restored this complex as his expression of devotion to Amun," Alberto said.

"Amun is the ancient god of the sun and air, correct?" I asked.

"Yes, that is right. He is one of the most sacred gods that rose to prominence at Thebes during the beginning of the New Kingdom," Alberto confirmed.

"If I recall correctly, the New Kingdom begins between the 16th and the 11th centuries BCE. Amun-Ra was the leader of all Egyptian gods. He evolved when Amun, creator of the universe and Ra, god of the sun and light, combined. He is symbolized with two vertices plumes and the ram-headed Sphinx," I said.

"Your knowledge of Egyptian history is impressive. Where did you learn all of this?" Alberto, asked.

"I'm really not sure. I remember returning from Cairo when I was only thirteen years old determined to learn more about Egypt. Without boring you with all of the details of my life, I will confess that I am still eager to explore everything that I can learn about *The Agap*. You mentioned that your grandfather knew my mother. Did she ever mention *The Agape*? Have you ever heard of this before?" I finally asked the most crucial question that I had wanted to know for days.

"There is really no easy response to that questions, Imani. It will take much more time than we have today. I would be quite honored to share with you whatever I can, but it will require us to take a short visit to Alexandria. It is the site of Cleopatra's sunken palace, on the island of Antirhodos," Alberto said, waiting for me to respond.

This invitation to Alexandria threw me totally off guard. I never expected that Alberto would suggest we leave Cairo. Unexpectedly it occurred to me that perhaps Sarah also knew about *The Agape*. Why else would she have returned to Egypt several times without telling anyone, especially me? But, now, I had an opportunity to begin some serious research into a topic that I was determined to learn more about.

"Alright, Alberto. I will let you make the necessary plans. I only need about twenty-four hours to finish up my story here, and then I will be ready to travel," I said.

Sitting on the Nile, sipping a chilled Karkadeh, the traditional Egyptian drink, I felt like life was now moving at a different pace. Perhaps the dried hibiscus flowers floating inside my glass, with the sound of the melodic harp in the background, were creating a mysterious ambiance. Whatever it was made this evening the ideal place to begin my pursuit.

The following morning, I proofread my final draft sending it off to cyberspace across several continents to its ultimate destination in New York before sunrise. Starting early this morning also allowed me to search the internet for details about Cleopatra, the last Pharaoh of Egypt.

Most of the information that I found was not anything new. After all, Cleopatra is more well-known than even King Tut. But sifting through the apparent details about her relationships with Caesar and Mark Antony also revealed some insights about the historical temptress.

Cleopatra's destiny required her to faithfully rule Egypt with the ability to strategically lead her country as it had been ruled for three hundred years previously by the Greek-speaking Ptolemaic Dynasty.

Born in Alexandria, Egypt, in 69 BC, Cleopatra was a polymath, a genuinely knowledgeable woman, and academically accomplished in many subjects, including medicine. Unfortunately, most of her narratives were destroyed by the Roman Empire, leaving her legacy to be that of a devious woman with the adept talent to tempt powerful men at her command.

Historically strong women rarely are known for their accomplishments. Mostly because literature and art have chosen to portray Cleopatra as a seductress mythologically, it has forgotten to remind the world how she survived after her father's death, Ptolemy XII.

When Cleopatra's younger brother Ptolemy XIII was presumed to be the next leader, she married her younger brother, and co- reigned with him to ensure stability. As this sibling rivalry continued between the two rulers, Ptolemy allied himself with their half-sister, Arsinoe, to dispose of Cleopatra, causing a civil war known as The Siege of Alexandria. During that time, Ptolemy drowned trying to cross the Nile, and Arsinoe, after been exiled for many years, was executed by Cleopatra's Roman allies.

With all of this hate followed by violence, it is unlikely that any *Agape* can be found in Alexandria. During my research of *The Agape* thus far, I knew that it included some carpet or tapestry with spiritual powers. Who named *Agape* is not yet clear. According to Scripture, *Agape* is transcendental love, the highest form possible. At the same time, Cleopatra, and the Alexandria site, appear to be a discrepancy to that definition, with plenty of Eros or erotic love.

There has to be some logical reason why Cleopatra is included in the mosaic tiles of missing pieces to this relic. Meeting Alberto was not a coincidence. Wandering into that cave at the Omar Khayyam Casino was not a mistake. My grandmother's last breath mentioning *Agape* is not an error. Alexandria does have some answers. It is up to me to ask the right questions.

Chapter Six

"Fool! Don't you see now that I could have poisoned you a hundred times had I been able to live without you".

Cleopatra
Cleopatra: from history to myth. www. the guardian.com

Imani Lewis
Cairo, Egypt 2017

The origin of my name has always been a mystery. Nobody seems ever to know how Imani, a redhead, green-eyed, freckled child, inherited this same Arabic distinguished epithet. Whenever I would introduce this subject, I was often told to simply appreciate the uniqueness of my moniker for life.

Then, thanks to my grandmother, I finally learned how my name was selected. In that mahogany box, with the collection of letters from my father, was the answer. While my mother was pregnant, she and Bran would research what the most appropriate name should be for their unborn child. Sarah wanted something distinguished, unusual, yet elegant. However, Bran was determined that his child, who he insisted was a daughter, would have a respected name. Historical! Memorable! Everlasting!

This was a contentious argument between the two lovers for many months. As my mother's due date was approaching, Bran suggested that the only fair way to select the name was to toss a coin into the air. Whoever won the toss would have the right to name the child.

Well, Bran won and he selected Imani. It took months of research before he finally settled on this name. Many people, including myself, thought it was chosen because in Arabic it means, belief or faith. However, Bran's explanation is much more authentic.

My decision to name you Imani, darling, originated after meeting with a high priestess who lived near the castle grounds of St. Davids.

Of course, she appeared to be more like a beggar than a priestess. Her clothes were tattered, and everything she owned was in a large carpetbag, including an artist's sketch pad.

I met her very coincidentally while I was strolling in the moors. It was something that I would often do to clear my mind. As I approached the castle entrance, the haggard lady offered me a place to rest on a stone bench.

When I explained to her that I was searching for an appropriate name for my daughter, who was due to be born any day, the high priestess, as she introduced herself, began to tell me about The Legend of Khaina. Without going into all the details now, I will provide you with the abridged version. Khaina was in search of a protected sanctuary to give birth to her royal child. She traveled long distances until she finally arrived at the enchanted island of Jacquet in the Atlantic Ocean.

While I was listening to this fascinating story, the Priestess was sketching on her blank tablet an image that I could not see. At the end of her story about Khana, she handed me this amazing drawing. As you can see, it is a picture of a young girl dressed in a white and purple warrior costume holding a bow and arrow. But, what I immediately noticed was the name, Imani. This character had long red braided hair with a slight golden crown on her head. Imani's eyes were verdant green, and her cheeks sprinkled with tiny beauty marks. This was my daughter. This was you, Imani! You were born five days later.

I was impressed at how much the portrait looked like me, of course, without the bow and arrow and crown. And, as I began to get used to my name, I found that other famous people shared this name.

First, I learned of an American singer, songwriter, and violinist, Imani Coppola, born April 6, 1978. She is older than me but also grew up in Long Island, New York. I am sure that this Imani always knew where her roots were. Both parents were also jazz musicians.

Then there was Imani Perry, an American interdisciplinary scholar of race, law, literature, and African American culture. Currently, she is a professor at Princeton University.

Imani Sanga, born in 1972, is a professor of music who teaches in Tanzania. In this case, Imani is a male. It was another reason why I began to appreciate my name. There was no gender prejudice attached. I concluded that Bran, my father, made a perfect choice.

There were times when I could only imagine what Sarah would have called me had she won the toss of the coin. Still, not knowing why my mother left my father was disturbing. Almost as irritating as not knowing why the letters stopped. Had Bran passed away, even before Sarah? Did he tire of writing all of those letters without any response? Or was there still something that I was missing? Nani's last words to me were never to ignore the Agape. But, I had no idea why she would say this to me.

Traveling to Alexandria to learn more about how Cleopatra fits into this mystery seems a long stretch. On the other hand, whatever I do discover there, just might make an interesting addition to the King Tut article.

There was something about that rug scene in particular when Cleopatra first meets with Julius Caesar. I always recall that moment as quite fascinating. When I first read George Bernard Shaw's interpretation in *Caesar and Cleopatra,* it was two of her assistants, Flatetta and Apollodorus, who wrapped the nude Egyptian Queen in a rug and delivered her by boat to Caesar. At that moment, Caesar is attempting a strategic maneuver to protect his outnumbered forces from being annihilated by the Egyptian navy. The carpet is not only Cleopatra's clever way to gain access to Caesar; it is Caesar's reaction next that is most important. Once it is clear that Cleopatra's forces are in charge, Caesar's guards throw the vulnerable Cleopatra over the barge into the water. It is then that the enamored Caesar jumps from the barge to rescue Cleopatra himself. Could this be in fact, an *Agape* act? I am not sure. But, it is worth looking further into Caesar's relationship with Cleopatra.

There is also the mystery of what happened to that infamous carpet. Certainly something this historic must have been preserved. It also appears in many famous paintings. What I am hoping to discover are some answers to these questions. *The Agape* carpet may very well still be moving around in the modern world without our knowledge.

Chapter Seven

There is no fear in love but, perfect love casts out fear. For fear has to do with punishment, and whoever fears has not perfected in love.
1 John 14:18

Imani Lewis
Alexandria, Egypt
2017

I was never sure why Sarah was always fascinated with Cleopatra, or Halloween, for that matter. But, like most of my mother's interests, I could care less. Her interests almost always resulted in my disappointments. This was no exception.

In the fall of 1991, the year before my first visit to Cairo, Emile, Sarah's travel editor, rented the Park Avenue Armory for a Halloween extravaganza. This is where *Tamera,* the avant-garde play by John Krizanc, opened in 1987. The story is about a painter, Tamera de Lempicka, a Polish Art Deco artist born in 1898, who spent most of her working life in France and the United States painting aristocrats, and the very wealthy in the nude.

This play is about Tamera's meeting with Gabriele d' Annunzio, an Italian playwright, poet, journalist, orator, and soldier. He has invited Tamera to his villa at Gardone Riviera, located in Lombardy, on the western shore of Lake Garda, the largest lake in Italy.

Tamara is hoping that Gabriele will commission her for his portrait. Kriznak portrays Tamera as a pawn in an influential culture. The audience is drawn into a labyrinth of conspiracy in civic responsibility. Although Tamera has the voice to make changes through her powerful connections to the upper society, she instead sells her art to the highest bidder without ever feeling any remorse.

What happens in this New York production is that the audience no longer has a barrier to the actors. The spaces begin to intermingle as the spectators follow the actors to many different rooms in the building. The audience becomes actors as well, streaming simultaneously through action in eleven other rooms.

Naturally, for a twelve-year-old, this type of audience interaction during a theatre production sounded extremely inviting

"You are going to love *Tamera,* my darling. And, since Emile has arranged for all of us to be dressed in costume, it will make the evening even more enchanting," Sarah said one afternoon.

"I agree that the idea of following characters throughout this mansion sounds quite appealing, but I don't understand why I must dress up as Cleopatra. I look nothing like her. People will think that I am a freak! You, Sarah, you look like Cleopatra. Not me," I insisted, trying to convince my mother of how absurd this idea was.

"Imani, as usual, you are exaggerating the situation. Halloween is a time when everyone has an opportunity to stretch their imagination, and for one evening become someone, or something, that they will never be in real life. If it makes you feel better, I will also be Cleopatra. We will attend as the child and the adult version. It will be perfect," Sarah said energetically.

I knew that I had lost this battle. Why couldn't I be Alice in Wonderland? Now there was a much better connection. I was certainly more of an Alice than a Cleopatra. Whoever heard of anyone with red hair and freckles looking like Cleopatra?

I did have to give credit to Sarah for trying. When our costumes arrived, and we tried them on, Sarah and I, for the very first time in our lives, looked like mother and daughter. It must have been my black wig. Sarah already had black hair, but her wig was exactly like mine; only mine was a mini version.

On Halloween evening, Sarah had arranged for a limousine to take us to the event. She very wisely predicted that Manhattan would be busy with many different parties making parking impossible.

The entire evening was indeed glamorous. I hated to admit that Sarah was right, but this Cleopatra attire somehow gave me more confidence than I ever felt before around strangers. The actors were so friendly and kind that some suggested that I consider theatre when I was ready for college. Unfortunately, once the evening was over, the costume removed, I was still Imani Lewis, the redhead, freckled, slightly overweight girl who preferred standing in the shadow of her quite magnificent mother.

Many years later, when I was attending Columbia University my roommate convinced me to take an art appreciation class with her. Although I was an English major, and all of my humanity credits were complete, another art class for enjoyment might be a nice change. It was my second introduction to Cleopatra.

During the third meeting in the lecture hall, there were probably three hundred students in attendance. My roommate, Marilyn, was home with the flu. Therefore I was taking notes for us both.

When the professor arrived at the podium, she informed us that we would be watching a selection of video clips from French artists, some better known than others. Once the lights were dimmed, everyone focused on the large screen on stage. Most of the artists I remembered from my previous art class, but then this Sotheby's film began to discuss classical art in the 19th century known as Egyptomania.

Immediately I recognized the Sphinx and pyramids in Cairo that I visited with Sarah several years earlier. Next was a painting by Jean Leon Gerome (1824-1904), a French painter and sculptor in the academic style. What indeed drew my attention to this art piece was Cleopatra, the only standing image in a room full of men. *Cleopatra Before Caesar* was the title. This style gave Gerome the freedom to explore both Classical and Orientalism. The quintessential first meeting between Cleopatra and Julius Caesar establishes her ability to control destiny when all appears to be lost.

Immediately, when I saw this, the historical context of the initial meeting with Caesar came back to me. Cleopatra had been exiled from Alexandria by her brother, Ptolemy XIII. Nonetheless, when she arrives inside a carpet as a gift to Caesar, Cleopatra is clearly in control of her life. It is this carpet that many scholars refute, saying that there is no objective evidence. Plutarch, however, may have been correct in referring to Cleopatra's dramatic entrance using a carpet rather than a sheet, as others claim. It certainly would have protected the Queen much better than any other material.

Now that I finally have an opportunity to speak with an Egyptian scholar about this "rug," it might be the missing link to the *Agape* puzzle. If the *Agape Carpet* can now be traced historically, and if it still exists, it will be much more critical today than during Cleopatra's infamous journey.

What I presume is that there are many of us researching this exact topic. We are all anonymous. You could say we are a secret society. So private that we have no idea of who anyone is. This is most definitely an exclusive quest. I know that there are more of us out there. I am not alone. But, thus far all my sources are silent. I have no idea how much I am progressing or merely idling. Hopefully this trip to Alexandria will provide some of those answers.

Chapter Eight

It is notable than when she is not condemned for being too bold and masculine, Cleopatra is taken to task for being unduly frail, and feminine.

Stacey Schiff
American Essayist, Pulitzer Prize Winner, Biography 2000

Imani Lewis
Egypt 2017

"Please, Imani, tell me again why it is so important for me to change your return tickets to New York? You do understand that Egypt is not considered a safe place for women who travel alone. Especially American women. Most Arabic men, my naïve friend, still believe that a woman is essentially a body created for men's pleasures. Tell me that you are listening to me, Imani."

Priscilla was sounding more like my mother on the other end of the phone than my administrative assistant. Well, maybe not like my mother, but like someone's mother.

"It's going to be fine, Priscilla. I am only extending my trip by three days. Just let corporate know that I am using a few of the many days that I have accumulate to visit with a family friend. They will be so happy with the King Tut article that they won't even miss me for a while," I said, trying to relieve Priscilla's anxiety.

"Alright Imani. I do hope that you know what you are doing. Where do you want me to FAX your tickets? Please tell me that you will at least need room reservations? Or are you going to take a camel caravan through the Sahara and stay in some exotic oasis?" Priscilla added snarlingly.

"As a matter of fact, Alberto has suggested that we spend one night at Fayoum Oasis, which is on the way to Alexandria. He claims that although it is only a few hours from Cairo to Alexandria, if we stop at this Oasis I will have a better appreciation for what the ancient archives will offer once I get there," I said, knowing well Priscilla would not approve.

"You are not serious now, are you Imani? Do you have any idea what trouble this could cause if you go missing? It will be an international blowup of terrible proportions. Please go to Alexandria the safest way possible, do whatever you insist on doing, and return to Manhattan where we can laugh all about this adventure sipping some fine wine at *Daniels,*" Priscilla said, her voice fading away.

"Everything is under control. Text me the Alexandria hotel reservations. I will be in touch," I said, ending the call.

Priscilla may be right about other women traveling alone through Egypt, but how many of them have ever been Cleopatra, Queen of the Nile, in their other life?

The following day, I was packed and ready to go when Alberto arrived in a minivan. Thankfully it wasn't his old Alfa Romeo. I wasn't sure if that vehicle would make it another ten kilometers.

"I'm impressed, Alberto. Where did you find this minivan? It looks quite comfortable," I said, opening my door.

"Oh, this belongs to my cousin. He owns a travel group. The business has been rather slow, so he agreed to let us use the van for the next few days," Alberto said, starting the engine.

I dared not ask how much this van would cost me for three days, but Egyptians love to haggle. Alberto would eventually quote me some outrageous amount of money for this transportation, and after some tough negotiations, both of us would agree to a fair market price. This happens whenever any finances are involved.

"I thought that you might want to read some information about the 750-year-old region that we will soon arrive at," Alberto said, handing me a couple of printed fliers written in English.

"That was very considerate of you, Alberto. Or, are you just trying to distract me from criticizing your driving?" I asked, flipping through the first brochure.

"Well, Imani, maybe a little of both," Alberto said, keeping his eyes on the road.

Since the drive to Alexandria via Fayoum Oasis was all desert, I did take the opportunity to read about the significance of this "tranquil retreat." I learned that although Fayoum is located very close to Cairo and is noted to be one of the most ancient areas in all of Africa, it is usually ignored, even passed by frequently on the way to Alexandria.

I also read that an oasis, in reality, is surrounded by capillary canals that feed into the Nile River rather than traditional springs. As we move closer, it is pretty resounding how the landscape changes from arid desert to wild sunflowers sprouting on the roadside, along with various date palms and water buffalo grazing.

"Have you got to the *Lazib Inn,* yet Imani? That is where we will be stopping for the afternoon," Alberto said while listening to some Arabic music station. It sounded like a strange adaptation of Prince singing *Little Red Corvette.*

"Yes, I am just now looking at the impressive gardens. That must be why people refer to this as an Oasis," I said.

"I do believe that once we arrive, Imani, you will truly appreciate why I insisted that we stay at least one evening. If you had additional time, a week does more justice. This Inn is considered a luscious example of outstanding Egyptian hospitality," Alberto added.

"I must say, Alberto, you are an excellent marketing advertisement. A walking, talking billboard for this establishment. Do you have any financial interest in this place that you are not revealing to me?" I asked, partly joking.

"Oh, I wish that I was able to have invested in this little gem years ago. Although there are only eight luxurious Oasis suites, they are always booked months in advance. Since I have known the owners since childhood, whenever there is a vacancy available, they let me know. We were fortunate on this visit," Alberto said.

"Excuse me for perhaps not sounding appreciative, but we do have separate rooms, correct?"

I certainly did not want to arrive at Fayoum without knowing our sleeping arrangements. There was nothing ever to suggest that this trip was to be a romantic interlude.

"No worries, Imani. The suite has two separate bedrooms. My wife would never have agreed to any other arrangements," Alberto said, pulling into the long driveway off of the highway.

That was the first time that Alberto ever mentioned he was married. He didn't even look like he had reached puberty. Not that there was any reason earlier to mention a wife. It just caught me unprepared on how to respond. There was no time now to answer since we had just arrived, and the valet was already removing our luggage.

"Welcome back, Mr. Mohammad, to the *Lazib Inn*. We have some cool refreshments in our reception for you and your guest."

The gentleman was dressed like the enigmatic Mr. Roarke from the once-popular *Fantasy Island* television series. We followed his lead to a magnificent indoor garden where everyone was sipping very pleasant-looking fruit beverages.

"Well, what do you think? Isn't it exactly how you imagine an Egyptian Oasis should look like?" Alberto said quite proudly.

It was impressive. But, for some strange reason, I kept thinking about *The Mirage Hotel and Casino* in Las Vegas, Nevada. This inn was the authentic representation that could have been used as the Vegas model. But, that Vegas image kept reappearing in my mind.

"Yes, Alberto, your owner friends have produced a magnificent retreat from the outside world," I said, quite impressed.

Just as we were beginning to enjoy the ambiance, a middle-aged man wearing a loose white linen shirt, jeans, and sandals approached Alberto, extending his arm. Rather than shake it, Alberto placed his arms around the stranger's shoulders, embracing him like a long-lost brother.

"Oh my God, Phoenix, what are you doing here? Why didn't you let me know that you were visiting Cairo? Are you coming or leaving Alexandria, my dear friend? ...Oh, forgive me? Where are my manners? I want to introduce you to a very gifted writer, like you Phoenix, Miss Imani Lewis, from the United States," Alberto said.

I stood up from the very comfortable rattan peacock chair and felt this stranger hold my hand with both of his as if we had known each other for years.

"It is a pleasure, Miss Lewis, to meet you. Alberto is a great guide for your visit to Alexandria," the gentleman said, taking a seat across from us.

Had Alberto or I ever told this stranger that we were going to Alexandria? I don't believe so, Although it might not be a far stretch to draw that conclusion on his own since it was a common route

But, why was he here? And, what kind of a writer is he? I must admit that this Phoenix is a superb-looking creature. That shiny black hair pulled back neatly in a short ponytail, and those mesmerizing blue eyes are intense, even somewhat alarming. This

Phoenix could intimidate the most confident man or woman in any arena he chose to compete in.

But, just as I was feeling rather uncomfortable, a heartfelt, authentic smile appeared nonchalantly on this stranger's face. Anyone who sees Mr. Phoenix smile realizes he does not need to be pompous. This charismatic attitude immediately made me relax, although I had no idea why.

"I am returning to Cairo after a very educational meeting with a philosopher scholar. He enlightened me to take a new direction with my thesis. I would love to sit and chat with you, Miss Lewis, but I have a plane to catch back to the UK. Enjoy your stay here and in Alexandria," Phoenix said, waving goodbye.

I was trying to absorb what all this was about when Alberto started to fill in the gaps for me.

"Phoenix Baldwin is an award-winning journalist from the United Kingdom. He graduated from Cambridge University with honors and is a Literature Professor on sabbatical. Mr. Baldwin speaks four languages fluently, comes from a wealthy aristocratic family, and is thirty-nine years old; never married. No children,"

Alberto said as if he was broadcasting a biographical documentary.

"Currently, I understand that some prominent British firm has hired Phoenix to find a very famous artifact," Alberto added.

"Is this antique that he is searching for, located in Egypt?" I asked Alberto.

"Well, yes, and no. I mean, it was once here. At least many archeologists believe this. But, there is no concrete evidence that we may still have it. It is the same object that many others are searching for. If there were more definite answers, this would no longer be a mystery," Alberto said.

"How long has Mr. Baldwin been searching for this antique?" I asked.

I realized that asking so many questions about a gentleman that I had just met sounded entirely improper. Yet, I was curious to know if we were now searching for the same *Agape*.

"All that I can tell you, Imani, is that I met Phoenix much as I did you. When he visited the Cairo museum about three years ago, I offered to assist him however I could. I agreed to be his eyes and ears when he was not here. But, I never heard from Phoenix again.

What I do know is that his search continues. Perhaps this visit may have finally produced some lucrative results for him," Alberto said.

"May I ask what it is exactly that Mr. Baldwin is commissioned to find?" I finally said explicitly what I wanted to know.

"I don't think that it is a secret, Imani. Phoenix is just one of an entire group of treasure hunters competing to be the first to find the actual *Agape Carpet*. Whoever accomplishes this fete will become extremely wealthy, but moreover will gain world-known respect," Alberto said, rising from his chair.

"I am going to check on the progress of our suite. You can remain here until it is time to move to our rooms," Alberto added, although, by this time, my mind was wandering in a different direction.

Agape! Agape absolutely is a carpet. I knew that there were several other antique carpets with historical significance, like the Cleopatra carpet, that continue to be debated. But, if that carpet was used to deliver the Queen of Egypt to Julius Caesar, the Emperor of Rome, and if it is also the *Agape Carpet,* where is it now? How was it moved from its original location? What powers did it have then, and what capabilities does it have now?

Alberto Mohammad may be a faithful, responsible guide, and I have no doubt of his integrity, but he is also a dedicated friend to Phoenix Baldwin. Who knows how many others? If I have an opportunity to compete with these treasure hunters, I must wisely retrieve the information I gather without revealing what I learn.

Phoenix has been to Alexandria for the past three years. I am hoping, that like a good journalist, I will discover what his final visit revealed. If I can do this successfully, Phoenix and I should be running the same course with no handicap.

Mr. Baldwin may be gorgeous, beguiling, and even charming, while I am a younger, plain redhead woman. Yet, I am sure Phoenix never received a signed copy of *The Rubaiyat of Omar Khayyam* from a mysterious Arabic little person encouraging him to seek *Agape*.

Chapter Nine

My heart is at ease knowing that what was meant for me will never miss me and that what I missed was never meant for me.

Imam Ash Shafi'i
Arab, Muslim Theologian
(767-820 CE)

Imani Lewis
Fayoum, Egypt 2017

The *Lazib Inn* did not disappoint, although I was anxious to arrive at Alexandria to learn more about this *Agape Carpet*.

"So, Imani, tell me honestly what do you think about our Egyptian Paradise? Are you ready to do some exploring around the grounds?" Alberto asked, eager to hear my reaction.

"Well, I certainly will admit that the owners did a fabulous job at reflecting Egypt's undisputed essence by using such vibrant colors that I know were reserved for royalty," I said, admiring the refined collection of handmade carpets throughout the suite.

What quality of carpet could survive centuries of constant foot traffic? Looking at the very bright citrine, turquoise, and sapphire threads that embellished the ones in this inn I tried to imagine what the carpet that Cleopatra chose to use looked like? Did it even matter to her that thousands of years later, people would be debating her decision to arrive at Caesar's feet in such a vulnerable manner? Somehow, I just felt that the answer would have to be yes. Everything that Cleopatra did was calculated.

"It is truly a tragedy that you won't let me share more days here with you, Imani. We have only barely 'scratched the surface'as you Americans like to say. There is an overpowering amount of shimmering sand flats in this pristine desert, with many archeological sites just waiting patiently to be explored. And, if that doesn't persuade you, maybe a magical horse ride on an Arabian steed in the moonlight is more your pleasure?" Alberto said, waltzing around the room like an enchanter.

"If I did not know better, Alberto, I would think that you are trying to seduce me," I said, hoping to bring our discussion back to a more reasonable level.

"No, no, of course not. I am a married man and faithful to my wife. I was suggesting that maybe one day you would consider returning to this romantic oasis with the appropriate lover to appreciate what it has to offer," Alberto said genuinely, now sounding embarrassed.

"That sounds like an excellent suggestion, Alberto, if I wanted to be wooed by an admirer. But, quite honestly, my life is moving now in a different direction. There is no time to be detoured into a frivolous relationship," I said, preparing to take a walk around the property grounds.

"I certainly hope that my comments did not offend you, Imani. They were not meant to. Your choice of personal, romantic partners, male or female, is certainly your preference," Alberto said, only making his proposals sound worse.

Rather than responding or even defending my remarks, I decided to leave things as they were. Soon I would be leaving Egypt, and it was unnecessary to justify or explain my sexual orientation to a stranger. We agreed to meet at the restaurant for an early dinner since I was anxious to arrive at Alexandria early the following day.

Nearby at the *Lazib Inn*, I commissioned a very eager Egyptian driver to take me to a place noted on the travel flier that Alberto gave me earlier. It was advertised as a fascinating wildlife preserve that included ancient fossils, named for King El-Rayan Ibn El-Walid, who was not an Arab ruler. He came to Egypt, I was told, during the Arabic conquest during the 7th century.

My knowledgeable guide, Bernardo, continued to tell me about this king that I had never heard of on our way to the Whale Museum.

"El Rayan Wade is a very famous ancient Egyptian king, if not the most famous one during the alternative popular Egyptian history era," Bernardo said.

"Really? I was just in Cairo writing an article on King Tut and never saw anything about this king. Why isn't he included in the historical archives?" I asked, now captivated.

"Oh yes, madam, El Rayan is in Cairo with his wife. There is a massive, colossal statue honoring him at the museum. But, most people do not realize that El Rayan Wald is also known as King Amenhotep III of the 18th dynasty in the Modern Kingdom of Egyptian history. He is the grandfather of Tutankhamen," Bernardo explained.

It was unfortunate that I didn't meet Bernardo earlier. I could have added some exciting footnotes to my King Tut article.

Although this young man could have spent hours talking to me about this region, we were running out of time. Unexpectedly I was being left off at my next destination. What I did learn in the few minutes remaining was that this obscure Egyptian pharaoh, or king, lived during the time of the Prophet Joseph.

I may not be a theological scholar, but I am familiar with Andrew Loyd Weber's famous musical, *Joseph and the Amazing Technicolor Dreamcoat.* As I recall, after Joseph was sold into slavery by his jealous brothers, he rose to become a vizier, the second most influential man in Egypt next to the Pharaoh. Some even claim that this Prophet Joseph lived in Fayoum.

But, before I could delve more into all of this Egyptian mythology/history, we were approaching the next most famous landmark, the *Wadi El-Rayan Waterfalls.* These are the only known waterfalls anywhere in Egypt. Not as impressive as our Niagara Falls, but certainly worth seeing.

"Of course to us, here in Egypt surrounded by the desert, with only the Nile as our source of water, this is considered magical to many," Bernardo said, stopping the van for me to admire.

I also learned, while sitting there watching the cascade flow, that, like everything in Egypt, progress is slow. This project began in 1968 and finished in 1973. What I found interesting was that in the 1830's Mohammad Ali Pasha, a governor, commissioned his chief engineer, Linet Pasha, to find a practical way to use the Nile River water as a reservoir. That attempt failed. In the 1880s and 1890s, both French, British and American engineers offered practical solutions. None were accepted until ninety years later.

Listening to this information reminded me of how young my own country is and what explorers might discover centuries later. Egypt offered a lifetime of exploration, but my focus now really must be on this *Agape Carpet.* I am just now beginning to understand the significance. If this carpet began here in ancient Egypt, then how many more historical details are still left to uncover?

My thoughts were interrupted once again by Bernardo, who was alerting me that we were approaching the Whale Museum.

"It has been a pleasure sharing with you a little history of my Egypt. Here is my card. If you find that you need a ride back to the *Lazib Inn,* dial my cell, and I will be at your call," Bernardo said pleasantly.

I handed him an American one-hundred dollar bill, knowing that it was probably equal to a month of earnings. The information that I learned was well worth the amount. And, although Alberto would object that I chose to seek another tour guide while he was available, it gave me a definite sense of freedom and control that I felt was needed at this moment.

The remainder of my afternoon I spent wandering through the *Fossils and Climate Change Museum* located inside Wadi Al-Hitan, known as the Valley of the Whales. It was designated as a UNESCO World Heritage Site in 2005. This valley is now part of the Egyptian desert and covered by a vast prehistoric ocean over 55 million years ago.

"Studies show that there were land mammals, including Walking Whales at that time. These mammals vanished because of climate change, a decrease in sea levels, and a rise in landmasses. The very same can happen to all of us if we continue to ignore all of the signs," a young girl said to her small group of followers.

I decided to approach the girl and ask her if I could follow along, although I was not a paid tourist. I offered to give her a significant tip at the conclusion.

"Are you American?"

"Yes. I am only here for one day and then continuing to Alexandria tomorrow," I replied.

Amelia, the tour guide's name, asked me how I got here without a tour guide. I explained to her that I was staying at *The Lazib Inn* and that a very nice driver, named Bernardo, had brought me here.

"Oh, Bernardo is my brother. Of course, you can join our group. We are also passing right by *The Lazib Inn* back to Cairo. We can drop you off, no problem," Amelia said pleasantly.

"That would be so kind of you. Thank you," I said, following behind the others.

There were many fossils located outside the museum that Amelia described in great detail. Later, our group was moved inside to explore the ancient seashells exhibited in glass boxes with informative explanations.

At the end of the tour, we all entered the minivan that resembled the same one that Alberto borrowed from his cousin. The trip back was less than thirty minutes. When we arrived, I offered Amelia a tip. She refused.

"You were very generous to my brother; I could not accept any more money from you, especially since my job is to speak to everyone anyway. Enjoy Alexandria, and I hope that you will find what you are searching for," Amelia said, embracing me goodbye.

Did I ever say anything about searching for something in Alexandria? I certainly don't recall. Well, regardless, today was actually a nice break from exploring.

At the lobby, I checked my phone for any new messages. There was one from Alberto reminding me about our dinner reservations at 6:00 pm, and the other one was from Priscilla confirming the room reservations for Alexandria.

I decided to Google *The Steigenberger Cecil Hotel,* where we would be checking in tomorrow. Priscilla, as I insisted, made reservations for two separate rooms, which avoided any further complications with Alberto.

From what I could see on the internet, this hotel is located directly on the Mediterranean Sea or nearby. Priscilla always tries to access the best locations when possible. I also noticed that the hotel is only a two-minute walk from Caesareum of Alexandria, an ancient temple.

"What can you tell me about Caesareum in Alexandria, Alberto?" I asked as soon as I sat down for dinner.

"Can't you ever relax and enjoy a marvelous evening, Imani? Sometimes to understand complicated issues with more clarity, you must allow your mind to explore in a different direction," Alberto said, pouring me a glass of wine without even asking.

"I did exactly that today. I was able to see the lovely waterfalls and the UNESCO Museum. It was just what I needed to refresh my mind," I said.

"Yes, I know. Bernardo and Amelia both told me that you had a delightful visit with them," Alberto said, smiling.

"How did you know that? Don't tell me that you are related to those two as well?" I asked, surprised.

"No, we are not relate just friends. But, it would help if you remembered Imani, that your safety is my top priority. It is also my reputation that I must make certain is protected," Alberto said, more serious now.

"Well, alright, but can you now tell me about Alexandria? After all, I am also paying you to be my tour guide, or did you forget?" I said, trying to get back on track with this conversation.

"Yes, I am very aware of my obligations. However, I also want you to take home great memories of this trip. Cleopatra VII built the Caesareum as a temple to commemorate her late husband, Julius Caesar's murder, and the devotion that she had for Marc Antony. When Caesar's son, Octavian, resumed power and took over Alexandria, he destroyed every statue that "the Egyptian Whore" constructed except this personal monument. He decided to rededicate that monument to himself. Travelers entering the harbor would notice the two fifteen centuries obelisks from the Temple of Ra in Heliopolis. Currently, you are familiar with these obelisks? One now stands behind the Metropolitan Museum in New York's Central Park. The other one can be found in London's Thames Embankment," Alberto paused to give our dinner order to the waiter.

"I had no idea that the one in New York was an original. How did it ever arrive in New York? Do you know, Alberto?" I asked, genuinely fascinated by this story.

"From what I understand, it was a gift from Egypt to promote increased trade between our two countries in 1877. But, what you will see tomorrow is only the remains. At one point, the center of this temple included ornate gardens, lecture halls, and satellites of the *Great Library*. In the 4th century, it was converted into a Christian church. The philosopher Hypatia was even murdered on the steps in March 415. Some believe that this may also have once been the home of the *Agape Carpet*. Yes, the very same one that Cleopatra chose to wrap herself in on that fateful day that she met Julius Caesar," Alberto stopped to watch my reaction.

This was the first time that Alberto directly referred to the carpet as a subject to explore.

"Do you know any of these historians that would be willing to let me interview them?" I asked anxiously.

"Perhaps. Since Phoenix appears to have left quite abruptly, I can only assume that he has spoken to someone also about this topic. I will make a few calls tomorrow and arrange some meetings with my connections," Alberto said.

"Thank you. Now I am ready to enjoy this lovely meal by candlelight with you, my dear friend. I know that this trip to Alexandria will be exactly what I have been waiting for," I said, taking a deep breath.

There was no way for me to have ever predicted what was coming next.

Chapter Ten

An ember burns crimson beneath the black coals. A fire left for dead, forgotten. I crouch and cup my hands. I remember its promise. In the rush of my breath, the ember glows brighter. It remembers too.

L. H. Leonard
Legend of the Storm Hawks

Alexandria, Egypt
Imani Lewis
August 2017

Arriving in Alexandria after spending a peaceful day at the *Fayoum Oasis* was most definitely an odd cultural transition. Whereas the oasis was quaint, serene, almost sensual, entering the city of Alexandria was dramatic.

I already knew that this was the second-largest city in Egypt, but I had no idea how magnificent it would feel to walk back into history. This was the city that Alexander the Great founded in 331 BCE. It is the home of the great lighthouse, one of the world's seven wonders, and *The Temple of Serapis*, part of the legendary library known throughout the world for its intellectual collection of scholars.

In 415 CE, Hypatia of Alexandria, the daughter of the mathematician Theon, was murdered by a Christian mob who claimed she was a witch. All historical accounts claim that this young, well-educated woman, tutored by her father at the University of Alexandria, was superbly skilled in science. By the time Hypatia began to use her knowledge to help progress Neo-Platonism, religious differences and rivalries were common, erupting violently among the masses.

"I am certain that you already know this, but, Alexandria has a lifetime of history that you cannot possibly appreciate in a few days," Alberto said, as we were deciding on what to see first in this ancient city.

"I wish that I could spend more time here. Alexandria, to me, appears to be much more exciting than Cairo," I said, obviously impressed.

"Both cities have much to offer. Ideally, since the two are located so close, tourists can enjoy the splendor of each," Alberto added.

"Yes, but as you know, I am not just a tourist. My purpose here is to gather whatever information is available to write an award winning article about this *Agape* mystery. Have you learned anything recently that I might be able to use?" I asked, trying to stay on focus.

"I have arranged for a meeting with a very brilliant scholar. His name is Shabaka. You may find him rather odd, even eccentric, regardless, he has many impressive credentials," Alberto said.

"Eccentric in what ways? And what exactly are his credentials? Does this Shabaka have a last name?" I asked skeptically.

Knowing that at least one other person was competing for this prestigious article was making me anxious and restless. Independent writers are well known for being friendly while aggressively pursuing a story. If I was going to have any chance to get the lead it is essential that this trip move rapidly, producing crucial insights. No time for errors.

"Shabaka is known as a mystic. Many others consider him a hermit. It is his critics that prefer to destroy his reputation in order to gain their own fame. I can assure you Imani that if anyone has any legitimate information on this *Agape* search, it is Shabaka," Alberto said, with conviction.

"Alright, Alberto, I am depending on you that this is all legitimate. When will I meet this man?" I asked.

"Tomorrow at 2:00 pm. Until then, may I suggest that you use this time to enjoy the city, learning as much as you can about Alexandria during your brief stay? You might find something interesting that can also be used later in your article," Alberto said before leaving.

With that last suggestion, Alberto left briskly. It was totally unexpected. Our arrangement did not include that he spends his evenings taking me to tourist attractions. Nevertheless, Alberto was correct. Ignoring the opportunity to at least visit part of this city would be foolish. I decided that my first destination would be to travel thirty-one miles west of Alexandria to a site called "Taposiris Magna." Recently I read that a team led by Kathleen Martinez, a well-respected archeologist claimed after fifteen years of excavating that her team was near to discovering the famous Cleopatra remains.

This was a very disputed assertion by many other scholars with expertise in Cleopatra's life. I tended to agree that the Queen would have insisted to be buried with Marc Antony in her personal tomb in Alexandria. Unfortunately, over the past two millennia, the coastal erosions caused parts of Alexandria to remain underwater, including Cleopatra's palace.

Regardless of all this skepticism, I was interested in visiting that site. Cleopatra identified with the goddess Isis, who was both the sister, and wife to Osiris. Osiris is one of the most important gods of ancient Egypt. He may have been considered a personification of the underworld.

Cleopatra may not be buried there, but it was well documented, that she visited that temple. If I could not be near Cleopatra's mummy perhaps visiting where she prayed would provide spiritual enlightenment.

Unfortunately, there was no one there to be found. The archeological teams were all working, excavating, refusing to allow any reporters access to their results. There was however, one young Egyptian student who divulged to me that after five years of laboring on this dig there were essential discoveries. Unfortunately, Cleopatra's remains was not one of these revelations. She advised me to return to Alexandria and explore the Caesareum. I decided to take her recommendation and visit there the next day.

At breakfast that morning, Alberto shared with me that the Caesareum was precisely the location where we would meet Shabaka at 2 pm. That rather surprised me since I expected my visit to be in some secret location after all of the hype.

"May I suggest Imani that we arrive a few hours early. This way we can take advantage of freely walking the grounds before the formal meeting with Shabaka?" Alberto, said.

"Yes, I agree. This will also allow me the opportunity to take a few photos. Will we need a guide?" I asked.

"Oh, not at all. I have been through here many times. Whatever questions you have I can answer, or if not I, Shabaka can," Alberto said.

When we arrived at the Caesareum, I was not surprised that there was nothing to see. Everything that I had read warned me about this.

There was, however, a map available depicting where the ruins may have been. This visual assistance did not make this visit less spectacular.

This grand metropolis founded by Alexander the Great, with congestion, honking cars, and traffic, including five million residents, soon disappeared once Alberto and I began to walk down a dilapidated ladder a few blocks from the Alexandria harbor. Unexpectedly the legendary city appeared below the surface.

"This is it. This is all that we can see. Unless, of course, you wish to put on some diving gear and immerse yourself into the cold Mediterranean ocean?" Alberto said.

"This is just so unbelievable. Here we are standing within a few feet of one of the most impressive archeological sites ever discovered, yet this is all we can experience?" I said, in awe.

"Exactly. Rather ironic isn't it? Beneath our feet are answers to so many questions, yet we have no possible way to retrieve them. Well, at least not at this moment. Many archeologists are discovering every day new fabled remains. Soon maybe even Cleopatra!" Alberto added.

"If there is nothing left of the Caesareum where are we going to meet Shabaka?" I asked, confused.

"Follow me. This will be an experience that you will never forget," Alberto said, taking my hand.

We continued to walk down a dirt path to the sea harbor, past the fish market, past all of the peddlers trying to sell fake Egyptian relics. Finally, we walked about a mile through a cave that led us to what appeared more like a cavern. Inside was an altar, candelabra, a statue of the Virgin Mary, and several pews made from solid stone. It was difficult for me to adjust my eyesight to this darkness. But then Alberto took my hand and led me to the first pew, whispering that Shabaka would soon join us.

"What is this place, Alberto?" I asked, feeling slightly uncomfortable.

"This is where Shabaka lives. He sees very few visitors. You are lucky that he agreed to meet with you today," Alberto said, handing me a paper that felt like papyrus. When I used the flashlight from my phone to examine the contents I realized that the writing was in elaborate hieroglyphics.

"How am I supposed to read this, Alberto?" I whispered, irritated.

"This will help you understand what Shabaka is going to share with you, Imani. Hieroglyphics is written in rows or columns. You may read it from left to right or from right to left. You will find the correct direction by following the human or animal figures. These always face towards the beginning of the line. Also, the upper symbols are read before the lower ones," he said, pointing to the text.

"Well that is very good information to know Alberto, but I still do not understand the context," I said.

Alberto turned over the papyrus sheet. On the other side was an English translation. It said:

Truth! Certainty!
That in which there
Is no doubt!
That from which is above
Is from that which is
Below, and that
Which is below is
From that which is
Above
Working the
Miracles of one
(thing). As all things
Were from one.
Its father is the sun
And its mother the
Moon.
The Earth carried it
In her belly, and the
Wind nourished it
In her belly,
As Earth which shall
Become Fire
Feed the Earth from
That which is subtle,
With the greatest
Power. It ascends
From the heaven

And becomes ruler
Over that which is
Above and that
Which is below.

Holmyard, Eric J
1923, "The Emerald Table"

"I am still not certain that I understand what all of this means, Alberto. What is this Emerald Table that is referred to at the end? Is it significant to my search for the *Agape?*" I asked, realizing how inadequate I must be..

"That will be something you alone will have to discern. I can tell you that *The Emerald Table,* or *Tablet* is also known as **The Tabula Smarsgdina,** a compact and cryptic Hermetic text. It is highly regarded as the foundation of alchemist philosophy. Translations of it have been made by several scholars, like Isaac Newton," Alberto said.

Now I wished that I had paid more attention to those lectures on the mysteries of the famous philosophers. I can only hope that whoever this Shabaka scholar is, he will explain how these ideas relate to *Agape.*

Just as I was about to read these words once again, I felt the presence of another person near me. Alberto had already vanished. In the pew behind me was a small statured person wearing a monk's robe and hood. Because there was no light, except from the candles on the altar, I could not see this person's face.

"I am so glad to see you again Imani. You have grown into a very impressive young lady over these past years. I was sorry to hear about your mother's tragic accident," the stranger said.

Who was this man? How did he know me, and how did he know about Sarah's death?

Then suddenly everything started to begin making sense. At least I recalled who this man was. He is the midget that I met in Cairo when I was only thirteen years old! But, how can this man be Shabaka?

"I know that you must have many questions, Imani. Unfortunately, I will not be able to answer most of them. That is something that you will continue to do as you move toward enlightenment. What I can do for you is help you move on to that next stage."

The next stage was not why I was here. I was here to get some answers about this *Agape Carpet*. Only recently did I even learn that *Agape* is a carpet.

"I am not sure why I am here with you, Shabaka. Perhaps it has something to do with the poems that you gave me by Omar Khayyam and that note about *Agape* the last time I saw you?" I asked.

"Our visit was very brief. I let you fall asleep on my blankets, but then when I returned from my short trip to the alchemist, you were gone. I really hoped that you found your way back to your room, but there was no way for me to make certain," Shabaka said, removing his hood so that I could now see him.

If it wasn't Shabaka then who was it that left me the collection of poems and returned me safely that evening?

"I understand that the reason you are here is to discover if Cleopatra's carpet is in fact, the famous *Agape Carpet,* is that correct?" Shabaka asked, changing the direction of our earlier conversation.

"Yes, you are correct. Although I am not exactly sure that I know enough about the carpet. Does it really have some hidden powers? Even more importantly, what are those powers?" I asked, hoping for some answers.

Although I did not receive any specific details, what I did learn is that my search for *Agape* will include much travel and research. Most importantly, I was learning that Hermeticism is definitely an important characteristic that contributes to the power that this carpet has gained over the centuries. Shabaka explained to me that the art of evolving is at the center of Hermeticism, as well as the transformation of human life and consciousness.

Shabaka read to me the following:

"Those who practice this religion, listen to the beating heart of the spiritual life of humanity. They cannot do otherwise than live as guardians of the life and communal soul of religion, science, and art." (Meditations on the Tarot).

"Are you trying to say that it is my obligation to show the world the miracle of the *Agape?* But, if this is why I have been chosen, I cannot do this by myself, Shabaka. Where do I go next in this journey?" I finally asked the one question I was afraid there was no answer to.

"You are correct Imani. The desire to share the *Agape* mystery with the world is crucial. But, it is also a burden that may cause you much grief and even harm. I would suggest that you allow Phoenix Baldwin to assist you with this tremendous task," Shabaka advised.

There was that name again. How can my nemesis be my adversary?

"I can't do that. I must discover where the *Agape Carpet* is on my own merits. Those with self-centered intentions, I fear, will only destroy what *The Agape* has accomplished. Mr. Baldwin is working for private investors that have no appreciation of what this carpet is capable of achieving. If you decide not to help me, I will have to find someone else who will," I said emphatically.

"There really is very little that I can provide you with, Imani. However, since you insist on pursuing this journey solely on your own, I will tell you the details that I withheld from Mr. Baldwin. The *Agape Carpet* was at one time seen at Machu Picchu. There you will find a tour guide, Dario Sanchez. When you locate him give him this coin. He will tell you all that he knows," Shabaka said, handing me a gold coin stamped with Cleopatra's image.

"Is this the same guide that Phoenix will be using?" I asked.

"Not from me. Mr. Baldwin has another mentor whom I have never met. I just know that he is on the same mission as you," Shabaka said.

I was not sure if any of this information was true. Trusting a little Egyptian person who lives in a cave doesn't seem like the most reliable source. Traveling to Machu Picchu might be a detour preventing me from competing with Mr. Baldwin. Although, I must admit there was also something quite exciting about exploring this fifteenth century Inca citadel located in southern Peru.

Now, all that I needed to do was find the time and the money to accomplish this next stage of my journey.

Chapter Eleven

Since it is impossible to know what's really happening, we Peruvians lie, invent, dream, take refuge in illusion. Because of these strange circumstances, Peruvian life, a life in which so few actually do read, has become literary.

Mario Vargas Llosa
Nobel Prize, Literature 2010

Imani New York 2017

Returning to New York City from Egypt after my meeting with Shabaka resulted in making some serious decisions. Up to this point, *The Agape* was only an intriguing idea, even mysterious, but never anything that I believed I would commit myself to exploring full time. Cairo was one thing. That was a writing assignment, and the opportunity to investigate *Agape* seemed relatively innocent. However, now that I understand that there is a real possibility to discover the true story, my decision to pursue this journey becomes even more problematic. Learning the path this carpet has taken, as well as the people it has influenced is overwhelming. If Shabaka is right about the spiritual powers, this adds another dimension to my odyssey.

Once I made my absolute commitment to follow these leads, committing my life to a new direction was not easy. As a freelance lance journalist, I have ample opportunities available to pursue a variety of jobs. All that changes once I start searching for *The Agape*. My comfortable life in New York will be transformed into the life of a nomad. Wandering the world like a lost soul searching for an elusive answer to Zeno's paradoxes.

In the fifth century BCE, a clever chap named Zeno of Ela designed several paradoxes to prove that contradictions are arguments where the assumption of plurality leads to incongruity or absurdity.

I recall one in particular. It is a very famous example known as *The Achilles and Tortoise Paradox*. In this illustration, Achilles, the greatest of all Greek heroes in mythology, is paired in a foot race with a simple tortoise. Naturally, to be fair, the tortoise is allowed a small lead. There is no doubt that Achilles is faster than the tortoise. However, if Achilles is at point A, and the tortoise is at point B, in order to win the race Achilles must traverse the interval AB. But, in the time allotted for Achilles to arrive at point B, the tortoise, which is considerably slower than Achilles, will nevertheless move forward to point C. And, as this pattern continues, Achilles will continue to be behind the turtle, which is of course quite absurd.

Zeno, being a pre-Socratic philosopher, has continued to challenge theories of space, time, and infinity for the past 2400 years. What is truly impressive is that there is no other method known today to solve these paradoxes.

This brings me to the conclusion that I am the turtle among many who could be considered equals to Achilles. I have no guarantee that any of my leads will ultimately be enough to discover *The Agape*. Yet, like the turtle, there is something that is definitely motivating me to continue with this race. Never again will this opportunity become available to me.

In times like this, I wish that I could speak to my Nani for advice. There is no doubt that she wanted me to accept *The Agape*. Those were her final words to me on her deathbed. But, did she want me to abandon my security for the opportunity to take this *Agape* journey?

Looking through my father's letters, I was also hoping to find some answers. Most of Bran Hughes life was an adventure. The letters he wrote always encouraged me to explore life beyond the usual horizons. Even the name he chose for me means a spirited warrior.

Although Sarah and I only had fifteen turbulent years together, I can now admire her tenacity more than ever before. There wasn't ever anything that Sarah would consider too difficult to undertake, including Mt. Kilimanjaro. Of course that choice did get the best of her. Nevertheless, had she refused to go with Laura, it would have been a personal defeat, one that she could never have lived with.

From the beginning I already knew what my choice would have to be. It was in my genes. At the very least I must compete in the pursuit of *The Agape*. The journey would be just as important as the final tribute.

Once my decision was final, preparing financially was just as paramount emotionally for this long adventure. I had no idea how long it would take, or how many countries I would need to visit. Thankfully, my grandparents left me a substantial trust fund. There was also my inheritance from Sarah's unfortunate death and some funds from an unknown benefactor. I always presumed it was my father, but I never knew this for certain. Those funds were in a Swiss account that only my personal financial advisor was privy to.

Sarah hired Mr. Bradshaw as her financial consultant many years ago. He was still taking care of my accounts today. I rarely needed to speak to him since my income was sufficient to live on until now. Once I decided to start traveling it was also necessary to be realistic financially. How much of these funds would be practical to use for this exploration. Unlike, Phoenix Baldwin I have no wealthy investors paying for my traveling expenditures.

"It is a pleasure to finally meet you Imani. I was beginning to believe that you were only a figment of my imagination. If it wasn't for the yearly taxes that I prepare for you, I don't think that we would ever communicate," Mr. Bradshaw said, offering me a seat in front of his desk.

"I have sent you a Christmas card and I believe also a gift for the past fifteen years. That should count for something," I said, smiling.

"Yes, you are absolutely correct. Always a very thoughtful gesture and always appreciated. But what has brought you here today? Are you considering some long term investments, like property?" Mr. Bradshaw inquired.

"No, nothing that simple. Frankly I am not even sure how much money I will need?" I said, watching Bradshaw looking confused.

I then explained to him my plans, hoping that he could provide me with some practical advice on how to plan for this journey.

"Well, I must say that you are a very mysterious young lady, Imani. You remind me much of your mother. She too was determined to explore the world. You must have inherited some of that desire from her. What I can do is arrange for funds to be wired anywhere in the world that you are visiting. We will set up an account with a balance of your choice. The funds will automatically transfer when the balance drops below an agreed amount. Unless you plan to purchase the Taj Mahal in India, you should have plenty of funds available," Mr. Bradshaw said.

After signing a few documents, I received my bank card. Next, I was on my way to join Priscilla for lunch. She would be the first one to know my plans, now that the finances were all arranged.

It was Priscilla's idea to meet at *Little Italy* since it is close to Mr. Bradshaw's office. At the last minute, she decided to change the place for our lunch meeting. I wasn't sure why Priscilla thought that we could get a table at *Emilio's Ballato.* The wait time was always hours.

"You leave all that up to me, Imani. You said this was a celebration luncheon, and there is no place in this city better to celebrate than Emilio's," Priscilla said, on the phone, as I was flagging down a taxi.

"Okay, Priscilla but, I don't plan on waiting three hours for a table," I said, slipping into the cab.

"Such lack of faith! You know me well enough. I always deliver when I make plans for special occasions," Priscilla said, her voice fading away.

"I will be there in about twenty minutes. Keep an eye out for me. *Emilio's* is always dark inside," I said, now paying attention to the route this cabbie was taking.

"You do know that I'm going to *Emilio's* on East Houston, right?" I said, confirming.

"Yes Ma'am. Traffic is heavier than usual. Just sit back and chill. We will be there as soon as possible," the cabbie said.

I knew by now that this meant that the driver was going to take his own special route, which always meant a larger fee. Whenever this happens I always adjusted the tip. Much easier than arguing. They don't like it, but they realize that I understand their scam and have never argued with me.

Emilio's Ballato inside looks like a tall box. There is nothing pretentious about this room except perhaps the faded walls lined with famous pictures of politicians and movie stars. Chandeliers provide a pleasant light once you pass the dark reception desk. The simple tables are lined with modest white linen table clothes.

I used to think that the waiters were intentionally rude, but then I soon learned that they simply have no personality. They don't need to. The food is so delicious that nobody even cares who serves you.

Any restaurant in New York, anywhere globally, with no telephone, takes no reservations and serves customers like Lenny Kravitz, Barack Obama, Joe Jonas, and Rihanna usually needs no other advertising.

Priscilla was right; as always, she did not disappoint. Once inside *Emilio's,* a hostess, who reminded me of a young Natalie Wood, led me to a table where Priscilla was already seated. All the other tables were also taken.

Immediately Priscilla got up and embraced me.

"I just can't wait to hear your celebration news, sweetheart. I don't see an engagement ring on your finger, so that can't be what this is," Priscilla said, sitting across from me.

I began to regret making this lunch sound like it was on the same level as a marriage proposal. But, to be absolutely fair, I never really said it was a celebration. That was all Priscilla's interpretation.

"What can I bring you ladies to drink?" the waiter said, abruptly.

"Bring us a fine bottle of your Chianti Classico. We are celebrating this afternoon," Priscilla said before I had a chance to respond.

"Now, Priscilla, I really want to share with you some important news, but it may not be in the same category as a celebration. What I mean is that it is more of an announcement," I said, waiting for Priscilla's reaction.

"You're not pregnant are you, Imani?" Priscilla asked, almost whispering.

"NO! Absolutely, not pregnant," I said, laughing.

I then continued to share with Priscilla everything I knew about *The Agape and my decision to search for it*.

"Do you even know if this Phoenix Baldwin is married?" Priscilla asked.

"What? I just told you that I am going to search for this ancient carpet that has mysterious spiritual powers. I have no idea how long I will be gone, and you ask me about Phoenix Baldwin?" I was stunned.

"If you are going to be traveling all over the world chasing some carpet that you don't even know exists, you might as well also take advantage of any opportunities that arise to meet a handsome, wealthy entrepreneur," Priscilla said sipping her Chianti.

"You do understand that Mr. Baldwin is my competitor, my nemesis, right? We are both after the same prize," I said, trying to make Priscilla understand that there was no physical attraction there.

"Many journeys turn out differently than how they start; you know this, Imani. It is quite possible that this Mr. Phoenix Baldwin could become an ally at some time, rather than a contender," Priscilla insisted.

Rather than to continue to persist that she was not understanding the situation, I decided to simply enjoy the rest of my Fettuccini. By the end of our lunch, Priscilla was beginning to realize that everything that I had told her was really going to happen soon.

"You are actually serious about traveling to Machu Picchu? Do you even understand how difficult that terrain is? I have a close friend that hikes everywhere in the world, and when she returned from Peru, she said that the trip to Machu Picchu nearly killed her," Priscilla said.

"I am aware of all the circumstances surrounding this trip. It isn't going to be easy, but if I don't go to Machu Picchu I will never be able to ever find *The Agape*. This journey is like a puzzle. Each missing piece that I find will lead me to the completed picture," I said, determined more than ever now to prepare for this first expedition.

Once I returned to my apartment I began to organize what I needed to complete before my voyage in three weeks. There wasn't much time. But, most of the preparations required packing and storing. After that, it would be a fifteen-hour flight to Peru. But, that was only the beginning. Once in Peru, I was required to take a train from Cusco and eventually a twenty-six-mile Inca trail trek. Finally, the mysterious monumental city would be my reward. That is if I survive.

Chapter Twelve

Machu Picchu seems to demand silence, like a love affair you can never talk about. For a while, after you fumble for words, trying vainly to assemble a private narrative, an explanation, a comfortable way to frame where you've been and what's happened. In the end you're just happy that you were there—with your eyes open— and lived to see it.

Anthony Bourdain
Kitchen Confidential

Imani Lewis
Machu Picchu, 2017

Preparing for my trip to Machu Picchu took as long as the time that I planned to be there. Although my tickets were purchased, the itinerary prepared, and supplies packed, my knowledge of this *Lost City of the Incas* was extremely limited.

Naturally I had seen pictures of what remained and was referred to as an Inca citadel, but this was the extent of my knowledge. It was time for at least a crash course. My focus was really on what I could learn about *The Agape,* not the history of Machu Picchu. Unfortunately, since I also knew very little about this mysterious carpet, it would be necessary to understand how and why *The Agape* ever resided in this temple if, in fact, it ever did.

In my Gratitude Journal, the one I used to write in daily years ago, my entry for today would include how grateful I am for whoever invented the computer system. With only a week before departing for Peru, I began researching, in the comfort of a nearly bare apartment, using my reliable, but dated Dell laptop.

There was no problem finding plenty of information on Machu Picchu. Not only was the information extensive, it included plenty of visuals as well. I already knew that this fifteenth-century ancient city was located on a 7,950foot mountain ridge in the eastern part of the

Andes in Peru. Still, when I saw the actual pictures of the ancient remains, it was truly breathtaking. The very thought that in one week, I would see this in person was difficult for me to comprehend. I also learned that to reach the ruins it is necessary to hike through the Sacred Valley of the Incas. I recall seeing this on the itinerary.

Understanding that most archeologists agree that Machu Pucci was originally constructed as an estate for the Inca emperor, Pachacuti Inca Yupanqui, still offered a variety of different theories. It also disputed earlier claims that Machu Picchu was the *Lost City of the Incas*. Hiram Bingham III, an explorer in 1911, was looking for a city called Vilcabamba. This was known as a hidden capital where the Incas escaped persecution from the Spanish conquistadors in 1532.

The fact that Machu Picchu was a royal estate makes the possibility that *The Agape* certainly could have found its way to this location. What remains a mystery is how the carpet, if it originated in Egypt, might have found a temporary residence in Peru. What powers could that carpet have provided for this dynasty? That may never be understood. But certainly, it is worth exploring.

Once I returned from Cairo and decided to search for The Agape, I immediately contacted Dario Sanchez, the guide that Shabaka advised me to hire. His agency sent me detailed instructions on how I was to prepare for this difficult multi-day hiking event. As I reviewed these recommendations, I immediately thought of those Olympic athletes in training for their competitions. Or, at the very least perhaps a military boot camp.

Priscilla suggested that I hire an exceptional trainer here in New York that could prepare me for this monumental adventure. There were, surprisingly, several reliable agencies that advertised preparations for hiking the Incas. Unfortunately, they all required a minimum of six weeks of preparation. That was far past my deadline. I was scheduled to leave New York in three weeks.

"Well then Imani, you will just need to adjust your schedule. Three weeks is not even a reasonable time for you to become physically fit for this type of hike. Have you even read what the tour guide sent you?" Priscilla said, handing me the letter from Dario.

"Yes, of course I have read his suggestions. It clearly states that, 'you don't have to be an Olympic athlete, but you should be able to walk 5-7 hours a day over relatively tough terrain for 3-4 days in a row.' I can do that. I mean, seriously, I have lived in Manhattan for years. Walking is what we do here," I said, feeling convinced that I was prepared.

"You can't really be serious, are you Imani?"

Priscilla took the letter from my hand and continued to read aloud the remaining instruction.

"...the biggest challenge you will find is that the Inca stairs are uncompromising up and down throughout the trail. This puts a lot of strain on the joint muscles, so building up stamina is key..."

"Okay. So I will start walking up the steps of The Empire State Building every day for the next three weeks. That is 86 flights and 1,576 steps. If the runners who compete every year for the *Empire State Building Run Up* are able to do this, indeed it will prepare me for this Machu Picchu trek," I said in rebuttal.

Priscilla simply shook her head in obvious frustration.

"If you want to believe that the Empire State Building is going to prepare you for one of the most grueling hikes imaginable, then all I can do is pray for you, Imani."

That was the last conversation that Priscilla and I had about Machu Picchu regarding my training regiment.

It even impressed me that I did follow my plan walking those 1,576 steps daily at The Empire State Building. There were moments that I thought that I might pass out, but then it was those athletes preparing for their competition which encouraged me to continue. By the end of my three weeks I felt fairly confident that I was at least semi-prepared for whatever the Inca trail would require.

On Sunday, July 10, 2018, Priscilla drove me to La Guardia Airport at 4:00 am to board my flight that left at 7:31 am on Delta. Since no direct flights were available, I would need to change planes at Atlanta, then at Lima, before arriving at Cusco at 5:50 am the following morning. The entire flight would be twenty-four hours, including layovers.

Thankfully, I was used to these long flights, sent overseas and even to Australia numerous times for journalist assignments. You could say that with my own experiences and traveling with my mother, airplanes became my second home.

Once we landed at Cusco, a charming man greeted me from Dario's tour group.

"Welcome, Imani Lewis, to Cusco! My name is Alejandro, and I will be taking you to the lodge, where you can freshen up, rest, and have a nice meal. Tomorrow morning Dario will be meeting with the entire tour group with details about the hike," Alejandro said, escorting me to a comfortable Lincoln Navigator parked directly outside the baggage claim.

"I do have one bag that I need to claim," I said before we exited.

"No problem. It will arrive at the lodge shortly," Alejandro said, opening the back door for me.

Inside there was some refreshing bottled water and a small bag of shortbread cookie sandwiches filled with dulce de leche. I was familiar with this filling. It is a caramel confection prepared slowly by heating milk and sugar for hours.

"These cookies are truly amazing, Alejandro. I have never tasted anything so decadent before," I said, taking another bite.

Alejandro laughed at my comment.

"And, I have never heard anyone refer to these cookies as decadent, but I will tell the baker that you approve," he said pleasantly.

"Well, if you were a lady, Alejandro, you would understand that anything that tastes this good and with these many calories is considered decadent. Especially when you eat too many," I said, ignoring my warning continuing to eat more cookies.

"Trust me, Imani, the hike you are about to experience will easily take care of any undesirable calories you may be indulging in now," Alejandro said, once again laughing.

The lodge was about forty miles from the airport, and although I did sleep a little during the flight, I could tell that jet lag was beginning to set in. I was looking forward to a warm shower and a comfortable bed.

Once we pulled into the parking lot, an elderly gentleman met us at the valet parking.

"Greetings, Imani Lewis, from all of us at MP Hiking Trails. We are excited to share with you all that we know about Machu Picchu," the gentleman said, extending his hand to assist me out of the SUV.

"Thank you. I am anxious to meet Dario and begin our adventure together," I said.

"You will find your luggage in your room when you arrive. This is your room key. I will briefly acquaint you with the hotel amenities. You will then have plenty of time to rest," the gentleman said, adding, "My name is Cristiano Salvador, at your service."

"I am pleased to meet you, Cristiano. You have a lovely name. Thank you for your hospitality," I said, trying to be polite despite being exhausted.

Cristiano must have sensed that I was moving very slowly since he said, "Please take the elevator to the third floor, and you will find your room two doors away. If you find that you are hungry later, our kitchen is open twenty-four hours for room service. Don't hesitate to call."

I followed Cristano's directions, and within minutes, I was in my room. With only enough energy to shut the drapes, I fell into the bed, wearing the same clothes I started the day with, and immediately fell asleep.

What are you doing here, Imani? Did you not learn from my death that there are limitations to how far you should push yourself? Do you remember when Peter Pan announces that "to die will be a huge adventure"? Well, it is not an adventure. Death is a problem. If anything, it sometimes invites us to live eternally while always providing us with ways to end our lives without notice. For Peter Pan, his fear of death forces him to live. My advice to you, darling, is to always live with love in your heart and ignore death knocking at your door. Make this Agape your journey, not a competition.

As quickly as I fell asleep suddenly now, I sat up startled, not knowing where I was or who was speaking to me. It took me a few minutes before I realized where I was. Waiting now to begin my pilgrimage, not knowing how it would end or what it would even accomplish, wasn't necessary. What was important is that for the very first time, I was beginning to realize that everything from this point forward was out of my control, and yet, somehow also totally under my control. Nothing else seemed to matter at the moment. I had a purpose that led me to accomplish a journey, and I was determined to do just that.

Chapter Thirteen

Male privilege is assuming that one has the right to occupy any space or person by whatever means, with or without permission.

Kate Bornestein
American Playwright

I was eager to meet with Dario Sanchez privately. Shabaka seemed to believe that not only was Dario the best tour guide for my Machu Picchu hike, but also he would be able to provide me with some essential information on *The Agape*. Since at this point I really did not have any other reliable leads Dario was a prerequisite to where my next move would take me.

The reception room downstairs where all the hikers were meeting this morning was already crowded.

Certainly, not all of these people are included in my group? I thought silently.

"Quite a lively motley crew we are, don't you think?" Said a gentleman who approached me from some unknown corner of the crowded room.

"Yes. I was just wondering if all these people are going to be traveling together with the same guide . I mean, it just appears like a very large group for such a perilous hike," I said, sipping my tea, trying not to sound pretentious.

"Oh, yes...you are correct. A group this large would be impossible to maneuver through the Qhapaq Nan safely."

"You must be one of the guides? My name is Imani Lewis, and I have signed up for the tour with Dario Sanchez," I said, extending my hand politely to shake.

"Ah, yes. I remember Dario mentioning your name. You are the reporter that is going to do a story on the mysterious carpet. I apologize for not introducing myself earlier. I am Dario's younger brother, Paulo; together, we will be your guides."

"Will it be just the two of you," I asked, a little concerned.

"Yes, most of the way, but, I can assure you Dario and I have been conducting these exclusive private tours our entire lives. And since Dario has indicated that you will want to speak directly to *Apu*, we are the only guides that have access to where he resides."

I wanted to ask Paulo if they also took Phoenix Baldwin to this Apu, but I decided against pursuing that question. My competition was not only with Baldwin it was also with them to meet Apu. We were all racing to find this carpet first and this must be my only focus.

"You are correct, Paulo; I am a freelance writer. Traveling here to Peru is where I hope to discover some critical leads to help me write a firsthand account about a very sacred carpet that has vanished," I said, trying to be elusive.

"If this *Agape* carpet was ever in Machu Picchu I can assure you that Apu will be able to validate this for you," Paulo said.

When I was about to ask more about Apu and how he knew about *The Agape*, our conversation abruptly ended. Several other tour guides took the stage, introducing themselves and explaining where their groups would be meeting for a brief orientation. Dario's team was meeting in a small room known as *Manco Capac*. We were later informed that this room is named after the legendary founder of the Inca Dynasty in Peru.

After a brief introduction that included two other travel guides, myself, a young couple, and three other young men, we all sat down to watch a video illustrating where we would soon be hiking. The film was quite informative. It also reaffirmed that the four-day Inca Trail trek would include twenty-six miles to compete, from start to finish.

Dario stressed that we would be walking on an extensive network of Inca footprints known as *Qhapaq Nan*. This was the same place that Paulo mentioned to me earlier. Dario added that the meaning of that Inca word is "Royal Road." We would enter Machu Picchu from this road that once led to the remote citadel. More importantly, we would be entering the sacred ruins through the Sun Gate. Later in a private conversation, Dario assured me that at this point, the group would take separate routes. That would be when I would meet *Apu*.

I was also reminded to bring with me the coin that Shabaka gave me. Dario never revealed how he knew about this coin, and I never asked him. Paulo would then proceed with the others on an alternative path. No further information was given to me about *Apu* at this time.

The evening before our departure, we were instructed to be assembled at 4:30 am to leave the hotel. Only one backpack was allowed. All other luggage would remain at the hotel. Once we arrived at the campsite, a hearty breakfast would be provided. We were encouraged to eat well. Our first two-and-a-half-hour hike would begin shortly after breakfast. I was thankful to learn that most of that hike would be on flat ground.

"When you arrive at Llactapata, our first stop, you will be given your first history lesson about Peru. After this brief rest break it will be another hour and a half before lunch. The final two-and-a-half-hour trek this first day to Ayapata will be where we will stay for our first night campsite. It is a short 3,300 meters," Paulo said.

This complete introduction was somewhat informative and rather overwhelming. I was beginning to comprehend the reality of this journey. By tomorrow morning this hiking tour would be real. Meeting Apu at my final destination is truly the reward for weeks of disciplined training. Dario assured me that any further information or questions would be addressed at that time.

The remainder of this presentation must have occurred while I was mind walking since Dario was still standing directly in front of me speaking, but I had heard nothing.

"I am so sorry but my mind just sometimes wanders off. I was trying to absorb everything that you just shared," I said, slightly embarrassed.

"That is quite natural. There is a great deal to assimilate. I just wanted to assure you that once we enter the Sun Gate, I will personally escort you to the site where your visit with Apu will begin. I do need to warn you that this visit will be short. Have your specific questions prepared beforehand. This is essential. Nobody knows how old *Apu* is, or exactly where he resides. But, I was able to locate him for you. I do hope he will be rational and accommodate your questions. There are no guarantees," Dario said reluctantly.

"Naturally. I understand the circumstances. There is no problem with being prepared. I have been planning this visit for quite a while. I was wondering, however, is Apu the only source in Machu Picchu that is an authority about *The Agape?*" I asked curiously.

Dario hesitated for a few seconds. I wasn't sure why. But, finally, he answered me.

"Strange that you should ask this question. A few days ago, there was another man here asking similar questions. I am not certain how many other wise men have knowledge about this carpet. But, what I do know is that *Apu* is very selective about who he speaks with. He respects Shabaka and will only meet with those who Shabaka sends him," Dario said.

Since Shabaka never spoke to Phoenix I felt fairly confident that my time with *Apu* would be exclusive. Whatever information Phoenix might have learned from his visit to Machu Picchu would not be as accurate as mine. I trusted that Shabaka was authentic. Why I was chosen to pursue Agape may never be revealed, but there are now enough people who have encouraged me to move forward that I now must proceed. One advantage that I do have over Mr. Baldwin is that he has no idea who I am or what I am capable of achieving.

My main objective is to learn if *The Agape Carpet* is the same carpet that Cleopatra used to present herself to Caesar. If so, how did it find its way here to Machu Picchu? The distance from Alexandria to Peru is 7,479 miles. It is difficult to imagine how this carpet could travel this great distance. Then there is the question as to why it even ended up in this location. All perplexing issues, recalling that Cleopatra's *Presentation Carpet* to Julius Caesar first appeared in 48 BCE, when she was only twenty years old. This initiates even more questions about how, when, and why the carpet would ever be in this Inca citadel.

The following morning I was eager to begin answering many of my questions, and of course, meet with Apu. Our day started with a stunning drive where the Andes mountain range was beginning to appear at sunrise. Everyone who had been sleeping when we left the lodge was now mesmerized by the natural beauty surrounding us. The campsite elevation at 3,300 meters didn't even seem important anymore.

As promised, the first two and half hours of the hike were reasonably flat until we reached the Inca site of Llactapata. We were greeted there by three men who introduced themselves as Inca descendants. The three storytellers, Apocatequil, Guacamaya, and Micos, each took turns sharing their histories with us.

Apocatequil, whose name means god of lightning, was the first to clarify that few facts about the Inca origin are available, even after years of studying genetic information. This was primarily because the mummies and bodily remains of those Inca Emperors, who were worshipped as gods, were all burnt or buried in unknown regions. This, he added, was due primarily because of political persecution by Christian conquistadors, as well as inquisitors.

Next, Guacamaya, also known as McCay, added that there were two popular myths about the origin of the Incas. First is the one related to Manco Capac and Mama Ocllo. They were the founding parents, who originated from the Sun god, Lake Titicaca. This theory also supports that Machu Picchu was more than a residential palace, but also a spiritual, religious temple.

Micos, also fondly nicknamed Monkey, provided us with an alternative myth. This one refers to four Ayar brothers with divine powers, who emerged from a hidden cave inside of Paccarictambo, 50 km south of Cusco. Of course, neither theory can substantiate that any of these Incas were related to Pachacutec.

The three storytellers then gave us a printed flyer with additional details about Machu Picchu and the 9th Inca ruler, Pachacutec Yupanqui. It was because of his successful conquests in the Cuzco Valley, and beyond that, he is credited with founding what remains today as Machu Picchu.

Although the storytelling was a nice addition to the tour, it really did not provide me with any new information on my personal quest. However, in the next few days, I might appreciate this rest time much more.

The first day continued with another hour and a half hike before lunch. This was followed by an additional two and a half hour walk to our first camp at Atapata. Our total walking distance thus far was 14 km, and I still felt reasonably strong. But, Dario suggested that after dinner we all retire early. Day two was going to begin at 4:45 am.

I really should have realized that when this hike was taking us to *Dead Woman's Pass that the worst was about to happen.*

Chapter Fourteen

After seeing the ruins of Machu Picchu, the fabulous cultures of antiquity seemed to be made of cardboard Papier-mâché.
Pablo Neruda 1954
Nobel Prize Winner for Literature 1971

Day two on my way to Machu Picchu truly challenged every fiber of my being. It was a 16km hike towards the highest point (4215 meters) to a place named *Dead Woman's Pass*. Dario explained that the name reflects an image resembling the supple form of a woman when seen from the valley below.

It soon became apparent that *Dead Women's Pass* is not recognized because of its image. Rather, it is the highest, most dreaded point of the Inca Trail. At nearly 5,905 feet, it is higher than the altitude of Machu Picchu, our final destination.

This trek requires that most of the next few days be spent at higher altitudes, with fewer trees for shade. Also, for the first time, the passes are rockier, uneven, making accidents more plausible. We were also warned that there might be unexpected weather conditions that vary from extremely hot sun exposure to cool rains with strong winds.

By this time, I began to lack confidence that I would ever make it to the Sun Gates. Dario, having sensed my anxiety, called for an unexpected rest break. Everyone appeared to be grateful for this.

"You are going to make it to our final stop for the day, Imani, although at this moment you may have some doubts," Dario said, sitting next to me on a rather large boulder.

"How do you manage to accomplish this trip several times a year, Dario? I mean, it is evident that you have the body of an athlete, but this does not explain how you can motivate us to continue," I asked, breathing quite heavily.

"Are you having doubts about making it to the Sun Gates, Imani? Because if so, it is understandable. But, let me assure you, that once we complete this segment of the hike, your spirit will become overwhelmingly refreshed, making everything much clearer. It would help if you remembered that this is not only physical endurance. It is a mental challenge preparing you to convene with *Apu,"* Dario said, looking deep beyond my eyes, into my soul.

When Dario walked away to prepare the others to continue for the next two hours without a break, I realized that all the physical training that I did in New York was also now mentally preparing me for a discovery that could change the course of my life. The following two hours I would rely on my study of Hermeticism.

Understanding and expecting that the universe moves on some fundamental natural laws help us deal with any obstacles, real or imaginary. When I remind myself that there is very little that we can control, or that we can modify, the idea that gravity exists, birds can fly, everyone lives, as well as dies, there is little in between to challenge.

Without getting into all the specific details, those who believe in empirical knowledge pursue mystical experience to communicate a more visionary reality. These thoughts lead to a mental plane, physical plane, and spiritual plane. I believe that this is what Dario was implying during our short pause from hiking..

Everything that Dario said during those few moments when I was feeling defeated encouraged me to make it to our next destination ultimately. Here we were able to visit our first two Inca cites, Runku Raccay, and Sayacmarka.

Rinku Raccay is translated to mean abandoned or collapsed houses. What makes this structure unique is that unlike other buildings in the Inca ruins these have circular enclosures among the structures that are not found anywhere else. Some archeologists have assessed it may be a final burial tomb, or perhaps a religious sanctuary. Whatever it might have been, seeing it now is an exciting preview to the main event, Machu Picchu.

Unlike Runku Raccay, Sayacmarka is thought to have been a rather cramped settlement laid out in a maze. The one factor that this site has in common with all the others is that the view is unobstructed. Dario also pointed out a line of observation platforms between here and Machu Picchu suggests that the Incas used a messaging system to send information and perhaps a way to warn of any potential invaders.

At the end of this day we were halfway to our final destination. Our guides assured us that most of the remaining trails would be easier to navigate. I didn't believe them. All that I wanted to do was to sleep in a bed for about twelve hours. That would not happen for at least three more days.

Before I retired for the evening, after a short dinner, I reviewed my notes for the interview with *Apu*. Since Dario emphasized that there would be limited time, I must be as prepared as possible under these circumstances. Tomorrow's hike, we were promised, would offer a unique view of the Vilcabamba mountain range. There was also a site called Winay Wayna, which means *Forever Young*. This place will have impressive buildings and terraces to scour.

As we begin moving closer to the Sun Gate and the end of this part of my journey, I am reflecting on how far behind in this trip I may be to the other treasure hunters. Although I am determined not to allow negative thoughts to discourage me from continuing, it is also necessary to be practical. This includes using empirical strategies to plan where my next travels might take me. I presume that Phoenix Baldwin has visited Machu Picchu, although I am not sure when. Nor, do I have any idea what he may have learned.

Then again, Phoenix is just another speck of dust in this universe. One that I must acknowledge but not allow to divert me.

The next morning at 6:00 am was the first time I joined the other four hikers for early coffee since we met at the lodge during our orientation. It was a substantial breakfast of scrambled eggs, sausage, potatoes, and baked beans. Today, everyone was gathered together, eager to continue our shared pilgrimage.

The young married couple from Australia, celebrating their honeymoon in Lima, pulled up a camp chair next to me. When the husband got up to get his breakfast, his wife, Mia said, "Good morning! I was just wondering if you are aching all over like I am?"

I remembered her name because I once had a parrot named Mia when I lived with my grandparents in Africa.

My first reaction to her question was to burst out in a hilarious laugh. This girl is half my age and looks like a model. It is difficult for me to believe that she has anything to complain about. Then it occurred to me that she might just want to start a friendly conversation.

"Yes, absolutely! I thought that my training would prepare me for all this, but that little jaunt over *Dead Woman's Pass* was almost enough to make me raise my white flag and ask for mercy," I said, not exaggerating.

"My husband, Tom ,it is still hard for me to believe he is really my 'husband.' We have only been married for a week. Well, Tom plays professional soccer in Australia, and this hike isn't anything for him to achieve. Your name, is Imani, am I correct?" Mia asked.

I was taken aback for a moment that she knew who I was. Not sure why since I remembered her name.

"Yes, I am Imani Lewis," I said, extending my hand.

"Glad to meet you, Mia, and, oh, Congratulations on your marriage," I said, trying to be polite and cordial.

"Thank you. We came to Peru for our honeymoon. Tom and I wanted to go somewhere different from all the other stereotypical honeymoon spots. After visiting the Amazon rainforests, I now know why they are referred to as 'Lungs of the world'. It was such an amazing adventure. That is when Tom suggested that we should visit Machu Picchu since it was so close," Mia said, waving to Tom from her chair.

Before I could even respond, Tom arrived back with breakfast for him and Mia.

"Oh, darling, come meet Imani. Remember, she is the writer that your friend, Phoenix, mentioned at the lodge?" Mia, said, taking her plate from Tom.

Hearing this reference to Phoenix immediately got my attention.

Was he here? Like right now? I know he isn't on this tour. And, is he really friends with Tom? Why does Phoenix Baldwin even remember my name?

"Excuse me. How do you know Phoenix Baldwin, Tom? We barely know each other," I said, trying not to sound agitated.

"Oh, I'm not really friends with Phoenix. We only met here at the lodge. On our first night, he bought Mia and me a bottle of champagne to celebrate our wedding. When I asked him if he could recommend a tour guide for Machu Picchu, he gave me Dario's name. He said that it must be a good tour company since you were using him and you are a well-known journalist," Tom said.

It all sounded quite suspicious. Why would Phoenix Baldwin even mention my name? Maybe Tom could also give me more information on who Phoenix Baldwin is.

When I returned to the table with my breakfast, Mia had already left, but Tom was still finishing his coffee.

"Do you have any idea what tour group Phoenix is using, Tom? I thought when I returned to the lodge maybe we could compare notes," I said, quite casually.

"No, I really don't know. But, I do recall that he was leaving on his excursion two days earlier than our tour. He had an appointment with some archeologists at one of the ruins. I thought that this sounded odd, but just presumed that he had exceptional credentials being an archeologist himself," Tom said.

Archeologist? I suppose that title works just as well as any other lie? But where are these other ruins that he was exploring all about? And, why was he returning before us?

There was only one person who might know anything more, and that would be Dario.

At our stop at Initpata, *The Terraces of the Sun*, I found Dario. When asked about these other ruins, he avoided my questions, turning his attention to the terraces. Dario explained that this was where mainly corn, potatoes and most of the produce were grown. Once harvested, they were then transported to Machu Picchu. our evening retreat was also going to be at this site.

Later I found Dario at the observation point by himself. The perfect time to approach him with my personal issues. The view from where we were was unbelievable. The sky resembled an artist's palette with blended colors that I had never seen before in my life. It was as if a rainbow exploded, releasing the unique shades of mint green emulsified with mustard yellows and streaks of purple, wrapping the visible color spectrum into new color magnitudes.

"By tomorrow Imani, you will be sipping tea with *Apu.* Are you beginning to get excited?" Dario asked?

"Yes, but I do have a few questions that were recently brought to my attention by Tom and Mia," I said calmly.

Dario stepped down from the elevated mound to hear me.

"Very well, what can I help you understand?" Dario asked.

"I was told that Phoenix Baldwin is here. I don't literally mean where we are now, but he is on a longer tour that will take him to other ruins prior to Machu Picchu. Do you know what route he is taking and what other ruins might he find that are important?" I said, trying not to sound demanding.

Dario walked around the site with his hands in his pockets for a few minutes, before he approached me. He then took my hand and led me to a rather large flat boulder where could sit.

"First, Imani, whatever Mr. Baldwin is doing on another tour is none of my business or yours. Many people visit Machu Picchu for various reasons. As long as it is not illegal, all of us tour guides accommodate without questioning. As I informed you before, *Apu* is the most respected guru known in Machu Picchu. He never speaks to anyone without a reliable reference. And, nobody but I can take visitors to him. If this Mr. Baldwin has found another source; I can assure you that you have the advantage. I hope this information relieves any anxiety that you may have," Dario said, standing, preparing to leave.

"Very well, Dario, I take you at your word. Whatever happens tomorrow with *Apu* will be my fate. I will forever be thankful for sharing this experience with you," I said.

Dario embraced me as we walked back to the campsite. It was all now in God's hands. I did appreciate the irony. Here I am searching for answers. I am trying to trace a carpet that may have the Agape spirit. A spirit that embraces universal, unconditional love. And, I am doing all this while hiking in the Andes Mountains of Peru, one of the most well-known sacred places on earth.

Chapter Fifteen

"The name of the story is "The all American Smile." And, it's by Hubbell Gardiner.

"In a way he was like the country he lived in. Everything came too easily to him, but at least he knew it."

Arthur Laurents
The Way We Were

Dario and I arrived at *The Temple of the Sun* on day four, while the others were taken to The Temple of the Condor by Paulo. As promised, my meeting with *Apu* would be private. At the conclusion, Dario would return and escort me back to the lodge ahead of the others.

I was slightly curious if Dario said anything to the other hikers about my absence. When I mentioned this, he assured me that it was not unusual for guests to request private tours and nobody would notice that I was no longer there.

So, here I am, at my final destination, *The Temple of the Sun*, standing by myself at one of the most important structures in Machu Picchu. At one time, only priests and noblemen were allowed to stand where I am now.

Before arriving in Lima, I recall reading during my research that this structure was meant to combine artificial and natural elements. As I drag my hand across the calm yet the rough surface of the semicircular outer wall of the Torreón (tower or turret), my senses are cognitively astute. This entire structure is a rarity among the Inca architecture.

This is when I notice a natural outcrop of rock inside this Torreón that many believe may have served as a ritual altar. Approaching the windows within the tower walls, I am aware, just as I have read, that these windows are aligned to the summer and winter solstices.

Could this be similar to the Stonehenge monument in Wiltshire, England? There is an image that I recall seeing in a book of drawings by William Stukeley. The engraving portrays druids paying homage to their Sun through sacrificing. This idea was disputed by the architect, John Wood, who surveyed Stonehenge in 1740.

His interpretation was that this was used as a pagan shrine. Stuckeley, continued to argue that the druids at Stonehenge were actually Biblical patriarchs.

Being so engrossed with my surroundings, I failed to notice an oddly dressed person wearing a hooded cape standing near an opening that appeared to be an entrance to a cave. As I approached this odd being, he extended a very boney finger out of his sleeves and waved me to follow his lead. Although this approach did seem rather strange, I kept reminding myself where I was and why I spent four grueling days climbing this mountain to reach my destination. This put everything in a more proper perspective.

Once inside the cave, there was somehow enough light to see this tiny creature leading me, but certainly not enough light to distinguish anything else. Subsequently, what must have been about one hour of silent walking at times felt like we were going in random circles; the little person stopped and signaled for me to take a seat on the cement bench across from what resembled an altar. I did what I was asked without questioning, preparing myself for just what might come next.

Actually, after so many days of mainly walking on the uneven rocky ground all day, this cool cave interior was an inviting sanctuary. But then, just as my eyes began to adapt to the darkness, I saw a very tall man appear from thin air. As he stood near the altar, I could see his long white hair and a matching white beard. Both were mostly hidden under the hooded cape. This attire also resembled that of the initial little person's outfit that I saw entering the cave. Perhaps they belonged to the same religious order? There was, however, an apparent distinction between the two men's robes. The taller man wore a cape that was a rich purple velvet with sparkling objects resembling stars randomly scattered. Whereas the little person's cape resembled a poor monks.

Gracefully gliding past me, the taller monk appeared as if he was a floating image. He then took a vessel from the altar, poured some liquid into a pewter flask, walked towards me, and said very pleasantl, "Greetings, Imani Lewis. I do hope that your trip here was not too difficult? Darios is a very competent guide. He does his best to make this journey as comfortable as possible." He then handed me a suspicious-looking libation.

My first reaction was to reject his offer politely. I remembered the last time when a strange little person offered me a drink in a cave. But, instead, I held the silver chalice in my hand, reasonably pondering what to do next. This entire scene was too reminiscent of what I recalled happened in that cave in Cairo when I was thirteen years old.

"Go ahead and drink the pomegranate beverage, Imani. It is quite safe. *Apu* only offers the best to his guests," the stranger added, noticing my reluctance.

"Are you *Apu?*" I asked before taking my first sip.

"Yes, I am known as *Apu.* Although not born *Apu.* This was the name given to me by my God. You see, Imani, the **Runasimi** language spoken by my people, the Quechuans, use the term *Apu* to refer to a mountain that has a spirit that lives."

By this time, I felt obligated to follow my host's instructions, so I began drinking from the chalice. Although still skeptical of what it was that *Apu* had given me to drink, it was relatively refreshing. After my hike in this warm Peruvian sun, I was beginning to feel somewhat strange, even before this libation.

Oddly this reminded me of when Alice enters *Squishville,* a game created by Fandom. Without going into specific detail, there is this scene, obviously lifted from the original *Alice in Wonderland* by Arthur Liddell. The original character, *Alice Liddell,* is the daughter of the writer Arthur Liddell. In this rendition, Alice is the only survivor of a house fire that kills her entire family. This results in Alice suffering immense trauma, which leads her to a distorted reality, an imaginary world that she calls *Wonderland.*

Years ago, I recalled writing an article on this absurd theatre interpretation of the original work written by Lewis Carroll. One of the fascinating aspects of this version was how Alice uses her imaginary *Wonderland* to escape her daily shattered psyche.

The quote that I now consider to be most relevant is when Alice meets Jules Verne and says, "I'm Alice Liddell. And, like you, I never refuse a…how do you refer to it, 'Voyage Extraordinaire'?

Suddenly my wandering mind was interrupted.

"Imani? How are you feeling now that your refreshment is settling inside of you?" *Apu* asked, waiting patiently for me to react.

"Mushrooms, Poppies, Sugar, and Spices. All those things are very nice. When combined, the proper mixture makes it like getting a small elixir," I said, quoting Alice Liddell without even trying.

"Excellent! Then we are almost ready to begin our session," *Apu* said, leading me deeper into the cave.

We were now sitting together in some very plush theatre-style chairs. Although it was even darker than in the previous room, it appeared we were here to view a movie, although there was no screen and obviously no network.

"Are you quite comfortable, Imani?" *Apu* asked.

Although he was seated directly next to me, it sounded as if *Apu* was speaking from afar. I concluded that the strange acoustics in the cave contributed to this.

"Yes, thank you. I am quite comfortable. Would you mind if I ask you a few questions?" I said, fearing that Dario would return and nothing would be accomplished.

"Of course, Imani. But, I do believe that I already know what you are inquiring about. You are here to ask me about *The Agape Carpet,* correct? *Apu,* said.

"Yes, that is correct. Shabaka strongly recommended you as an authority on this matter," I whispered, sounding as if my voice was echoing.

"What I am about to reveal to you, Imani, nobody else has seen. Others may have similar information, but I can assure you nobody has the correct details. I have chosen to share this with you only because I am sure that when the appropriate time comes, you will know what you must do," *Apu* stated solemnly.

Why did he believe that I would know what to do? Honestly, all that I am certain of at this moment, is the closer I get to this Agape carpet, the closer I will be to the Pulitzer.

"I will do my very best to be the keeper of this essential information that you are entrusting to me," I said.

"Very well. I do believe you are ready. Let us begin from the earliest known story of this carpet before it was blessed to be *The Agape Carpet*. As you know Cleopatra used a rug to wrap her body with the intention to surprise Julius Caesar. That carpet was then sold to a local carpet maker who was told the significance of the rug. Not sure what to do with it, the elderly gentleman rolled it up and stored it in a safe place until he could determine how to make a profit from this gift," *Apu* stopped waiting for questions.

Since I already knew most of this story I had no questions. It was the following story when everything started to become interesting. *Apu* explained that Egypt was practicing many different interpretations of Christianity before Christ was born. The essence of the Christian belief was centered in the Egyptian faith of resurrection after death, the reckoning of sins and, distinguishing between heaven and hell.

About sixty years after the death of Cleopatra her carpet was used to weave a gift for the child known as Jesus. The original carpet maker was no longer alive but when his son discovered this carpet he decided to use the remnants, which were in excellent condition, to create a new carpet for this baby Jesus who was coming to Egypt.

Unfortunately, the carpet was never presented to Jesus until many years later in Galilee. No one is certain how it arrived there, but there were Egyptian symbols that remain today. These symbols support the theory that this was originally the carpet used by Cleopatra.

"But, there is no real evidence that documents this hypothesis, is there?" I asked.

"Nothing but this papyrus certificate. It was included with the carpet when it was discovered here at Machu Picchu," *Apu* said, pointing to the cave wall that projected an image of this letter.

"Where did that come from, and is it authenticated? Do you actually have this letter here in your possession?" I asked.

There wasn't even any projector that I could see in this cave. How was *Apu* able to provide this theatrical presentation? Even if he had access to the newest technology, known as *Gobi Source,* a computerized version of the old projectors, it still would not explain how this papyrus was restored.

"It really doesn't matter Imani, how this papyrus document was found, or where it is now. What I want you to observe is the symbols that are etched on the diagram of the carpet. Egyptian symbols are used in magical and religious rituals throughout Egypt. Now, notice the following ones that were selected to decorate this carpet. These were going to be presented to Jesus." *Apu,* using a long wooden branch, pointed to the following symbols.

"First, there is *The Ankh.* Notice the showcase position. This is because it represents the concept of internal divine protection. It is a cross with a looped top. Giving homage to eternal life, the morning sun, and most importantly, the union of opposites, such as the earth, heaven, or male and female.

Next is the *Djed.* It is a pillar-like object that represents stability. This is also known as 'The Backbone of Osiris', because of the strength and balance needed for resurrection and eternal life.

Finally, the last Egyptian symbol that was chosen to be included in this new carpet was *The Lotus Symbol.* Also known as a Water Lily. This flower closes at night, sinks underwater, and in the morning, it resurfaces refreshed. This is why it has become a widely accepted symbol to represent the sun, creation, and regeneration.

We will never know exactly why the carpet maker chose only these symbols, since there were many available and more likely many different ones on the original Cleopatra carpet. But, it does seem to establish a pattern that others have recognized as powerful." *Apu* waited for my reaction.

Although all of this information was fascinating, without corroborating evidence, or at least a photo of this papyrus, it would not be easy to write anything that could be taken seriously.

"Is there any way that I would be able to take a photo of this document, *Apu?*" I asked reluctantly.

"Unfortunately, no Imani. But, there is still so much more that you must understand about *The Agape* before you continue on your journey," *Apu* added.

I listened attentively as *Apu* continued sharing this story. What I learned next certainly explained why so many treasure hunters are also in pursuit of this relic.

"When *The Agape* arrived at Machu Picchu, by around 1460, it was no longer the original carpet. It now had unbelievable powers weaved throughout the years by many other generations. Although it is impossible to trace all the locations that this carpet traveled before being brought here, we do know that it finally made its way to Jesus in Galilee. A scribe, known as Benicio, copied the testimony of a young woman. When she arrived one day with this gift for Pachacuti Inca Yupanqui, this mysterious gift bearer, stated that only "a reformer of the world" with the status of this magnificent ruler could appreciate *The Agape Carpet*. She then shared with the emperor that this carpet was woven from the hair of Jesus and his disciples.

Once the carpet was unwrapped it now looked more like a tapestry. Pachacuti was truly impressed. The emperor listened attentively to how Jesus eventually blessed this carpet.

When *Agape* later somehow surfaced at a home in Galilee, it had some interesting Egyptian symbols. The new owner had no idea what those symbols meant. But, it did remain in his unique collection of prized investments for many years. When this carpet maker was told that the prophet, known as Jesus, was in town with his disciples, he was eager to hear him speak. As fate sometimes intercedes, later that afternoon, Jesus and his disciples stopped at the carpet makers' humble home for some water from his well.

When the carpet maker saw Jesus, he ran inside his home and brought the most valuable gift he could find, his Egyptian rug. He told Jesus that it was not complete yet, but he wanted him to have it as a testimony of his faith in Jesus.

When Jesus heard this story, he instructed the man to complete the carpet with the Christian symbols that would later be associated with Jesus' teachings. Jesus then asked for a pair of shears. The carpet maker accommodated this request. When Jesus received the scissors, he clipped small pieces of locks from all the disciple's hair, including his own.

According to the notes later found by scholars but never included in any scriptures, the carpet maker was instructed to weave the carpet with the hair he was given and include these Christian images. Jesus then blessed the carpet, saying that it would be forever now known as *The Agape Carpet*.

Although the carpet maker felt the spirit of Jesus, he had no idea of this carpet's energy. Nevertheless, he followed the instructions given by the Messiah as directed." Apu paused, waiting for me to ask questions.

"This is a fascinating story, but once again, there is no documentation that can be validated. Why isn't any of this included in the scriptures by the disciples?" I asked.

"You do know Imani, that there are many accounts about Jesus that were never found, or accounts that have chosen to be excluded by those who were in authority. Those same men ultimately decided what should be included in the Bible. For example, ten books are excluded from the Bible, and fourteen books were removed. There are many important religious texts that scholars unearthed that were never included in any formal documents. Some were previously unavailable artifacts and even written chronicles. One of the most well-known are Gnostic Gospels, discovered in 1945. Or, even the Gospel of Judas, just recently discovered. A great number of these non-canonical gospels were also once accepted by various Christian groups as sacred Scriptures. Then it was concluded by anonymous religious leaders that some of these stories were considered bizarre and must be prohibited. Many of us believe that this is what happened to *The Agape* story." *Apu* stopped once again, waiting for my reaction.

What I was hearing did sound plausible. I really wish that I had spent more time studying at least the apocryphal texts. *Apu* was correct that there were many missing pieces to what most Christians accept as *The Word of God.* But, is there enough evidence available to support *The Agape Carpet* theory without church documents? Perhaps, if I could locate this carpet and document the powers that it claims to possess.

"You are correct, *Apu;* I am familiar with those text that you are referring to. But, at the very least I need something to identify *Agape.* Without photographs, there is no reasonable way to document the actual object, if I can even locate it," I said, feeling rather desperate.

"Oh, that is not a problem. Here is the most reliable image that you will find," *Apu* said referring once again to the projection on the cave.

There it was! Well, at least the way it appeared in 1460. It included all of the earlier Egyptian symbols that I was told. These are located on the outer edges, while the center of the carpet included additions by the last carpet designer.

"Now, Imani, you will notice how the carpet looks today. There is no additional data to support that any new symbols have been added. Observe that in the center of the carpet, all the images are in very dark purple are outlined in gold. That is what will alert you to the authenticity when you see it in person," *Apu* said, quite naturally.

I still had my doubts about ever finding this exact carpet. Tracing it just to where it has traveled, thus far, would be a significant accomplishment. Discovering the spiritual powers it possesses would be like capturing a brass ring on the carousel.

"I will begin to identify for you each of the new symbols. You may then sketch a copy of those images. The notes will help you understand why they were selected, as well as what powers they may have.

First, there is *Chi Rho*. Based on the studies by philosopher, A. N. Whitehead, these tangible symbols have the power to change history. In this example the symbol is formed by superimposing the first two letters of the word Christ, in Greek *chi,* and rho=r. Together it invokes the crucifixion of Jesus and Christ's status as the savior.

Next is *Ichthus*. This is the Greek word meaning "fish". Jesus is known as the fisher of men. It is interesting to note that, like the other Egyptian symbols, this one is introduced from Alexandria, Egypt. Ironically, where we still believe the carpet originated.

This third symbol you will recognize is the *Dove*. It is the symbol of the *Holy Ghost*. It represents the Lord's baptism, as well as the release of the soul in death.

The fourth symbol, is known as *The Borromean Rings*. The three interlocking circles symbolize the Christian Trinity. In Latin the word Trinitis means three in one. God is one being made up of three persons.

Notice how this image is larger than all the others, indicating its importance.

Next to the *Dove,* you will notice *The Horn*. This represents God's divine power. It is the principal being of defense as well as an attack. *The Horn* also symbolizes dominion, triumph, strength, intelligence, dignity. All the necessary elements to create change while offering protection.

Finally, surrounding *The Horn,* you will notice the *Palm Branches*. These remind Christians of victory while also honoring the martyr that sacrifices his life for the sake of God. In early Christian doctrine *The Palm* was also referred to as *The Tree of Life*.

Now, as far as we scholars know, there are no other symbols. This doesn't mean that we are correct. It only supports that there have been no other sightings that can dispute our conclusions. Do you need any further time to complete the sketch, or notes?" *Apu* asked.

I was definitely spent. It may have been the libation or all of the overwhelming data I just witnessed. It felt like I walked through miles of historical terrain without absorbing any of the content.

"Do you have any idea where and when the last sighting of the *Agape* was documented?" I asked reluctantly.

Apu began to escort me back to the cave entrance where Dario had left me earlier. With his dark monk-like garment and hood, Apu appeared now more like that Star Wars Jedi Master, Obi-Wan Kenobi, than an Inca Spiritual Philosopher.

"My advice to you Imani is to abandon this journey. Find your own *Agape*. But, since I already know that you will not heed my advice here is a name that might assist you. If Angela is still alive she will be your best resource. God's speed, Imani."

Before I could respond or even thank him for all that he shared with me, Apu was no longer here. I could only presume that he returned to the cave that we just exited.

When I turned around to walk outside of *The Temple of the Sun*, Dario was at the entrance waiting for me.

"Greetings, Imani. I presume that your visit with *Apu*, went well?" Dario said, offering a hand to help me step up to the next level.

"Yes, Dario, everything went better than expected," I said looking at the card *Apu* gave me. In the daylight it was easier to read.

Angela Kiek
Absolute Antiques
Prinsengracht 230
Amsterdam, NH
020-6241524

"Apparently, Dario, I am taking a trip to Amsterdam," I said.

Chapter Sixteen

I think women are foolish to pretend that they are equal to men, they are far superior, and always have been. Whatever you give a woman, she makes it greater. If you give her sperm, she'll give you a baby. If you give her a house, she'll give you a home. If you give her groceries, she'll give you a meal. If you give her a smile, she'll give you her heart. She multiplies and enlarges what is given to her. So, if you give her any crap, be ready to receive a ton of shit.

Sir William Golding
Nobel Prize Literature 1983

Imani Lewis
August 2017

I just barely caught the last bus down from Machu Picchu to SUMAQ Lodge. This is where I began my trip, at Aguascalientes nearly five days ago. Being on the hiking trail made me forget how appealing this lodge is.

When I walked into the lobby my first instinct was to immediately go to my room where a warm bath and a comfortable bed were beckoning me. But, for some unusual reason I detoured to the reception lobby, took a seat near the full glass window and was amazed by the Peruvian authenticity that was surrounding me.

There were no other guests to disturb the sound of silence. This allowed me to totally appreciate this location. There was a fresh new elegance that I never appreciated earlier. The rich textiles, among red and gold palettes, swirled freely among the vast, impressive artworks. These were all inspired by original Inca design. It was the perfect setting for me to call Priscilla and let her know of my progress.

Although I was no longer a corporate employee, Priscilla always assured me that she would still book my reservations anywhere in the world that I needed to travel. Considering there was no reliable travel agent nearby counting on on Priscilla was paramount.

I checked my phone, which is always set on dual time zones. New York is only one hour ahead of Peru. Perfect! This will allow me to first make dinner reservations at the very publicized Pachamanca feast. Everyone was encouraged to experience this ritual prior to leaving Machu Picchu. Not knowing how soon Priscilla could get my airline reservations to Amsterdam, I didn't want to take any chances of missing this banquet.

Thankfully, this event did not begin until 8:00 pm. Allowing me plenty of time to rest before returning and reaching Priscilla.

In my room, after a wonderful hot bath, I sat outside on the balcony in an inviting lounge chair. I was now facing the same Machu Picchu mountain that I earlier traversed. Seeing it from this vantage point I was able to appreciate all that *Apu* shared with me. It was much easier to understand these mystical attractions now from a distance. Being a part of those ancient surroundings can be quite overwhelming. Nevertheless this entire experience was worth all the weeks preparing. And now to conclude this journey with a wonderful meal seemed quite appropriate.

The concierge that made my dinner reservations for this evening, gave me a card explaining what to expect when I arrived. The historical significance of this ceremony was both profound and stunning. Reading the meal details, it became clear why it is an appropriate closure to my visit here.

First we are taught that Pachama is the Earth Mother and that this meal is a communal social rite. We participate by eating delectable vegetables and meats that possess the energy of the earth. No other style of cooking shows such a strong connection to the forces of nature. This did sound very similar to a Hawaiian Lua. That culture also celebrates nature by traditionally cooking the Imu in the ground. Also, an Andean tradition.

We are then told that the remains of these underground ovens are anywhere from seven to eight thousand years old. And, the term "Pachamanca" is a Quechua word that combines the word earth (Pacha) with the word food (manca). These feasts in the Andes sometimes last a week or longer.

Here, in this restaurant, they have also included an Andean Shaman to authenticate the celebrations. My research on this group of spiritual healers has been enriched since meeting *Apu*. I am curious to see how this guru compares to *Apu*.

In this case the shaman belongs to a group community known as QEROS. They are dedicated to preserving the authentic way of living while practicing the knowledge of Spirituality. In doing this, they have pledged to have no contact with anyone outside of their limited community. This has continued since 1950.

If I had more time here, I would interview these exceptional healers who have devoted their lives to exclusive programs that interact with the energy world. It is a strong belief that we are all energy beings. There is no doubt that there is a strong connection here. It also explains why *The Agape Carpet* became a part of this legendary civilization. Unfortunately, I do not have the time to pursue many of these interweaving mysteries. With the details that *Apu* provided me with, I must now move forward. Any outside distractions could result in me losing the race for this story. This is another reason why booking my Netherlands flight as soon as possible prevents me from being tempted otherwise.

Just as I planned, my alarm alerted me that it was time to phone Priscilla. It was now exactly 5:30pm. She should still be at work, unless she slipped out early for drinks with some new love interest.

"Hey, world traveler, how do you like Peru? Meet any interesting male companions that might be worth holding on to?" Priscilla asked, obviously in a good mood.

"There are no attractive or even boring men here. I have been hiking for four days. Don't even ask me about the hygiene facilities. Anyway, more importantly, I survived. My visit with the guru went really well. He gave me my next assignment for the carpet. So, please make reservations for a flight to Amsterdam as soon as you can. I will give you all the details later," I said.

"Well, I must say girlfriend, I am impressed. When you left New York City last week I had my doubts that you could complete the hike. This is quite an accomplishment, Imani," Priscilla said sincerely.

"Thanks, but I have a feeling that this may have been the easiest part. Anyway, I have dinner reservations tonight for some traditional Inca celebration, so, leave me a message with the itinerary, please, hon? I will check my messages when I return," I said.

"Will do. This could be your one last attempt to meet some dreamy Prince Charming in the Andes," I heard Priscilla say just before I clicked the off-key to my cell phone.

Men were absolutely not on my mind at this moment. I was even beginning to doubt my decision to attend this Pachamanca event tonight. The only semi-formal attire that I brought with me was an emerald green strapless dress that Priscilla insisted I bring for occasions like this one. I hated to admit that she might have been right. Thankfully, during my short stay in Lima, waiting for the train to take me to Cusco, I found this unique gift shop. Although there were several items I was tempted to buy, the travel instructions stressed to pack lightly. The only article that I decided on was this lovely tapestry shawl. With its vibrant Inca colors, I correctly predicted it would be an excellent addition to my emerald sundress. It covered my bare arms perfectly, creating a more formal impression.

And my small clutch bag was the perfect accessory. Since I opted to wear my hair in a classic French twist, there was no need for me to bring even a tiny comb. My cellphone and room key carefully stored away in the purse and I was ready to enjoy this final evening.

The hotel lobby was where all the guests with reservations waited to enter the dining room. It was filled to capacity. Nearly all the open seating was taken. After walking around the room awkwardly I came across a small empty cocktail table with two chairs. Immediately I sat down. At least if anyone else asked to join me it would only be one person. I was not feeling very cordial this evening.

Then from absolutely nowhere, I saw him. It was only the second time, yet I knew it was him. Years ago, my grandmother insisted that I watch one of her favorite Robert Redford movies, *The Way We Were*. In that opening scene, when Barbara Streisand recognizes Hubbell, a former college student sitting at the bar in New York, I understood how stunning Redford was. Phoenix Baldwin draws that same attention.

There are just some people who are blessed with charisma, charm, talent. There are not many, but when you meet them, it is profound; "The Privileged." In literature, they are Jay Gatsby (The Great Gatsby)), Rhett Butler (Gone with the Wind), Oliver Barrett IV (Love Story), and Sterling Powers (Destiny Revisited).

Certainly there are also female characters that fit this similar profile, but at the moment watching Phoenix work the crowds around him; none come to mind. Indeed, I clearly am no competition for this man. He appears to have god-like powers, no less admirable than Apollo.

I am only hoping, no, not hoping, praying, that the banquet room is large enough that we won't ever cross paths. Just as I was about to move away from my direct view of Phoenix, a waiter handed me a Cosmopolitan.

"Oh, excuse me. I never ordered this drink. There must be some confusion. I just sat down," I said, stunned.

"It is from the gentleman standing near the window, Miss," the waiter said, placing the drink on the table.

Before I could object, Phoenix, dressed in cream-colored matching linen pants and a button-down shirt, walked towards me. He was tan from obviously days of hiking and his raven black hair was pulled back in a tight ponytail. He was still wearing his aviator sunglasses.

"Imani Lewis? Am I correct?" Phoenix asked, taking a seat before I could object.

"Yes, you are correct. I am impressed that you remembered me. We barely met in Egypt," I said, trying to sound calm.

"How was your trip to Machu Picchu? Oh, I hope you like the Cosmopolitan? It was something that I thought quite appropriate. If not, I can get you whatever you like," Phoenix said.

His slight accent was not as pronounced as it was when Alberto introduced us the first time. He must methodically decide when it is beneficial to sound British and when not.

"This is quite suitable. Thank you," I said, avoiding the first question.

Why was this stranger fishing randomly around my pond? He was obviously a mighty deep-sea fisherman. You know, the ones that are after the larger Marlins. So what was it that he expected to learn from me?

"The Maitre de is signaling that the dining room is opening. Would you mind if I join you at your
table?" Phoenix asked politely.

What was I to say? If this was a chess game Phoenix would at least have me at check.

"Yes, of course. That would be lovely," I said, trying to be gracious.

Phoenix rose from his seat, offered me his arm, escorting me into the formal dining room. It was not apparent until we arrived at our table that although it was set for a party of six, no other people joined us. That should have been my first warning that I was dealing with an expert.

Before the introductions earlier this evening, most of our talk continued to be rather general until, out of nowhere, Phoenix made his first move.

"I think that we both know that searching for *The Agape* is not going to be an easy journey. You certainly understand that we are not the only ones pursuing this story, Imani, correct?" Phoenix asked me directly.

It was really the first time that anyone formally confronted me with this question. It did take me by surprise.

"Well, what I do know is that you have been hired by some very wealthy business men who are expecting you to deliver an extremely valuable item. My goal is not quite that enterprising," I said, careful not to divulge too much.

"You are only somewhat correct. I am working on commission. But, *The Agape* doesn't belong to anyone and it never should. My benefactors have hired me to find this carpet so that the world can appreciate it. *The Agape* is a spiritual relic, similar to the Holy Grail or Jesus' shroud. It must be preserved in a museum," Phoenix said, speaking quietly, not to be overheard.

"If I were to believe you, what does any of this have to do with me? You certainly are much more of an expert at this adventure than I am," I said, refusing to give him any leads.

"Did you notice all those men gathered around me before I sat down with you? They are all *Agape* hunters. Mercenaries that only want profit. Beware of them. We are of a much more noble cause, Imani," Phoenix said.

This man was most definitely gorgeous. I could easily drown in those ocean blue eyes without anyone knowing where I vanished.

It was important for me to ignore those dangerous attributes that Phoenix had in his toolbox. What I did know is that he was far beyond my grade level, even if I found him attractive.

"I really have nothing to share with you, or anyone else, Mr. Baldwin. I am a freelance writer. I travel to places of interest to write my stories. But, I will keep you in mind if I come across any news on *The Agape,*" I said, sounding quite reasonable.

"Very well. At least take my card. It has my private number. If you change your mind, or if you need anything, do not hesitate to call," Phoenix said, before leaving.

His departure was as sudden as his entrance. I did not expect him to leave before the dinner started, but it was now less stressful. Once the ceremony began, I was quite grateful that I stayed. It was well worth the earlier distractions.

When I arrived back to my hotel room, a few hours later, there was a message from Priscilla on my phone.

I have booked you on a KLM flight that leaves from Lima tomorrow evening at 5:00pm and arrives in Amsterdam twelve and a half hours later. That is the next day. I also reserved a room for you at the Waldorf Astoria. It is located in the Grachtengordel neighborhood, near the Celebrated Canal Ring, known for 17th century houses, diverse cafes, and several museums, including Anne Frank's House. Be careful out there Imani, and definitely reserve some time for fun.
❤ *Priscilla*

Fun? I can't remember when the last time I did anything for entertainment. But, I do know that Priscilla has good intentions. Now, let's hope that I can get on a direct train to Lima early enough tomorrow morning. It will also be interesting to see if Mr. Baldwin will be on the same flight as I am. I cannot imagine that there are that many flights from Peru to Amsterdam the same day. However, I should never underestimate a Phoenix. They are known for rebirth, eternity and renewal. Why else be named Phoenix if you can't be born again from the ashes of death?

Chapter Seventeen

Love is the offspring of spiritual affinity, and unless that affinity is created in a moment, it will never be created for years or even generations.

Nikki Giovanni
American Poet

Imani Lewis
Amsterdam, The Netherlands
August, 2017

When we landed at the Schiphol, Airport in Amsterdam, all that I was focused on was finding my hotel it and sleeping for a few hours. International travel has never been easy for me. When I traveled with my mother it was even worse. Sarah never had any problem adapting to the time difference. But, it always took me at least twenty-four hours to adapt.

Everyone always advises me of their own great methods at overcoming the time change, but none of those suggestions seem to work for me. Honestly, it always takes me at least twenty-four hours before my mind begins to function properly.

Once we arrived at the customs passport control inspection, I was still expecting Phoenix to appear miraculously, all refreshed, ready to continue his search for *Agape* with no obstacles in his way. Well, except for me, that is.

Especially after our last little "rendezvous" at the SUMAQ Lodge, about forty-eight hours ago, Mr. Baldwin must be feeling quite satisfied with himself. He has no idea how complicated I am about to make his life. During this early stage in our competition, we will be cautious about covering our tracks. For my sanity, I have decided to ignore any other fortune hunters. I will choose to move at my own pace with my own leads. If I dwell on how open this competition is, indeed, I will lose the small amount of confidence that I am slowly rebuilding.

As my driver approached the Waldorf Astoria, I realized that Priscilla did not exaggerate. It is definitely a magnificent hotel.

"You are an American, am I correct?" The friendly taxi driver asked.

"Yes, that is correct. It is my first visit to the Netherlands, and I must say in just these few moments, I am very impressed," I said politely.

When the car pulled up to the valet drop-off, the driver handed me a business card.

"If you need a driver while you are here in Amsterdam, I am available at a very reasonable price," he said, waving goodbye.

I placed the card in my wallet, with only one thought at the moment, and that was to check in to my room.

Naturally, the lobby was crammed with international travelers like me, all wanting their rooms to be quickly available. Since Priscilla unofficially used the corporate account to reserve the room, I did have a priority pass. This allowed me express access.

"Welcome to The Waldorf, Ms. Lewis. We have prepared an excellent room for you. One that faces the canal," the friendly young lady said.

"Will you be using the credit card on file for all your purchases while being our guest?" she asked.

"Yes. Everything will be charged to my American Express. That is accepted here, I presume?" I asked.

"Absolutely, Ms. Lewis. If you sign here agreeing to these terms, I will have the bellman take your luggage to your room immediately."

That was when I noticed what my room rate was for one deluxe Queen room. I was being charged $750 a night. And, this was a corporate discount price.

What the hell was Priscilla thinking? No wonder the desk clerk was asking me how I planned to pay for my stay. I was booked for seven nights! That is $5250 without any amenities. Never have I spent that much money on any business trip. And, now there isn't even an expense account I can turn in at the end of this trip.

Alright. It is too late now to panic. If I am lucky I will finish my trip here sooner than expected and be able to check out early. If not, my future room accommodations might have to be with the homeless in the local park.

I signed the document, received my key, and took the elevator to the twentieth floor. When I opened the door, the first thing that I noticed was how large the room was. I could throw a party here every night. This suite had a separate living room, giant balcony, kitchen, and a massive bedroom. Maybe Priscilla forgot that I am a writer, not a member of a rock group.

Whatever it was that made her imagine that I could afford these digs did not matter at this moment. I immediately drew the drapes, put a "Do Not Disturb" sign on my door, and collapsed onto my $750 a night mattress. Just as I began to feel that excellent point where reality fades into that world of slumber, I heard a young girl's voice say my name.

"Why Imani Lewis, do you know that I've believed as many as six impossible things before breakfast," the unfamiliar voice said.

"Do I know you? Have we ever met? And, even more importantly why are you visiting me here, in my room?" I asked.

"To be perfectly clear, my friend, you are in my territory. And, don't even ask where that is, because nobody, certainly not even I, know the answer to that question. But, what I can tell you, is that if you asked me to join your tea party, you must know that I have some very odd friends who always travel with me," the mysterious girl replied.

"But, I haven't planned any tea party. At least not one that I recall. Can you at least tell me who these other people are that you say will be joining us, if there is a tea party, of course?" I asked, continuing to feel very confused.

"You are such a silly Imani. All of those who are joining us you have met many times before."

It was right then that the first character began to prance through a large, elaborate Victorian mirror that somehow appeared from nowhere in my room.

"My dear Imani, or are you Alice in disguise? Well, it doesn't really matter, in the gardens of memory, in the palace of dreams, this is where you and I will always meet."

This odd character, who appeared to be no older than a middle school age boy, was wearing oversized clothing, and a large top hat;

so large that it covered his entire head. He handed me a card that identified him only as Hatta.

"Why do you have a card on your hat that reads 10/6?" I asked, recognizing this character as The Mad Hatter. I always wanted to know what those numbers meant.

"It is of course what this hat is worth, silly child. I am a walking advertisement, always trying to sell my wares for a nice profit, and never wandering off to some wonderland where crazy tourists catch you off guard," The Mad Hatter said, very proudly.

The next character who appeared from the looking glass I recognized as the quiet timid Dormouse. But, he was dancing around to a famous song by Jefferson Airplane, named after the white rabbit that joined him.

Suddenly, Alice took my hand, and we were all singing "We're in Looking Glass land now, And, you have just had some of those tasty mushrooms, you know the ones that make you small, then big? 'Go ask Alice, I think she'll know, remember what the dormouse says, go feed your head, and start to grow. (Jefferson Airplane).

Right then I bolted up from the bed, startled, almost incoherent. What the hell was that all about? When everything I heard and saw began fading, I determined it must be nothing but nerves causing these hallucinations. Yet, it felt as if there was something that I should be remembering about this dream. What? I was not sure.

Then I recalled that during one of my visits to London, as a foreign exchange student in college, I was studying literature at Oxford University. I enrolled in this fascinating class that offered a new perspective on the famous *"Alice Chronicles,"* by Lewis Carroll, the pseudonym for Charles Dodson. Since all these stories are attributed to *"All in a Golden Afternoon,"* taking a boat trip from Oxford to Godstow provided an exciting perspective. The Oxford professor was also quite entertaining.

Even now I can still recall some of the lines from the poem, *All in a Golden Afternoon.*

Anon, to sudden silence won
In Fancy they pursue,
The dream child moving through a land
Of wonders wild and new
In friendly chat with bird or beast-

And half believe it true.

*Thus grew the tale of Wonderland
This slowly, one by one,
Its quaint events were hammered out
And now the tale is done
And home we steer a happy crew,
Beneath the setting sun.*

Why was all of this surfacing now into my subconscious mind? Perhaps because Alice follows that strange rabbit while burning with curiosity just like me? There certainly have been plenty of those same rabbits in my own life that I have accompanied down unknown rabbit holes, searching for explanations. *The Agape* is just my latest adventure, and apparently my most expensive one. I try not to admit that this journey has no safety net, but to be perfectly honest, there is no safety net.

Now that I have successfully self-psychoanalyzed myself, perhaps I can still catch a few hours of rest before my alarm goes off. Amsterdam certainly will offer many new insights that I must be prepared to analyze.

Startled by the loud knocking on my bedroom door, I reach for my sweatshirt nearby. I am careful only slightly to open the door with the safety chain still attached.

"Good morning Mademoiselle," says a man with a very heavy Austrian accent. He is wearing a white formal waiter's uniform.

"Excuse me. You must have the wrong room. I never ordered breakfast last night," I said, slightly disturbed.

"Yes, Madam, but Madam Kiek ordered this for you last night. She insisted that it be delivered no later than 10:00 am," the waiter said rapidly.

"But, I do not know any Madam Kiek," I argued.

Then suddenly the name sounded familiar. I asked the waiter to wait a moment while I verified my assumption. He looked confused but followed my orders.

I went to the dresser, removed the card I was given at Machu Picchu, and realized that the waiter was referring to Angela Kiek, the lady I was to meet here in Austria. But, how did she know I was in this hotel?

Everything was still rather foggy in my brain. Nevertheless, I allowed the room service waiter to enter with his breakfast cart.

After giving him a substantial tip, more than I usually do, I looked under the steel domes to inspect what was there. Beneath the first dome was a very delicious-looking blueberry crepe, and the other one had a variety of Austrian sausage and bacon. Angela must think that I eat like a small army. I decided to pour myself a hot cup of coffee before tackling any of the food items.

That was when I noticed a small note in an envelope with my name on it. I opened it now, anxious for some answers.

Welcome to Austria Miss Lewis!

I look forward to our meeting and have taken the liberty to order your breakfast. In Austria, breakfast makes us much more precise in our decisions as we begin our day's work.

Also, please be aware that a driver is at your disposal. He will pick you up in the lobby at about noon and be your tour guide this afternoon. Later this evening, once you have rested, he will return you to your hotel. Later, we will have a late supper at my home. I hope this is to your satisfaction? If you have any questions or wish to change these plans, kindly inform Daniel, your driver.
Sincerely,
Angela Kiek

That was definitely a surprise. I expected to search the city for this antique shop, and then wait days to arrange a meeting with Madam Kiek. This was almost too easy. Although I now understood why the big breakfast was ordered. It appears like I am going to be preoccupied for the entire day.

After a quick shower, I dressed in some comfortable travel clothes, not sure where Daniel was planning on taking me. I also brought a very reliable black jacket on the slight chance that I might be somewhere that requires a tourist dress code. Many European cathedrals and even museums have strict rules regarding appropriate attire. I always like to be prepared.

Downstairs in the exquisite lobby, I took a seat, waiting patiently. On the coffee table was an interesting magazine that featured The Waldorf Astoria. The first page explained that the exterior of this building is six palaces built in the 17th and 18th centuries, with the double front canal palaces, joined together. But, it is the unique grand staircase built by the architect of Louis XIV Daniel Margot that guests always admire. There were several pages included in the article that showcased the many people who have taken photographs standing on that elaborate staircase.

However, what drew my attention was the famous trompe-l'oeil painting reproduction of Frabitius hanging in the hotel's Goldfinch Brassiere. According to this article, the goldfinch reflects the city's 17th century Golden Age, when golden finches were popular companions in the private gardens of canal cottages.

It is the Pulitzer Prize-winning novel, by Donna Tartt, in her book, *The Goldfinch*, that immediately comes to mind. Tartt writes a Bildungsroman, coming of age tale, about a thirteen-year-old boy, Theodore Decker. When he survives a terrorist bombing that kills his mother at an art museum, Theodore rubbles through the debris frantically, only to discover a small Dutch Golden Age Painting called the Goldfinch. Like the reproduction here, at The Waldorf, the Goldfinch painting is an example of Trompe-l'oeil.

Tartt's story traces how Theodore, now an adult, must fly to Amsterdam in an attempt to steal back his Goldfinch painting. Although Theodore is not in search of an *Agape,* he certainly does have an epiphany ending. It is when Theodore contemplates why people, who love beautiful objects, are dedicated to preserving these objects that seems most relevant at this moment. Theodore concludes that people will even risk their lives to save rare items from destruction. I am one of those people. I am now dedicated to preserving the *Agape* spirit at whatever cost.

Chapter Eighteen

Caring too much for objects can destroy you. Only—if you care for a thing enough, it takes on a life of its own, doesn't it? And, isn't the whole point of things—beautiful things—that they connect you to some larger beauty?

Donna Tartt,
The Goldfinch

Imani Lewis
Netherlands, 2017

"Good afternoon, Ms. Lewis. My name is Daniel. I believe that Mrs. Kiek informed you that I am to be your escort today. Is this your first visit to our beautiful Amsterdam?" Daniel asked.

I was curious how he was able to recognize me since Angela, and I had never met. Then I realized that I was the only female in the lobby. Most tourists and even business people are gone much earlier than midday.

"Yes. This is my first trip to Amsterdam, and I am sorry to admit that I know very little about the Netherlands," I said, rising from my seat.

"No problem. If you won't mind, Ms. Kiek has asked me to take you to some very specific locations. If you should have any questions, I will certainly try my very best to answer them. Shall we start our tour now? My car is with the valet," Daniel said, leading the way.

Once outside, I was taken to a very impressive black town car with dark tinted windows. It reminded me of the ones that the paparazzi always chased to get a photo of some celebrity. I was beginning to believe that Angela Kiek must be quite wealthy to be treating me like a VIP.

"Our first stop is going to be at the Dam Square, now the Royal Palace. Unfortunately, we will not have much time to explore. But, this will allow you to see the most important historic buildings erected during *The Golden Age of Amsterdam,* 1585-1672. Notice the Westerkerk Tower across from the Royal Palace? This is our biggest church in Amsterdam. The bell tower remains the pride of Amsterdam. Many consider it as the symbol of our town. Quite beautiful, don't you think?" Daniel said proudly.

"Would it be possible for us to go inside for a few minutes? I understand that the Dutch painter Rembrandt is buried here," I asked, walking toward the entrance.

"Of course, we may visit Rembrandt. It is one of the locations Ms. Kiek insisted that I share with you." Daniel confirmed.

Inside the church I first noticed the big organ with shutters painted by Gerard de Lairesse. He was a well-known Flemish painter who lived from 1640-1711 and painted scenes from the Bible.

"Notice, Ms. Lewis, on the left panel, King David is playing and dancing in front of *The Ark of Covenant.* Do you know what that Arc is, Ms Lewis?" Daniel asked, whispering.

My first reaction was to let him know that he was not talking to some moron. I may have never visited Amsterdam, but I certainly know what *The Ark of Covenant* is.

"Absolutely. It is often referred to as, *The Ark of the Testimony.* What I recall during my studies is that this is a gold-covered wooden box with a lid cover. In *The Book of Exodus,* it states that the two stone tablets inside are *The Ten Commandments,"* I said, making my point.

"That is correct, Ms. Lewis. The biblical account also states that one year after the Israelites' exodus from Egypt, Moses instructed that the *Ark* be created. It was to be a gold-plated acacia chest carried by its staves approximately 2600 feet. The Ark was always hidden under a large veil made of skins and purple cloth," Daniel added.

By this time, I was no longer angry. Daniel was simply following Angela's orders. I wasn't sure why she wanted me to see this painting or know about *The Arc,* but I am sure it will eventually make sense.

"Would it be possible now for us to visit Rembrandt's grave?" I asked, hoping to move in another direction before leaving.

"Yes, of course. But, you do realize that nobody is certain exactly where Rembrandt is buried, don't you?" Daniel said, waiting for my reaction.

"But, I read that he was buried right here in the graveyard," I insisted.

"Follow me, and I will show you what has been placed in memorial for the famous artist," Daniel said, leading me to the left hall wall. There I saw a very modest oval-shaped white plaster plaque.

Hier Ligt
BEGRAVEN
REMBRANDT
HARMENSZ
VAN RYN
B 15 JULI 1606
D 4 OCT 1669

"I don't understand, Daniel? Why isn't there a headstone on Rembrandt's grave?" I asked baffled.

"Rembrandt lived a very turbulent life, reasonably standard for artists of his time. Once he arrived in Amsterdam in 1624, he was well recognized for his reputation as a historical painter and portraitist. Unfortunately, by 1669 this great painter was so poor that when he died, he was buried in an unmarked church grave, along with many others. These sites remained only for twenty years before it was time to recycle them for other poor people. Since no one, and I can assure you there have been many who have tried, can find Rembrandt's remains, this plaque is all we have."

Although Daniel was eager to move on to another attraction, I insisted on taking a few moments to walk the outer grounds where the graveyard remained. To acknowledge how death blends us with the most unexpected circumstances is always worth a few moments of pause. It was hard to imagine how Rembrandt's paintings have survived centuries of instability, yet, the artist has vanished into dust. It all seems quite tragic.

On the way back into the church, I found some wildflowers to place under the Rembrandt shrine. Apparently, this was a common practice since there were several small bouquets along with mine.

Walking back to the town car, I asked Daniel if he knew of any historical paintings that Rembrandt painted that might include a carpet or tapestry. I knew that Rembrandt did have an entire collection of oriental and Indian art that reflects his spiritual journey.

"If you genuinely want to learn more about the diversity that Rembrandt expresses in his art, I might suggest that you take an art appreciation class offered here in Amsterdam. Or, if that requires more time than you are able to spare, I can assure you that Ms. Kiek is your next best source, Ms. Lewis," Daniel said.

I decided not to pursue my theory about Rembrandt's carpets any longer. If there is some connection between the artist and *The Agape*, it will be something worth footnoting in my mind for later.

"Where is our next stop, Daniel?" I asked, anxious to move on now.

"Not very far from here. We are now going to visit *The Anne Frank House and Museum*. We could actually walk, but driving will allow us to move on to our final destination in plenty of time. Ms. Kiek has asked me to follow this particular schedule," Daniel said.

It was becoming quite clear that Angela Kiek, just like *Apu,* was someone who was an authority on many different historical levels. I was still not convinced why either of these intellectual geniuses was willing to help me search for *The Agape* if it even still exists. Since it is also worth an astronomical amount of money, why wouldn't these experts join forces and discover it themselves? The only logical answer is that neither of them desires publicity, nor do they care about any monetary reward. The only person I know that is doing this search for money is the suave Phoenix Baldwin.

"I should warn you, Ms. Lewis, *The Anne Frank House, and Museum* can be very poignant. I, myself, have visited it often and walked away emotionally drained afterward. This will be our last stop before a brief picnic in the park. I have arranged a a lovely meal that we can share in a much more enjoyable atmosphere following the museum," Daniel said.

"Is there anything in the museum that I should take particular notice
 of?" I asked, not really knowing what to expect.

When I visited The Holocaust Museum in New York, it was incredibly moving. There were so many details in each exhibit that I was never even aware of before then. It was hard to imagine that

Holocaust survivors and their families donated over 30,000 items on exhibit. These items were juxtaposed with Nazi rhetoric and propaganda dedicated to removing every living Jewish person.

Regardless of how extensive that Holocaust museum was, visiting the actual hiding place of the young Anne Frank would be more personal.

"I will be with you during the entire visit. It is best to allow the experience to flow naturally. There will be time later to express your emotions," Daniel said, leading me to the entrance.

Unlike a traditional museum, I immediately noticed that this story was being told with quotes, directly from Anne Frank's Diary, photos, videos, and original items. It was similar to walking into a time warp, where for a short time, you could experience the same sensations as those who lived here.

On July 6, 1942, Anne and her family went into hiding in this building, Prinsengracht 263. Two other families later joined them; the Van Pels and the Fritz Pfeffer families.

Otto Frank, Anne's father, realized early that to save his family, they must leave Munich, Germany. He was able to start a business that traded in pectin, the gelling agent for making jam. That new business was located in this warehouse in Amsterdam.

When the Nazis started to make all the Jewish people wear a Star of David to identify who they were, Otto decided to move his family into hiding. They would all now be in very close quarters.

While I was reading the details that surrounded Anne Frank's exile into her annex sanctuary for two years Daniel insisted that we move directly into that secret area.

"It is tempting to spend hours here reading all of the historical data. There are even several videos that are strongly suggested. We, however, are going to move directly to Anne's room. I want you to see, as expressed in her own words, what this experience meant to her."

Although I would have preferred seeing this museum on my terms, I followed Daniel without objecting, past the massive bookshelves that opened into the secret annex.

"Anne was forced to share her room with Fritz Pfeffer. Can you imagine how many arguments they must have had in here?" Daniel said, walking around the small empty room.

"When Otto Frank returned here after the war, he insisted that no furniture be added. He wanted to show the shallow leftover area that once was inhabited by his talented daughter. What I do want you to notice are the photographs that remain and especially Anne's own words that explain how important those photographs were to her," Daniel said, leading me into the room.

On an opposite wall from the photos was an excerpt from Anne's diary.

"Thanks to father, who had brought my whole collection of picture post cards and movie stars here. Beforehand I have been able to treat the walls with a pot of glue and a brush and so to turn the entire room into one big picture." (Anne Frank, July 11, 1942).

Daniel was right to insist on coming directly here. There was a definite sense that Anne's spirit visited this room frequently. Although it was such an impossible, difficult circumstance in this small area, I can also understand how her diary writing allowed her a temporary pass to the outside world.

"There is one last room that you must see, and then we will go on to lunch. This is the *Diary Room*. This is where you will be able to see the original red-checked diary that Anne received for her thirteenth birthday, only a few weeks before she went into hiding," Daniel said.

"I do remember reading that she decided in 1944, I believe, to rewrite her entire diary. Do you know why?" I asked, wanting to understand as much as possible.

"This is because Anne learned that the government would be collecting diaries after she was free. She dreamt about being a famous writer or journalist and thought that her diary might finally be recognized as important," Daniel added.

He then took me to the room that showcased Anne's Diary. In here there was once again several important passages that expressed her hope for the future. The first quote that I found highly insightful was:

"Although I am only fourteen, I know quite well what I want, I know who is right, and who is wrong. I have my opinions, my own ideas and principles, and although it may seem pretty mad from an

adolescent, I feel more of a person than a child. I feel quite independent of anyone." Anne Frank

Ironically, this was written only a few months before the Nazis captured her. Her diary encapsulated the ordinary aspects of emotional upheavals that influenced her very short life. These routine daily events included friendship, love, desire, and aspirations.

In one passage, Anne expresses her dream to be "a journalist, and later on, a famous writer." I could not help smiling when I read this. If she only knew how that dream was to evolve. Even her horrendous treatment by the Nazis in the concentration camp that led to her dying of typhus at the age of fifteen could not change her fate.

"You know something Daniel? I believe that Anne Frank and I would have been best friends," I said, following him past the crowds that were now gathering to enter the first room of the museum.

"I have no doubt that you would have been great companions," Daniel said, smiling.

Chapter Nineteen

There is potential for boundless good in the boy I knew. Trust that the man you see now is a shadow of what lies beneath. If you would, give him the love that will enable him to see it for himself. To a lost soul, such a treasure is worth its weight in gold. Worth its weight in dreams.

Renee Ahdieh
The Wrath and the Dawn

Phoenix Baldwin

Some may say that I have lived a privileged life. I always say, never make any judgments until you have worn my shoes and have walked on my path. Nevertheless, I cannot deny that some of what is perceived as privilege is correct.

Following the Norman Conquest in 1066, the Baldwin migration from Normandy was imminent. Based on the Germanic elements, the first part of our name, *bald,* translates to bold, while the last syllable, *win,* means friend or protector.

Although my heritage may be traced back to 1100 AD, with Archbishops and guardians of William the Conqueror, I will not bore you with all the historical details that I was taught at a very early age. Let's say that my family was, and still is, recognized as one of nobility. Unfortunately, I would be considered the rebel, the black sheep of a very well-respected lineage.

It all started relatively normal. Being the firstborn son of Alastair and Charlotte Baldwin, I was celebrated with all the pomp and circumstance that one might imagine the heir of a wealthy empire to receive. Preparations for me to attend the most influential schools were decided even before my first steps.

During my primary years, I attended Wetherby and Ludgrove. These are the very same schools that the future King of England, Prince William, attended. And, just as William later enrolled at Eton

College, in Windsor, at age thirteen, my parents followed the same protocol for me.

I give credit to my mother for being the one to move outside the traditional box and insist on naming me Phoenix. What I learned later is that decision almost led to a divorce. My father was furious. He insisted that Phoenix is a commoner's name, not appropriate for a dignified man of stature. Nothing that he could say would change my mother's mind. Her beloved son, the one who she knew would someday be a great leader, should have a name that signifies eternity. In the end, Charlotte won that battle but lost the war. My parent's relationship was never mended.

When I was seventeen years old I decided that it was time to see the world. Naturally my parents objected. Not only did they protest, but they also threatened to disown me, leaving me penniless with no inheritance. Considering that I was an only child, this was quite a drastic decision, even for my parents. Strangely those threats were not enough to prevent me from demanding my independence.

A week before the spring holidays for Easter break, Bobby, my best friend and I, decided to take a short bus trip into Windsor village on a one-way ticket. The plan was to then take the train to Dublin, Ireland and eventually earn enough money for a ticket to America. In the United States we would join a band and travel the world. The fact that neither of us ever seriously played guitar or drums, nor could either of us sing, never even crossed our minds. We just wanted to be free of this very rigid life. Without being granted this freedom, we made the decision to explore the world before it suffocated us.

"No worries Phoenix. I know a bloke that lives in Clontarf, only 6km away from Dublin, Ireland. He knows one of the stage hands for Rod Stewart. We can hit him up for an audition."

I still remember Bobby's words after all these years.

Well, he was right about the distance between Clontarf and Dublin, but there was no bloke there when we arrived at that address. There was, however, the lovely Maggie May. And It was Maggie's husband who ran off to Liverpool with Bobby's pal.

Was it a coincidence that Maggie May was also the same name as Rod Stewart's famous Maggie May? Maybe.

Bobby must have got confused. That bloke never knew any stage hands for Rod Stewart. All he knew was that Maggie May was named after that wench that stole Rod's innocence.

But, here we were in this small village, known mainly for the castle hotel and strong rugby teams, with little money, no plans, and just confused. Yet, neither Bobby nor I was ready to concede that this plan was a total failure. It didn't even matter that we had no alternative plans.

"You two lost souls have any idea what you're going to do now that there is no plan to meet Rod Stewart," Maggie asked me, wiping the bar down thoroughly.

I looked over at Bobby. By this time, he was throwing darts with a buxom blonde. When he hit the bullseye, the blonde babe jumped up into Bobby's arms and wrapped her long legs around his waist.

"I don't think your Bobby is going to have any problems finding a place to sleep tonight. Shannon has had her eyes on him since you two walked in here. Now, we need to find a safe place for you, Laddie," Maggie said, coming over to me from behind the bar.

In the light I could now tell that she was older than I first thought. Not old, just "older" than the girls near Windsor Castle. What I really liked was her long red hair. It flowed like lava spouting from a live volcano. It should have been my first clue that Maggie was a firecracker.

I won't go into details about my six months with Maggie, but that night I moved upstairs into her apartment over *The Fountainhead Pub*.

I never learned how old Maggie really was, but during that time, she trained me well on how to please a woman. This may not be Rod Stewart's Maggie May, but *"mother what a lover,"* she turned out to be.

Honestly, it was so easy living at the bar with Maggie that if that private detective that my mother hired had never found me, I would still be there today. But, fate moves in strange circles, often with odd companions.

"Your mother has instructed me to give you this letter, Sir Phoenix," the detective said, handing me the note. There was nothing written on the outside of the envelope to prepare me for what I was about to learn.

Dearest Phoenix,

Your father is in his final stages of life. Death is imminent. We discovered days after you left Eton that father had untreatable cancer in his left lung. Last week he was no longer mobile. We are now all sitting vigil for that final moment. If you do not want to be here for his passing you must be prepared on how you will feel once it is over. Now is the time to amend all ill feelings between the two of you.

I have arranged for Mr. Anderson to escort you home as soon as you have made your final preparations.
Your loving mother,
Charlotte

I placed the note in my shirt pocket, trying to access my choices. These past six months with Maggie May definitely made me appreciate life. But, mother was correct. I was obligated to close the pages that were left open in my previous life. When I abandoned all those responsibilities as a son there was a void. Ignoring this commitment will ruin all that I have learned about myself these past months. This journey would be meaningless.

"I have a few obligations here that I must take into consideration before I leave. Give me twenty-four hours, and I will be ready to return home," I said to the detective.

"It is not clear to me how long your father has, but I will notify your mother of your decision. Unless she gives me further instructions, I will arrive here tomorrow morning for our departure at 10:00 am. Is that agreed upon?" Mr. Anderson asked.

"Yes. I shall be ready tomorrow morning," I said, still uncertain how I was going to tell Maggie.

First, I called Bobby. For the past six months he had settled in with Shannon. Bobby had no intention of leaving. When I told him that I really had no choice but to return home his reaction was odd.

"You, my good friend Phoenix, are destined for outstanding accomplishments. Being here with Maggie, working at *The Fountainhead Pub,* was a nice prelude to your life, but it certainly is not where you belong. But, this is exactly where I belong. But, not you, my pal. Keep in touch if you can. This has been a great joy ride, hasn't it?" Bobby said, embracing me for the last time.

He was right. I came to Clontarf a boy escaping the rigid life of nobility, and now I was leaving, a man who is prepared to make his own choices for the future. When I told Maggie what I had to do she was not surprised.

"I knew that this day would come, Phoenix. What we had was a great romp. You saved me from being alone while satisfying my sexual desires, but honestly, I'm ready for a new outlet. Maybe I'll take up crocheting," She said, leading me into the bedroom for one last intimate moment.

When it was over, I felt different. Like Rod, I wanted to tell Maggie that, *"...she stole my heart...and made a first class fool out of me..."* But, Maggie May, was my first lover; the one I will love forever. But, I said nothing of this to her. My last memory of Maggie is seeing her lying naked on the bed, looking just like Francisco Goya's model in The Nude Maja. In that portrait, like Maggie, the model is unashamed of her nudity. I mainly now find this image appropriate because I later learned that the painting was commissioned by a wealthy patron, rumored to be Goya's mistress. Although my Maggie was smoking a cigarette, the other two women in Goya's portrait appeared erratically charged, pushing the boundaries of ethos.

Ten hours later, I was back in London sitting next to my father, watching him take his last breath of life.

"Phoenix, promise me only one thing, before I die? Promise me that whatever you choose to do with your life, you will make it worth something."

I was grateful that he didn't ask me to commit myself to politics, like he had always insisted when I was younger. Because, regardless of my mother's advice, I would not have agreed to that, even if it was my father's dying wish.

What happened after the funeral was almost prophetic, if not pathetic. Everything surrounding me was back to normal. It was as if the past six months never happened.

Thankfully, I did not need to return to Eton. There is some advantage to living a privileged life. The next semester I enrolled at Oxford University.

Although the Dean insisted that I declare a major, preferably political science, I refused. Finally, however, to avoid any further arguments, I selected Literature as my major. It was the only subject that I truly enjoyed. It also allowed me to study the humanities, which was more pleasant than argumentation or political theory.

Mother was just thankful to have me home. She decided wisely not to object to my choice. Although I do believe she said, at one time, that it was a frivolous waste of money.

Nevertheless, I continued to attend Oxford with quite some success. I enjoyed it so much that when the opportunity arose, I decided to continue at Cambridge for eight additional years. This is where I finally earned my Doctorate. Although, to my mother's chagrin I refused to be recognized as Dr. Baldwin. She always insisted in public, to introduce me as her "brilliant son, Dr. Baldwin".

When there were no longer any other degrees to be earned, I was offered a Professorship at Cambridge. Money was never an issue, making this offer even more tempting to accept. It would allow me to become completely independent from the Baldwin estate. Notably, since my father's associates continued to insist that I take an active role, even after many years of declining their offers.

Unfortunately, I soon became quite bored with teaching. It was never the literature, or the students that bothered me. It was all the bureaucracy. It was precisely why I never wanted to study politics, yet I was practicing it daily.

Occasionally, my mind would wander back to those six months that I spent with Maggie. They were still the best months of my life. So, why did I never return? Was it really Maggie, or was it what she represented? If it was not her, then what exactly was the attraction that kept pulling me away from my base? It was a question that haunted me.

I did finally resolve that I needed new inspiration. Anything. Everything. Life had to be more interesting than this. My current path was moving me in the direction of Dante's Inferno. Each year was bringing me closer to Judecca, or better known as Hell.

Then from almost nowhere, I found the answer. A close friend of mine, an anthropologist, told me about this ancient sacred carpet. Apparently, some believe it has spiritual healing powers. Although the carpet or tapestry has not been seen by anyone recently, there is evidence that the carpet has surfaced in the modern world.

"Do you believe that these sightings are accurate?" I asked, Dr. Morris skeptically.

"I'm not ready to form any definite conclusions yet, Phoenix. But, what I will share with you, is that there is much interest in this theory," Morris answered.

"Like what type of interest? It sounds to me as academia is promoting this fantasy," I said in response.

"It is much more than a philosophical quest. Several very wealthy gentlemen are offering millions of dollars, maybe even billions, to have access to this carpet known as *The Agape,*" Morris stated.

"If all that you are telling me is true, what value does this carpet have for these mysterious men? Do they somehow intend to make a profit from their enterprise? It seems rather frivolous to me. You would think that powerful men would want guarantees before they waste their money on treasure hunting," I said.

"Not true, my boy. These entrepreneurs are searching for an elite status that money cannot buy. It is the one recognition not for sale. Whoever locates this *Agape* and delivers it to the mysterious coalition will assure them a place in history forever," Morris added.

"And, how does someone get in contact with this coalition?" I asked, now becoming more interested.

"Well, for you Phoenix, it should be no problem. From what I have gathered, they are in the same circle of associates as your family's firm," Morris added.

I am not sure why this surprised me, but it did. After my discussion with Dr. Morris concluded. I pondered what it might be like to search for such a mysterious relic as *The Agape*. Since I had no idea where to start, the idea of spending months, maybe even years, traveling the world to find a carpet seemed somewhat reckless. But, as I thought more about the possibilities, the idea became more appealing. Then it became almost an obsession.

What wasn't very inviting was the prospect of meeting with the family firm. For the past twenty years I did my very best to avoid meeting with any of these members. If I make the decision to search for *The Agape,* I will have to be prepared to request their assistance in locating this mysterious coalition. First, I will need to learn all I can about the history of *Agape*. To do this, I requested a year's leave from Cambridge. My sabbatical started in one month, at the end of this semester. This allowed me to focus entirely on learning everything that has been published about *The Agape* and, if necessary, travel to where the experts are.

It was the first time in many years that I could feel the adrenaline flowing through my veins once again. Up until now I was on a life support system. Now, once again there was a purpose for living.

Although discovering *The Agape* is the ultimate reward, it will be the search that is truly rewarding. Never really appreciating the term 'treasure hunters' I must admit historically there have been many who have discovered some amazing items. The one common similarity that we all have is passion.

This passion became even stronger once I learned about Giovanni Battista Belzoni. He was an Italian explorer, treasure hunter and pioneer during the time of the Egyptian archeology in 1817. Some of his accomplishments include a giant sculpture of Ramses II's head and a sarcophagus that he stole. Both items are now in the British Museum in London.

Even Sir Walter Raleigh was in search for a different type of treasure; the golden city of El Dorado. Somewhere across our great pond he insisted there was a city flooded with gold. Unfortunately for Sir Walter Raleigh he was beheaded by King James for clashing with the Spanish. Did any of these explorers perhaps come across *The Agape?* Not that I could find as of yet.

By the time I finally met with my millionaire investors, several months later, I was able to outline an extensive plan that would assure them *of The Agape* acquisition. My first stop, like Belzoni, would be to Cairo, Egypt, where there was a mystic guru well known and admired for his knowledge about *The Agape*. From there I would inform the investors of my next lead, as well as any new circumstances.

In return for my search, the coalition would pay for all my travel expenses. Once *The Agape* is delivered I will receive a 1.5-million-dollar commission. Although I knew of no other treasure hunters at this time competing for the prize, I felt very confident that I could deliver *The Agape* regardless of the competition. Quite frankly, the money was an excellent addition, but it was the adventure that thrilled me the most, especially against unknown rivals.

But then I met Imani Lewis briefly in Egypt and once again in Machu Picchu. This was the first time I could identify a competitor. At this point, I am still quite confident that she is far more inferior than me. She may be a slight irritation, but certainly nothing more than a pesky distraction.

Have you ever heard of the *Queens Gambit?* If so, then you will enjoy this tournament between myself and Imani Lewis. Let the game begin!

Chapter Twenty

Chess isn't always competitive. Chess can also be beautiful. It was the board I noticed first. It is an entire world of just 64 squares. I feel safe in it. I can control it. I can dominate it. And, it's predictable, so if I get hurt, I only have myself to blame.

Beth Harmon
The Queen's Gambit

Imani Lewis
The Netherlands, August 2017

By the time I returned to the Waldorf it was nearly 6:00 pm. My dinner meeting with Angela Kiek was scheduled for 8:00 pm. Barely leaving me enough time for a fast shower. I was beginning to question Ms. Kiek's motivation. Why would she ask Daniel to keep me occupied all day sightseeing and then schedule a late supper that same evening? Perhaps she was testing my grit. Well, if that were the case, she would soon learn that I have a significant amount of personal perseverance combined with a substantial amount of passion. It is called survival strategies when living with an eccentric mother.

Exactly at 7:30 pm, Daniel was waiting for me in the hotel lobby. This was the meeting I was anticipating all day. Thus far, there was no clue as to what I could expect. I was hoping that at the very least Ms. Kiek would be able to provide me with another piece to this mysterious puzzle.

On my way to this meeting, Daniel offered no foreshadowing. And, I asked no questions. As we approached a street with a guard who controlled the electronic gate, I assumed that Ms. Kiek lived in one of those communities where neighbors felt it necessary to protect themselves from the outside world. What I was about to witness was totally unexpected. Once we passed the gate, Daniel drove quite a distance under a magnificent tree tunnel, a large lake, and a substantial-sized barn that resembled a horse stable. The entire pasture was fenced, but no horses were obvious. Possibly because it was the evening. Also not visible were any other houses along this dirt highway.

Nearly ten minutes after driving well past the entrance gate, I saw a huge mansion lit up like a fairy-tale palace. Daniel pulled into the circular driveway and stopped the car.

"We have arrived! When your meeting with Ms. Kiek has ended this is where I will be," Daniel said.

"Will you have to wait here the entire time that I am inside?" I asked.

"Oh no. I have my own small residence on the estate. I will return once Ms. Kiek texts me her instructions."

Estate? Oh my...I had no idea there was more past this point. But, before I could ask any further questions, an elderly gentleman dressed in a black tuxedo, who I assumed was the butler, opened my car door and helped me out of the sedan.

"Good evening, Ms. Lewis. I am Herr Muller, Ms. Kiek's personal assistant. Welcome to Amsterdam."

Before I could even say goodbye to Daniel I was being led into a massive hallway with marble statues and coats of arms. As we walked past several large portraits and a few more marble statues, I was beginning to feel like this was another museum rather than a private residence.

Once I arrived at the library, there was a much warmer, inviting atmosphere.

"Please make yourself comfortable, Ms. Lewis. We will be serving supper in the library tonight at Ms. Kiek's request. She will be here to meet with you shortly," Herr Muller said, leaving me by myself.

On three of the walls, there was floor to ceiling bookshelves, all filled with various book sizes, organized by theme. There was probably a card catalog somewhere nearby. I was tempted to explore but thought otherwise.

The one wall without a bookshelf had a massive window facing the gardens. Although it was already evening, the gardens were well lit. I could see that it was designed in an intricate labyrinth.

On one of my visits to England with my mother, I remembered us visiting a maze garden, offering many different paths to follow. Our guide compared this garden to the journey of life, or rebirth. We were told it was a symbol of reincarnation. One that we all experience at different periods in our lives.

Later I learned that in Medieval times the labyrinth represented man's hard road to God. We were told that metaphorically this road eventually leads us to salvation, or at the very least enlightenment. Even the maze built for ancient King Minos of Crete, specifically to imprison the man-eating Minotaur, still fascinates readers in this generation.

But, it was the onyx chess board, embedded with gold and silver that drew my attention away from the garden. The chess pieces are even more impressive. They are at least 18cm tall, three-dimensional, with extreme details. It appears that each piece is made of solid bronze, 24 karat gold, and silver. I once saw something similar in a chess magazine. It was a Medieval Venice Chess set valued at $50,000. I am presuming that this set is worth at least the same amount.

Seeing this chess board today brings back memories when I was twelve years old, staying with my grandparents in Africa. During one of my mother's frequent freelance writing expositions, my grandfather introduced me to this game. Chess is sometimes referred to as "the gentlemen's game." My grandfather was determined to extend that definition to ladies. He wanted me to understand that lack of courtesy breeds cowards. Win or lose when the game of chess is over you shake hands and move on to the next competition.

"I don't know; Poppy chess seems like a waste of time. Down at the village I watch the older men sit there for hours just staring at the board. And, then when one of them finally moves those odd pieces, the staring game continues again. I just don't understand why you find this fun," I said.

"Chess, my dear Imani, is much more than a board game. It is a strategy that you will need to master if you are ever going to be successful in life," Poppy said, with conviction.

"But, Poppy it is only a game? How can a game ever determine my accomplishments?" I asked, honestly confused.

That is when I was given my first history lesson on how chess originated and its juxtaposition to political power. At the time, most of what Poppy tried to teach me was far beyond my comprehension, but he never gave up on me. Once it was time to leave Africa, seven years later for college, everything Poppy was trying to teach me about chess made sense.

What I remember most is when Poppy compared chess to a Mandelbrot Set.

"It is just like the complex numbers that randomly appear in this new concept referred to as *The Mandelbrot Set*. At times also known as the 'thumbprint of God.' And, yes, there is a spiritual significance as well," my grandfather said.

It was not until I took an advanced mathematical theory class many years later that I learned that any fractal pattern, when viewed as an image, will retain that same visual effect even when cut into parts. These will appear to be a smaller version of that original picture. Trees, snowflakes and even coastlines are examples of natural fractals. All of these also form a *Mandelbrot Set*.

Benoit Mandelbrot, a Polish-born French American mathematician, is credited for this theory, sometimes regarded as "the uncontrolled element in life."

In terms of our world, like a chess game, or *The Mandelbrot Set*, there is always more to see than what the eyes provide. Specific chess pieces are restricted in movement and our freedom is almost always dictated by whether we are the "black" or "white" pieces on a chess board. Once I learned that the white pieces have control of the action and are always allowed to move first, my objective in life has always been to be the white pieces.

As I continued to learn the game of chess and life, it soon became apparent that the Queen, my favorite piece, is a horrifying example of how women are always underrated. It seems ludicrous that although the Queen is the most powerful piece on the chessboard, she can never gain the ultimate reign of power since once the king is defeated, the game ends.

No wonder the Queen of Hearts in *Alice in Wonderland* is always angry; she is always fighting for respect. But then I learned about *The Queens Gambit*. This is the oldest method of opening a game of chess. It is considered a gambit when white chooses to sacrifice the pawn. But as in any gambit strategy this sacrifice is specifically aimed at achieving a substantial positional advantage.

This opening is one of the oldest ones known in chess. It is mentioned in the *Gottingen Manuscript* in 1490, the earliest known written document that is entirely devoted to modern chess. What I found most important about *The Queens Gambit* is the ability to force my opponent to respond to my threats rather than working on their strategies. By using this same theory in my search for *The Agape* I hope to create chaos in Phoenix Baldwin's world.

"Are you a chess aficionado, Ms. Lewis?"

The voice from across the room startled me. I did not realize how deep I was immersed in my thoughts until that moment.

"Oh…well, yes and no. I haven't played for many years. But, I do enjoy the competition," I said, standing to greet my hostess.

"Well indeed I am sure you are also a worthy competitor, or we would not be meeting this evening," Ms. Kiek responded cleverly.

"Yes, I suppose you are correct. Chess does prepare us for many other mental challenges that we encounter in life," I said, feeling confident with my retort.

"Very well then. Let us enjoy our supper, learn a little more about each other, and then discuss the topic that has brought you here, *The Agape,*" Ms. Kiek said.

Almost as if this was a well-written script, the servants came in with a variety of food items, placed them on an elegant yet intimate dining table with candle lights. They then left promptly leaving us to enjoy our feast.

"Bon Appetit!"

Chapter Twenty-One

Avoid the crowd. Do your own thinking independently. Be the chess player, not the chess piece.

Ralph Charles
American Boxer

Imani Lewis
Netherlands, 2017

As it turns out, Angela Kiek's life is nearly as fascinating as Anne Frank's. Rose, Angela's grandmother, was friends with the Frank household. Originally from Vienna, Austria, like so many other Jewish families, the Kiek's fled to Amsterdam once the Nazis invaded. Here they met other Jewish families in their new neighborhood, including the Frank family. Maria, Angela's mother, was nine years old, the same age as Anne. They soon became friends. Angela recalled her grandmother saying that Anne was much more outgoing than her mother, Maria.

Many years later, when Anne Frank's Diary was required reading, Angela's grandmother shared the relationship between their families. It did not last for very long, but what Anne's mother, Edith Frank, gave to the Kiek family was priceless.

"Days before Otto Frank decided to move his family into hiding, Edith was told that she could only take items of extreme necessity with them to their new apartment. It was difficult to discard many heirlooms especially treasured by the Frank family. Nevertheless, Edith followed her husband's instructions. One of the first items to be given away was an ancient carpet that Edith's mother gave her on her wedding day. Edith was told that it had spiritual healing powers," Angela paused to assess my reaction.

I of course was stunned.

Was Angela Kiek in possession of The Agape? Could this be the end of my journey?

"Are you suggesting, Angela, that Edith Frank actually had custody of the real *Agape Carpet?*" I asked skeptically.

"Well, it does seem likely, although Edith never trusted that this carpet had any powers. For years it was so old and hideous, that Otto refused to allow Edith to lay it on any of the floors in their home. But, since it was a wedding gift from Edith's mother she stored it in the attic for years. When my grandmother heard this story, she asked Edith to take it off her hands. Edith agreed. Rose carefully cleaned the carpet. What appeared was many beautiful images with vibrant colors…"

"I apologize for interrupting, but this is crucial. Do you know specifically what images were on that carpet," I asked, eager to know.

"Yes. My grandmother was able to describe the carpet in great detail. One of the most distinct areas of the carpet was the deep purple center with gold threads outlining special symbols, such as a white dove, palm branches, and a fish symbol," Angela confirmed.

I could not believe how accurate this description was. It was nearly exactly what *Apu* shared with me at Machu Picchu.

"Are you certain about these symbols, Angela?" I asked, not wanting to sound doubtful, but I also wanted it to be precise.

"Absolutely, Imani. I saw these images with my own eyes. And, one of the most fascinating symbols that drew me to the carpet in the first place was a tiny unicorn. It was an exact replica of the famous Unicorn Tapestries known as, *The Unicorn Rests in the Garden.* It was similar to the original complex art forms of the Middle Ages. Like the famous one that is hanging in the New York Metropolitan Museum of Art, this unicorn was woven in fine wool and silk with silver and gilded threads," Angela added.

Knowing from my studies that the unicorn represents Christianity, as well as immortality and wisdom, I was not surprised to hear that this image was added to *The Agape.* What I was curious about is who decided to include the unicorn and when.

"You said that you actually saw this carpet, Angela? Where is it now?" I finally asked the most critical question.

"Yes, I did personally see the carpet. It was included in our antique shop on Prinsengracht, when I opened *Absolute Antiques* twenty years ago. It was after my grandmother passed away that I decided to showcase a few of the priceless items in the store to arouse interest and as a legacy to my grandmother. It was great advertisement. Everyone that visited was anxious to see the quite famous carpet that once belonged in the home of Anne Frank. Ironically, that carpet, if Edith Frank had insisted on saving it, may have spared all their lives. As it turned out, that is exactly what it did for my family," Angela stopped briefly, collecting her thoughts.

It was clear by Angela's tone that this discussion was getting difficult for her. But, I knew that it was crucial for me to hear all the details if I had any chance of discovering where *The Agape* was now.

"What exactly do you mean? How could that carpet have saved Anne Frank and her family," I asked, quietly.

"When Rosa finished cleaning the carpet she proudly placed it in the small living room. But, soon, all of her Jewish friends were preparing to leave the country, if they could. My grandparents instead started their preparations to stay in hiding. While they were exploring various locations, my grandfather finally made the decision that the best place would be right where they were. That is when my grandmother, mother, aunt, and grandfather removed everything from the apartment, except for the carpet and the small kitchen table with four chairs. That carpet and only the remaining furniture was placed directly over a hidden trap door that led to an underground tunnel. Apparently, when the Nazis eventually discovered the empty apartment, they never searched for the hidden tunnel. My family remained hidden in that cave for six months until the Russian army in 1945 found them. Why the Russian army chose to move the carpet, and the Nazis did not is a mystery nobody could explain. Regardless, my grandparents were now free and immediately made plans to travel back to Poland. But, my grandfather passed away, before he could make that trip. Rosa blamed the lack of circulation in the caves for his death. In fact, all of the survivors did experience some emphysema-related illnesses later in their lives. When my mother passed away I was only twelve years old. Rosa, my grandmother, continued to raise me. I then spent the remainder of my life caring for her, until she passed away a few years ago at the age of 102. She made me promise never to sell the carpet that saved her life, and I kept that promise," Angela said proudly.

"Then you still have it displayed in your antique store?" I asked, sounding enthusiastic.

"No, my dear, unfortunately not. Five years ago the original antique shop burned down. The carpet was assumed to have burned along with many other priceless treasures. But then, I began researching those items that I needed to replace. This is when I discovered *The Agape*. This was my carpet. I now have no doubt. What I soon learned is that it really never was my carpet. Nor was it my Grandmother's carpet. *The Agape* belongs to the world. Its power comes from God, and only God can control where it goes next," Angela said, pouring me another cup of coffee.

"But, Angela if *The Agape* was destroyed in the fire, how could it still be traveling," I asked, confused.

"I certainly do not have all the answers Imani. The time that *The Agape* was in my possession brought my family great happiness and peace. What I can tell you is that if *The Agape* is still traveling in the modern world I would suggest that you visit Spain. If I was much younger, I might join you, but it is time that *The Agape* be located. Our society needs some guidance from the spiritual world, before we destroy ourselves," Angela said.

She then walked over to an ancient but well-preserved early 18th-century Escritoire writing desk. I watched Angela shuffle through a few loose papers before locating what she was looking for.

"These letters that I have been saving, I printed from my internet conversations with a historian who lives in Aviles, Spain. His name is Señor Tejeda. From our conversations, I do believe that he will be an excellent contact for you,"

Angela said, handing me all the papers that she had compiled.

By this time, I was beginning to feel like a nomad gypsy Hippie. I was traveling from country to country with the intent to spread peace and kindness while still expecting these strangers to provide me with information about a mysterious spiritual carpet. One that very well may be nothing but ashes by now. But, then again, if a Phoenix can rise from the ashes, why not The Agape?

"You want me to book a flight from Amsterdam to where?" Priscilla asked.

"Aviles, Spain. And, Priscilla, I don't need a super luxurious hotel. A four rated accommodation will be fine. I really need to start watching my budget," I said, hoping she could hear me through all the static.

"I haven't even heard of Aviles, Spain, Imani. It may take me at least twenty-four hours, considering we are now also in different time zones," Priscilla calculated.

"I don't mind staying here in Amsterdam for a while. It may be a good place to do some reflecting prior to leaving for Spain. Just please do your best to get me on a flight by next week. My phone is dying so I will check back with you tomorrow. Thank you, Priscilla, for being so patient with all my requests," I said, hoping that she could still hear me.

"No problem, sweetheart! I will get on it first thing tomorrow morning. Try to enjoy Amsterdam while you are waiting."

That was the last I heard before my phone turned black.

Chapter Twenty-Two

I've died a thousand deaths, each time reinventing myself brighter, stronger, and purer than before. From the midst of destruction, I became the creator of myself. From the midst of darkness, I became my own source of light.

Cristen Rodgers
Keys to Freedom

Phoenix Baldwin
Aviles, Spain 2017

This Imani Lewis creature is definitely a conundrum. I would add that she is quite annoying, although that observation may be biased. Yet, quite accurate based on our first formal meeting at Machu Picchu. Miss Lewis was downright rude when all I was merely trying to do was suggest a friendly alliance.

It must be her striking ginger hair hanging loose around her shoulders that create a frightful image. Yet, she is also quite similar to those Titian's models from the 19th-century Pre-Raphaelite art movement. I must admit that is exactly what attracted me to her at first. Perhaps, attract is not the correct word choice. I am certainly not romantically drawn to this young lady. Certainly, nothing like I was to another redhead beauty, my Maggie May! Now she was an absolute gem!

No, a better word to express my attraction to Imani is that I am intrigued by her. Yes, I am intrigued by her tenacious personality. The very nerve on her part to suggest that she could compete with me or any other legitimate male treasure hunter is quite incredible.

Some may consider my attitude chauvinistic or outdated, but I am a strong supporter of the women's rights movement. I have always admired what strong women can accomplish when they are focused. But, when women like Imani Lewis are just stubborn, it isn't enjoyable. They aren't even capable of admitting how incompetent they are. How can she ever expect to compete with my expertise? Imani's naïve attempts are totally ludicrous.

During one of my most dry seasons at Cambridge, when everything was tasteless and even regurgitatingly dull, I decided that if things did not improve, it might be time for early retirement.

To spice up my curriculum, I prepared a very detailed class course to teach a series of Ernest Hemingway novels the following semester. American Literature on this side of the pond has always been considered inferior. Nevertheless, I was determined to convince Dean Hopkins that Ernest Hemingway was an exception to that stereotype.

I agreed to take a one-year sabbatical to allow intensive research and prepare a plausible dissertation supporting my claims. Dean Hopkins would then consider the merits.

To complete my thesis, I decided to visit as many possible settings that Hemingway chose for his novels. During that time, I became obsessed with the man. Not only the seven novels he published in his lifetime, but it was also the women he spent time with that were fascinating. All of those women that he loved, married, had affairs with not only contributed to his success but also were the reasons for his nightmares. That is what finally destroyed him.

During that year of research, I knew so much about Hemingway that I began to resemble him. I grew a beard, wore plaid shirts and even turtlenecks. Drinking became a natural habit every day, everywhere. The only conviction I could not mimic is hunting. It was something that I always abhorred and even Ernest couldn't convince me that it was a "manly" sport.

As I traveled through Europe, letting Hemingway's novels lead the way, I began to understand why his works were so universal. His characters are real people that he met. Strangers, friends, fellow writers all were recast into many of his stories. These were all people that readers already knew or wanted to know. But, it was the adventures that he created for those characters that people hungered for.

There were wars, running with the bulls in Pamplona, and even a simple sea village in Cuba where an older man's struggle with a great marlin depicts courage and grace under pressure.

By the time my sabbatical was over I understood why Hemingway was called by friends *Papa*. Ernest Hemingway was my surrogate father. He was the model I wanted to become. He inspired me to leave Cambridge and search for *The Agape*. I would not let him down. There would be no competition during this race. Imani Lewis was not even a viable adversary.

One of my favorite quotes from Hemingway can be found in his short story collection, "Men without Women." That self-reflection truly is what I fear the most. These words resonate with me daily.

"The most painful thing is losing yourself in the process of loving someone too much, and forgetting that you're special too." Ernest Hemingway.

I will never allow myself to be in that dilemma again. The best way to avoid heartache is never to love a woman completely. They should always love you more. This makes for a very safe relationship.

The pilot has just announced that our plane is at its final descent. We should be landing at Valladolid. From there, it is another three to four hours before reaching Aviles by train. I am certain that Imani must be at least a day behind me. Her visit to Amsterdam took longer than mine, as expected. If I could only convince Imani that this isn't a competition, we could both save precious time.

I will admit I am curious about her leads. What I discovered in Amsterdam is that *The Agape* controls its own destination. Dr. Schneider, an anthropologist who was referred to me by my friend Dr. Morris insists that anyone searching for *The Agape* must clearly understand its power.

"You see, Phoenix, most people are mistakenly looking for leads to where the physical carpet surfaced recently. This will result in chasing an elusive object with little satisfaction," Schneider said.

"But then what is the alternative? If we can verify that *Agape* has been seen in a designated site, isn't that bringing us closer to discovering where it may be next? I have found that there appears to be a recurring pattern forming. Is this a viable conclusion, Doctor?" I asked.

"The answer, my chap, is both yes and no. What you are discovering is that *The Agape* has many different facets. But, have you ever asked yourself if it is the situation that leads *The Agape* to its next crisis, or is it merely a coincidence that one carpet with such spiritual powers allows circumstance to dictate where it is needed?"

Schneider poses a very interesting question. Perhaps trying to follow *The Agape* on a linear trail is causing me to misunderstand its true potential. Dr. Schneider strongly encouraged me to study *Christian Hermeticism* before continuing my trip to Aviles. Although at the beginning I was somewhat skeptical, Then I realized that to ignore any leads might be a disaster. What I discovered was quite insightful.

The Hermeticism philosophy encourages the art of enlightenment by understanding what the transformation of human life and consciousness is. What I learned from *Meditations on the Tarot: A Journey into Christian Hermeticism* is that "Christian Hermeticists listen to the beating of the heart of the spiritual life of humanity. They cannot do otherwise and live as guardians of life and communal soul of religion, science, and art," (First letter of *A Journey into Christian Hermeticism*).

The ancient Egyptian Hermès Trismegistus initiated this tradition and is credited for writing the *Emerald Tablet*. This text gives a very concise summary of the ancient view of a catalyst for growth and evolution. *The Emerald Tablet* is later the foundation for the entire school of spiritual exercises.

In the twentieth century, an anonymous author wrote Meditation on the Tarot, reflecting on his spiritual journey fusing Christianity with the Hermetic tradition.

All of this information was fascinating and confusing. What exactly was it that Dr. Schneider thought I needed to learn from these lessons? Perhaps this is why traveling now to Aviles is essential. Without the knowledge of the Hermetic tradition this visit can only offer me another clue without any guidance. I was beginning to understand that locating *The Agape* is more than accomplishing a goal. Finding *The Agape* just might be a personal awakening. Somewhere in the deep layers of my human soul, there must be a profound understanding of spiritual truths.

La Casa de Presidente is located six hundred feet from Torreón de Los Guzmanes and forty-seven miles from Salamanca Airport. It is an excellent location to stay while in Aviles. Imani Lewis will also be registering at this hotel a few hours after I arrive. It was not difficult to trace her itinerary; after all, that is what I am being paid well to do. I am quite certain that Ms. Lewis will not find any of this amusing. Mainly that we are lodging at the same establishment.

I must convince this very stubborn woman that it would be a benefit for us both to join forces. I really am not her enemy, merely her competitor. And, like any wise competitor, it is to my advantage to act on any opportunity that arises.

"Welcome to La Casa Presidente, Señor Baldwin. Your room is ready to occupy. Please let us know if we can assist you in any way during your stay with us," the desk clerk said as I signed in and gave him my passport.

It is always customary to leave your passport while you remain in the hotel, although I never liked the idea.

"Thank you. There is one thing that I would request. Would you please see that Ms. Imani Lewis receives this letter once she arrives later today? I would kindly appreciate it," I said, handing the clerk the envelope.

"Oh, and one more request. Can you recommend a nice intimate restaurant nearby for later this evening?" I inquired.

"Of course Señor Baldwin. *Pasama La Sal* is an excellent choice. It is walking distance. Excellent cuisine with an intimate setting. Would you like me to reserve a table for two, Señor?" The clerk asked.

He imagined that Imani and I were having a romantic interlude. If he only knew how amusing that assumption was.

"Yes, I would appreciate you are reserving a table for 9:00 pm this evening. Gracias," I said, departing to my room.

What I wouldn't give to be a fly on the wall in that reception room when Imani Lewis checks into the hotel, receives my letter and realizes that I am here.

Chapter Twenty-Three

I cannot prove to you that God exists, but my work has proved empirically that the pattern of God exists in every man, and this pattern in the individual has at its disposal the greatest transforming energies of which life is capable. Find this pattern in your own individual self and life is transformed.

Carl Jung
Swiss Psychiatrist

Imani Lewis
Aviles, Spain
2017

"The drive from Salamanca Airport to downtown Aviles will be approximately forty five minutes, Señora. 100 Euros. Best deal in town!"

The driver was waving at me, trying to outshout his competitors.

Before I could even haggle a deal with him on the price, my luggage and laptop were already in the trunk, and I was sitting in the backseat.

"Buenos Diaz, lovely Señora, or is it Señorita?" the driver asked before pulling away from the curb.

How did I end up in this car so quickly?

"Oh, it doesn't really matter what title you use. I need to go to La Casa de Presidente hotel in Aviles. Do you know where that is located?" I asked while searching for the address in my backpack.

"No problem, lady. I have been there many times. It is a lovely hotel. Near all the important sites. My name is Pedro. Now you can just relax and enjoy the ride. If you have any questions, I will be happy to answer them if I can," he said, exiting the airport carefully.

"Is this your first visit to Spain, Señora? Pedro asked, looking at me through the rearview mirror.

"No. I have visited Madrid, Barcelona, and Seville, but have never really explored the smaller cities," I said, staring out the car window at the very plain landscape outside.

"You will find Aviles considerably less exciting than any of our major municipalities. But, there are some interesting places to visit. We also have some popular beaches close by that you might enjoy. Salinas is the most frequented by visitors," Pedro said, this time keeping his eyes on the highway.

"Unfortunately, I do not think that my plans will include a beach outing. Although, I must agree that sounds tempting right now," I said, realizing that the past several weeks, I have had no time for any personal recreational activities. Unless I count mountain climbing and museum junkets. Maybe after my meeting here, I should take several days off to enjoy the ocean.

"Well, I certainly hope that you will allow at least some time to visit a few of our historical sights. Although Aviles is mostly an industrial city, it does have several important churches, like St. Thomas of Canterbury, located at Plaza de la Merced. Nonetheless, perhaps what Aviles is best known for is the home of Pedro Menendez, a soldier in the Spanish army. He is best remembered for exploring Florida in the 16th century," Pedro said."

"Is it merely a coincidence that your name is also Pedro?" I asked, jokingly.

"Not at all. Many people who live in this region are named after the famous Pedro Menendez. The house where he was born still exists today and is accessible to visitors. Pedro was born to an old established noble family in the Asturias kingdom. He was also one of twenty children. Pedro's life was quite complicated until he joined the military and went off to fight in a small armada against France. There he became recognized as a potential leader. Make certain that you visit the monument to Pedro Menendez. Locals believe that his spirit guides them through many difficult times," Pedro added.

I could definitely use some of that guidance now. Lately, I was beginning to feel like I was chasing an elusive object that would never be found.

"If you are staying until the weekend you must join the locals to celebrate *The Descent of Galiana*. It is our *Mardi Gras* and worth participating in," Pedro said with conviction.

"Although it sounds tempting, I doubt that I will still be here. My business requires much dedication with little time for entertainment or recreational activities," I said, avoiding too many details.

The last twenty minutes, Pedro found a radio station that played contemporary Spanish rock. Although none of it sounded familiar, it all sounded universal. Everything from the classical guitar to the similar rap sounds combined with bebop style jazz developed in the early 1940s in America. I must not have been paying much attention to the time because soon Pedro was pulling into the driveway of La Casa del Presidente.

"We have arrived, lovely Señora. May your stay with us here in Aviles be memorable," Pedro said, helping me out of the car.

Immediately a friendly gentleman in the traditional guayabera, or "wedding shirt," welcomed me.

"Buenes Tardes Señora. Sincere salutations from our humble historical establishment. You must be Imani Lewis? Correct?" The gentleman said behind a friendly smile.

At first I was slightly taken aback that he would know my name, but then again I didn't need a sign around my neck saying I was American. It was fairly obvious from the location that most of the guests in the lobby were from other regions in Spain or Europe. Aviles was not a popular American tourist attraction.

My host escorted me inside the airy hotel, where I completed the formal registration papers. Before I was about to walk away, I realized I had no keys.

"Oh, I nearly forgot. I have a letter here for you," the clerk said reaching into the guest mail slots, fetching an envelope with my name on it.

I presumed that it was some instructions that Priscilla left for me about souvenirs or tourist hot spots that she thought I might want to visit. Placing the envelope in my bag I started to leave just as the clerk said,

"We have selected a beautiful suite for you, Señora Lewis. It faces our lovely garden courtyard. As you may already know this hotel was once the home of our first President of the Spanish Democracy. This house has been the witness to many historical events, as well as mysteries. Our exceptional house is also a retreat from the outside chaotic world that sometimes is difficult to escape."

This acclamation sounded more like an advertisement commercial.

"Gracias, Señor. I am certainly looking forward to all your amenities once I have completed my business here in your lovely city," I said.

With the antique hotel key in my hand, I noticed that my room number, 444, was boldly imprinted.

"You may take the elevator around the corner. The bellman will retrieve your luggage shortly," I heard the attendant say as I continued to walk in the direction he pointed to without looking back.

Once inside my room, I opened the window coverings. It revealed a lovely balcony facing the pool and gardens just as the clerk had promised. I took a seat on the veranda and opened the envelope that I placed in my bag earlier.

Dear Ms. Lewis,

I am reaching out to you once again with an olive branch hoping that you will meet with me at supper tonight across the street from our hotel, at Pasama La Sal. I have made reservations for 9:00 pm this evening, knowing that you might want to take a short nap after your long flight. I also thought you should be aware that we are both here to meet with the same gentleman, Señor Tejeda. Perhaps now would be an excellent time to join together in this journey rather than stepping on each other's toes all the time?

I am looking forward to a pleasant evening with you, Ms. Lewis.
Cordially,
Phoenix Baldwin

Phoenix Baldwin and I are in the same hotel? How did this happen? And, how did he know when I was arriving here? This does complicate matters and certainly muddies the water. I can't simply ignore his request to meet for dinner. Strategically that would just make me appear weak. No, I must meet with him; there is no other alternative. Interestingly, he must believe that I have some knowledge about *The Agape* or why even bother contacting me at all? Unfortunately, I am in the same situation. Nothing that I have learned about this mysterious carpet the past few months has brought me any closer to locating the elusive Agape.

I planned on spending the evening reading through the collection of letters my father compiled for me. Prior to beginning this trek, I had those letters bound into a journal. There was just something about those letters that I felt Bran Hughes wanted me to know beyond his reflections on losing a daughter and lover. I just haven't been able to discover exactly what it is yet. Unfortunately, tonight I will need to postpone my original plans. This meeting with Phoenix Baldwin must take priority.

Before closing my eyes on the very inviting mattress for a short nap, I set my alarm for 8:00 pm. Since this meeting was not until 9:00 pm and only across the street from the hotel, I still had several hours to recover from any jet lag. Having a clear mind when meeting with this strange competitor is crucial. The tone in his letter indicates that he believes he is in complete control of this contest.

The alarm went off exactly on time. Without hesitation I bolted out of bed prepared for combat. Just like the Imani warrior, I am not a force to be ignored. This meeting would make Mr. Baldwin not only respect who I am but also realizes that I am his equal.

Once again I chose that emerald green strapless dress Priscilla insisted that I pack. I really didn't care that it was the same one I wore at Machu Picchu. Besides, there was no other choice.

I still had time to open *The Bran Hughes* journal. This is how I now referred to it. I turned to the page where my father first describes the Imani of his imagination; the Imani that he believed I would become.

This section vividly describes Bran's idea on how I would naturally evolve into a worldly woman. He writes,

"She is a woman who is willing to share her intellect with anyone willing to listen. She is a traveler with an open mind, yet a fierce competitor who refuses to accept defeat. I see my Imani with blazing red hair flowing like a fiery river. She has the ability to slay any demons that confront her. Imani is wise beyond her years."

I close the pages. I confidently slip on my tightly fitting gown. It glimmers with a fire opal translucent shimmer reflecting various hues. As I twirl in the light, my flaming, fiery red hair appears more scarlet tonight than ginger. It is carefully piled on the top of my head, with strands cascading loosely framing my face. If I were fearless, I would use Indian war paint on my cheeks, but then again, it is much better to be discreet.

I do believe that Bran Hughes would approve of me tonight. The Imani warrior is prepared to meet the Phoenix. Although it is a well-known fact that the Phoenix is immortal, it is also vulnerable to iron. When a Phoenix is touched by iron it will burn.

I opened a small velvet pouch and removed a lovely antique eternity bracelet given to me by my grandmother when I turned sixteen. The bracelet is forged and fabricated from one piece of iron without welding or smoldering. Originating from a solid bar of iron there are two cuts that form an X shape. These two additional extra ramifications form the bridge of a violin. The brass pegs hold a steel cable with a piece of amber in the center.

This piece of jewelry is inspired by the violin mechanism.

"One day, my child you will read the great *Metamorphosis,* by Frank Kafka. In this story, Grete's violin is one of the few objects of beauty. What Gregor wants to do more than anything in his life is pay for Grete to study violin at the Conservatorium. Although there is so much more that you will learn about Grete and Gregor later in your life, for now this is all you need to understand. This bracelet is an eternal violin, symbolizing a loving bond, a generous, sympathetic characteristic that I always want for you. My lovely Imani strive for perfection!"

Those words spoken by my Nani on my sixteenth birthday resonate each time I wear this bracelet. Tonight, I am counting on this power, which will provide the light to shine within me.

Chapter Twenty-Four

> Calm —indeed the calmest—reflection may be better than the most confused decisions.
> Franz Kafka, *The Metamorphosis*

Phoenix Baldwin and Imani Lewis
Aviles, Spain 2017

It has been ten days since I have reported back to "the Roaches". That is my latest name for the Firm that hired me to find *The Agape*. I am reminded by their agent, since nobody really knows who the Firm really is, "That time is of the essence." Whatever the hell that means.

Just as I told the *Roaches* agent, all documents were submitted as per our agreement to support the progress that I have made thus far. I have discovered that most of the other treasure hunters are amateurs. They really know nothing about *The Agape*. They are following circular leads that will only result in more useless information. The only real competitor I am aware of is this Imani Lewis, who somehow finds sources leading her to my trail. The fact that we both have a meeting with Señor Tejeda is definitely a sign that Ms. Lewis is a potential threat. What I want to discover this evening is why *The Agape* means so much to her. If it is the money, we certainly can come to a suitable agreement. But, if she is working for someone else, I need to know that as well. Maybe with any luck I can pry away what leads she has that might be useful to me. The easiest way to exclude Ms. Lewis from any further competition is, of course, to buy her out. If the money attracts her to this treasure hunt, I can easily persuade her with excellent compensation.

I must admit that our first meeting did not go well in Machu Picchu. Most of the time, I have no problems convincing lovely ladies that my intentions are honorable, even when they are not. But, this woman does not play by the obvious rules. Tonight I have reevaluated my strategy. Miss Lewis will soon conclude on her own that she has no possible chance at finding *The Agape*. I intend to make it easy for her to concede graciously. With my financial backing and superior professional skills, this will no longer be a fair pursuit. Even Imani Lewis will finally admit to this. To save embarrassment, I will offer Imani the one-time opportunity to join me in a mutual arrangement. Offering her a fair percentage of the reward should "seal this deal." A typical American phrase, I believe.

Usually after wining and dining with a lovely companion at a romantic seaside restaurant, the remainder of the evening turns more intimate. If it were anyone other than Imani Lewis, she would be my dessert for this evening. There is no doubt that I could use an evening of sultry lovemaking.

Unfortunately, this lady is not my type. Not even for a one-night stand. What I am looking forward to is moving past this awkward tryst quickly, leaving maybe a few hours after to frequent some of the other local taverns. There should still be plenty of time left to meet some truly sultry Señoritas.

At *Pasama La Sal* I was about twenty minutes early. It was my strategy to be seated where I could see Ms. Lewis as she arrives. I had no doubt that she would be here exactly on time. All the plain-looking girls I have ever known always arrive either early or on time to avoid being noticed. This girl is no exception.

The restaurant was quite elegant, with inviting candlelight creating a very seductive atmosphere. Precisely what I was counting on. Not for romance but for ambushing. I wanted to make this Imani Lewis realize from the very beginning that she is out of her element.

The chimes from the church across the street rang nine times, and just like clockwork, the front door opened to the restaurant, and Imani Lewis graciously walked past the reception desk to my table. A small band was playing, a famous love song by Andrea Bocelli. *Besamo Mucho*. Although the words were naturally in Spanish, I was fairly familiar with the English version.

Besame, Besame Mucho
  Kiss me, Kiss me a lot

Como si fuera esta la noche
  As if this was the night

But, before I could even translate the next verse in my head, there she was. A strikingly attractive woman that reminded me of a young Ann Margaret and the singer Rihanna melded.

"Good evening, Mr. Baldwin."

That was all I heard. Her hand outstretched, I stood up from my chair, feeling foolish and looking awkward.

"Good evening. I am so pleased that you accepted my invitation for dinner," I said, pulling her chair out politely.

"Even I need to eat somewhere. Might as well be here," Imani said, staring right past me, looking at the troubadour.

Thankfully the wine steward came immediately. He offered us the best pairings for a variety of menu choices. Once our eyes connected to the *Besame Mucho* song, I could not free myself from her trance. There was an involuntary reflex in the size of her pupils that invited me deep into her soul. I was losing all control.

Once I regained my composure, I clumsily apologized for my rudeness at our last encounter at Machu Picchu.

"I really am not that brash most of the time, Ms. Lewis. Perhaps it was the altitude. Nevertheless, let us make a toast to new beginnings, with better outcomes," I said, feeling slightly back in control.

Imani raised her glass and added,

"May the best of the past be the worst of the future."

We both took short sips and returned our glasses, as if this was a test of valor. This was followed by an embarrassing moment of silence. Finally, I made the first move to release the tension.

"Was your flight from Amsterdam to Seville pleasant," I asked cautiously.

"Yes, quite pleasant," Imani answered, not offering anything further in her comments.

It was now becoming quite evident that my perfect plan was not working. Imani Lewis was not going to concede easily. Somehow she already knew what this meeting was meant to achieve.

We both moved our pawns. Was I prepared to release my knight at this moment? If so, what could I expect from my opponent? Unlike the long-range bishop or even the popular rook, my strategic movement at this moment must be cautious. It would be the only way to regain control of the center without alerting any retaliation. Now was the time to offer some bait.

"I hope we can take this opportunity, Imani, to understand each other better. Perhaps sharing a bit of our background might make this evening even more pleasant," I said, perusing the menu casually, waiting for her reaction.

Imani appeared to be absorbing what I said, rather than listening. Her attention was being filtered by the music playing. The soft illumination created by the candlelight was not enough to distract Imani from her mission. She always remained in control. Imani Lewis knew precisely where she was and why she was here.

"Have you ever tasted glazed octopus?" Imani asked, avoiding my previous questions.

"No, I must admit that I have never even considered eating an octopus, although I do quite respect them when I am scuba diving. Do you enjoy scuba diving, Ms. Lewis," I asked, bringing us back to my original purpose; to learn more about Imani Lewis.

"Yes, I have gone scuba diving, but, this time I will play it safe and have the special fish stew. I presume all your fish is local, correct?" Without elaborating, Imani was now talking directly to the waiter.

"Absolutely, madam. You will not be disappointed," the waiter said, then turned to me for my selection.

"Well, I will take the bait, and order your glazed octopus," I said, staring directly into my guest's magnificent green eyes. They were now more radiant than the emerald gown she was wearing.

"This way you will have an opportunity to taste a true delicacy for the first time, my dear. It will be a memorable moment that the two of us virgins can share," I said, wanting to add touché, but left that caption to be understood.

The waiter naturally was amused with what he believed was my obvious foreplay to a romantic evening. Imani wet her lips and raised her right finger as if to say that the first round went to me.

"You definitely do not disappoint Mr. Baldwin. I am not sure that I can compete with your charades, but I will guarantee you that my stamina is unrivaled. I am looking forward to a delightful evening," Imani said with conviction.

Just then, as if scripted by a clever director, a lovely young lady approached our table with long-stemmed roses. I gave her a twenty-dollar Euro and handed the roses to Imani. It just seemed appropriate at the moment. What I didn't expect was what Imani did next. She took one of the roses from the bouquet, snapped off the long stem, stood up, leaned across the linen table, and placed the rose in the lapel of my jacket.

"Red roses should be shared, Mr. Baldwin. Since ancient times, in whatever circumstances, the rose gives us a glimpse of a masterful creator gradually revealing the spiritual wisdom that surrounds us," Imani said.

She then sat down waiting for me to react.

I reached for her hand, which was cool and steady. She did not resist my touch. It was as if she expected it.

"It is this spiritual wisdom that we share that will benefit us both. Once you agree to be my partner in this remarkable opportunity, everyone wins. We must share with the world the power of *The Agape*."

I couldn't believe that I ever could suggest that Imani and I become partners. Well, it doesn't matter much now. I sincerely doubt that Imani will ever agree to such a commitment.

Slowly Imani withdrew her hand from mine. But, I hardly noticed. It was her head slightly tilted that caught my attention. Those Merlot tresses piled randomly on the crown of her head glimmering like a seductive model who might have just stepped out of a Titan portrait; sensual, yet innocent.

Tiziano Vecelli, better known as Titan, a Renaissance painter from Venice, captured this mystery of red-haired women in many of his portraits. And, at this very moment, I was seated across a young lady who had the power to either destroy me or embrace me. Not knowing the outcome is disturbing. It was a situation that I had not ever faced before.

"Certainly, Mr. Baldwin, you aren't suggesting that you need me to fulfill your contract?" Imani said with confidence.

Was she giving me an opportunity to rescind my original proposal? If I did this now it would definitely appear as a weakness. But, if I affirm my position, it also confirms that I need her. Clever move.

"Perhaps the term 'partner' may have sounded rather presumptuous. In our situation, whether we choose to acknowledge it or not, we ARE both joined by the same endeavor. I am merely suggesting that if we shared our findings, it would accomplish a much more pleasant environment," I said, once again gaining control.

Imani, lifted her glass towards mine in a gracious sign of collaboration. Her eyes sparkled as if she was the victor. I decided to allow her to believe that she was, at least for the moment.

After our meal, several hours later, I learned as much about Imani Lewis as she would allow me. Still, it was much more than I had previously known. We mutually agreed to meet with Señor Tejeda the following morning. After that meeting, we agreed to reconsider what our next strategy would be.

I no longer had any desire to search for Spanish Señoritas. Whatever I was hungering for earlier was somehow satisfied with an intellectual orgasm beyond my imagination.

Chapter Twenty-Five

There are some people who live in a dream world, and there are some who face reality; and then there are those who turn one into the other.

Douglas H. Everett
British Chemist and academic author

Imani Lewis
Aviles, Spain 2017

Crystal visions wrapping around my eyes enhance an echo of a heartbeat, a dripping faucet washing my eyes with lonely, lucid dreams. My arms embrace a broken bird that has landed on my lap. Its blazing red feathers are oozing with a gold leaf and shimmering flakes of silver. He buries his weary head into my bare bosom, weeping, as I rock back and forth to give him solace. His body has been badly beaten, but he refuses to relinquish: he refuses to perish. His weary eyes meet mine.

"You are the chosen one, Imani. You must be the one to help me build my best and set it on fire. Without you, I am unable to be reborn from the ashes of my flames".

"Why am I the chosen one? I ask, confused.

"Because you, Imani are the midwife to Death. You will bring the birth and rebirth needed to fulfill God's highest mystery. Listen to the words of Miyamoto Musashi...There is nothing outside of yourself that can ever enable you to get better, stronger, richer, quicker, or more intelligent. Everything is within. Everything exists. Seek nothing outside of yourself."

Before I can respond, a brilliant white light enters my atmosphere. It is so powerful that it is all-encompassing. The suffering bird is no longer in my arms. It has been replaced with a bouquet of flowers. Then, a voice says that I should never confuse 'love' with 'like.' People who like flowers pick them, as the ones I am holding. But, those who love flowers are dedicated to watering and nourishing them.

"One who understands this, Imani, will understand their purpose in the world," an omnipotent voice whispers.

I try to move away but sitting next to me, on the marble floor, is the famous psychologist Carl Gustav Jung. Without saying a word, he hands me a card. I read it aloud,

"One does not become enlightened by imagining figures of light but by making the Darkness Conscious."

When I have finished reading, I realize that once again I am all alone.

As I begin to feel myself moving from one dimension into another, I again hear a voice barely audible, saying,

"The mind and the world are not separate. All space and time are in the mind. There are many levels of the mind, and each projects its own vision...just as what you dream is your own dream, and no one else can see it, so the world you see is your own."

I do recognize that these are the words of Nisargadatta Maharaja, a Hindu guru of nondualism.

Now it is my opportunity to exit through a short door located behind a black velvet theatre curtain. I run towards it anxiously, confused, exhausted, only to fall through a trap door that lands me in the center of a stage surrounded by darkness. A spotlight is now on a horrendously ugly creature, portraying a Franciscan friar.

On the opposite side of this stage, directly in front of me, stands a tall man wearing a scholar's cloak, decorated with a cross. His face is hidden by the hood, but what is visible is tragic. It is the visage of a distorted human, rotting from the inside out.

But, it is the thunder and lightning that appear without warning that make me tremble. There is no escape. I am now part of this tragedy. A tragedy that I am extremely familiar with. Like Faustus, am I willing to relinquish my soul for knowledge and power? Is Phoenix pulling me toward the gravitational center of human temptation? Faustus is the human archetype striving to reach beyond his natural restrictions. Is my search for The Agape leading me to Hell?

Before I can assess this situation, everything begins to fade into a whirlpool sending me back to a loud knock on my bedroom door.

"Imani! Imani Lewis? Are you in there?" I heard the sound of a familiar man's voice.

I rise from my bed, stumbling toward the sound, to look through the peephole. I see Phoenix Baldwin standing outside, holding two styrofoam cups.

"Yes, I'm here. What time is it?" I ask, still feeling odd from awakening unexpectedly.

"We need to leave here in thirty minutes for our appointment. You didn't answer any of my calls," Phoenix said.

I slightly cracked the door ajar to accept the coffee cup.

"I am so sorry. My phone must have died during the evening. I will meet you downstairs in twenty minutes," I said, refusing to allow him to see me in this vulnerable state.

"Very well, twenty minutes, no longer, or I will have to leave without you. I was warned that Señor Tejeda is adamant about being on time," Phoenix warns.

"Don't worry, I am never late. I will be there, Mr. Baldwin, in precisely twenty minutes," I said, taking a last sip of the hot coffee that I find in my hand.

There is no time now to consider what my dream meant. My grandmother always said, "that dreams are a foreshadowing of a future that we should never know."

I may not trust this man but, Mr. Baldwin was right; if I miss this appointment over a ridiculous dream, I will have no credibility.

How could I ever allow myself to be controlled by some useless dream?

I looked at my watch. It was 7:55 am. Five minutes to spare. I chose the stairs and sprint down the steps to the lobby. There he is, looking fresh in his crisp khaki pants and mango-colored linen shirt. On his head is a classic cream-colored Panama hat. Phoenix Baldwin could have stepped out of a James Bond thriller movie.

Before I can even think of something clever to say, Phoenix grabs my hand, rushes me out the door and into a car parked outside.

"You look quite stunning this morning, Miss Lewis," Phoenix says, never looking directly at me.

I wasn't certain if he was sarcastic or merely rude. It certainly was a different look from how I appeared last evening. Today, with no time for makeup, my hair is barely brushed in a ponytail. I look more like Wilma Flintstone than Boudica of the Iceni.

Boudica was one of the many strong women that my father wrote about in his collection of letters to me.

"I do apologize Mr. Baldwin for my rather messy appearance, but I can assure you that beneath this exterior, I am well prepared for our meeting with Señor Tejeda," I said, sounding defensive.

"And, by the way, some have even compared me to Boudica," I said.

Did I really just say that?

Phoenix Baldwin turned his head slightly toward me, lowered his sunglasses, and said, with a slight grin, "I can see that as a possibility."

"Really? You don't even have any idea who Boudica was, do you?" I said, now genuinely arrogant.

"Surely you are jesting, Ms. Lewis, aren't you? Have you forgotten where I come from?" Phoenix said, amused.

"In Welch, Boudica is known as Buddug, Queen of the British Celtic Iceni tribe. She led the uprising against the forces of the Roman Empire in 60AD. Do you intend to lead a revolt here in Spain, Imani?" Phoenix said, smiling, obviously pleased with himself.

Phoenix Baldwin, you might be more intelligent than I first gave you credit, but never believe that you are superior. I thought silently.

"It, would be impossible for me to ever forget your origin, Mr. Baldwin, it is prominent in everything that you execute. But, let me remind you that knowing the history of Boudica does not mean that you appreciate her tenacity. It is that perseverance that runs through my veins," I said, staring right back into those powerful blue eyes.

"From this day onward, in honor of Queen Boudica, I will forever refer to you as Lady Bud!" Phoenix said, raising his right hand as a pledge.

Before I could answer back, the car was pulling up to an impressive building. I presumed this is where Señor Tejeda's office was located. Phoenix paid the fee to the driver before I could insist on paying my share. A doorman allowed us into the lobby, where we were required to check-in at the reception desk.

"Señor Tejeda is located on the ninth floor. Each of you will need to wear this badge your entire visit. At the end of your time, please check back here before you depart," the gentleman said.

Following Phoenix's lead, we walked to the elevators. It was only the two of us now.

"Do you have any idea why all of this security?" I asked, Phoenix.

"Not sure. I can only presume that this is a research institute working on many competitive projects. They must want to protect their investments."

Tejeda's office was at the end of the hallway. After all of the previous security I was surprised how simple his office was. There was no receptionist to greet us, only a sign in Spanish that instructed everyone to take a seat and wait patiently.

"Does this seem odd to you?" I finally asked.

"Nothing seems odd to me anymore. I only hope that Tejeda is legitimate," Phoenix replied.

After about ten minutes, an older lady with short white hair called our names. It felt more like a doctor's visit than a meeting with a historian.

She asked us to follow her down the narrow hallway to the end of the corridor.

"I am pleased that the two of you have finally agreed to unite. It will make our discussion much more pleasant," the gentleman behind the desk said, inviting us to take a seat.

I was not sure what he meant by unify or how much he knew about Phoenix and me. It would be better at this moment to say as little as possible. I was more interested in listening to what he would share with us.

"We are grateful Señor Tejeda for agreeing to meet with Ms. Lewis and myself. I can assure you that both of us have only the best intentions in locating *The Agape*," Phoenix said.

I wanted to correct this eloquent introduction by adding that only one of us has good intentions. The other is making a considerable profit from this journey. But, as always, I knew when to stay silent.

The same lady that escorted us into the office was now back again with a pot of coffee, tea, and an assortment of sweets.

"Please, partake in some refreshments as we begin to discuss the best approach to take in your quest," Señor Tejeda graciously announced.

"What I am about to share with both of you is not conventional. Surely you know that there are others searching for *Agape*? Many have strategies that trace *The Agape* from conception yet are still unable to locate it. In my research I have learned that chasing *Agape* is futile. One must understand that it is *Agape* that decides where and when it appears. There is no real pattern. In practical terms, one must first understand why *Agape* has even continued to surface . This is much more powerful than where it has been," Tejeda said, sipping his tea.

"Everything that I have learned about *Agape* thus far is that the spiritual powers are life-changing. But, are you suggesting that those powers are also able to dictate where it travels?" I asked, wanting to be clear that I understood this new revelation.

"Exactly, Miss Lewis. The difficulty is understanding how *The Agape* makes its choices. With so many places where it is needed how do we know why it appears in one place of the world and not another? How does one determine the method used to prioritize miracles? Some have even suggested that there are more than one *Agape*. Maybe many. We have not yet determined that theory," Tejeda said.

"If this is true, then it certainly changes the dynamics of the search," Phoenix added.

"Exactly. This is why it is much better to have us all working together toward a universal goal, rather than competing for personal laurels," Tejeda emphasized.

"May I ask if either of you has ever studied the Nostradamus?" Tejeda asked us.

"I certainly am aware of his contribution to the theory of predicting future events. Although astrology during his time was considered a scientific method to predict the weather. Nostradamus used numerous methods, including astrology, to foretell the future. However, I do not see the relevance of any of this related to our search for *The Agape*," Phoenix responded.

I, too, have studied the mysterious Nostradamus. But, I assumed that what Tejeda was about to share with us would be much more apropos than anything that I could add.

"Yes, Nostradamus is still being studied today by many scholars hoping to discover anything that can prepare the modern world for the catastrophic future we might be traveling toward. But, it is how Nostradamus was able to see the future that many ignore. In one private letter, discovered only recently, Nostradamus admits that it is through his dream visions that he is motivated. Those Divine inspirations originated through Divine angelic spirits. This allowed him to see the future like a burning mirror through a cloudy vision.

If we accept what Nostradamus shares with us, we must also understand that it is *The Agape*, not us, that is in control. My advice is that once you accept this mandate, your mission will be complete," Tejeda said.

Suddenly everything in this journey was beginning to shift. The journey was now a mission. Whereas I was preoccupied with searching, now I recognized that I must be dedicated to fulfilling a purpose or commitment.

Will Phoenix Baldwin also be dedicated to this new mission?

Chapter Twenty-Six

The body without soul is no longer at the sacrifice. At the day of death, it comes to rebirth. The divine spirit will make the soul rejoice seeing the eternity of the world.

Nostradamus
Les Propheties

Imani Lewis and Phoenix Baldwin
Aviles, Spain 2017

There was a moment of awkward silence. You know when nobody wants to be the first one to respond because then they will be signaled as the object of the conversation. I felt that pressure to react. Then I caught a slight glimpse of Phoenix. He appeared completely calm, simply scribbling something in his leather notebook.

Who still takes notes by hand when we have cell phones and laptops?

Anyway, whatever Phoenix was jotting down made him appear quite relaxed.

Why was I then nervous?

That is when I took control of the deafening silence and said,

"I have no objection to working with Mr. Baldwin on this journey. However, I believe that both of us expect, or perhaps a better way of phrasing this may be that we are both hoping that you will be able to provide us with some additional details about *The Agape* carpet."

Phoenix never took his eyes off the notebook he was scribbling in. Did he intend to watch me fly solo, hoping that I would nose dive into a crater and explode?

"No...no, Miss Lewis. I absolutely intend to share anything and everything that I have researched about *Agape* with both of you. But, I also strongly feel that it is imperative to make you both aware and fully understand that *Agape* requires a union, not a tournament," Tejeda said.

This was the first time that Phoenix looked up attentively.

"We assure you, Señor Tejeda that whatever information we receive will be highly appreciated. Miss Lewis and I have mutually agreed to travel together from this point forward. And, it is because of you that we now fully understand what our mission will be," Phoenix said, like an ambassador.

When did I ever agree on this arrangement? Although, I understood his tactics. We certainly cannot insult Señor Tejeda by arguing with him that our intentions to find Agape are extremely different. Once this meeting has ended, I am pretty confident that our relationship will return to its normal distance.

"Excellent, Mr. Phoenix. Then since we all understand the basics, I will continue sharing the latest research our institute has acquired," Tejeda said, sounding much more relaxed.

The following three hours Phoenix and I were taken on an historical tour of Aviles, Spain. We were shown rare artifacts, maps and even ruins throughout the city that were interesting but did not seem relevant to our *Agape* journey.

Then, everything changed.

"Now that you have had a few hours to absorb the history that surrounds Aviles we are going to take a short flight on my private jet to the coast of Santander. It is a most beautiful ocean resort. The Palace de la Magdalena was once the Royal summer residence. It is quite a charming town and the perfect place to conclude our visit," Señor Tejeda said.

"This is a very generous offer, Señor. Everything that we have seen thus far has been certainly rewarding, but what is the *Agape* connection?" I asked, confused.

I looked at Phoenix, hoping that he might also support my inquiry. But he said nothing.

"I understand why you are anxious, Miss Lewis, but believe me everything will soon become quite obvious. Our flight is a short forty-five minutes. When we arrive to our destination a driver will take us to a lovely hotel on the ocean. Reservations have been made for overnight. The next day my jet will return you to Aviles. There you may plan your next quest," Señor Tejeda said.

"We are both extremely thankful for your generosity and hospitality. Everything that you have shared with us has been tremendous. I am looking forward to discovering the final piece to this puzzle," Phoenix said, leading me up the steps to the jet.

Once we were inside, sitting next to one another, I turned to Phoenix and whispered,

"We have been gone all day touring Aviles. Have you found any connection to *Agape?* What have we actually learned? And now we are flying to Santander for an overnight stay? I don't even have a toothbrush, let alone a change of clothing," I said, frustrated.

"Buckle your seatbelt, Lady Bud, and calm down. Santander is a beach resort. They will have everything that you need. Chill out, girlfriend," Phoenix said, with that amusing smirk on his face.

"Girlfriend? Excuse me Mr. Baldwin, you are beginning to sound like some international playboy. Let me remind you that simply because we are traveling together on a private jet does not make me your girlfriend. Not only am I not your girlfriend, but it is also difficult for me even to acknowledge being your friend. So get rid of this arrogant attitude, or you will return to flying solo," Imani said.

Those mysterious eyes reflecting the vibrant red color of her hair was overwhelming. I said nothing. Instead, I took her hand. The one she had a death grip on the side of her chair. I placed that hand in mine.

"Take offs and landings are always the worst part in these small jets. Once we are in the clouds it is smooth sailing."

I wasn't sure if Phoenix was saying this for my benefit or for his, but whatever anger I had previously felt was definitely replaced by fear now. For the next five minutes, all I could feel was Phoenix's strong hand wrapped around mine like a comforting glove. It kept me steady.

Once the pilot announced that the remainder of the flight would be smooth, Phoenix immediately released his hand from mine.

"Well, my compadres, it will be just another forty minutes, and you will begin to see the lovely mountains surrounding the Santander Bay," Señor Tejeda said, taking a seat across from us.

"Why exactly are we traveling to Santander?" I finally asked.

"I suppose that much of our visit today has been quite confusing to you, Miss Lewis, and I apologize for that. But, you see, if you wanted just the facts about *Agape,* I assumed you would have gone to another source. You see, I am a historian and I firmly believe that whenever a person has the opportunity to retrace the steps of significant events, they should embrace that. You might compare me to a method actor. I wish to emulate a complete emotional attachment to the circumstances that I am studying. I hope that you will experience a similar sensation," Tejeda said.

"Please forgive me if I appear not to appreciate all that you have done for us. Perhaps it is just that I am having difficulty making these connections that you have so thoughtfully furnished," I said, trying to be more humble.

Phoenix, who remained silent, as he did most of the day, finally turned toward Tejeda as if an epiphany had just occurred.

"We are visiting Santander because this is where Pedro Menendez died after he founded St. Augustine, Florida. This must be where *The Agape* carpet originated from at one time. Am I correct?" Phoenix asked Tejeda promptly.

"Yes, and no Señor. *Agape* was once here in Santander, but how and why it came here is the real story. I will be your guide, providing you with the facts, but once you have all that you need, it will be your decision on where to go next."

The pilot was announcing preparations for landing, and before I could ask any further questions, I could feel the tires touching.

"Are you prepared for this scavenger hunt, Miss Lewis?" Phoenix asked, amused.

"As prepared as you are, Mr. Baldwin. Although, I don't believe I would refer to this as a scavenger hunt. It feels more like a Great Race, with no rules," I said quietly.

The drive from the airport to The Hotel Real was a very short twenty minutes. As we approached the impressive Neo-classic grand hotel, it appeared as if we were in the boulevards of Cannes or Nice rather than a Spanish seaside resort.

"This hotel is frequented often by the Spanish Royal family. I hope that you will be impressed by the Cantabrian Mountains as well. They are a spectacular backdrop to the bay. There is no need to check in or out tomorrow. Here are your keys. If you find that you will need an extra day or week, call this number. My pilot, Pierre will be available at any time to return you to Aviles. Enjoy your stay, and I truly hope you both find *Agape,*" Tejeda said, waiting for us to depart.

"You won't be joining us, Señor?" I asked.

"There is no longer any need for me to accompany you, my dear. Everything that you will need is located in this folder," he said.

Tejeda must have been referring to the manila folder that he handed to Phoenix on the runway.

Before I could object, Tejeda walked away, never looking back.

"I guess it's just you and me, kid," Phoenix said, taking a seat in the closet chair he could find in the deserted lobby.

"Well, are you going to open the envelope?" I asked, anxious to discover what we were supposed to do next.

Phoenix carefully tore the seal off the back of the sealed manila folder. It revealed several maps and two sheets of paper that appeared to be a plan.

"It is already 7:00 pm. How does Tejeda expect us to accomplish anything on his itinerary tonight?" I asked.

"This is a resort town, Imani. Most places will remain open until daybreak. I saw a small boutique around the corner when we drove up. Let's take care of whatever you need first. From what I am reading here we don't need to be anywhere until 10:00 pm. Plenty of time," Phoenix said, waiting for me to follow him.

"Can you at least let me know where it is we are expected to be at 10:00 pm?" I asked, insisting on knowing before agreeing to go anywhere else.

"We are meeting a Señor Mendoza at the pier. He will be providing us with everything we need before we leave tomorrow," Phoenix said.

"All of this just seems like a waste of our time. But, okay, I will follow your lead until it leads us to a

dead-end," I said, trying to keep up with his long strides.

The corner store only had the bare essentials, but it was enough until I got back to Aviles tomorrow. While I was at the cash register checking out, I turned around to tell Phoenix that I was almost finished, but he was nowhere to be seen.

Where could he have gone, and why?

After a few moments waiting outside the store, I turned back around toward the path to the Hotel Real. That is when I noticed Phoenix standing on the corner wearing a new Panama hat and aviator sunglasses. He resembled a much-improved version of Harrison Ford in Raiders of the Lost Ark.

"Wow, are you traveling incognito?" I asked, trying to avoid any compliments that he might be anticipating.

Phoenix ignored my reaction.

"Here, this is for you. I guessed at the size. The Señoritas said if you don't like it, or if it doesn't fit, you can exchange it. We are right around the corner from the boutique," Phoenix said.

I was rather surprised at the idea that Phoenix would buy me anything. As a matter of fact, I have never received a gift from any man before. Not that I didn't have some interesting relationships in the past. Unfortunately, they were all candidates for the Loser Hall of Fame. Thankfully I was level headed enough to leave before any gift exchanges.

"What made you decide to buy me anything? Working with you on this journey is clearly nothing more than a business relationship," I said, regretting immediately how ungrateful that sounded.

"Oh, but this is a business expense. Nothing more. You need to be dressed appropriately. At this moment, you look like someone who might be living on the streets of Santander," Phoenix said, nearly throwing the paper bag at me.

He was right. I looked miserable. It had been hours since we left Aviles where I had no time to dress appropriately. Phoenix stood in front of me silent. I carefully removed a turquoise colored garment from the paper bag. Immediately I recognized the traditional *traje de flamenco*. Señorita Spanish dancers most often wear the dress during festivities. This version was layered with ruffles at the hemline, as well as the sleeves. In addition, there was a matching *Manton de Manila (shawl) and a pinetum (a hair comb made of a tortoiseshell)*. If I recall correctly, this outfit is typically worn during weddings and Holy Week processions. Neither of these events was I planning to attend any time soon.

"I apologize for sounding ungrateful, Phoenix. This is quite lovely. And, you are correct. I am not looking my best at the moment. This outfit will be a significant improvement," I said sincerely.

Phoenix smiled, uncrossed his arms and said, "You have approximately ninety minutes to reinvent yourself. I will meet you in the hotel bar. Don't be late."

As I watched him walk away from me toward the hotel, I shouted,

"I am NEVER late to any appointment!"
Phoenix never turned back to answer me.

Chapter Twenty-Seven

"She was the third beer. Not the first one, which the throat receives with almost tearful gratitude; nor the second, that confirms and extends the pleasure of the first. But the third, the one you drink because it's there, because it can't hurt and because what difference does it make?"

Toni Morrison, *Song of Solomon*

Phoenix Baldwin and Imani Lewis
Santander, Spain 2017

Imani Lewis is my enigma. She certainly is not my type. I am not even certain what 'type' she is. But, if I am to be fair she is quite intelligent. I was impressed when she met me at *Pasama La Sal* in Aviles. That Imani Lewis was confident, assertive, and quite mysterious. But, then the following day, when I had to practically pry her out of the hotel room to meet with Señor Tejeda, the magnificent "Fire and Ice" Goddess overnight transformed into a Raggedy Ann doll. Nevertheless, Imani somehow was able to continue with our plans, even at times contributing insightfully to the discussions. What I must decide soon is how valid is the advice Tejeda is offering. Is it to my advantage to join with Imani on this journey, or is it more advisable to part our ways now? I will revisit that thought once I learn why we are really here in Santander.

"Señor, can I buy you another ice cold beer?" The gentleman sitting next to me offered.

"Gracias, Señor," I said, thankful for the company while waiting for Imani.

"Are you on holiday from Great Britain? We have many Brits visiting us during holiday. Santander has numerous beautiful beaches and also other cultural opportunities," the man said, sounding more and more like a travel agent.

"No, I am here on business. Will be leaving tomorrow morning," I said, cautiously.

"If you ever return, here is my card. Call me anytime. Our tours are the very best in Santander," he said.

Before I could respond he was gone, obviously searching for other clients. Just as I turned around to pay for my bar bill, I noticed Imani walking through the front door. Every male head in the room turned toward her. The tight fitting turquoise gown accentuated every feminine curve in her body. When she glided past all the admiring men and women, it was as if an international model was working the room. What I immediately noticed was how Imani's Titan red hair cascaded like hot molten rock past her shoulders. Like an empress with a crown on her head the tortoise shell hair clip added just the right amount of elegance.

Rather than wait for her to see me or be approached by a stranger immediately, I met her halfway. When I took her hand, it left no doubt from the admiring crowd that Imani was with me.

"Let's sit down over here, away from the others and have a drink before we go on our meeting," I said, trying not to appear like a drooling fool.

Imani looked quite amused at my reaction.

"Can I assume that you approve of my attire? I hope it is an improvement from my homeless garb," Imani said, smiling.

"I apologize for that rude statement earlier. Sometimes I can be very insensitive," I said, noticing once again how emerald green Imani's eyes were.

"Apology accepted. I have had to put up with many unpleasant allusions to my red hair. Did you know that in ancient Egypt men with red hair were sacrificed at Osiris' grave to help fertilize the fields? And, in medieval times any child with red hair was assumed to have been conceived during a woman's menstrual period," Imani said, insisting on giving me a history lesson.

"No, I must admit that I never knew that. But, I do know that during the Spanish Inquisition redheads were believed to be witches since they clearly stole the fire of hell for their hair. But, you have nothing to fear, my Lady. I will be your Champion, never allowing any harm to cross your path," I said, standing up, then on one knee bent in front, I lowered my head.

Imani reached for a silver knife on the table and said,

"With that honorable pledge, I knight you Sir Phoenix."

The crowd in the cantina began applauding and cheering as I raised my beer mug in approval. Imani, of course, could not have known that the title Sir was more accurate than she realized.

Although this role-playing was amusing, I looked at my watch and recognized that in one hour, we needed to be at the pier.

"Are you planning to let me know what else was included in Señor Tejeda's notes, or am I to continue to play the damsel in distress for the remaining of the evening?" Imani asked anxiously.

It didn't take long for her to return to those familiar feminist roots. I wanted to tell her that there was no competition. I wanted to assure her that we were partners. But, the truth is, I wasn't yet ready to believe any of that. All the women that I have ever known understood that they could not compete with men. With the exception of maybe my mother. Most of them found other ways to excel that were acceptable to everyone. Everyone other than Imani. However, this was not the time to challenge her.

"Naturally, it is all here," I said, handing her the manila folder.

There are no surprises. We were to meet at the pier to receive further instructions. However, since we were also provided the location to meet Señor Martinez at 10:00 pm, I suggest we bypass the dock and continue directly this evening to *Palacio de la Magdelena*.

"Are you sure that we will not need any further instructions?" I asked reluctantly.

"Everything that we need appears to be in this folder. This is the summer residence of the Spanish Royal Family. The introduction continues to identify the current Royal Family as King Felipe VI, the Queen consort Letizia, the King's parents and of course the couple's children. In 1977 the Count of Barcelona sold this property and the peninsula back to Santander. Since it is the most visited site in Santander, Señor Martinez requested that we meet with him after hours when we would have complete privacy," Phoenix added.

"These notes really don't tell us very much. Are you sure that Tejeda didn't give you anything else," Imani asked skeptically.

"I can assure you Ms. Lewis, that there is nothing else. Teheda made it extremely clear that we should be at this meeting together. I for one do not intend to challenge that request. Do you, Miss Lewis?" I responded, agitated at her ridiculous assumption.

"Very well. I suppose once we arrive to the palace this mystery will be solved. Do you have any idea why Tejeda insisted that we come to Santander? Certainly at this time of the evening I cannot imagine that we will be doing much sightseeing," Imani said, anxious to get started on this next stage of the journey.

It was I that suggested that we take the opportunity to eat supper now since we might not have another occasion after the meeting. Imani agreed.

We decided to share *ragas* (calamari) as an appetizer. This was followed by a generous platter of *Tudanca Beef, veal, and lamb*. But, it was the *Paella* that impressed Imani and me. This *Paella Valenciana* included rabbit with saffron and runner beans. After an hour of sharing this meal, neither of us had any desire to argue any longer.

"I believe that I can now go for the next week without ever being hungry," Imani said, sipping her wine.

"Well, let's hope we won't need to test that prospect, but I certainly feel much better knowing that we won't starve for a while," I said, feeling quite satisfied.

"Maybe we should leave now and walk some of this meal off. The Palace can't be that far away. What do you think?" Imani suggested.

This turned out to be a great decision. It was a lovely warm evening, with many people out enjoying a late summer walk. It also gave Imani and I an opportunity to relax with one another.

"What made a nice girl like you want to travel the world in search of an ancient carpet that may not even exist," I asked.

"I suppose I could ask you that same question Mr. Baldwin, but then again I think I know the answer," Imani said, walking slightly ahead of me.

"Well, if you are implying that my motives are solely mercenary, you would be quite wrong. It may have been my objective at the beginning, but there is much more that I am learning every day. This journey is an awakening. Are you aware of what that means, Ms. Lewis?" I said, stopping at a fountain outside of The Summer Palace.

Imani turned around and took a seat on the bench next to me.

"If you are suggesting a spiritual awakening, or an epiphany then yes, I do completely understand. I have experienced this as well. I have shifted my perspective on how I see the world around me since I have been on this mission," Imani said, sincerely.

"Exactly. This enlightenment is a duality between time and space. In Buddhism this would be a place where paradoxes exist. Relative and universal truths are resolved at that time and even understood," I said, now looking directly into Imani's eyes.

She completed my thought.

"In this stage we are connected in a state of total and unconditional love."

This was a moment when I wanted to reach out and hold that natural spirit in my arms, but I knew that once I touched her intimately the moment would be lost. I wasn't ready to take that chance. I backed away.

"It's time for our meeting with Señor Martinez. Are you ready?" I said, reaching for her hand.

I was rather surprised that Imani did not pull away from me. She didn't even object to me touching her. The energy between us was there but it did not last long.

"Ready and eager. Let's learn what Señor Martinez has to share with us," Imani said, now walking next to me.

When we reached the front gate, I gave our names, and we were escorted to the receiving room. There we could see from the windows Mouro Island with its Lighthouse at a distance and the horse stables that have been now converted to residences for international students.

"If you look through this other window on the opposite side, you can see the city with its twinkling lights at a distance," I said, watching Imani move from one side to the other.

"Did you know that there is also a mini zoo and an open air museum? It is known as 'The Man of the Earth'. It says here in this pamphlet that you can see the reproduction of Columbus' caravels," Imani said, turning toward me.

Before I could respond a gentleman entered the room. He introduced himself as Señor Martinez.

"I apologize that we had to meet so late this evening, but, it is necessary for ultimate privacy. If you will follow me, we will go upstairs to the library office. I can assure you that there we will be completely isolated from any disturbances," Señor Martinez said, leading the way up the massive staircase.

Once inside the office we saw a rather large round table. Imani and I said nothing. But before being seated I handed Señor Martinez a sealed envelope, from Tejeda that was in the manila folder. He took a few moments to read the letter silently and then removed his glasses turning his attention on us.

"Miss Lewis and I made the decision to come directly here rather than meeting at the pier. I hope this did not cause any confusion," I said, wanting to clear any confusion prior to starting our meeting.

" No worries. There will be plenty of time for you to meet Jesus, my assistant, later if you decide to continue. Are you both sure that you want to learn the truth about *The Agape?* What you might discover may not be what you are expecting," Martinez said.

"Señor. I assure you that both Ms. Lewis and I are prepared for any new information that you can share with us. We have been traveling for months around the world in search of this *Agape,"* I said, trying to be firm in my response.

"Very well. I will tell you what we have discovered, and you may decide on how this will assist you. I want to clearly state that we have no idea how accurate this information is. Others have attempted to validate these claims without much success. Nevertheless, the information is yours to explore," Martinez stated.

What we learned after hours of discussions, videos, and restored letters was extremely fascinating. Pedro Menendez de Aviles, in the years of 1543-45 served as a pirate for Don Alvaro de Bazan y Guzman. At the age of twenty-nine, Menendez had his own vessel. He began capturing French fleets in the Bay of Biscay on the western coast of Spain and France.

In 1552 Pedro Menendez was captured by French pirates off the coast of Cuba. During that time, he learned that the French were planning on raiding the Indies. Once he was rescued, Menendez was recognized for his bravery by King Philip II. When the king realized there was a potential threat on a strategic part of the Florida coast by French Huguenots, he sent Pedro on an expedition July 1565 with eleven ships and about two thousand men to claim for Spain the territory. On August 28, 1565, he entered the bay and named the property Saint Augustine. A fort was built to protect the new colony. On September 20, after a bloody massacre, Pedro Menendez took possession of Fort Caroline killing the entire population.

At the age of fifty-five, after returning to Santander, Pedro Menendez de Aviles died of typhus.

Finally, I asked Señor Martinez why all this historical information was essential for us to know.

"Now that you understand the relevance of this explorer, I can show you these letters from his wife that we have recovered and restored," Martinez said.

I still was not clear how any of this made any sense. When I looked at Imani I could tell that she also had the same concerns. But then Martinez went to the credenza, removed a glass box, placed it on the table. He asked us to move closer. Imani and I followed his instructions.

Martinez then opened the glass box, placed latex gloves on, and reached for a letter.

"This letter was written by Pedro's wife, Maria de Solis. She refers specifically to a unique carpet that she gave to Pedro when he left for Florida. She describes it as having "God's spirit." The images include a dove, fish symbols, crosses, and a strange horse with a horn. In several other letters, she advises Pedro to always keep the carpet close to him for safety. We can only assume that Pedro left the carpet in St. Augustine when he returned to Santander, since he was intending to return to St. Augustine. What we do not know is what happened to that carpet once Pedro died," Martinez said, carefully placing the letters back in the case.

"That was six hundred years ago. Even if *The Agape* once was in Saint Augustine, there is no logical reason to assume it is still there. Have you ever visited St. Augustine, Señor Martinez? I would have no idea where to look for an ancient carpet in this city in Florida," Imani said, frustrated.

"I understand your hesitation. And, yes I have visited St. Augustine several times. Many brilliant historians live there. Many others are well versed in this ancient city. They are all there studying so many interesting historical evidence. I can provide you with some of the names of these scholars. They will be very helpful to you," Martinez said.

"I certainly would appreciate that information Señor," I replied.

"Of course, compadre. Are you planning to stay in Santander for a few days? Our beaches are amazing. You both should take advantage of what our small city has to offer. Who knows if you will ever return!" Martinez said, sounding very inviting.

I looked toward Imani for her reaction. She still seemed to be disturbed.

"What do you say about taking a few days off here at this beach resort before continuing on to Florida? It will probably take that long for us to make arrangements anyway," I said, already deciding that I was going to stay.

Before Imani could respond, Martinez was telling me that he could arrange our flight to Florida and would send everything to us at the hotel by tomorrow evening.

Once Martinez left the room, Imani walked over to where I was standing. She did not look pleased with any of these decisions that had just been agreed upon.

"Are you seriously suggesting that we remain here for two more days? Doing what? Feeding the pigeons in the town square? And, what are we going to learn in Saint Augustine? I feel that after all these months, there has been no real progress," Imani said, quite disturbed and disappointed.

"You, of course, are free to leave Santander tomorrow, that is if you can book a flight to wherever your destination might be. We accomplished meeting with Tejeda, as agreed. You are not obligated to any other contract with me, Ms. Lewis," I said, knowing that she would respond accordingly.

"Naturally, I am free to move forward without you. All of this idea about collaborating for the sake of finding *The Agape* is nonsense.
But, I certainly could use forty-eight hours of recovery before deciding on what to do next," Imani said, sounding fatigued in her argument.

"That is a very wise choice, in my humble opinion. Just allow Martinez to make the arrangements now, and if you change your mind later, we will let him know. In the meantime, I will also share with you the contacts that he will provide," I said, feeling that my negotiation tactics were splendid.

"You are such a polite gentleman Mr. Baldwin. Like a clever fox," Imani added.

I chose not to respond. Every successful politician realizes when it is strategically wise to be silent. This was my moment of silence.

Chapter Twenty-Eight

"Do not go gentle into that good night, old age should burn and rave, at close of day; Rage, rage against the dying of the light."

Dylan Thomas
Do not go gentle into that good night.

BRAN HUGHES
Cincinnati, Ohio
2017

"Hey Boss...what is the plan this week? Are we going *Over the Rhine* tonight to visit?" Michael asked as he stocked the food pantry with the latest donations.

"That's the plan. I was hoping to stop by the church pantry and clothing closet to pick up a few items the crew might need. It won't be long before this weather starts chilling up again. We need to make sure that everyone has what they need by then," I said, taking a seat on the stone bench that one of the volunteers made for us a few years ago.

It has been ten years since I arrived here. After a short stint in Florida that was truly life-changing, Cincinnati, Ohio, became my final destination.

"How *did you ever manage to find this strange city 3,793 miles away from your home in Wales?*" I was often asked once people heard my Welch accent.

"Oh, laddie boy, you would never believe me," I always told them.

The absolute truth is I have no idea why I chose Cincinnati? Or why Cincinnati chose me. When I received the letter from South Africa informing me that Sarah had passed away in 1995, my first reaction was to immediately leave Wales and insist on getting custody of my daughter. Imani by then was sixteen years old. Old enough to make her own decisions. But, did she even know who I was? Did Sarah even give her all of those letters that I wrote? All of those letters that I sent? If Imani knew who I was, why had she never written me back? No. As much as I was aching to hold Imani in my arms, I knew that appearing after fifteen years might be a disaster. What was clear now was that I could no longer remain here in Wales.

Sarah was dead. She would never return. It was time for me to do something, anything, to make my life worth living.

While contemplating this decision, a Lutheran minister arrived in town searching for a room to rent. The living quarters at his church were being renovated. Church council members asked me if I would be willing to let the Pastor stay in my home for a short time.

Was God finally intervening? Was this Pastor the answer to all my self-doubts? Perhaps. Just maybe.

Pastor Jamison was a young man answering a call to take charge of a quaint Lutheran Church here in St. David's. The previous Pastor, quite elderly, passed away six months earlier. The congregation specifically requested a younger, more vibrant Pastor to fulfill the position. When Pastor Jamison arrived from a small town called Batavia, Ohio, in the United States, I was immediately impressed with how young this man of the cloth was. Probably, I am guessing, no older than twenty-five years. What immediately caught my attention is how much he resembled Richard Chamberlain, the actor who portrayed Ralph de Bricassart, a priest in Colleen McCullough's movie adaptation of *The Thornbirds*.

Unlike Father Bricassart, in the *Thornbirds*, our young Pastor was not sent to a remote town in Australia as punishment for insulting a bishop. Pastor Jamison arrived anxious to establish a strong relationship with his congregation.

When a group of women of all ages started arriving at my house with fresh loaves of bread, muffins, casseroles nearly every evening, I knew that this young pastor would not remain single for very long. Perhaps God was also asking me to help Jamison.

After Sarah left me, taking with her Imani, I too abandoned my faith in God. But, now it seemed that God had found me. I could no longer reject His presence.

During the six months that Pastor Jamison lived with me we became as close as brothers. He is the much younger, more handsome one. And, just as everyone expected, all the available lassies would find any excuse to visit us. Some would bring homemade gifts, while others would invite Jamison to their homes for Sunday dinner. The first month Jamison was with me, I must have gained ten pounds. But, it was his spiritual inspiration that I gained the most.

"Bran, my good friend, you mustn't leave St. David's with grief in your heart. This will only result in misery. Wherever you decide to go, Jesus tells us that if you are experiencing agony, you will need to allow yourself time to mourn. God permits us to weep. What you must learn is how God teaches us is to transform our sorrow into good intentions," Jamison said one day when I was lamenting.

"How am I to know what to do? I have been grieving for so many years that my soul is an empty vessel," I said.

"Then perhaps now is the time you should start filling your vessel with good deeds," Jamison said, handing me an article from a newspaper that a friend sent him from Florida.

The story reported how the community was organizing an outreach program to help the homeless in Saint Augustine, a small town in Florida.

"Have you ever been to this city in Florida, Jamison?" I asked, quite intrigued.

"No, unfortunately not. But, a good friend of mine is the Pastor at Memorial Lutheran Church in that city. He sends me the local newspaper. I am always impressed by how different parts of the country deal with similar obstacles in their communities. I thought that this article might interest you," Jamison said, leaving me to ponder the possibilities.

What I read about this community, named Saint. Augustine was inspiring. The first place mentioned in the article was St. Francis House, and Port in the Storm. For over thirty years, these organizations have been dedicated to taking families off the streets and keeping them safe. But, it was the Homeless Coalition, determined to break the cycle of homelessness and poverty, that immediately caught my attention. The article stated that,

"Many St. John's county children live a life of constant hunger. Some live with their families in woods near your neighborhoods. If lucky, abandoned cars could be their shelter from the elements."

I had no idea that this could ever happen in America. Here in St. David's, we have those in poverty, but there is always someone who will care for these people. Living on the streets or in the woods? No, not here.

But, what if this was my daughter living without food? How could I walk away without even trying?

That is when I made my decision. This was my calling, and I knew it. St. Augustine, Florida was where I was going to learn how to change the world, or at the very least maybe improve someone's life.

When I told Pastor Jamison about my decision he said that he truly believed that this was my destiny. I wasn't yet convinced for sure that this was truly my predestination, but for the very first time since Sarah left, I felt that there was a purpose in my life. I decide that now was the time to write my final letter to Imani. Only I would not finish it until I knew what would happen in St. Augustine, Florida. That is where I would mail it from. If she ever wanted to find me, she would know where I was. That is all I could do.

"Remember Bran, when I arrived here at St. David's and you would call me Father Briscarrast all of the time? I had no idea why. Then I looked up the name on the internet and decided to read *The Thornbirds*. It was quite an enlightening story," Jamison said one afternoon.

"Well, Pastor, I only meant that you reminded me of the actor Richard Chamberlain. I hope you won't take any offense. Since you have arrived at St. James, there have been so many remarkable improvements. And, your sermons are always spot on," I said, hoping for forgiveness.

"Oh, Bran, I know that there was no ill will intended. But, what I found is this excellent quote from the novel. I had it printed for you and framed. I hope you will place it in your new home in St. Augustine and always remember our friendship," Jamison said, handing me the gift.

I held it up and read the words out loud:

There is a legend about a bird that sings just once in its life, more sweetly than any other creature on the face of the earth. When it leaves the nest, it searches for a thorn tree and does not rest until it finds one. Then singing among the savage branches, it impales itself along the most extended, sharpest spine. And dying, it rises above its agony to out-carol the lark and the nightingale—one superlative song, existence the price. But, the whole world stills to listen, and

God in his heaven smiles. For the best is only bought at the cost of great pain...or so says the legend.

Colleen McCullough, The Thornbirds.

I could feel the tears fill my eyes. This was my story. For the very first time, I realized why Sarah left me and why I must find Imani. Sarah was always searching for a "thorn tree" without realizing it was always right here. Imani must not make this same mistake.

Chapter Twenty-Nine

We set our own limits on love. Some of us bind our hearts like Chinese women bind their feet. The binding is painful at first, but eventually you get used to it and the pain goes away. The saddest part of all is that binding yourself to the choices you make, you forget that there was ever another way to live.

Kate McGahan
The Last Adventure of Life

Imani Lewis and Phoenix Baldwin
Santander Spain
    and
St. Augustine, Florida
September 2017

"That's great news, Imani! I can't wait to see you. It's been nearly two months since you started this odyssey. When do you want me to book your airline tickets for New York City?" Priscilla asked, excited.

I really didn't want to tell her about Phoenix. And, I definitely didn't want to share with her that we were traveling together. But, since Priscilla was the only person I really knew, I had to tell her something. If my body ended up mysteriously missing at least, Priscilla would be suspicious activity.

"I'm not exactly coming home yet. But, I am at least headed in the right direction. My meeting here at Santander went extremely well. I genuinely feel like I am moving closer to discovering where *The Agape* is," I said, trying to avoid the obvious.

"Well then, if you aren't coming home to New York City, where exactly do you want me to book your flight?" Priscilla asked, moving back into her professional mode.

"I am flying into Jacksonville, Florida in a few days. But, you don't have to arrange the accommodations. My contact here graciously insisted on taking care of everything. Since I am spending a few days sightseeing, I determined it best to allow him to make all the reservations," I said, relieved that my explanations at least sounded reasonable.

"Jacksonville? You traveled all around the world for all these months, and now you think this crazy carpet is in Florida? That's nuts," Priscilla said.

"Not exactly Jacksonville. I am traveling to St. Augustine. That is where my next lead is. It actually makes perfect sense since Pedro Menendez was given *The Agape* here in Santander by his wife before he left for Florida to discover St. Augustine," I said, sounding quite knowledgeable.

"I love St. Augustine! It is such an amazing little town. Maybe I will fly down there and meet you. There are great places to party and a fabulous waterfront," Priscilla said, excited.

"Perhaps another time, girlfriend. This trip is still business. If everything goes well, my stay will be short. After I write my Pulitzer Prize article, we will have plenty of time to celebrate," I said.

"Alright, but don't forget we have a date. You will love St. Augustine. Let me know when you get there. And, oh, by the way, book a room at Casa Monica; *it* is the best location," Priscilla added before she signed off.

At the moment, I was not thinking about anything except how the next two days traveling with Phoenix Baldwin would be. Martinez was correct in his assessment. We were both exhausted from months of traveling. However, removing the guard rails from our relationship, that might take more than two days of seaside recuperation even if Santander boasts at being a recluse for lovers.

Whenever I feel challenged or even insecure, it is always Bran Hughes' letters that I turn to.

Wow! A group of psychiatrists would have a great time assessing that. The young woman who her father abandoned turns to him when in despair? No wonder the lady is psychotic.

Bran Hughes, also known as my father, never really abandoned me. If anyone can claim that, it would be my mother. Although I am quite sure she would be yelling at the top of her voice, objecting vehemently in her grave. If she were here I just know that she would be on her soapbox preaching that she was the best mother any young girl could ever have.

It is too late to debate that topic, so I turn to *The Bran Collection* for some temporary consolation. Without searching, I turn to the middle of the collection. Years ago, I had all the letters bound like a priceless antique book. To me it has been a priceless discovery and connection to my lost world.

My dearest Imani,

There are days like now that I imagine the two of us taking a holiday to Criccieth. It is located at the seaside resort town called Cardigan Bay. I am including some photos of your mom and me. I took her there when she had you in her belly. I used to jest with her that she ate so many fish and chips on that trip that you must be a dolphin.

Oh, how I remember that trip! It was spectacular. We both had so many dreams that we wanted to share with you, Imani. And, the medieval castle would have been a place that I imagined you would immediately claim as your own. In the 14th century, a Welch bard, Lolo Goch, wrote a poem that celebrates "the bright forth high on a rock and the sophisticated court of Syr Hywel of the Axe."

Whenever you need your spirit to be revived, my dearest child, find the nearest ocean, where a menagerie of sea creatures are waiting for you to shake away the fresh red sargassum seaweed and whisper secrets that will soothe your soul. If you ever have the opportunity, I encourage you to read Tides, The Science and Spirit of the Ocean by Jonathan White. He was my mentor when I lost you and your mother. These words restored my faith in life:

"The moon may move our hearts today, but her first love was the ocean, stirred millions of years ago. The attraction may have grown stronger or weaker through time, but the affair has never ended. Like any relationship, it has complexities and baggage. The moon calls out to the earth's oceans in the form of gravity, and the oceans call back, their pulsing energy holding the moon close while pushing it away."(Tides)

Your mother was my moon, but I could never accept that I lost her to such a vital energy source that was much stronger than my love.

Now I know that there was nothing left for me to do but love her while I could and let her go when the gravity pulled her away from me. But, you my lovely child you are a wonderful result for both of us. I will always believe that somehow I will find you once again.

Love, your father,
Bran Hughes

I closed the book, placed it in my suitcase, thankful that I decided to bring my father's advice with me on this quest. We may have been separated by years and miles, but the words that he has written are etched in my memory as if he was sitting in this room with me at this very minute.

My cell phone began vibrating, warning me of an incoming message. I opened the text. It was Phoenix reminding me to meet him at 10:00 am in the garden sanctuary.

Once again, I stated that I AM NEVER LATE.

When I agreed on extending my stay by two days, I had to pick up a few more changes of clothing c. Since we were spending at least one day at the beach, a swimsuit was a necessity. But, everywhere I went, close to the hotel, they only sold bikinis. I refused to let this arrogant playboy see me wearing a skimpy suit, knowing well that there would be an entire beach filled with beautiful models walking around perfectly confident and more likely nude.

"Well, Imani, if you can't find anything that pleases you, just remember that in Europe, many women feel quite comfortable going topless at the beaches," Phoenix suggested.

I naturally refused to respond to his advice. The final store that I entered offered some reasonable suits that were an excellent alternative. I chose a vibrant yellow bandeau top, and high-top bottoms. The salesperson showed me a lovely sheer sunflower cover-up, straw hat, and sunglasses to complete the "incognito" appearance.

I took one last look in the mirror before leaving. It was the first time in many days that I felt pretty. I am not a beautiful woman by any imagination, but at this moment, I could at least fit in with the others. That is good enough for me!

Señor Martinez insisted on providing us with his private driver who outlined a tentative schedule of places to visit.

"These are only recommendations my dear friends. Select what you like, and Jesus will take you wherever you decide. We want you to leave our city with beautiful memories that will lead you back, God willing, someday," Martinez said last night before we left.

In the garden, Phoenix was seated at a café bistro table, sipping his coffee, reading the local newspaper. I could see several women eyeing him with interest until I took the chair across from him. Then all his admirers turned their attention to another gentleman on the other side of the room.

"I had no idea that you could read Spanish? Is there anything interesting that you want to share with me?" I said, removing my sunglasses.

"Do you mean share interesting facts about me, or facts in general?" Phoenix answered.

"Either one will do. Is that basket of sweets exclusively yours, or are you going to share?" I asked, pouring the coffee into the empty cup in front of me.

"Whatever is mine is yours Imani. Did you have a restful night's sleep? You look very lovely this morning although, I still feel that you should try going topless when we arrive at the beach," Phoenix said, passing me the breadbasket.

Once again, I ignored his topless comment and turned my attention to the array of pastries, all tempting me to try them.

"What is on the sightseeing agenda today?" I asked, finally selecting a decadent Chocolate-filled croissant.

"Take a look, and let's discuss what we want to prioritize. Our driver will be here in forty-five minutes, so you have plenty of time to enjoy your sweets," he said, handing me the activity sheet.

I immediately noticed that some of the attractions had stars next to them, while others were noted with question marks.

"Did you annotate this list, Phoenix?" I asked.

"I did. But, feel free to decide what activities suit you. I just decided that it might be easier to discuss once we narrowed it down to those that appear to be the most engaging," he said, turning back to his newspaper.

It was clear that Phoenix Baldwin was a man that expected to be in control of every decision that affected him. Although his strategy appears "flexible," I doubt that he has ever truly experienced that behavior. This might be an excellent opportunity to teach him the result of such behavior.

"I appreciate that you took the time to indicate your preferences. It will make it much easier for me to make my choices," I said, taking my yellow hi lighter and marking my favorites, followed by a priority number sequence.

Phoenix watched me methodically, trying to determine if my choices were compatible with his own.

Finally, when I had finished, I gave him the list and took the newspaper.

While Phoenix contemplated his next move, I spent a few minutes completing the crossword puzzle in Spanish. When it was filled, I handed it back, smirking.

"There were a few words misspelled. But, don't fret; I corrected them for you," I said, standing up, waiting for his reaction.

There was none. He placed the newspaper in his backpack, saying nothing. But, once in the car that Señor Martinez sent us, Phoenix handed me back the sightseeing list. All my choices had happy faces next to them. I could not hold back my laughter.

"You are a most interesting and amusing gentleman, Mr. Phoenix. Just when I expect one reaction, you surprise me with another," I said.

"Well, Ms. Lewis, I live by the words of Ralph Waldo Emerson, 'Shallow men believe in luck, or in circumstances. Strong men believe in cause and effect'," he answered back confidently.

Before I could react to his response, Jesus, our driver, pointed out some of Santander's famous landmarks.

"The city and main beach, *Playa de Sardinero,* are situated between the lovely *Cabo Mayor,* where you visited last night, *Peninsula of Magdelena.* We are going to return after you visit the Museum of Prehistory and Archeology," Jesus said, parking near the entrance.

"Will you be waiting for us, Jesus?" I asked.

"Si, Senora. You may leave your beach bags with me. It will be safe," he assured us.

I had nothing of value in the straw bag, so I gladly left it. But, Phoenix insisted on taking his backpack with him. It did make me question what he was carrying. It couldn't be that important since he ended up checking it in at the museum desk anyway.

"You don't mind that I selected the museum as our first stop, do you?" I asked, trying to be polite.

Phoenix looked at me surprised.

"Your first choice? It was on my list as the number one place to visit," he said, leading me through the front gate.

"Really? That's not how I recall the list. The first item you listed was the maritime museum. I am quite sure of that!" I insisted.

"Yes. It was the first one listed, but I carefully coded the places I wished to visit. Just because you weren't able to understand my code doesn't make you right," Phoenix said, walking ahead of me to the first exhibit.

I was immediately impressed at the extensive collection of 1200 objects displayed from the Paleolithic and Iron Ages. Many of these items were retrieved from Cantabria Caves. There was also a virtual visit through the caves that helped us understand how these artifacts were discovered.

But, it was the interactive exhibits that brought to life many of the places we were unfamiliar with. This resulted in Phoenix asking the docents many questions about the Spanish archeologist Jesus Carballo Garcia. Phoenix thought there might be some additional information about Pedro Menendez discovered in the same caves that Garcia excavated early in the twentieth century. Unfortunately, the docent either did not know or wasn't willing to share any information with us .

"What made you suspect that there was anything here about Menendez?" I asked.

"I didn't. But it was worth inquiring. For some reason, Pedro Menendez does not seem very important to any of the historians here at Santander. Hopefully St. Augustine will reveal more evidence," Phoenix said.

After nearly two hours at the museum we both agreed it was time to move ahead. And, thankfully Jesus was right where we left him.

"I believe that our next stop is *Parque de Cabo Mayor,*" Jesus said as we left the museum.

By this time, I wasn't sure where we were going nor did I really care. It didn't seem to really matter now. This was a time to relax and enjoy some well-deserved rest. I had a feeling that it would be a long time before this opportunity would happen again.

"Cabo Mayor is a lovely seaside village where there are many entertaining activities. We are going first to the point known as El Faro de Cabo Mayor. It is the lighthouse that has been greeting ships since 1839," Jesus said as we began to approach a large cliff.

We were both surprised when Jesus turned away from the lighthouse and drove down a dirt highway. When he stopped the car, I wasn't sure what was happening next.

"Por favor mi amigos. I wanted to select the perfect place for your picnic," Jesus said, opening the trunk that had all the necessary commodities.

"Was this also on your list?" I whispered to Phoenix, waiting to hear what he would say next.

"Not on my list. I just assumed it was your idea," Phoenix said, grinning.

I refused the lure. We both followed Jesus to the open space where he was carefully positioning a blanket, umbrella, pillows, and a wicker basket.

"Come, come, my friends. Inside the basket you will find a meal suited for royalty. There is also a chilled bottle of Santander's best wine. It is a perfect blend of Albariño, treixadura, (a local grape) and Chardonnay grapes. These wines are so very fresh that they bustle with subtle bursts of citrus and eucalyptus. Take your time. Enjoy each other's company. Here is my cell number. Call me when you are ready to leave for the beach," Jesus said, walking away before either of us could react.

"I suppose we should take advantage of this Royal meal, and this breathtaking view," Phoenix said, uncorking the chilled bottle.

While preparing the wine, I removed several platters, crystal wine glasses, elegant china dishes, and linen napkins from the basket. This was no typical picnic. I carefully revealed each covered dish. There was a platter of local cheeses and meats with a can of fresh anchovies. The next platter offered a grilled sirloin with a beret of foie on a crusty slice of bread and a touch of caramelized onions. The final platter was a collection of sweets. *Quesada Pasiega,* Spanish cheesecake, Spanish flan, billie de mantequilla (butter buns), and chocolate sugar cookies.

"Jesus was not exaggerating when he said this was a Royal meal. Have you ever seen such a spread served at a picnic?" I asked, impressed.

"This wine is also superb. I intend to enjoy every moment. Maybe even a short nap. I think it's called a
siesta?" Phoenix declared, handing me my glass of wine.

"I hate to admit this, but sitting here in our private oasis, watching the waves from a distance, admiring the beacon on the lighthouse, I am beginning to feel alive once again," I said, really to myself rather than to start a conversation.

"Any theories as to why Señor Martinez chose this picnic on the cliff?" Phoenix asked.

It was something that I was curious about myself. But, I could never tell if Phoenix was asking to hear my thoughts or just using my response as a sounding board. One that he could contradict.

When I didn't respond, he laid back on the pillow and closed his eyes. It took me a few minutes before I decided to follow his lead.

Just as I was beginning to doze off, I heard him say,

"Martinez wants us to unite. To unite, we must agree to an alliance. To agree on an alliance means we must form a friendly entente. Are you willing to move forward without assuming that I am your enemy?" Phoenix said bluntly.

His unexpected analysis caught me off guard.

Was he implying that we should work together to find The Agape? If so, how was the Firm, who was funding this venture, going to react to this new development?

"I never thought of you as my enemy, Phoenix. Maybe, a fierce adversary. Sometimes ruthless, but never vicious," I said, sitting up.

"You asked me what Martinez' motive was, not mine?" Phoenix replied confidently.

"Honestly, Phoenix I am beginning to agree with him. I am not naïve. Many others are searching all around us. We may not be the best treasure hunters, or the wisest, but together our motivations may be what gives us an advantage," I said, waiting for his reaction.

Phoenix took my hand in his. I felt an energy move through my fingers as he caressed each one gently.

"Visual dominance causes us to feel things differently than when we rely on touch. This is why vision can be distorting. It redirects the tactile perception, so no conflict is experienced," Phoenix whispered in my ear while his lips kissed each finger gently; I was mesmerized.

"There is this vision of chauvinism that falsely tends to indicate our need for a single narrative of the world when there are so many ways to interpret our emotions."

I could hear his voice fill my body like a hollow soul that had been empty, craving, yearning to be fondled. It was too late to object. Too late to dissent. For that very moment, the high energy between us magnetically held us concurrently. How long it would last, I had no idea, and I didn't care. Here and now, Phoenix was mine.

Chapter Thirty

Love as a concrete foundation for an authentically functional civilization requires the around-the-clock labors of forgiveness. Without it Love fails, Friendship fails, Intelligence fails, Humanity: fails.

Aberjhani, Journey through the Power of the Rainbow

Phoenix Baldwin and Imani Lewis leave Santander and arrive at Saint Augustine, Florida.
September 2017

Yestetday at the lighthouse with Imani was life-changing for me. It was not meant to be. It made no sense. Women in my life come and go like fireflies in June. This was different. This was frightening. There is something about this *Agape* journey that has changed me. It is not anything specific, but there is a different direction shifting inside without any way to control how far that shift will move. I am confident now that if this carpet still exists, my only chance of finding it is somehow connected to Imani. And, after yesterday, we are definitely connected to one another.

It was at the golden sand beaches with an array of sun worshipers lounging under colorful parasols after the lighthouse when everything started to get confusing. Jesus suggested spending a few hours watching the surfing competition at El Sardinero Beach, with its Belle Époque atmosphere. This was to be our final stop before returning to the hotel. And, it definitely lived up to its French history, synonymous with peace, tranquility, and artistic freedom.

We first waded in the shallow waters of the Bay of Biscay; then, Imani insisted that we take a stroll through the verdant gardens nearby, called Piquio Gardens. We learned from a jogger that it was given that name because it is shaped like the beak of a ship that enters into the sea.

It was after that walk when everything went unexpectedly wrong, and not gradually, suddenly. One moment Imani was laughing, joking, cuddling close to me. Then as if a tsunami hit, she pulled away. There was nothing that I could attribute to this odd behavior.

"Hey…stranger, what is going on?" I asked, practically jogging to catch up with her stride.

Imani said nothing. It was as if two different people were residing in that same body.

When we reached the car that Jesus parked nearby, I finally confronted Imani before she could get in.

"Okay! We are not leaving here until I get an explanation for why you are reacting in this irrational manner," I demanded. My hand was holding the car door shut, waiting for an explanation.

"An answer to what, Mr. Baldwin? Did you assume that just because we had a few moments of careless flirtation at the park that I was going to succumb to your advances? Well, I am sorry to disappoint you, but we are on a mission. A journey to discover one of the most incredible artifacts that religions throughout the world have been searching for centuries. Nothing, not even the suave, sophisticated Phoenix Baldwin, is going to prevent me from that moment of enlightenment," she said, her eyes on fire.

"And, you really believe that I am attempting to prevent that from happening? Did you ever try to consider that what we were feeling at the lighthouse might just be what we need to complete this mission?" I said, genuinely astonished at her assumptions.

The crowds surrounding us were beginning to gather to watch the "love quarrel" ignite around them. It was beginning to appear like a very engaging spectacle, worthy of a small audience.

That was when I knew it was time to move somewhere private. I released my hand from the car door, and Imani immediately moved inside. I was close behind her. Nevertheless, our audience did not move. It was as if they were waiting patiently to see the next scene play out in this soap opera.

"Oh, my! What has happened? Everything seemed perfectly cordial after we left the picnic. Now there is a dark cloud following the two of you," Jesus said, starting the car to let the air conditioner clear the friction.

Imani sat silent. I already knew I had said enough. But, it was what Jesus said that made the most sense.

"Will you allow me, in good faith, to share with you both something that I have observed while listening to your dilemma," Jesus said, waiting patiently for both of us to concede.

Imani finally nodded, yes, but said nothing. I verbally agreed to hear what Jesus was willing to share.

"If you don't mind, I will first take us away from these crowds that have now assumed that the two of you are some celebrities on hiatus," Jesus said, laughing.

We soon left the El Sardinero Beach vicinity through some winding roads that appeared to be leading us to some quaint residences. During the fifteen-minute ride there was a deafening silence. All I could hear was breathing periodically.

When we were parked, at last, Jesus asked us to follow him through a wooded area that was approximately one mile I assessed. When we arrived at our destination, there was a small brick chalet surrounded by fragrant flowering bushes and an outside veranda that offered an unobstructed view of the majestic Atlantic Ocean.

"Who lives here?" Imani asked after being silent the entire ride.

"I do, at least for now. Eventually it will be willed to the government after my time on earth. It has been in my family's possession since the early sixteenth century. Very few visitors have ever been invited here," Jesus said, insisting that we sit, relax, and enjoy the view while he went inside for some cool refreshments.

I was tempted to take this opportunity to continue my inquiry as to what caused Imani's sudden meltdown, but I was unprepared for her reaction if it was to be volatile. Best to wait for Jesus to explain why we were even brought here.

Jesus quickly returned. I assume he also did not want to leave the two of us alone for an extended amount of time. Walking quickly toward us he held three chilled wine glasses and a bottle of *Cormoran Tempranillo Rioja*. I recognized that from a winery advertisement in the town.

"Perfecto! Here we are seated in a secret paradise, sipping wine from the best vineyards beneath us and enjoying the magnificent view of Santander. No doubt, this is why my great descendant, Pedro Menendez, purchased the property for his wife. When he departed for America under the orders of Prince Philip in July 1565, he insisted that Maria, his wife, would have a suitable residence during his absence," Jesus said.

I was intrigued at what Jesus was implying. How did a descendent of Pedro Menendez, if this is true, become a tour guide? Imani was the one who asked what I was speculating.

"Are you suggesting Jesus that you are related to Pedro Menendez? But, why have you been chauffeuring us around this city like a typical worker?"

"My dear, we are all common workers of God. I have never felt superior merely because my last name is Menendez. Pedro was not an innocent man. You will discover that his life was filled with many tragedies, as well as horrific acts. My life has been dedicated to sharing the spiritual teachings resulting from many experiences with The *Agape Miracle*.

This was the first time that I had heard anyone express that *The Agape* was a miracle. Imani's voice was clearly still filled with anger. Her tone toward Jesus was borderline contentious.

To divert away from this negativity I continued to ask more questions.

"Have you actually ever seen the famous carpet?" I inquired.

"No. Not I. But, every generation of my family has been told about its power. Nevertheless, we have all benefited from *The Agape's* influence in our home at one time. When Pedro married Maria de Solis she was very young. They had very little time together before he was given his orders to sail to Florida. Maria feared he would never return home to her. It was then that a street beggar approached Maria with a gift, a spiritual carpet. She was told that her husband must take the carpet to the new world. When she hesitated, the beggar assured her that the carpet would protect Pedro on his voyage, returning him safely to her. Maria brought the carpet home. It stayed, right here in this house for several months before Pedro's departure."

If what Jesus was telling us is true, it makes sense that Señor Martinez directed us to St. Augustine. But, how was I now going to convince Imani that it was essential for us to trust each other?

"Now that you understand how *The Agape* arrived at St. Augustine, you must also realize it's power. Are you a religious man, Dr. Baldwin?" Jesus asked me.

It was a very long time since anyone referred to me as Doctor. Why Jesus chose this moment was not apparent.

Questioning my faith was also not anticipated. There was no answer that I could give him. Formal religion was a part of my early life. My parents attended every services on Sunday, at St. Stephen Walbrook in London. I often felt that the only reason they patronized this church was its prestigious history and, of course, because it was politically correct.

In 1672 Christopher Wren began the commencement of St. Stephen Walbrook, a church that he would attend in his neighborhood. He later designed the famous St. Paul's and a total of fifty-four other famous churches in London. My parents were proud to be listed as charter members. But, did they truly live by the word of Jesus? I never felt that they did.

"I certainly cannot speak for Mr. Baldwin, or Dr. Baldwin," Imani said sarcastically,

"But, I am an agnostic. This is not to say that I don't admire Jesus. My objection is with the hypocrisy of traditional religious organizations. They no longer respect any of the fundamental beliefs that Jesus tried to teach Christians," Imani said.

"This may be true in many parts of the world, Imani. However, rejecting the critical ideas that Jesus strives to imbue in every one of his disciples will alienate you from ever discovering where *The Agape* currently resides. Are you familiar with any of the scriptures?" Jesus asked Imani directly.

"I have studied all religions, including what the Bible claims Jesus taught his followers," Imani answered.

"Then, you must understand that Jesus treated the poor with compassion. He provides us with many parables where beggars teach us the truth that Jesus speaks about. In Proverbs 19:17, 'Whoever is kind to the poor lends to the Lord, and he will reward them for what they have done.' So, you must understand that as long as your motivations, Imani, are self-centered, you will never discover *The Agape,"* Jesus announced.

I listened attentively. If what Jesus was telling us was accurate neither Imani nor I could find this spiritual carpet.

"If we are to believe what you are telling us, Jesus, why did Señor Martinez suggest that we travel to St. Augustine, Florida? Without true faith, it appears that *The Agape* will never be discovered," I said, trying to assess my next strategy.

"Yes, and no. Jesus confronted many nonbelievers during his short time on earth. He never walked away from that challenge. What you and Imani must resolve is how you will tackle the obstacles that have now surfaced. Imani must address that her reaction to you, Phoenix, is motivated by fear. In this case, Imani's fear is a result of losing control. Many people attempt to remedy this feeling by gaining control. This is achieved by an action of 'fight' or 'flight'. Therefore, Imani, which will you choose?" Jesus asked.

Imani looked perplexed, as well as disturbed. Had Jesus just exposed Imani's Achilles heel? Was Jesus correct? Did Imani truly have the courage to determine what she must do next? Ironically, if she can overcome this flaw, she will have complete control over both our fates.

"What you have shared with us has been truly inspiring. It has reminded me of a favorite poem that I was introduced to by my father, Bran Hughes," Imani was finally moving past her aggressions.

"I would be very pleased if you could recite it to us, Imani. It might be the same answer that we have been searching for," Jesus said.

"Unfortunately I have not memorized it, but I do carry it with me always. This does seem like an appropriate time to hear it once again read aloud."

There was a definite transition occurring. I had no idea why or how, but the earlier emotional storm was now quelled. Imani removed a small sheet of paper from her backpack and began to read. It was quite moving to listen to her speak.

Hermetic Happenings
By Brian Swann

It is not turning the corner
and biting the wind off at the root
nor letting it lead you
to a Forest in full fledge
throwing yourself on it
as if that would absorb
It's green fire.

Imani stopped, placed the notepaper on her lap, and looked directly at me.

"I will not apologize for my attitude, Mr. Baldwin. Whatever bond you have created in me was an invasion of my privacy that I was not prepared to share. But, I now know that I am strong enough to adjust and accept a cool gap 'among my green fire'. *The Agape* is waiting for us in St. Augustine. Let's claim it and introduce it back into this modern world."

Jesus appeared to be content. I was relieved that everything appeared back to normal. The remainder of our time in Santander was uneventful yet pleasant.

The following evening, we would fly 4,258 miles to continue our *Agape Journey*. From this point forward, we were unified. Although Imani did not share the rest of her poem with me, I took the liberty to find it online. Brian Swann captured the feeling that I had at this moment. Imani and I were, entering a *"buffer zone"* into *"no man's land" where* events, I was certain would bring, "autonomy closer to experience" and, "shape those thoughts and acts" into a self-reality beyond our comprehension. Would we be prepared to accept this responsibility? We would both find out shortly.

Chapter Thirty-One

Faith is to believe what you do not see; the reward of this faith is to see what you believe.

Saint Augustine
Philosopher

Bran Hughes
St. Augustine, Florida
September 1996

"Sometimes when sorrow dissects your heart, God leads us to a place where healing restores your soul. He breathes life into the heart that lies lifeless, my dear friend, Bran."

Those were the final words that Pastor Jamison said to me as I boarded my plane, leaving behind my beloved Wales to begin a new life in an ancient city in America. It was my first time traveling to America. It would be an understatement to suggest that I was nervous. After all, I was leaving behind not only all my friends but a very different lifestyle.

At forty years old was I too old, or too young? Was I truly prepared for these changes? If I failed, what would I do to recoup?

The answer to all my doubts is also known as the power of faith. Pastor Jamison in the very short time that we spent together taught me that fear is a human obstacle. Once overcome, it may be used to strengthen our moral framework.

"Do you even know who Saint Augustine was Bran? It is not a mere coincidence that the city you are moving to has quite a powerful and memorable history, starting with its namesake. I want you to understand the story of Augustine because it is a lesson that will provide you with the strength needed to complete your evolution," Jamison said.

"It is a powerful story that I have often referred to whenever my spiritual disposition requires enlightenment.

During the early 400's Augustine served the church as a priest, bishop, and theologian, in Hippo, which is now the present seaport city of Algiers. What was most interesting to me was that Augustine was not an early follower of God. Quite the contrary. His struggle with morality led him to experiment with many non-Christian faiths and philosophies. Much of his frustration was reconciling his desire for intimacy with the church doctrine for godly living.

Similar to St. Paul, who struggled with these same insecurities, Augustine claimed that he heard God say to him, "Tolle, lege". Translated from Latin this means, "pick up and read."

When Augustine did what God directed him to do, he turned to the Letters of St. Paul.

What interested me the most about Augustine was his devotion to the poor. But, more than practicing a pious life he also wrote some powerful rhetoric including *Confessions* and *The City of God*. Centuries later, an American writer, Thomas Cahill, deemed Augustine's writing "a crucial turning point in human consciousness from classical to a modern way of thinking." (*How the Irish Saved Civilization*).

But, it was Pedro Menendez, 1100 years later, who chose to honor his patron Saint by naming this town St. Augustine. Menendez founded this property on August 28, 1565, the exact date the Roman Catholic Church dedicated a feast to Saint Augustine to honor his death in 430AD.

From the moment that I arrived at this ancient town, there was this intense surge of energy that penetrated deep into my everyday activities. Without any doubts or hesitation, I knew that St. Augustine is where I belonged. What I didn't know was what my calling would be.

At the Jacksonville Airport, after I cleared customs, I was greeted by a friendly gentleman carrying a sign with my name.

"You must be Bran Hughes. I am Pastor Marcus. Jamison speaks highly of you. I hope that you will be happy here with us at Memorial Lutheran," the gentleman said, placing his arm around my shoulders.

"Yes. I have also heard wonderful accolades about your ministry from Jamison. Unfortunately, I will warn you that I lack personal direction, but if you point me on the right path, I am indeed a hard worker," I said, following Marcus to the baggage claim.

"No worries, my friend. There is always something that needs to be improved on in the city and the chapel. St. Augustine is a friendly community that will gladly welcome you with open arms," Marcus assured me.

And, Pastor Marcus was definitely correct. Everywhere that I went, there was plenty of work to be accomplished. Memorial Lutheran had many outreach programs. I soon learned that even with all the community help there were many poor and homeless people that needed more. I was determined to find ways to improve their circumstances. Unfortunately, I also needed to earn a living, or I would be one of the "untouchables" who live on the streets during the day but fade into the dark wooded camps in the evening.

Old Town Augustine Trolly hired me during the morning tours. I would then work as a waiter at *The Ale House* on the weekends. Between these two jobs, I earned enough to rent a small one-bedroom cottage on Anastasia Island near the Lighthouse. It was a comfortable community. My neighbors often planned picnics in the park nearby. It was much like a commune where we all looked out for each other, sharing whatever we had. For the first time since I lost Sarah and Imani, I felt accepted. Maybe not happy, but at peace.

Then one afternoon Pastor Marcus visited me at *The Ale House* after my shift.

"This is a surprise Pastor. What can I get for you," I asked, even though I was finished for the evening.

"Sit down my friend. Let me buy you a burger and a beer while we talk about some proposals I have in mind," Marcus said.

It had been several weeks since I was at church. Unfortunately, *The Ale House* needed me to work on Sundays since they were having difficulty hiring steady waiters. My original reason for coming to St. Augustine was to help the needy not to work in a restaurant. Somehow I found myself changing course.

"I want to make you an offer Bran one that I hope you will seriously consider. The church council has voted to hire a community liaison to organize suitable programs to remove the homeless from the streets. It has been brought to our attention by several welfare organizations that the homeless population is expanding, not decreasing. With your desire to help I believe this will be a perfect fit for you. It will include visiting homeless camps, preparing and distributing meals, encouraging the business community to donate to a bicycle fund, and much more. All of these improvements will help more homeless people to stay mobile with the long term goal being permanent housing. You were our first choice," Marcus explained.

There it was finally my calling. But, what experience did I have to accomplish this? Marcus was asking me to reach beyond my abilities. All my previous visits to the homeless camps were spontaneous. Often if I came without food or money, I was rejected by this very exclusive community. There were even many homeless people who avoided going to those camps in fear of being beaten or even killed. There was no doubt that this was the survival of the fittest camp. Very competitive. There was even a hierarchy among those men and sometimes women, who dictated the rules. Some respected them; others feared them.

"I am not sure that I have the experience needed to successfully accomplish all that you are asking, Marcus. Perhaps the council should interview someone with a degree in Welfare or even Psychology," I said, skeptical about my ability to accomplish this assignment.

"You are exactly the right person, Bran. The homeless community does not trust anyone they regard as *The Establishment.* They blame those people for their predicament. And, quite honestly I can understand their resentment. In many cases, it is The Establishment that gave them no alternative. It is this society that pushes them to the outer limits where they are today. But, you Bran are not associated with any of that stereotype. You don't look or even speak like the rest of us. To them, you appear to be an outcast, similar in many ways," Marcus said, smiling.

I never felt like an outcast in St. Augustine. Everyone treated me with respect. But, Marcus might be correct. Once a rather frail young girl invited me to follow her into the woods. She introduced me to the others at the camp as an "alien." I believe she meant immigrant, but there was no need to correct her. I was touched that she was willing to share anything with me. Several days later, I searched the streets for her. Finally, someone who I was serving food in the park told me that her body was found floating face down in the intercostal waterways. Nobody even knew if she was buried. That memory still haunts me.

"I cannot promise you, Marcus that I will be able to accomplish much, but I am willing to do my very best," I said.

One week later I gave notice to the Trolley Company and *The Ale House*. Marcus found me a used Volkswagen bus that looked like it belonged at Woodstock. But it ran well. More importantly, it was perfect for transporting tents, clothing, food, water. Every essential item needed to live in a counterculture. And, the homeless soon recognized me wherever I was driving around nearby.

When I wasn't meeting with the city council, service organizations, like the Elks Club, Moose Lodge, and Rotary Club. In addition to my outreach job, I was the maintenance manager at the church. This left me little time for any social life. But, I didn't care.

I never stopped thinking about Imani. Although my letters were not as long or detailed with illustrations, I continued to write her every month. I never specifically said where I was, but if she ever noticed the postmark, it would be evident that I was no longer in Wales. I even told her about the deceased young girl. I included a charcoal portrait of how I remembered she looked. It may seem morbid, but it was my way of trying to parent my child. There was so much that she needed to know. I had no idea who was even caring for her now that Sarah was gone?

One afternoon while I was polishing the wood floors in the sanctuary, Marcus came.

"Bran, take a break for a few minutes and share a cup of tea with me in the fellowship hall," he said, waiting for me to stop the floor polisher.

I followed him into the empty room and took a seat at one of the round tables. Marcus brought over a tea pot, two cups, milk, sugar, and several pastries. It reminded me of my tea time back home in Wales.

"I am sure this isn't as delicious as what you were used to in Wales, but it's not bad for an American version," Marcus said, pouring the tea.

"Not bad? This is quite delightful, Marcus. I haven't had tea like this for several years now," I said, grateful.

"We haven't really had a chance to talk very much about your family, or why you left Wales. There are people from everywhere in the world that relocate to St. Augustine for a variety of reasons. I am curious to hear what motivated you to leave your motherland," Marcus asked.

There was an awkward moment of silence. I was not expecting to share my private life with anyone. Pastor Marcus had done so much for me I didn't want to be rude. Maybe it was time to share with him some of my history. I told him all about Sarah. Later I shared with him my frustrations about losing Imani. When I was finished, I felt a strong sense of relief.

"It is sometimes difficult to understand God's plans for us, Bran. But, what you have accomplished here with the homeless has been extraordinary. What I am about to suggest may seem like another leap of faith, but please trust me. If I didn't feel so strongly that this is God's decision, I would never confront you with such a proposal," Marcus said.

I was thoroughly confused.

Had I not accomplished everything that the church council asked me to? What more did Marcus want from me?

"I am not sure what you are asking me to do, Marcus?"

"There is a community in Ohio known as *Over the Rhine*. It is located in Cincinnati. They are in desperate need of someone to help them with their homeless community. I have a close friend, Pastor Liam McDermott. His congregation is located in West Chester, a suburb of Cincinnati. *God's Grace Lutheran Church* desperately needs help with its outreach program. *Family Promise* is an organization that collaborates with local faith and civic groups to provide housing, education, meals, and transportation to families that have become homeless. They need you, Bran. If I make all the arrangements would you be willing to relocate?" Pastor Marcus asked.

"Relocate to Ohio? I have no idea where Ohio is? Is it anything like St. Augustine? You do realize Marcus, that I am not even a citizen of your country. They may not even allow me into this place you call Cincinnati?" I asked, bewildered.

"No, Cincinnati is nothing like St. Augustine but it does have snow like Wales. And, no worries about citizenship. You will be an ambassador of the Lutheran church. What do you say? Will you at least think about it?" Marcus asked.

"Yes. I will consider it. Give me a week. I need to do some soul searching and a few conversations with God first. I will give you my answer next week," I said.

Marcus agreed that a week was a reasonable time limit. I already was beginning to regret even the thought of leaving St. Augustine. But, I did owe Marcus an appropriate reflection on the prospect of relocating. Maybe some of my hippie friends at the Lighthouse neighborhood could at least tell me what Ohio was like.

"Ohio? Are you out of your f***ing mind, Bran? Nobody leaves Florida for Ohio. The weather alone is reason not to go. And, you know there are no beaches, right?" Mick said one afternoon while we were sitting on the porch drinking a couple of frosted Guinness.

"I'm not worried about the weather. I actually miss the snow. The beaches I might miss. Our walks with Mateo in the morning always clears my head. But, Marcus says that this *Family Promise* group really needs help. I read an article about how it got started. It is an important organization," I said.

"Sounds to me like you already have made up your mind. I suggest that you talk to Faith. Do you know Faith? She lives around the corner. We are having a little party Saturday night. I will introduce the two of you," Mick said.

Mick's parties throughout the neighborhood are notorious. Not for any specific reason other than they attract a variety of people from different walks of life. There is always plenty of pizza, pasta, beer, wine, and cannabis. Several musicians stop by during the evening to play classic rock'n roll. When they take a break the karaoke machine suddenly appears from nowhere. Everyone loves Mick's parties.

For three days, I tried to recall meeting Faith. But with that name I would not have forgotten her. Is it just a coincidence that Imani also means faithful? I decided not to wait until the party. Friday afternoon I took a walk around the block to find Faith for myself. It was dusk and many of the small cottages were beginning to light up with twinkling stars.

When I was going to give up my search, I stopped in front of a small house surrounded by a rather tall white fence with an arbor gate. On the porch I saw a wooden sign that said, *Faith's Menagerie*. I hesitated before entering.

What could be the worst thing to happen if this wasn't Faith's house? Then again how many Faiths could live in this neighborhood? Anyway, I would apologize for any inconvenience and return home.

Before I reached the front door, I was greeted by a giant tortoise, a white rabbit, a Siamese cat, and a white cockatoo.

"Hey, be careful you don't step on any of the puppies on your way up the steps," I heard a voice say before I noticed who the speaker was.

When my eyes began to adjust to the subtle light I saw a young woman standing in the doorway wearing cutoff jean shorts, and a razorback peach colored shirt with the words *SaltLife* printed across the front. I recognized the standard uniform worn at the popular beach restaurant.

"Hi! I'm Bran Hughes…a friend of Mick's," I added as if that might give me some credibility to be here on her porch.

"Yah…Yah… I know you. You're the guy that drives around in that Hippie van, right?" She said..

I laughed, shaking my head.

"Are you, Faith?" I decided to take the plunge and ask.

"Yes, I am. Mick said you might stop by."

She began to clear a path for me to the rocker on the porch. "Can I get you a beer, soda, water," Faith asked, as I managed to sit down finally.

"No, thanks. Mick thought you might be able to tell me something about Cincinnati?" I said, getting directly to the point.

Faith sat down next to me on a matching rocking chair. A small dog that resembled a beagle pushed his way through the screen door and jumped on Faith's lap.

"Sorry for so many animals. I spend all my free time helping at the pet shelter. We do a lot of dog rescues. When it gets really busy I bring a few here while we try to find foster homes," Faith said, managing now a kitten and puppy at the same time.

"It looks like we have similar objectives. I do the same with humans," I said, stroking one of the loose puppies on the head.

"I know," was all Faith said.

I finally did decide to have a cold beer. Probably more like three. Faith told me about her dream to open her own rescue haven. She also gave me a good idea of what to expect in Cincinnati.

By the time I left her house, we knew more about each other than any other person on this planet. It was just a natural friendship.

After that day there were several other visits with Faith. Soon we were spending almost every day together. I soon learned that she was originally from a small city, "a village," as she called it, known as Glendale.

Although Faith moved to St. Augustine five years ago, she also commuted to the Midwest relatively regularly. Most of the time transporting abandoned dogs to their "forever homes." She was the one who suggested that maybe we could blend both of our missions. I liked that idea, and I really enjoyed Faith's company. That is what I was going to propose to Marcus today.

"Unfortunately, Bran, we are unable to transport our homeless population to other parts of the country like Faith has been able to accomplish with her animals. She is pretty admired throughout the community for her tenacity and dedication to all animals. I wish that we could find "forever" homes for many of our displaced humans," Marcus said reverently.

"So, do I, Marcus. But, what I was suggesting was perhaps something similar in the logistics. Would it be acceptable if I travel back to St. Augustine when needed? I still have many people here that depend on me. I don't want them to add me to the list of people who rejected them," I said, hoping that Marcus would accept the compromise.

"If you can find a stable balance between the two commitments, I am certain that Pastor Liam will agree," Marcus said, pleased.

Faith was organizing a caravan with several different dogs that families recently adopted in Kentucky, Indiana, and Ohio. We decided to travel from Florida together making the trip more enjoyable. Since Faith was more familiar with the route, she made the arrangements for all the safe, appropriate campsites.

The afternoon prior to our departure Marcus asked me to stop by the church. There were a few items that he wanted Pastor Liam to have. I was hoping that it wasn't much since my Hippie Van was already filled with items for camping and transporting four dogs that needed crates.

"Oh no worries my friend. This item will easily fit in some corner, taking up little space," Marcus said, carrying out a rolled-up carpet that was carefully tied with strong twine.

"What is this, Pastor?" I asked, curious why an old carpet needed to be taken across the country.

"This relic has a very lengthy history. Perhaps one-day Pastor Liam will share it with you. But, for now, please consider this precious cargo," Marcus said, finding an appropriate place in the van.

Our last night in St. Augustine Mick threw one of his popular parties. It was Hawaiian-themed, with everyone wearing floral shirts, flowered leis, and, of course, drinking plenty of rum beverages while smoking "prescription marijuana," which is legal in Florida.

"I'm gonna miss you, man! We all are. Don't stay away too long. I can't wait to hear all about your new adventures," Mick said, embracing me on my way out.

"Thanks Mick for the Aloha send off. If everything works out well, I plan to be back in the spring," I said.

There was one last thing that I needed to do before I went to bed that evening. Write my final letter to Imani. I wasn't giving up hope that we might still meet in the future. But, realistically, and for my own mental health, it was time to let her go.

My dearest Imani,

I have spent the past two years in this lovely ancient city known as St. Augustine. Someday I hope that you will have the opportunity to visit. Since this will be my final letter to you, I want you to always remember that if you ever need to find me, Pastor Marcus, at Memorial Lutheran Church of the Martyrs, here in St. Augustine will always know where I am.

God Bless you my beautiful child!
Your father, Bran Hughes.
October 1998

The following morning, on our way out of the city, I wanted to drive once more through the ancient town that changed my life forever. The final stop was the local post office where I dropped off Imani's letter through the drive-up mailbox. It was now time to look forward with no regret.

Goodbye St. Augustine. Stay strong forever!

Chapter Thirty-Two

To get over the past, you first have to accept that the past is over. No matter how many times you revisit it, analyze it, regret it, it's over. It cannot hurt you anymore.

Mandy Hale
The Single Woman

Imani Lewis and Phoenix Baldwin
St. Augustine, Florida
October 2017

Everythng that Jesus said about fear, obsessive control, flee or fight mentality was true about me. I can admit this, but I do not know if I am able to change this behavior. I am not even sure if I want to expose myself to the vulnerability that follows. What has become clear, since arriving at St. Augustine, three days ago, is that this ancient city has survived many crises. Millions of visitors from around the world arrive here on a yearly pilgrimage to discover the amazing euphoria that the city elicits. I have felt that attraction. It is a sense of overwhelming peace. Much different from what I shared with Phoenix at the lighthouse in Santander. That experience is known as, The Principle of Vibration, the third of seven Hermetic principles.

Not that Phoenix knew how to use that principle that made me nervous; it was my reaction to his touch. The theory associated with "vibes" has existed for centuries. *The Kybalion* was introduced in 1908 to teach the modern interpretation of the teaching of Hermès Trismegistus, a legendary Hellenistic figure to a new generation.

When Phoenix began caressing my fingers he was perpetuating my physical and mental energy simultaneously. This resulted in my heart beating, stimulating an energy source that I had never experienced before. It was as if fire and ice were being transfused into my body at the same time without my control. What was just as confusing to me was why?

Unfortunately, this was not the time or the place to continue to dwell on that one moment. There was much to accomplish here, and The Agape was my priority.

Señor Martinez arranged for Phoenix and I to meet curators at several local libraries and museums. Neither Phoenix nor I knew how much information would be useful or how long we would be staying at St. Augustine.

I was pretty skeptical when our driver from the airport told us that we were staying at a quaint Bed & Breakfast downtown that also permanently housed "shadow people."

"What exactly do you mean by 'shadow people'?" I asked the driver.

"Shadow People are mischievous spirits…you know, dead people!" the driver tried to explain.

I looked at Phoenix, hoping that he would say something brilliant, or at the very least contradictory. But instead, he added that *Casa de Suenos* was listed in all of the literature available as the most haunted property in St. Augustine.

"This only makes sense, Imani. Prior to its renovation the property was considered one of the most successful funeral homes in the area. It was not until the 1990's that the old building started to house live people, like us," Phoenix said, nonchalantly.

"I must tell you that the location is one of the best for sightseeing. We have a real parking problem in town. But, you two will have no trouble visiting all of the local exhibits, stores, and fantastic restaurants. Oh, my goodness, doesn't let me get started on how great the food is here," the driver said.

That first evening at the Inn I had no idea, nor did I care to know what Phoenix did. The jet lag kept me in bed until late the next morning. When I woke up, there was a note that I found under my door.

"Coffee, tea, fresh fruit, bagels downstairs. I have an appointment at the Mission De Nombres at 10:30 am, with or without you."
Phoenix

My cell phone clock indicated it was 9:00 am. Plenty of time for a shower. How did Phoenix arrange an appointment? Then I remembered the names and contact numbers that Martinez gave us. We decided to visit the first museum together, then later divide our leads to accomplish more groundwork. It sounded reasonable. Once we had everything documented we would evaluate our results. *Mission De Nombres* must have something relevant to our search, or Phoenix would not be anxious to go there first.

I opened my notes on my tablet. There was something that Jesus mentioned about Pedro Menendez and the *Mission De Nombres*. Whatever it was I know I included it here. Yes! There it was. It was Jesus telling us the story about his ancestor that lead us here. All of this was documented on my tablet.

When the Spanish King Phillip II, summoned Menendez back to Spain from Florida in 1574, he died of typhus in Santander. That is where he was originally buried. However, in 1924, Menendez's casket was moved to San Nicholas Church, in Aviles Spain, where he initially noted he wanted his final resting place.

I recall Jesus telling us that,

"Even when Menendez's casket was laid to rest in his hometown, it was not the end of his posthumous travels."

My response was classic.

"Pedro relocated as much as I have. Perhaps even more considering how often his remains have been moved," I said, somewhat amused at this story.

"To even complicate matters, Pedro's body was reposed several more times before it was finally laid permanently to rest. You see, for reasons ranging from leaks in the parish church to fears of his body being desecrated during the Spanish Civil War, there were times that only a few Franciscan priests knew for sure where Menendez's casket was. To add to this confusion, there were two churches located about half a mile away, off the plaza, that one time or another also were called, St. Nicholas Church. So, now you can begin to understand Imani, what a historical nightmare this became," Jesus explained.

Finally, it made sense why there were no burial markers for this great Native Son at either Aviles or Santander.

My notes reconfirmed that in 1924, there was a carved marble urn with the remains of Adelantado Pedro Menendez found in a niche high above a wall near the pulpit. This is where there is a discrepancy regarding who actually possesses the final remains. According to Spain, the urn was not found until after the Spanish Civil War in the 1930's. It took another thirty years for that urn to be moved back to its original 1924 location.

"If this information is accurate, Jesus, what is in the casket at St. Augustine? Is it empty? Why would we need to travel there merely to view an empty casket?" I asked hesitantly.

"As intriguing as the story is about Pedro Menendez life and death, it is *The Agape* connection that is drawing you to St. Augustine, Imani. Consider every small historical tile that you are provided as a piece to the final mosaic. And, I cannot stress enough that it is *The Agape* Journey that will lead you to your final destination. Allow it to take its course," Jesus stressed.

Those were the final words that I recall Jesus saying to me before I departed. I wasn't even sure if Jesus shared that same advice with Phoenix. But, I was now more than ever anxious to explore St. Augustine. For some reason, I just felt that this city would offer some inspirational insights unlike any of the other historical sites that I have visited. I was now convinced that this is why Jesus and Martinez wanted Phoenix and I to first begin our search at *Mission De Nombres*.

"Good morning, Ms. Lewis. I am pleasantly surprised that you could tear yourself away from your *Shadow* companions to join me for what I expect to be a fascinating exploration later this morning," I said, waiting to see how the unpredictable Imani would react today.

Imani took her seat across from me looking quite casual, yet professional. Much different from the beach attire that she was wearing only a few days ago. Even her alluring red hair today was subtly braided. There is just something quite exotic about this enigmatic lady that frightens me and yet beckons me to her, like a lost ship looking for that alluring lighthouse in the distance. But, am I willing to enter that harbor surrounded by deadly current and hidden rocks? I am not sure yet.

"No *Shadow* companions, Mr. Baldwin, just a few Hollow men. Do I have time for a cup of tea before we leave?" Imani asked, politely.

"Plenty of time. And, I certainly hope that your comment about *Hollow Men* was merely a literary allusion?" I said, wanting her to appreciate that I was familiar with the famous poem by TS Eliot.

"That will depend on how the morning progresses. Measuring 'my life with coffee spoons' lately is becoming quite annoying. I am not sure how you are feeling about this race that keeps leading us back to the starting line, but I am hoping that one of us will soon discover something relevant to our journey."

I could sense in Imani's voice frustration. It certainly was something that I could relate to.

"All that I can suggest is that you listen to the 'mermaids singing, each to each'…and, ask yourself at the end of the day, 'if it has been worth it after all, would it have been worthwhile after the sunsets and the dooryards, and the sprinkled streets, After the novels, after the teacups'?"

I said, watching Imani smile for the very first time since the fiasco at Santander lighthouse.

"That was quite lovely, and poetic, Mr. Eliot. Were you ever going to mention to me that you had a Ph.D? Or, that you are a professor at Cambridge? Perhaps someday, when we have 'real' time to enjoy reminiscing, we can return to this moment?" Imani sounded strangely sincere.

"I would enjoy that, as well. But, just FYI, I never use the title Dr. By the way, you look quite radiant today, Ms. Lewis. I hope that you will accept this as a genuine compliment and not as a 'come on' as you Americans like to say."

"I appreciate an honest comment. You too look quite dapper Mr. Baldwin. Although if I had earned a Ph.D., I would be flaunting my Dr. title everywhere. Anyway, I have a good feeling about this meeting," Imani said.

I was pretty relieved that our conversation was at least pleasant. Yet, I could not help being cautious as we decided to walk our way to the Mission.

It was tempting to take the many side roads that were busy with tourists, but Imani and I had no time this morning to enjoy the outstanding historical sights. When the host from Casa de Suenos told me that Mission De Nombres was only a pleasant 5-minute walk down Castillo Drive via Cordova Street, we took advantage of the crisp October weather that many snowbirds travel from the Midwest and East coast to enjoy each year here in Florida.

I personally knew nothing about these odd "snowbirds" until I met one of them last night while I was exploring the pubs nearby. I soon learned to appreciate why St. Augustine is such a favorite attraction. There is no scarcity in watering holes or restaurants. Anyway, this snowbird found my English accent appealing. We ended up closing the bar. The darling invited me to her room, but as alluring as she was, I gave her some tongue and, like a good boy, went to my room alone.

"There it is, *Mission De Nombres* behind the wrought iron fence. Who do we consult once we arrive?" Imani asked.

"I believe that the name on this card is Mrs. Armstrong. Yes, Mrs. Elizabeth Armstrong," I confirmed, handing the card to Imani.

"Nice. Finally a woman. Everyone thus far have been men. Not that it really matters, but I do, at times, find that the European mentality is quite chauvinistic. It will be pleasant to hear an intelligent woman's perspective on this *Agape* carpet," Imani said, walking ahead of me for the first time.

"I am not sure who you are referring to by that comment, but in Spain, everyone, including myself, treated you with equal respect," I said, refusing to allow Imani to make such exaggerated claims.

"We can discuss that at another time Phoenix. Right now we have an important meeting to attend," Imani said arrogantly.

The only image that came to mind almost immediately, watching Imani walk off was Dante Gabriele Rossetti's, *La Ghirlandaio*. The portrait of a stunning red haired woman that symbolized for me, and obviously Rossetti, promiscuity, sensuality, and mysticism.

I decided to allow Imani her time on this stage. Being an attentive observer actually might reveal essential insight that could be lost if I become part of the plot. At least for now, she can take the lead.

Watching Imani interact with Mrs. Armstrong was impressive. There was no doubt that Imani was well prepared.

"Would you mind sharing with us the historical significance of that cross at a distance?" Imani asked.

"Of course. Why don't we take a walk outside to view the cross where it now stands? I believe that when you hear the story it will answer all your questions," Mrs. Armstrong said, leading the way across the bridge silently.

Once we arrived at the base of the gigantic cross, Mrs. Armstrong invited us to take a seat. I still was not convinced that any of this background was necessary, but since I agreed to allow Imani complete control, I kept silent.

"On October 1966, to celebrate the 400th anniversary of Mission Nombre de Dios, the Archbishop dedicated *The Great Cross* right here where you are seated. Just imagine that this 208-foot steel structure can be seen above the Matanza marshes from almost everywhere. We refer to our cross as a "Beacon of Faith". You see, when Pedro Menendez in 1565 landed right here, the first item he placed on Florida soil was a wooden cross. We Catholics consider this gesture the beginning of Christianity in this new land," Mrs. Armstrong said proudly.

Imani stood up. She walked close to the edge of the water, turned around and asked a question that made me immediately take notice.

"Do you consider it Christian to slaughter one hundred eleven Frenchman who refused to denounce their religion, Mrs. Armstrong? And, doesn't even the word *Matanza* mean
slaughter?" Imani asked bluntly.

Mrs. Armstrong's face appeared as if it had been drained of all its color. It took her about a minute to react.

Very diplomatic, Imani. Is this the technique you use to encourage cooperation? I thought quietly, waiting for the following reaction.
"That event that you are referring to has been disputed by many scholars. There are letters from Pedro Menendez denying any inappropriate action taken against the French. We prefer to celebrate the many wonderful contributions made by the Franciscans that followed," Mrs. Armstrong said, once again composed.

Bravo, Mrs. Armstrong, for retaining your calm composure.

It was now time for me to intervene before Imani decided to debate this sensitive topic.

"We were told by a credible source that Pedro Menendez's final resting place is right here, at *Misssion De Nombres*. Am I correct?" I asked, intervening.

Imani said nothing. But, I could sense her disgust toward me.

"To be as accurate as possible we are not certain if there are any remains in the coffin. However, you are correct that the casket is in our museum. We will walk back now, if you would like to view it?" Mrs. Armstrong was now determined to ignore Imani's earlier comments.

The walk back to the museum was much faster and completely silent.

"On September 4, 2010, Pedro Melendez's 445th Birthday, there was an elaborate celebration, including the reenactment of the landing that originated in St. Augustine. Mark Menendez, a descendant of this famed explorer was also invited. The painting that you see here, was created by Mark Menendez. It is a copy of an oil painting created by Titan, a great Venetian painter," Mrs. Armstrong said.

"Are you aware of any artifacts that were found here in St. Augustine that may have been traced back to Pedro Menendez?" Imani asked, now politely.

"There have been many artifacts found throughout the years in St. Augustine. If you would like I can arrange an appointment with a gentleman at the Florida Museum of Natural History? The staff there is constantly updating their electronic database," Mrs. Armstrong offered.

I knew what direction Imani was going, but I really didn't want her to directly mention the carpet. If the museum has *The Agape*, game over. I was betting that they were in search of it just as we were.

"Well, Mrs. Armstrong really didn't offer us much, did she?" Imani said as we exited the Mission.

I wanted to point out that after Imani's conflicting remark about Christianity, we were lucky to finish our visit to the Mission.

"Do you want to have lunch and decide what we should tackle Next?" Imani asked, sounding surprisingly pleasant.

"On our way here I saw an inviting pub. It faces the Marina. I think it is called Meehan's Irish Pub," I said, leading the way before Imani could object.

"That's fine. I think I see it right there on the corner," she said, catching up with me.

We decided to split a plate of fish and chips and a large plate of oysters Rockefeller. The Guinness made me homesick, but I wasn't sure why since there was nothing to return home to.

"Okay. Why don't you call the museum, and determine if it is worth our time to drive there? I will check out *The Villa Zorayda*. There is some exotic ancient cat carpet there with a rather mysterious history. You, can follow up with that Massacre of the Huguenots. Our notes also suggest that we visit a church called *Memorial Lutheran Church of the Martyrs*. What happens if nothing leads us any closer to *The Agape?*" Imani asked.

"Then, we spend the remaining days of our visit sightseeing, shopping, and drinking cold Guinness," I said, raising my glass.

Chapter Thirty-Three

I have been in Sorrow's kitchen and kicked out all the pots. Then I have stood on the pesky mountain wrapped in rainbows, with a harp and sword in my hands.
Zora Neale Hurston, Dust Tracks on a Road

Imani Lewis and Phoenix Baldwin
St. Augustine, Florida
October 2017

Today I woke up early. Since Phoenix and I were moving in different directions. Stopping downstairs for a quick cup of tea "to go" seemed like an excellent idea.

St. Augustine is definitely a different environment at 6:00 am. The tourists are all recovering from their previous evening shenanigans, while all the service workers are only beginning their morning shifts. The streets are quiet. Occasionally I see a feral cat sipping from a saucer of milk on the doorstep of a quaint cafe.

"If you want to see the sunrise, I suggest you walk over to *Castello de San Marco*. There is a walkway that will take you through the back. It faces the bay. During this time of the year, it offers a fantastic view," a young man said while we were both stopped at the traffic light.

"Thanks," I said, following his advice.

The stranger was correct. There was no one else even close to where I chose to sit. I had no idea how many years had passed since I witnessed this daily event. It was a moment I appreciated yet often taken for granted.

When the dark clouds started revealing the sky, it was like a theatre curtain slowly exposing this impressive setting to a captured audience. It was a mesmerizing show that Mother Nature performs daily that many people ignore.

Once the sun slowly begins to move the sky's tapestry reveals a mere sunbeam that struggles to expose any glowing light. Then miraculously when the sun beam gains the courage to expand its horizon it lightens the universe with new sparks, offering endless opportunities. I want to grasp each of those sunbeams, hold them in my pocket until it's time to release them into sunsets later in the day.

Such a simple phenomenon when every shining moment that the sun rays offer invites us to explore a new occasion. One that we may choose to accept, or reject. This is our daily reminder to return later to the fleeting moments of twilight and dawn. That is the time when opposites once again merge into a day of enchanting moments. It is when reality and dreams dance harmoniously as one.

I checked my cell phone for the time. It almost felt sacrilegious even to be concerned about the shackles of time. But, as pleasant as this detour from my schedule has been, I do have an appointment with a famous cat rug at The Villa Zorayda in a few hours.

When I exited the *Castillo,* there was a road construction crew taking advantage of the early morning to remove some strange obstacles from the roads. To avoid crossing their path I made the decision to walk through the *Colonial Village* and somehow found myself on the corner of *Ponce de Leon* and *King Street*. By this time, it was about 8:30 am. Being unfamiliar with the area, I decided to sit down for a few minutes on a bench in the corner of an unexpected garden oasis to get my bearings.

A few feet away I noticed a historical marker. Just as I was about to move closer to read what was written, a relatively short, stout man placed his dark hand on my shoulder.

"Isn't it just a marvelous morning to take a walk through the park?" he said.

At first I thought that he must be talking to me, since I was the only other person nearby. But, before I could answer him, he was having a conversation with another voice that sounded like a French inflection. When I realized that there was no one else in our vicinity it became clear that this strange man was talking to himself in different accents. He was also talking in a variety of imaginary conversations.

When he took the seat next to me, I also noticed he was pushing a shopping cart filled with many different objects, from pillows and blankets to books, magazines, and canned food, as well as plastic bags with small bars of soap, like the ones in hotel rooms. That is when I realized this man was homeless.

His hand moved now from my shoulder to gently touching my hair pulled back in a long ponytail.

For some reason, it didn't bother me. Nor was I frightened.

"My name is Imani. What is your name, sir?" I asked, hoping that I would get his attention.

"Oh...people call me Professor. I guess because of all these books. It also maybe because I have claimed this bench as mine," he said, sounding reasonably normal for the moment.

"Is there something special about this bench," I asked, trying to follow the logic trail he was leading me on.

"Absolutely it is special! And, I will share it with you. This is where *Their Eyes are Watching God.* You know that as long as we stay here or in the garden space behind us, the demons will leave us alone," the Professor said.

Was this poor man referencing the novel by Zora Neale Hurston? I had no idea how this man could know this author. Is it possible that she lived in St. Augustine at one time? Maybe. I had to admit that I certainly didn't know anything about this ancient city.

"Are you familiar with that novel by Zora Neale Hurston?" I asked, hoping that he would stay in one personality.

"Are you asking me if I know that story? I know everything that the beautiful Miss Hurston ever wrote. She had a tragic life. Very much like mine. Two failed marriages; the first marriage took place here in St. Augustine, as well as her second divorce. If all that wasn't bad enough, the poor woman was falsely accused of molesting a ten-year-old mentally disabled boy."

At that moment, the Professor started telling his story by recreating a female voice, who I presumed was supposed to be Hurston. In that dialogue, Hurston's voice explains that she has her passport as proof that she was out of the country during those accusations. She also explains that because of this terrible experience, she lost her desire to write, although later it was discovered that the boy had lied.

I also remember reading that in 1960, Zora Neale Hurston died with no money and was buried in an unmarked grave. Later it was discovered by Alice Walker, the author of *The Color Purple* and literary scholar Charlotte Hunt in 1973. A tombstone is now in place commemorating Hurston at *Garden of Heavenly Rest in Fort Pierce, Florida.*

"Miss Imani what homeless camp are you staying in? You know it can be very dangerous out there in the woods. The Sheriffs usually leave me alone here in God's garden. I don't let anyone stay here. But, you can stay until we find you a safe spot."

I was touched by the Professor's offer. And, I realized for the first time this morning how awful I must look.

"Thank you, Professor. I wish I could stay longer and chat with you more about Ms. Hurston. But, unfortunately, I am already late," I said, getting ready to leave.

"Oh, my...I am sorry to hear this. I wanted to share a building that a true gentleman from across the pond restored for us homeless people. He was our hero. He saved many of our lives until Those Eyes that are watching God decided that he was needed in another community."

The Professor stood up and wrapped his arms around me.

"You know where I am if you have a chance to visit with me again. It gets lonely here, even with those friends that like to come out and visit with me without an invitation, I might add," the Professor said as I started walking away.

After I left him, I wished that I could have given him some money, but I had only my credit cards with me. During that entire time, the Professor never asked me for anything. I must plan on returning here before we leave to give him at least enough to purchase a meal.

On the way back to the *Casa de Suenos,* I noticed a used book store. I decided to see if they had any books by Zora Neale Hurston. There was one copy. I bought it. When I arrived back to my room, I turned to the quote that will always remind me of my meeting this morning with the Professor. It is in Chapter 18 when Janie and Tea Cake must find shelter from a dangerous hurricane. Like Hurston's characters are waiting to accept their fate, the Professor, and even myself "...seem to be staring at the dark while our eyes are watching God". None of us have control of our own destiny. I may as well be as homeless as the Professor.

Now at last I understand that the sunrise I witnessed earlier, "is the Sun, who scattered into flight, The Stars before him from the

Field of Night, Drives Night along with them from Heav'n, and strikes The Sultan's Turret with a Shaft of Light." (Omar Khayyam)

The Agape carpet has been here. I know it now. What I must learn is who else knows this?

The Villa Zorayda was closed to the public today. Mrs. Armstrong had arranged for me to have a private tour, with a historical guide. Thankfully she did not let my comment about Menendez's
The Inhumane slaughter of the French Huguenots interfere with my research.

Prior to touring the Villa, I was escorted to a private office where my host, Mr. Thomas Masters greeted me.

"I hope that you won't mind me giving you a short introduction to the historical significance of this quite fascinating piece of property. Since you only have a short time here at St. Augustine, I will not delve too deeply into all the mysterious parts that our ancient history has to offer. But, I also don't want you leaving without understanding a few of our most outstanding achievements," Mr. Masters said.

After we visited the Mission yesterday, I was skeptical about how much of what Masters had to share would be beneficial. Nevertheless, I did have the time to listen to his information politely.

"I certainly appreciate that you understand that my focus is on locating *The Agape*. And, it is not that I lack interest in how special St. Augustine is to all of the people who travel here, and especially to those of you who reside here. It is just that my partner, and I are working diligently to complete our expedition," I said, warmly.

Phoenix would have been impressed how diplomatic I can be when necessary.

"Your search for *The Agape* is not unknown to me. There are various paths that one may take in discovering its location. It truly depends on an individual's expectation. I certainly hope that what I share with you today will help you to achieve your goal," Mr. Masters said.

I did not hesitate to ask the obvious.

"Have others been here before me requesting the same information?"

Mr. Thomas turned to a portfolio located on the credenza behind him and handed it to me.

"What you are holding, my dear is a collection of photos and paintings of various Agape carpets located throughout the world. Those who have been fortunate enough to come in contact with it, even for a short period, have claimed a significant improvement in their personal lives," Masters said.

As I turned the pages in the bound portfolio, I was impressed at the detail of each image. Although the carpets were all significantly different in shades of color, what they did have in common were similar symbolic images. Everything from the cross, to the Star of David, to Khanda (symbol of the Sikh faith), Ankh (Egyptian key of life), Alpha and Omega, The Faravahar, (a sign of Zoroastrian, an Iranian religion, a crescent, (in Hinduism it represents a moon on the head of Lord Shiva, symbolizing that the Lord is the master of time).

What I held in my hands was totally unbelievable. Was this proof that *The Agape* has many different versions? If so, where are they all presently?

"How did you ever compile such an impressive collection?" I asked.

"This has been my passion for many years, Imani. The reason that I am sharing this with you is that I hope it will help you understand that your journey is a private one. Do not allow the temptation to make it anything else, or you will fail," he said thoughtfully.

I wanted to assure Mr. Masters that failure is not an option, but rather than defend my position, I took another approach.

"I would truly appreciate hearing more about how Villa Zorayda evolved, as well as, how the famous *Cat* carpet arrived here, Mr. Masters," I added.

"Let's start by you addressing me as Thomas, shall we?"

What I learned in the two hours that I spent with Thomas gave me a new vantage point. It was the first time I understood that Agape has many facets, each offering an opportunity to discover self-awareness.

I was now walking among a variety of priceless artifacts collected by a gentleman, Franklin Webster Smith, who created a winter residence here in St. Augustine. He was inspired by a 12th century Moorish Alhambra Palace that he recreated, naming his new home Villa Zorayda.

It was an impressive endeavor, but what interested me the most was the small room on the second floor that is now referred to as *The*

Egyptian. Showcased on the far right wall as you enter the vestibule is *The Sacred Cat Rug.* It is identified as both an ancient and haunted object.

When I was in Cairo, which now seems to have been a lifetime ago, I learned about this exotic item. Seeing it here now made me slightly nervous. It was as if I was traveling in a perpetual circular motion, never moving too far from my original starting point.

I recall being told that this Sacred Cat Rug was removed from its rightful place over 2,400 years ago by tomb raiders or perhaps treasure hunters. Nobody really knew the real story, only that it went missing unexpectedly. It was Abraham S. Mussallem somehow acquired this relic from a man known as Ben Yakar. The Mussallem family are also the current owners of *Villa Zorayda.*

Now this story that Thomas told me starts to become fascinating. First, there is little known information about Ben Yakar, who bought this rug for one franc in 1861. Prior to Yakar's possession, all that is known about the *Sacred Cat Rug* is that a fisherman found it on the banks of the Nile in a floating mummy casket. Most people know, although often ignored, that any item removed from the final resting place of wealthy Egyptians is going to be cursed. For an obsessed culture with immortality, it does seem logical that interrupting the natural progression to the afterlife would cause serious repercussions. As one Egyptian archeologist pointed out, "It would be similar to you Christians if you witnessed the devil yanking angels from heaven and started displaying them in the exotic animal exhibitions at your local zoo."

Some other notable facts that Thomas pointed out is that to the Egyptians using cat hair to weave the rug was considered god-hair since cats were considered gods. The fact that all the cat hair used also creates a cat image should be noted. I cannot ignore at least one of the similarities between this *Cat Carpet* and the *Agape Carpet.* Whereas the Egyptians used what they regarded as sacred cat hair to weave their carpet, *The Agape's* power of healing and spiritual power may be attributed to the hair used by Jesus and his disciples.

When I mentioned this to Thomas, he referred me to a carpet illustration in his portfolio that I must have passed without noticing.

"Take a good look at this pencil sketch of a carpet that one of the survivors from the Menendez massacre illustrates. It includes a carpet on the floor of the room where Francisco Mendoza, the chaplain accompanying Menendez is pleading to spare the lives of Jean Ribault and his soldiers. Unfortunately, the pleas were ignored," Thomas said.

I looked carefully at the crude drawing, noticing the familiar symbols that I recognized from the carpet photograph in Amsterdam. They were both the same. It was unbelievable, yet true.

"I have seen this carpet before in another country. Well, not the actual carpet, but a photograph," I said, sounding overwhelmed.

"Yes. It has appeared in a variety of different situations. What is exceptional about the *Castillo de San Marco* carpet is that it is still here. We just don't know where," Thomas said.

"What do you mean? How can you be sure that *The Agape* is here in St. Augustine?" I asked, anxious to hear his response.

"You may not like my answer since it isn't scientific. But, you must understand that St. Augustine is not what you might call a conventional city. We are used to many oddities that surround us, from the supernatural to the spiritual. Several mediums will attest to the fact that The Agape is still active in our community, or that at the very least, its influence has remained. I can refer you to an excellent psyche in nearby Cassadaga that might be able to give you more details," Thomas offered.

I was skeptical, but I had to admit that nobody else thus far had provided me with anything as specific as Thomas Masters.

"How far is Cassadaga from St. Augustine?" I asked.

"Not far seventy-six miles. But, if you give me a date and time, Lady Catalina can meet you at your convenience," Thomas added.

"Let me confirm with Mr. Baldwin and I will let you know tomorrow. I truly appreciate everything that you have shared with me," I said thankfully.

Now it was time to meet with Phoenix and compare our notes. If his day was as productive as mine, we are moving in the right direction. My only regret is that I could not do more for the Professor. Tomorrow I will make it a point to deliver him his own copy of *Their Eyes are Watching God.*

Chapter Thirty-Four

Do you think because I am poor, obscure, plain, and little, I am soulless and heartless? You think wrong! - I have as much soul as you, - and full as much heart! And, if God had gifted me with some beauty and much wealth, I should have made it as hard for you to leave me, as it is now for me to leave you.

Charlotte Bronte
Jane Eyre

Bran Hughes
Over the Rhine
1998-2017

Driving eight hundred and eighty-five miles with anyone will test your patience. It also forms forever friendships, if you are lucky. Living in Wales, I rarely drove anywhere. Traveling was always by train. It was enjoyable having someone else responsible for selecting the best route to take. But, perhaps my favorite memory of riding a train is the dining car. There was always a variety of freshly prepared sandwiches, crisps, chips, assorted cakes, and of course hot tea.

Faith called this a road trip. Before we left, she decided to map out our route. Twelve hours didn't sound like a very long drive, until I was reminded that we were traveling with several dogs that ranged in different ages. None of them, just like me, had ever been on a "road trip."

"It will be essential to make appropriate pit stops every few hours somewhere safe for the dogs to relieve themselves. And, naturally, I will prefer to be relieved in a restroom, not in a park," Faith said.

That journey was nineteen years ago. I never would have placed a bet on me staying here this long. Perhaps one reason was Faith, and the other Imani. In that order.

Faith used all of her savings to open a dog rescue. She purchased a fixer upper ranch house on five acres of land near her hometown, Glendale. I offered to help restore the house and barn. In return I was offered a rent free room for as long as I wanted. It was a fair exchange.

In reality I didn't need a place to stay. Pastor Liam arranged a lovely one-bedroom cottage that was located on the church property. Originally it was used as a recreation house for the Lutheran youth that met there for various activities. When the main building was eventually remodeled, the congregation decided to keep the tiny residence. Later It was designed as living quarters for any future interns. Unfortunately it was really too small for anyone except a bachelor. Thankfully, it was perfect for this bachelor.

When I accepted the new position as Lutheran Liaison, it came with a suitable income, housing, and SUV. This became very important later since Faith needed my Hippie Gypsy Van for transporting animals, as well as all the bags of food required to feed a growing kennel.

My living arrangement was quite suitable. Several days during the week I would stay at my church dwelling, the remaining time I spent with Faith and the canines. We stopped counting how many different dogs were rescued. Finding them *forever homes* became the real challenge. But, somehow, most of them miraculously were placed in a reasonably timely manner. Those who were not became part of our family. And, after nineteen years with Faith, the furry children, and I, we're a family.

I was thankful for my new life. Whenever I became depressed, which was often, I was reminded of my many blessings. While watching the desperate homeless increase each month on the streets, I knew how easily it could happen. For most, it was only one catastrophic event that found them with no home. I always wanted to do more. It never seemed like enough was being accomplished. That was when Faith would remind me of all the progress that I made in *The Over the Rhine* Community since we arrived. She was right, but it just wasn't enough.

Timothy Thomas was a nineteen-year-old black young man shot and killed by Cincinnati Police for an outstanding traffic violation and other nonviolent misdemeanors. When the community learned that Thomas was unarmed, the community's anger exploded into some of the worst riotings since those in Los Angeles, known as the Watts Riots.

By 2009 *Over The Rhine* was labeled, rightfully so, as one of the most dangerous communities in America. Like most areas that were neglected in the 1920s, this was an anti-German neighborhood. Thanks to the First World War and Prohibition, many people who lost their jobs moved away from the area, inviting a new group of migrant workers from the Appalachian regions to replace them in the 1940s.

However, by the 1960s, when highway construction started to displace, many African American residents moved to the only affordable alternative, Over The Rhine. Unfortunately for this community, it is also where Hamilton County's homeless population has migrated.

I found this similar to the situation at St. Augustine only much more diverse.

Cincinnati's most significant landmark, *Music Hall,* houses 3,600 men. Down the street, known as *The Drop in Center,* houses 2,900. Sometimes, even more, when the temperature goes below 0.

"Do you remember, Bran when we arrived here, and you visited *Over the Rhine* for the first time? I thought that you would pack up and go home to Wales. But then you started to work with Pastor Liam and the others. Now *OTR* is once again a place with so many diverse activities. People don't mind sitting in the park, listening to concerts, or visiting the community theatre and art galleries," Faith said.

"Those were definitely challenging times. But, you are right. Since 1978 one hundred and forty-two new properties have been added. The types of housing now include Permanent Supporting Housing for those people that were once homeless. And, of course, the Family Promise at Lord of Grace Lutheran Church has created phenomenal opportunities. Maybe we should take another one of those little "road trips" that you always hint about. You, know...to celebrate nineteen years?" I said, walking over to Faith and giving her a short kiss.

"Like that will ever happen. Did you forget that I live in a dog zoo?" Faith said, laughing.

"Aren't there professional dog sitters that we could hire," I said, offering a solution.

"Not any that I would trust," Faith said.

I could tell how this was going to end. It happens any time I make a suggestion to take a short trip. Faith couldn't leave her fur babies behind.

"If you change your mind, you know my number, cutie," I said, walking away toward my SUV.

I was already late for my meeting with Pastor Liam.

"Maybe we can go listen to Liam's band Saturday night at *The Blue Wisp?*" I heard Faith say from afar.

"I will ask him if I make it on time to our meeting," I said, waving goodbye.

Pastor Liam is a Pied Piper that everyone follows. Some call him a rock star; others refer to him as Pastor L. All I know is that when I arrived here from St. Augustine, *Lord of Grace Lutheran Church* was merely a small city church with mostly an elderly congregation. This church was in serious need of being resuscitated with the breath from the Holy Ghost.

There were three services but none of them had more than twenty-five people each Sunday. What was worse, was the lack of children. Without young ones there is little opportunity for growth. But, this Pastor was never discouraged. Each week he would always provide an interactive children's sermon for the four or five children led up to the front of the church by their parents. And each child would walk back to their parents, smiling.

"Do you ever get discouraged, Pastor, by the lack of members attending each week?" I asked once.

"Not really Bran. I know that people will start to come once they understand that *Lord of Grace Lutheran Church* is a place that welcomes everyone who walks through this door. Just like what we always say at the conclusion of our service, "Go forward! Live, laugh, and celebrate," Pastor Liam said.

He was right. After one year of his calling, Lord of Grace Lutheran Church tripled its membership. Families flocked like sheep to sign their children up to attend Vacation Bible School. Then later they enrolled them in the Parish Church School. Soon, those children were bringing their parents on Wednesday evenings to a potluck. That was a direct pathway to Sunday services.

Lord of Grace Lutheran Church offered an 8:00 am conventional service, followed by a 10:00 am contemporary service, and finally, an 11:30 am worship for families whose children attended Sunday School. After five years the church was barely large enough to accommodate all the members. The Church Council voted on a significant expansion project that would include room to house Family Promise regularly.

But, it was always Pastor Liam's sermons that energized his parishioners. They were gentle stories that inspired everyone to seek their own calling. Often times the congregation would be treated to the Pastor accompanying the music director by playing drums, or bongos. This was another added dimension to the spiritual energy that was always inviting.

Today, I was meeting with the Pastor at a new coffee shop in Hamilton. It was recently opened by one of our own members. *The Fringe Coffee House* originated with the desire to empower inmates, ex-felons, and anyone or everyone that is at "the fringe of society." The goal is to provide opportunities to live healthy lives. The unique décor with various murals on the walls is a vivid expression of a commitment this establishment has made to our community. Every time that I meet someone here, I recognize some new art that has a moving message.

Not only is the art a reflection of the music that is dedicated to the famous musicians, but it also invites local talent to share their vibes with the neighborhood. This is supported by one central mission statement that predominantly reminds everyone who visits that *You Are More Than the Worst Thing You Have Ever Done.*

"Bran, over here, man...take a seat," Pastor Liam said when I walked in the door.

"Sorry for being late, Pastor. Faith and I started reminiscing about the past and before I knew it, the time just flew by," I said, apologizing.

"I know exactly what you mean. Every time I come here to meet someone I end up staying for hours. There is just something about all these great pictures that surround us that makes it difficult to leave. Did you know that over twenty-four local artists have contributed their art inside this building? It just makes me want to share all of this with the world," Pastor said energetically.

I also thought it might be the third caramel latte that Liam had that contributed to his enthusiasm.

"So, what's the exiting news that you said you had? Inquiring minds, like mine, want to know," I asked.

"Okay. There are actually several items on our agenda that are exiting. First, now that the reception hall in the annex is complete we will be hosting the *Family Promise* guests at least once a month. The administration has approved us. That means we need to make the room welcoming. Years ago Pastor Marcus gave you a carpet in St. Augustine to deliver to me. We placed it in the attic until there was proper time to unveil it. Now is the right moment," Liam said.

"Do you even have any idea what condition that carpet is in? I mean, Liam, it was in the attic at Memorial Lutheran for so many years that nobody wanted to open it. I am afraid that before we can use it for those families, it will need to be inspected and maybe even fumigated," I said reluctantly.

"Oh, my dear friend you have no idea what *The Agape* has seen during its lifetime. That carpet has stories beyond your imagination. All that I can tell you now is that when that carpet is ready to be opened, it will be something so spectacular that it will take your breath away," Liam said, touching my shoulder.

"I hope that you know what you are doing, Pastor. Naturally, I will follow your instructions, but I want to be on record that I warned you if anything goes wrong," I said, quite skeptical.

"Noted, 'Doubting Thomas.' You do know where that term comes from, don't you?" Liam asked.

I had to sadly admit that I could not recall what that phrase meant. But I suspected that Liam was about to educate me.

"Thomas was the disciple that refused to accept that Jesus was resurrected until he had first hand evidence. You should read John 20: 24-29 for the specific story. Anyway, moving right along to the second agenda item. We will be hosting visitors in a few days from St. Augustine, Florida. They are searching for *The Agape* carpet which you now know that we have. From what Marcus tells me the two travelers have been on this journey around the world for months. He has not told them that their odyssey is about to end shortly. This is because they still have no idea of its power. Just like you have no idea, Bran. So, when they arrive it will be important for us to reveal the carpet at the right moment. Do you understand, Bran?" Pastor Liam said.

"That should not be difficult, since I really have no idea why that carpet is of any importance to anyone. May I kindly inquire who these visitors are and where they will be staying?" I asked, feeling fairly confident that they would not be housed in my quaint cottage.

"Their names are Ms. Lewis, and Phoenix Baldwin. I don't have much more information than this to share with you other than Mr. Baldwin is British and Ms. Lewis is American from New York, I believe. Anyway, they will be staying at the Marriott in West Chester, near Lakota West High School. I believe that they are planning to rent a vehicle releasing you from being their chauffeur. Anyway, as I get more information about their arrival, I will let you know," Liam said.

I nodded in agreement. It was time for another latte.

"What could possibly be as important as the previous two items?" I asked, realizing that it was getting late.

"The third item is that tomorrow night at *The Blue Wisp* our band *Stratum* will be the third group. Are you and Faith doing anything tomorrow night? Mandy asked if both of you could come. I know she would love to see Faith," Liam asked.

Liam's wife Mandy and Faith became friends as soon as they met. I was sure that she already knew about the gig before I even left her house. Over all these years both Liam and Mandy must have adopted at least six of Faith's rescue dogs making the bond between us almost like family. The only oddity is that, ironically, Faith refused to join the church.

"How can someone whose mother named her Faith be so skeptical about God's calling," Mandy would say.

"I can't resolve in my mind that God would allow all the unfortunate, evil events to happen to so many innocent animals, Mandy. When you can give me an honest answer to that, maybe I will change my mind," Faith would argue.

Nevertheless, Faith did participate in all the church programs, as well as volunteering whenever they needed her. She also contributed to many different committees. When I asked her why she would agree to everything else, and not membership, her response was that,

"Every new person that I meet is a prospective dog owner that I can call on to be a forever family. You know Bran that really is my calling."

That was a fact. Faith loved each of the dogs that she rescued more than any other human that I ever met. Whenever she saw stray dogs wandering the streets she would pull off the road to rescue them. She also worked with other nearby rescue teams to find dogs abused by their owners or abandoned. Many of the dogs she brought home were given to the shelters only because they were too old, and the owners didn't want to watch them die.

Faith would comfort each of the rescue dogs every day. When death was imminent, she would lovingly hold each one of them until they passed on. Faith may not have publicly affirmed her belief in God, but every day she demonstrated it by the life she chose to live.

Chapter Thirty-Five

Faith cannot be inherited or gained by being baptized into a church. Faith is a matter between the individual and God.

Martin Luther
German Professor of Theology

Phoenix Baldwin and Imani Lewis
St. Augustine, Florida
2017

While Imani was out exploring the exotic *Villa Zorayda*, I somehow got the short end of the stick. My morning was going, to begin with breakfast at the *Salcedo Kitchen* on St. George Street with Pastor Marcus of Memorial Lutheran Church of the Martyrs. Since we had never met before, I was not sure how to recognize him.

When I got the call last night confirming our appointment Pastor Marcus suggested that we start the morning with a traditional Spanish breakfast only a four-minute walk from the famous Castillo de San Marcos. I didn't feel that it would be appropriate to tell him that I had just spent a couple of weeks in Spain eating authentic meals.

When I arrived at the *Salcedo Kitchen*, my first impression was that the small building, with its white stucco-styled roof, was true to its Spanish roots. Inside there was an open hearth that also added to the comfortable, inviting ambiance.

"Welcome! Welcome, Mr. Baldwin! I am Pastor Marcus Welles. It is truly a pleasure to have you join me for breakfast. I was hoping to also meet Ms. Lewis?"

Since I was the only customer in the restaurant it was easy to assume who I was.

"Please, Pastor, call me Phoenix. No need to be so formal. Miss Lewis is visiting the *Villa Zorayda* this morning. She is pretty excited to be on a private tour. The quite infamous *Cat Carpet* is an item that she is particularly interested in. She will meet us for dinner later this evening," I said.

"That is something I look forward to. Perhaps she will be able to answer some of my questions about that mysterious artifact. I hope that you don't mind meeting here for a traditional Minorcan breakfast. I thought that it would be a great place to introduce you to what we will be soon visiting," Marcus said, handing me the breakfast menu.

"It is very thoughtful of you to spend the day sharing some of this rich history that surrounds us," I said, quite impressed.

"I am always grateful to be living in this historical time capsule. Where we are now sitting was constructed during what historians refer to as the First Spanish Period. That period is documented as beginning in 1565 and lasting until 1763. When Spain regained Florida in 1783, Pedro José Salcedo, a Captain of the Royal Corps of Artillery, bought this lot.

By 1805 a Minorcan fisherman and farmer Pablo Sabate purchased the house. In 1962 during archeological excavations, the St. Augustine Historical Restoration and Preservation Commission undertook this property as their project. At one time the *Salcedo Kitchen* was a part of the living history museum. Bakers Bessie Bargmon and Lizzie Murray became famous for their orange, vanilla, lemon, almond, cinnamon, rum cookies, turnovers, and fresh bread. I would strongly recommend the sweet potato turnover and, of course, the scone," Marcus said.

"My goodness! Does every restaurant in this city have such impressive credentials? I could eat my way through the centuries. It certainly would be much more entertaining than sitting in a research room," I said.

Marcus was not exaggerating about the bakery. Even the scones, which I must admit I was skeptical about, were outstanding. The rustic atmosphere may have contributed to the delightful taste. Regardless what the reason might be I was impressed.

"Now that we have had our caffeine boost and our sugar adrenaline we are ready to move on to *Castillo de San Marcos* just right across the street. What do you say?" Marcus asked.

"I am definitely prepared for my next lesson, Pastor. Aye, Aye, My Captain," I said, saluting.

"Very well, then. Please let me know if I begin to get carried away with historical facts. I know that *The Agape* is your primary investigation. Still, because this carpet is much more complicated than many people realize, I will attempt to give you as much insight as possible. This will provide you some additional insight that may help you recognizing it.

It was encouraging that at least there was someone who acknowledged that *The Agape* does exist and that I might have the opportunity to find it.

Any person that visits St. Augustine knows where *Castillo de San Marcos* is located. It is often the very first structure seen when entering the city. Located on over twenty acres of land on a small hill overlooking Matanzas Bay, Pastor Marcus and I walked past all the visitors waiting in line. At the front, we were allowed immediate access once the attendant saw our VIP Passes.

"There are definitely advantages having a few influential people who work for the city council," Marcus said, leading the way.

As I followed the Pastor it was soon obvious that we would not remain on the traditional path intended for the tourist. We passed several large rooms which I presumed were soldier barracks. The vast interior courtyard, where the cannons were located, was probably a popular site for visitors to stop, watch the firings and weaponry demonstrations. But, we just kept walking.

At last, Marcus lead me up some stone stairs to an observation deck. It was an excellent view of the sailboats on the horizon.

"There is so much history surrounding us here that I often come simply to meditate. The voices of those innocent souls that were massacred for their faith echo through these chambers. It is a sobering feeling; I must confess," Marcus said quietly.

This was the same incident that Imani addressed Mrs. Armstrong with when she was paying homage to Pedro Menendez. I was curious to hear how Marcus, a man of the cloth, justified honoring the founder of this historic city. But, I decided against asking too many questions that might make my host uncomfortable.

"I brought you here first, Phoenix, to specifically help you understand how Memorial Lutheran of the Martyrs church contributed to *The Agape Journey*. When I have concluded my story, I hope that you and Ms. Lewis will be prepared for the final revelation," Marcus said.

What I was about to learn, sitting here surrounded by 17th-century coquina stones, would change the course of my life, but at this moment, I had no idea how dramatic that change would be.

"I am curious why your church included the reference to the Martyrs," I asked.

"That is an excellent place to begin. First, and most importantly, our church wanted to honor the three hundred and fifty French Huguenots/Lutherans who were slain directly beneath where we are now sitting. This is why the surrounding waters are called Matanzas, translated it means 'massacre.' Many people still believe the innocent Frenchmen's blood still runs through the inlet."

"Were there no survivors?" I asked.

"Menendez did spare the lives of a select few men, including some musicians. Apparently, Pedro was a music lover. One very fortunate young man who played the fife became a legend in his hometown twenty-one years later. When Sir Francis Drake approached St. Augustine in 1568, Nicolas Bourguinon, now known as the fifer, paddled his small boat toward Drake's vessel, playing as loudly as he could *The March of the Prince of Orange*. It was clear to the French soldiers that no Spanish Catholic would play this tune. The crew identified the musician as one of the few surviving Huguenots.

Later Drake burnt down St. Augustine and returned Nicolas to his French village. In honor of his bravery *The March of the Prince of Orange*, also known as *Wilhelmus van Nassouwe*, became the national anthem of the Netherlands. The words are pretty moving once you understand the background," Marcus said, handing me the famous lyrics to that tune.

He was right. Reading the lyrics, particularly in this iconic setting was quite poignant.

Alas, my flock! To sever
Is hard on us. Farewell,
Your shepherd wake wherever
Dispersed you may dwell
Pray God that he may ease you
His Gospel be your cure.
Walk in the steps of Jesus
This life will not endure.

Into the Lord His power
I do confession make
That ne'er at any hour
Ill of the King I spake.
But, into God the greatest
Of majesties I owe
Obedience first and latest
For justice wills it so.

"May I keep this, Marcus? The words are quite powerful," I said, surprisingly moved.

What I wanted to avoid now are any further emotional roller coaster distractions. It was time to move forward. I decided to share with Marcus what we learned in Spain.

"When we were in Santander I was informed that before Menendez left for Florida his wife presented him with a carpet that she received from a beggar. That carpet, she was told, had powers to protect Menendez from any harm. Have you ever heard this story?" I asked, hoping for clarification..

"Yes, and no. There are many stories about a carpet with supernatural powers. Remember Phoenix that I live in one of the most haunted cities in the world. Everywhere we go, someone has a new story about a ghost or a sacred stone. What I can tell you is that Memorial Lutheran was gifted a remarkable relic by an original member of our congregation. It was in her will that this family heirloom is kept in a safe place until the proper time came to unveil it once again. Of course this was prior to the very first Lutheran church in St. Augustine. That church originated on December 14, 1924. First, it was a small group of close friends, really neighbors, who decided to meet in different houses for their religious services. When the chapel on 54 Saragossa was completed, three years later it remained a worship sanctuary until 1977. At that time our current church was built," Marcus explained.

"Does anyone know if this special relic was ever moved when that previous building was sold?" I asked.

Marcus still said nothing that identified this relic as a carpet. It could be just another red herring.

"Before we move ahead too quickly you should also know that in the new Narthex there is a six-foot painting by a local artist, Jean

Wagner Troemel. This illustrates the Martyr's story that continues to honor the French Lutherans who arrived here in 1564. Also throughout our church there are symbols to commemorate those Frenchman who refused to disown their Lutheran religion. The stained glass window above the door includes the French, Spanish, and sword symbols with the Lutheran rose.

In addition, the hand carvings on the front door and the pulpit remind us of our heritage. It is our mission to always celebrate God's message. And, yes, the historical relic that was gifted to us was moved to our new church. It remained in the attic until 1998, about nineteen years ago," Marcus stopped at that announcement.

What did he mean until nineteen years ago? Where did it go? Does he even know the answer?

"Are you suggesting that no one has ever seen this carpet? How could you not know where it is? Certainly Marcus, you must be aware that this carpet is over 2000 years old. Many people are searching for it. That famous *Cat* carpet hanging in *Villa Zorayda* does not even come close to the value of *The Agape*," I said, seriously.

Marcus moved silently away from me toward the end of the walkway. At first, I thought that he might leave. But, he did not. With his hands clasped behind his back he finally turned around and faced me.

"Phoenix, *The Agape* is safe and will soon make its debut. But before I tell you anything further Ms. Lewis needs to join us," he said.

"I absolutely agree that she needs to be here to hear this. But when will the exhibition happen? We would prefer, if possible, to get a private showing before its public unveiling," I said, knowing very well that I had no leverage to request this exception.

"There is still much you must learn about *The Agape* before it is viewed. Would it be possible for us to meet later this afternoon for a nice supper? Let's say at 6:00 pm at the *Casa Brava?* It is located on the first floor of the quite famous *Casa Monica Hotel* not far from where you are staying," Pastor Marcus suggested.

"Splendid. I know exactly where that is. When we leave *Castillo* I will text Imani and let her know the agenda for this evening. She will be as excited as I am about this new development," I said.

"Would you like to hear a little more history about the *Casa Monica*, or have I bored you enough with my stories?" Marcus said.

"Nothing that you have shared with me today Pastor has been boring. I might even say that during my entire adventure trying to find *The Agape* my visit to St. Augustine and listening to your stories has been the most enjoyable," I said politely.

"Very well. You can't leave St. Augustine without learning something about Henry Flagler. He is the next most influential man, after Pedro Menendez, to discover St. Augustine. Flagler was certainly charmed by this ancient city. His trademark can be found everywhere. I am sure that you already know that Henry Flagler was the co-founder of Standard Oil corporation? But, of course, he is also remembered for being a railroad pioneer, hotel magnet, and successful entrepreneur.

It was in 1887 that Flagler sold a parcel of prime land to Franklin W. Smith. He considered this to be a great business decision. At the time Smith was only regarded as an amateur architect from Boston.

Smith opened his hotel, *Casa Monica,* on New Year's Day 1888. It only took four months later for Henry Flagler to make an offer to purchase this new business, complete with all furnishings, including all the silver pieces, for $325,000. Immediately Flagler renamed his new hotel *Cordova.* Flagler wanted the name of his hotel to reflect a strong noble family; one with a family crest and coat of arms that dated back to the 15th century in Spain. Mr. Flagler always liked the idea to connect his life with sovereignty," Marcus said, pausing to allow me to ask any questions.

"I did read that at one time there was a bridge built that connected the *Cordova* to the *Hotel Alcazar,* in 1902. Is that correct? I believe that building is now known as *The Lightner Museum?"* I asked, quite fascinated by all the details that Marcus knew about.

"Yes, you are absolutely correct my friend. Unfortunately, after Flagler's death and the Great Depression, the Alcazar Annex became dilapidated. Eventually that bridge was completely destroyed. It wasn't until St. John's County Commission, thirty years later that the decision was made to purchase the facility. This famous building was restored to be the county courthouse," Marcus added.

"Is it also true that Flagler experienced personal tragedies that even his wealth could not prevent? How did this influence the remainder of his life?" I asked, now genuinely curious.

"Great observation, Phoenix. That story will lead us to another connection that St. Augustine has with *The Agape*. When Mary Harkness, Henry's first wife, passed away in 1881 from health complications, she was only forty-seven years old. Henry was left to raise a young son by himself. Many believe that this was the main reason he married his second wife, Ida Alice Shrouds, so soon after Mary's death. There is also a third wife with many murky details. But, it was the death of Jennie Louise, Flagler's daughter with Mary, and his granddaughter, Margery, who died at childbirth that contributed to Flagler's truly tragic life. He was never able to overcome that sorrow.

There is a magnificent mausoleum that was added to the Presbyterian church downtown. Inside it includes Mary, Jennie, and baby Margery. Henry Flagler himself was also interred in a separate tomb when he died.

Soon after the deaths of his daughter and granddaughter, Flagler began to search for a carpet that possessed spiritual powers. He was hoping that *The Agape* would be able to console his grief. Nowhere was he able to find any peace of mind. Even with all of his wealth Flagler was unable to locate this carpet. Ironically, it was not far from where he lived," Marcus said.

"Why is *The Agape* so elusive?" I finally asked.

"Now Phoenix, you are finally beginning to appreciate the true power of this carpet. *The Agape* makes its appearance without prejudice. We have no idea what the criteria is. All we may expect is the unexpected," Pastor Marcus shared.

"If what you are telling me is accurate then how do you know that it is about to surface?" I asked.

"That is an easy answer. We have been provided with a foreshadowing; you may wish to call it a prediction. This prediction prepared us for you and Imani's arrival. All will be made much more apparent this evening," Pastor concluded.

Before I even got past the exit of the fort, I stopped to call Imani on my phone. Just when I was about to tell her how close we were to *The Agape,* I could hear Imani screaming on the other end of the phone.

"Phoenix! This is just unbelievable! My father, who I haven't seen for forty years, is here! My Dad is right here in St. Augustine. At

least he was in 1996. Can you believe this! And, I think that maybe I can finally find him!"
Imani announced.
My news could wait.

Chapter Thirty-Six

Miracles are a retelling in small letters of the very same story which is written across the whole world in letters too large for us to see.

C. S Lewis

British writer and lay theologian

Phoenix Baldwin and Imani Lewis
St. Augustine, Florida
West Chester, Ohio
October 2017

At the corner of St. George St. and St. Francis, I discovered a very inviting sanctuary surrounded by many shade trees. There was a sign that proclaimed the area *St. Francis Park*. Past the sign, there was a brick path leading to a water fountain. As I continued walking to the corner there was a moss covered statue of St. Francis of Assisi. He was holding two doves. The old plaque at the foot of the statue reads like:

"God make me an instrument of your peace...Where there is hatred let me sow love...Where there is injury, pardon...Where there is doubt, faith...Where there is despair, hope...Where there is darkness, light, and where there is sadness joy."

St. Francis Assisi

As a young boy my mother read this same message to me. It was one of those lessons that made sense to me at one time. Why did I forget these simple words? Perhaps because they are much more challenging to live by when you are an adult?

On the bench I took a seat near the St. Francis statue. I tried to reflect on the course of my life. When Imani rejected my affection it was not directed entirely towards me. It was her fear that caused that reaction. Not entirely unexpected once I take into consider the cause for her apprehension. Why should she trust me? I have given her no reason to trust me.

In retrospect, I have the same lack of trust toward my own family. They may not be nearly as wealthy or famous as Henry Flagler, but even Flagler could not escape the demons that finally destroyed him.

Was Pastor Marcus also trying to warn me that searching for *The Agape* could also result in tragedy? Marcus did warn that the purpose for searching *The Agape* must be a righteous endeavor. If not, the journey will be futile. This certainly is something to consider. Maybe, just maybe, our meeting this evening at *Casa Monica* will reveal the final solution to this puzzle.

When I arrived at the steps of *Casa de Suenos,* it was Imani's room that I went to first..

"What took you so long to get here? Do you think that the Pastor will have time today to see me? I can't believe that this is happening so quickly...and, I have tons of questions to ask Bran," Imani said, sounding like an excited child.

"Just calm down first. I know how thrilling this news is, but maybe you can just clarify what this is all about. And, just in case you are still interested, I think that we may have found *The Agape*. Do you remember? That 2,000-year-old carpet that we have been trying to track down for months. I have some exciting news to share with you also," I said, finally getting Imani to sit down and listen.

"Of course I am excited about your news! I apologize if you thought that my news meant that *The Agape* was any less important. It is just that since my mother's death and then when my grandparents both passed, I have felt that any roots I might have had were taken away forever. But now, with this letter, I know that Bran wants to see me again. I have kept his letters in this binder ever since I was fifteen years old. The only one I never opened was this one," Imani said, handing the envelope to me.

I read the short note and then noticed the postmark. It was from St. Augustine, dated 1996. That was nineteen ago. I didn't want to point out the obvious to her, but she must also wonder why this was the final letter. Imani needed to be prepared for the worst. Marcus may very well tells her that her father is no longer alive. I will avoid that scenario now.

"Well Imani it is your lucky day. Today I am also the bearer of good news. We have a dinner meeting at *The Casa Brava* tonight with Pastor Marcus. He wanted you to be included when he was ready to reveal where we would find *The Agape*. This will also give you the perfect opportunity to ask him about your father," I said, relieved.

"Oh, yes. You are absolutely correct. The timing could not be better. Depending on what we learn tonight I also have a tentative appointment with a psyche who claims to know where *The Agape* can be found. I know that doesn't sound very scientific, but from what I understand, supernatural soothsayers in St. Augustine is a very reliable source," Imani said.

"I will keep this in mind if tonight ends up a fiasco. At the very least, we will enjoy a nice meal," I said, walking toward the door.

"It shouldn't take us more than thirty minutes to walk to *Casa Monica*. The pleasant Florida weather should make it very enjoyable. I will meet you downstairs in the garden, on time, as usual," Imani said.

I was tempted to point out all the times that I have waited for her, but knew it would only result in an ugly scene.

Once, Phoenix left my room, I held the letter my father wrote me. It smelled like vanilla with a slight aroma of cinnamon.

Does he smoke a pipe? Does he like lemon meringue pie? Is his red hair the same as mine? When he falls asleep does he turn on his right side? What is his favorite color?

All of these questions are running wild through my mind. Is it too late to start believing in God? I certainly hope not.

At exactly 5:30 pm, I entered the private garden. Under a giant magnolia tree for just a few seconds I hesitated moving any further. A rather elegant man with raven black hair a few feet away from me was reading a local tourist magazine. When the stranger noticed me, I recognized that the gentleman I was admiring was Phoenix. He immediately smiled at me as I approached his table. It was a smile of confidence. The type of confidence that no one dares challenge. It is that same, charming, irresistible demeanor that is both comforting, and at times annoying. No man should have that much chutzpah.

"Right on time. Very impressive, Lady Bud. I particularly like what you have done with your hair. The French braid gives you just a slight amount of mystery. Shall we start our walk, my lady?" Phoenix said offering me his arm.

I accepted. Nothing was going to ruin this evening. For the very first time in my life I felt like I belonged on the arm of a handsome man.

We were greeted at the restaurant by Pastor Marcos, and his wife Elizabeth.

"Would you like a cocktail before dinner? Or should we be seated and then order?" Marcus directed the question to both of us. I allowed Phoenix to make the decision.

"Whatever you decide will work for us," Phoenix said, volleying the answer-back.

After a few minutes of introductions, the hostess signaled that our table was ready.

Elizabeth reviewed with us the various cultural opportunities that St. Augustine has to offer. I didn't want to be rude, but my mind was preoccupied with locating my father. Marcus must have sensed my anticipation, although it was Phoenix that changed the topic.

"Imani has just learned that her father, Bran Hughes, is a member of your community. Can you perhaps tell us how we may contact him?" Phoenix inquired.

There was a slight awkward moment of silence. I could feel my breath being sucked out of my body. But then, Marcus finally replied.

"I was hoping to gradually lead into this subject. How did you learn that your father was here? "Marcus asked.

"Years ago I was given a collection of letters. My father sent them once a month. I was never aware of them, or even him, until my mother passed away when I was fifteen. For years I have read each one of those letters many times. It was just the last one I refused to open. It never seemed to be the right time to read that final message. But, today, for some reason, it just felt like the right time. I just hope it isn't too late," I said, thankful to be able to share this news.

"I can only imagine how excited you must be, Imani. First let me assure you that your father is alive and safe. Unfortunately, he is not in St. Augustine," Marcus waited for all of this information to settle.

"But, you do know him, correct? And, if he isn't here, where is he?" I asked, confused but also relieved to learn he was alive and well.

"Oh, yes, Bran and I have been friends for many years. His outstanding contribution to this community improved the homeless situation significantly for so many people. Many regard Bran Hughes as a messiah for the needy. It is because of him that we now have a homeless shelter downtown. It was able to be staffed with professional health workers who volunteer their time. All because of your father," Marcus added.

"I met a homeless man on King Street this morning that mentioned that haven," I said.

"When your father left St. Augustine, many people, regretted his move, including your father. But his mission meant that he be sent to a new location. I must ask you Imani to be patient just a little longer. Everything about *The Agape* and your father will soon be revealed," Marcus said in his comforting pastor voice.

Phoenix reached his hand under the table to hold mine. I could feel his fingers wrapped around mine. It was the first time since Santander that I had felt his touch. This time I did not fight the sensation. For just a slight moment I caught his eyes. I knew what they were saying to me without hearing the words. But then Phoenix discreetly whispered, "We got this, Imani. Stay strong."

I merely nodded my head slightly assuring Phoenix that I was still in control of my emotions. At least I was trying to be.

Dinner would have been much more enjoyable if I had not been so anxious to finish. It was difficult to concentrate on food, or even those around me when all I wanted was answers regarding my father. What kept me grounded was my obligation to Phoenix, as well as myself. It was *The Agape* that brought us here to St. Augustine and I were determined to complete this journey. I am sure it is what Bran would tell me to do also.

"I must say that in the past forty-eight hours I have spent in this city everywhere I go leads me to a new epiphany," I said, trying to relax.

"If you were able to stay longer I would introduce you to many groups of people that would all attest that their moving to St. Augustine was a calling from God. Naturally at the time none of them realized this. It takes time to truly understand what our true quest in life is. Once we accept this challenge, the Holy Spirit takes charge," Elizabeth said.

"I am not sure if one dinner, regardless how spiritual, can convince me that the Holy Spirit will change the course of my life. Although, I admit I wish it was that easy," I said, trying to be honest respectful.

"Actually it is that easy, once you allow the spirits to guide your choices," Elizabeth said, with conviction.

It was Phoenix, the natural diplomat that attempted to clarify what I said.

"Isn't it St. Augustine of Hippo that affirms God as the father, the son, and the Holy Spirit? Although it may appear we are addressing three Gods, it is St. Augustine teaches us that this 'Supreme Trinity' is omnipotent. Recently I have personally learned right here in this city that the Holy Spirit acts as a comforter, God's advocate during times when it is difficult to accept our human limitations."

"Quite eloquently expressed, Phoenix. I couldn't have said that any better, my son. Have you ever considered studying theology?" Marcus asked.

I could not wait to hear how Phoenix was going to answer that question. There was never a doubt in my mind that he was brilliant. But, a quasi playboy transforming into a man of the cloth? That was beyond even my imagination.

"You are too kind, Pastor. But, I think that we will all be better off spiritually if I leave the difficult job of ministering to experts like you," Phoenix said, once again with humble grace.

I was watching a true match of intellectual dialogue. It was very entertaining. There was no doubt that Phoenix was an expert. He could have been the model for the very popular 1973 movie *The Sting,* with Paul Newman and Robert Redford. In that Hollywood movie the two con men are determined to orchestrate an elaborate scheme. Let me make it clear that I don't believe Phoenix is a con man, but he certainly could be if he ever chose that profession.

"May I suggest that this is an excellent time for us to move on to our next destination? We are parked in valet. Memorial Lutheran is too far for you to walk. They will bring the car around the side exit. Just follow Elizabeth around the corner. I will give the parking ticket to the driver and meet you out front," Marcus said, leaving us to follow his instructions.

On the way to the church, Elizabeth previewed for us what we were about to witness.

"As I am sure my husband has informed you already our church is named for the French Huguenots who were slain in the 16th century here in St. Augustine. Pedro Menendez gave his Spanish soldiers orders only to save those men willing to denounce their Lutheran religion. Although at this time anyone who was not Catholic was considered Lutheran, those men strongly believed their faith was worth dying for. We recognize the convictions of these early Protestants by including their memory in our church.

You will see the carvings on the pulpit and lectern. They were contributed by Dr. Carleton Calkin, a St. Augustine resident. All twelve of the apostles are included in the carvings."

As I was about to ask if we would also be viewing *The Agape*, Marcus pulled into the parking lot.

"I recall you telling us earlier that this new church was built to reflect a Moorish architectural design. Even the sixteen stained glass windows are filled with symbolism," Phoenix said.

"Yes, correct. You have an excellent memory my friend. But, it is inside that I want you to take special notice. While we were at the fort earlier I mentioned the large horizontal historical painting that artist Jean Wagner Troemel titled *La Caroline*. You will notice when we enter the sanctuary that it depicts the origins of our Lutherans in St. Augustine," Marcus was addressing me directly.

While I was admiring all of the artwork it was also worth noting how modest this historical church was inside. For some reason, I imagined that it would be much larger, almost the size of a cathedral. Instead, it was quite the opposite. There was a warm sense of belonging as if I had been here before. The church was familiar and inviting. There was no logical explanation for this familiarity, but it was present.

"This is quite lovely," I said, turning to Elizabeth. She was the closest person to me.

"Many people have expressed that there is a peaceful atmosphere. Marcus and I are always encouraging our visitors to enjoy that peace within these walls. I am pleased that you are experiencing this now," Elizabeth said.

Through the sanctuary we walked to the fellowship hall which was empty. The round tables and chairs were arranged for larger groups. We took a seat. Marcus moved to the front where a screen was projecting a picture. I assumed that it was the earlier church located downtown.

"Don't worry. I'm not going to show you our summer vacation photos from the Grand Canyon. Although, Elizabeth and I, of course, think they are delightfully entertaining," Marcus said, obviously amused with his comment.

Elizabeth turned off the lights. The first few photos were mostly St. Augustine landmarks. Similar to what you might see on a tourist channel. But, then, totally unexpected, there was a picture of a rather large, muscular man with hair the color of rose gold. It appeared he was busy planting vegetables in a garden. Nobody said a word.

Finally, Marcus explained that this young man arrived here from Wales nineteen years ago.

"He dedicated his life to helping the disadvantaged. Because of his commitment, our church is now able to reach many of the homeless who were destitute." Marcus stopped, waiting for my reaction.

"Is that man's name Bran

Hughes?" I asked, already knowing the answer.

"Yes, Imani. That man is your father. I wish that he was here now to meet you. Everything he accomplished here was a tribute to his love for you," Marcus said.

I didn't want to ask the next question, but it was inevitable.

"You did say my father is still alive, am I correct?"

I could not control the tears forming in my eyes.

It was Elizabeth that walked toward me. Her embrace was tender, yet ominous. I was ready for the worst scenario.

"Yes, Imani, your father is very much alive. He is spreading God's message to more untouchable people that need him."

But, I need him!

I wanted to scream, but my voice was gone. *How could I have found my father after these many years, just to lose him again? What type of God was I dealing with?*

Phoenix finally was the one to ask what the connection was between Bran and *The Agape*.

Marcus intentionally ignored that question. Instead he continued to show the photos on the movie screen. Most were illustrations of the Minorcans that were recruited by a cruel property owner named Andrew Turnbull.

"It was only because of this thirty-eight-year-old pastor, Pedro Camps, that these immigrants survived in such harsh conditions. When they could no longer take this abuse by the overseers, hired by Turnbill in 1777, the Minorcans began their exile. In November of that same year, a ship finally came to take any survivors to St. Augustine.

When they finally arrived, one of the Minorcan women was carrying a heavy object tied with twine. Frail from lack of food, lack of water, and fatigue somehow she found an Irish priest in the crowd. Before collapsing to the ground, she muttered the words, Agape, Agape!"

The next picture on the PowerPoint was that carpet.

Nobody said a word. I got up and walked closer to the screen to see all the images surrounding the outer edges. They were all there. Chi Rho (the crucifixion of Jesus), Ichthus (fish), Christian Trinity (three interlocking circles), a dove, horn, palm branches, a unicorn, Ankh, the sacred beetle.

"How did you ever get these pictures, Pastor?" I asked overwhelmed by the images.

"Years ago, before my time, the carpet was delivered here wrapped in plastic with specific instructions that it should remain under wrap in a safe place. It was not until your father, Bran Hughes, received his calling to leave for Over-the-Rhine that any of us knew about this carpet," Marcus explained.

"I am still confused," Phoenix said.

"Has *The Agape* carpet ever been opened? We were told in Santander that the carpet was with Pedro Menendez. Is this the same carpet?" Phoenix asked.

"We were not aware of any spiritual powers attributed to this artifact. When I received a call from Pastor Liam in Cincinnati, Ohio, he enlightened me on the importance of this carpet. Once it was explained how *The Agape* was to be used, I agreed to send it with Bran when he left," Marcus said.

"What you are telling us is that for nineteen years this carpet has resided in a small community church in Ohio? And, this is where my father is right now?" I asked.

"*The Agape,* is in Ohio. During the renovation process at *The Lord of Grace Lutheran Church* the carpet has remained in storage. I am told that Pastor Liam is preparing a celebration where the carpet will be seen for the first time," Marcus added.

Marcus told us that there was still plenty of time for us to be there during the unveiling. I was more concerned at this moment, how my father would react when he was told that I was one of the treasure hunters.

"Have you been in contact with my father since we arrived at St. Augustine?" I needed to know what to expect.

"No, Imani. Bran has no idea that you are here. He also knows nothing about *The Agape*. I will let you make the decision when and how you want to inform him. I do, however, want to emphasize to you and Phoenix that the carpet was never the purpose of your journey. It was the catalyst. At the end, you will both realize the true miracle of *Agape,*" Marcus said solemnly.

The evening ended quite pleasantly. It was a relief to know that my father was alive and well. Now I must decide how to let him know that I will be in Cincinnati.

"It is still early. Do you want to take a walk and talk about how we are going to approach this next trip? If Marcus is right about *The Agape,* and it really is the same one our expedition will be over. I will need to convince this Pastor Liam to let us purchase the carpet. For the right price, I am sure that this will not be an issue," Phoenix said.

"I saw a jazz club earlier today on St. George. I think it is called *Stogies.* Not too far from here. There is an outside patio, away from the crowd that we can sit and talk about our strategy," I said, leading the way.

I knew that offering to buy *The Agape* from the church was wrong. If my father left Wales to travel here intending to improve the lives of the impoverished, making a profit from his hard work seems sacrilegious. But, convincing Phoenix that his plan was wrong would not be easy. Maybe even impossible.

I found a seat near the garden while Phoenix went inside for some wine. The sounds from the jazz instruments were a combination of smooth and raspy, the perfect backdrop to a sultry October evening.

"The Chardonnay is from The Sebastián Winery, on King Street, chilled." Phoenix said, handing me the glass.

"Thanks. I never had a chance to tell you about this odd man I met this morning. He lives on the streets. There is a small park dedicated to Zora Neale Hurston where he sleeps. He goes by Professor. I would like to find him before we leave. I think he might remember Bran," I said.

"Your dad hasn't been here for nineteen years. I can't even imagine any of these homeless people are the same ones, Imani," Phoenix pointed out.

"Regardless. I would like to give him something. Maybe we can bring him some food before we leave. Just something, I don't know exactly what. I also have a book for him. He needs to understand that some people care," I said, feeling frustrated.

"I know that today has been really difficult for you, Imani. But, let's try to come to some agreement about how we are going to get this carpet. It's your chance for a Pulitzer, and quite honestly, it will be a personal achievement for me," Phoenix said, sipping his wine and enjoying a cigar.

"Let's first make sure that this carpet is *The Agape*. Do you think that we can get a flight by tomorrow afternoon? Cincinnati is only about a three-hour flight from here, I believe," I said, ignoring Phoenix's comment about leaving with the carpet.

"Yes, I believe you are right. I can make the reservations when we get back. When are you going to tell Bran that you are coming?" Phoenix asked.

"Marcus gave me Bran's personal cell number. When the jazz music stops, I am going to make the call," I said.

It took five rings before I heard a male voice answer.

"Is this Bran Hughes?" I asked.

"Yes…yes, it is. Who is this calling?"

"Imani, Dad…it is Imani, your daughter!" I said, shaking.

There was dead silence on the other end.

Chapter Thirty-Seven

Never be afraid to trust an unknown future to a known God.
                                             Corrie ten Boom
The Hiding Place

Phoenix Baldwin and Imani Lewis
Cincinnati, Ohio
2017

"Impossible…who are you? How do you know my Imani?"
The voice on the other end sounded like he was in pain.
How was I going to convince Bran who I am? Then the answer came to me.
"Dad…you named me Imani after a story told to you by the high priestess, Kahina!" I said.
Once again the phone was silent.
"You ARE my IMANI. I have never told that story to anyone but your mother and you," Bran said, finally.
"Yes, Dad. I am your Imani. I have been in St. Augustine for a few days. Your friend, Pastor Marcus told me where I could find you. I will be arriving tomorrow afternoon to West Chester. When can I see you?" I asked, anxiously.
"As soon as possible of course. Let me know what airport you will be landing at, and all the details. I will be there to pick you up, my darling," Bran said, thrilled.
"Yes. As soon as I have all the details I will text you. Dad…I love you," I said, my voice still trembling.
"And, I love you, Imani." I heard my father say as we concluded the call.

Phoenix arranged for a flight from Jacksonville to Dayton, with one layover at Nashville the following day.

"Are you sure you are ready for this meeting with your father?" Phoenix asked me as we were waiting for our airport van to arrive.

"I certainly hope so. I have been preparing for this day for thirty-seven years. I just never really believed that it would ever happen," I said.

"Just don't put too much of your soul in this first meeting, Imani. It may be difficult for both of you," Phoenix said.

Phoenix had shared with me the volatile relationship he had with his father. His reaction to me meeting my father was not surprising. But, this was my moment to reunite. I had no expectations that meeting with Bran now would wipe away all my years of uncertainty. But, it was a new beginning. Just knowing that this man wanted to show me love, after so many years of separation was enough at this point in my life.

Our plane was scheduled to land at the Dayton airport at 11:38 pm. We were renting a car this time since it was anticipated that we would need to drive between West Chester and Over-the-Rhine. Marcus was uncertain of the current location of the *Agape*. It seemed that only two people knew the exact location, and nobody wanted to share that with us yet.

"Are you sure you don't want me to drive you to the hotel? It is pretty darn late for a family reunion," Phoenix said when the plane landed.

"No, thank you. Bran will be here to pick me up. By the way, you do know how to drive on the right side of the road, don't you?" I asked, just realizing that this might be a problem.

"Absolutely. Do you really think this is my first trip to the US? I have probably driven more than you have. You live in Manhattan don't you? Nobody who lives in the City ever drives if they want to live. Regardless, call me if there are any problems with your ride," Phoenix said, looking for the car rental office.

"I will call you when I know what the plan is. You get some rest. I have a feeling that the next few days are going to be exhausting," I said.

As soon as we were able to retrieve our luggage from the baggage carousel, we parted ways. Since the Dayton airport was much smaller than I expected, there were far less people waiting for arrivals.

Before I even made it to the lobby exit, an attractive lady with platinum blonde hair walked directly towards me.

"Hello, Imani. I am Faith. Your father asked me to make sure that I meet you," she said, placing her arms around me.

I wasn't confident how to react. The first time I was to meet my father and he sends a stranger? Well, I guess if I want to be honest, Bran is also a stranger.

"I am so sorry sweetheart. It has been a crazy afternoon. I will try to explain everything on the way home," this petite lady said, taking my luggage.

Outside the terminal I asked Faith how she was able to recognize who I was.

"Are you joking? You are the spitting image of your dad," she said as we walked to a Volkswagen van painted with peace signs and hippie flowers.

"Is this my dad's car?" I asked, trying not to laugh.

"Kind of…I mean, we drove from St. Augustine in this baby, nineteen years ago. I use it now mostly for transporting the dogs. But when I got the call from Bran asking me to pick you up, I was on my way home from a delivery. I didn't want you to have to wait," Faith said.

I was curious about her relationship with Bran. Obviously it was close or he would never have asked her to meet me. I decided that this was not the best time to ask her.

"Your dad really wanted to be here. But, when he got that call from the suicide crisis center there really was no chance that he could make it here on time. You need to know Imani, that only a life or death emergency would prevent him from being here himself," Faith added, keeping her eyes on the road leaving the terminal.

I knew this was uncomfortable for her. We were both trying to be as friendly as possible under difficult conditions.

"I'm staying at the *Marriott* in West Chester. I hope it isn't out of your way?" I asked.

Phoenix was right. I should have gone with him. My naive expectations were making this situation very awkward. Now I have no idea what time I will make it to the hotel.

"Hotel? No way. Bran would kill me if I didn't bring you home. We have a guest room already set up for you. No debate on this subject," Faith declared openly.

She used the word "we" when she said home. I guess that answers my question. Of course Bran was in a relationship. Why not? He has every right to live his own life.

"I don't know if Bran had the opportunity to tell you, but Sunday is an important day of celebration at The Lord of Grace Lutheran Church. They are opening the new recreation room that will be used to expand the *Family Promise* program. Everyone in this community has been waiting for years for this day," Faith said.

Those were the last words that I remembered hearing.

When Bran carefully lifted Imani from the front seat of the Hippy Van, it was difficult for him to take his eyes off of her. He was hoping that she would wake up, but she was sleeping so soundly.

"This is where you belong, baby." It was all he could say at the moment.

Once he gently placed his daughter on the bed, her head safely on the pillow, and covered her with the warm comforter, Bran sat on the rocking chair next to the bed. A few times he gently stroked her hair just to insure that she was really here. When Imani began to move restlessly Bran reached for her hand and caressed it until she was once again still. He then picked up his guitar and began singing the same lullaby he did many years ago.

Do not fear
It is nothing but a leaf
Beating, Beating on the door
Do not fear, only a small wave
Daddy is here, my darlin' babe, Your daddy is here, to
Watch you smile.

When the sun filtered through the blinds, I saw him for the first time. His hand resting on his chest, a guitar at his feet. Bran Hughes was breathing the same air as I was; our hearts were beating at the same pace. Finally, all was right in the universe.

When his eyes opened and met with mine we were both silent. Neither of us said a word. But, it was Bran that moved toward me first. Instinctively his strong arms pulled me to his chest. It was the first time in my life that I ever felt complete.

"I have no idea how we found each other, Imani, but I will promise you that today my life is worth living again because of you, my darling," Bran said, looking into my eyes.

It took me a few moments to be able to articulate. There was just so much to say that I was speechless. Finally, I said, "I have all the letters that you sent me. Wherever I go, those letters are with me. I never felt that you were far away. But being with you now, I understand everything that you wrote to me so much better."

"Father Liam told me that you are here with a friend. Where is your friend? Is he someone important to you?" My father asked.

"His name is Phoenix Baldwin. We met when our paths began crossing. Both of us are searching for a spiritual carpet, *The Agape*. Pastor Marcus says that it is here, somewhere in Cincinnati. Maybe a place called Over-the-Rhine. I will tell you all about this later. First, tell me how you got here? Why did you leave Wales? I have so many questions?" I said, enthusiastic to begin our first day together.

Bran stood up excited also to share with his daughter what he planned for them this first day.

"I hope you like fishing. We are going to spend the day on the lake. Faith has a friend that is loaning me his boat today. Winton Woods is about nine miles from here. Close enough but far away from the masses," Bran said.

I never fished in my life. I wasn't even sure that I wouldn't get seasick. But the chance to spend hours alone with my dad was worth the risk.

When we arrived at the dock both of us agreed on silencing our phones for the duration of our boat adventure. Phoenix was probably ready to call the police. With all of this excitement I forgot to let him know where I was. Phoenix is a smart man. I did not doubt that he would figure out the details without any further explanations.

Eight hours on the lake provided us with plenty of time to talk honestly. We held nothing back. It was as if Bran knew what I was doing my entire life. I shared with him secrets that nobody else ever knew. Bran listened, never making any judgements. Finally, he did ask me directly about my relationship with Phoenix. I told him what happened at Santander when Phoenix touched my face and how frightened I became.

"You must not allow fear to dominate any passion that this man expresses toward you, Imani. Your mother never allowed herself to experience how magnificent and how powerful love is when it is equally shared with another. You Imani are a product of that love, and unfortunately also the result of Sarah's obsession with fear. Allow Phoenix into your heart now before you make the ultimate mistake," Bran said profoundly.

"Is that what you did with Faith?" I had to know how he felt about her.

"Yes. I never stopped loving your mother, but Faith gave me a new philosophy about love. And, let me tell you, Imani if anyone has the right to fear loving me, it is that lady. I had no direction in my life. Yet, Faith was willing to lead me in the right direction," Bran said, handing me his fishing rod.

"I think you are about to catch your first fish, Imani. Hold the rod tight, it feels like a fighter. Reel it in when you are sure it is ready," Bran said, guiding my every move.

Bran was right this fish was a fighter. But that fish had no idea how long I had been fighting.

"Congratulations Imani. Let's get a photo. I'd say he's about 5lbs. Too bad we need to throw him back," Bran said, removing the hook and tossing him into the river.

"That makes absolutely no sense. Why do people fish if they are just going to throw the fish back in the river?" I said, disturbed.

"Because Imani it is not the fish that is important, it is the challenge. Maybe an important life lesson as well," Bran said, offering me a beer to celebrate my victory.

That reminded me of what my Grandpa used to tell me about chess.

When we reached the dock I asked Bran about the important ceremony tomorrow at the church.

"Oh my goodness. I almost forgot. Pastor Liam has invited us to preview the recreation room tonight. The message that he left on my phone says that it is a VIP showing and you and Mr. Baldwin must not miss it. I am not sure what he means by that, do you?" Bran said, confused.

"Not really, but I better let Phoenix know. I haven't talked to him since we left the airport last night," I said, regretting now that I didn't call him earlier.

"Oh, wait a minute, Imani. Liam's text says that Phoenix already knows. He has been with Faith all afternoon. A play day with rescue dogs can change your life. I can't wait to hear how he survived that," Bran said, smiling.

"Phoenix surrounded by dogs? Now that would make an entertaining photoshoot," I said, amused at the very thought.

When we arrived back home Phoenix was outside with Faith sitting on the porch. I was not sure what to expect when I walked up the steps.

"Where are all the fish? Don't tell me they all got away," Phoenix said, offering me a seat next to him on the porch swing.

"It's not the number of fish that you catch. It is how you approach the challenge that is important," I said, winking at Bran.

"That sounds like your father's ideology on life. Can I get you two a beer, coffee, cider?" Faith asked, moving toward the front door.

"No, thank you, Faith. A hot shower before our evening at the preview sounds more inviting," I said, still not moving from the swing.

"I almost forgot to introduce you to Mr. Baldwin, Bran. He is a natural with animals. All the dogs want to go home with Phoenix," Faith said.

"Nice to meet you, Mr. Baldwin. I understand we are both subjects of the Queen," Bran said, extending his hand.

"Yes, that is correct. Are you now an expatriate? I know quite a few British subjects that are now calling America their home," Phoenix said.

"Not yet. But, it is Faith that makes a living in America the most beautiful country in the world," Bran said, placing his arm around Faith's waist.

It was definitely time to change the topic.

"Can you tell us a little more about what we can expect tomorrow when the Recreation Room at the church makes its debut?" I asked.

"I think that is exactly what Liam wants to tell us tonight. I just got another text that instructed me to have us all meet in the sanctuary at 7:00 pm. Since I was not included in any of the arrangements, I suppose we all will be enlightened together," Bran said, walking away with Faith to the kennels.

This left Phoenix and me alone for the first time since we landed at Dayton last night.

I took the lead before he could admonish me for leaving him alone with Faith and her menagerie.

"Look, Phoenix, I know I owe you an explanation. A text was the very least I could have sent you. But, honestly everything happened so fast, I really had no time," I said, sounding very guilty.

"This is a man you haven't seen for nearly your entire life. Imani. I know that you regard me as...I don't know, maybe a Mr. Darcy figure? You do know who I am referring to, don't you?" Phoenix said, smug.

"Oh, yes! What an ideal caricature. You are absolutely a carbon copy of Fitzwilliam Darcy. Do you have any idea how many times Jane Austen refers to 'Pride' in that novel?" I asked, feeling smug.

"No, but I am quite sure that you are going to inform me, aren't you, Miss Bennet?" Phoenix retorted.

Well, no I don't think I will share that with you. It will just make your head expand even more than it is," I said.

Phoenix started to reach out for my hand but then withdrew it quickly. That is when I did something entirely unexpected. I laid my head gently on his shoulder waiting for a reaction. It was the first time that I recall not feeling vulnerable, except earlier with Bran.

Phoenix stroked my hair with his hand without saying another word. The silence was powerful. We both admired the sun sinking behind the horizon, knowing that whatever it was that just happened was only the beginning.

"You do realize that there are two sides to a coin that are in opposition to one another? The significance is similar to your allusion to *Pride and Prejudice.* There are different ways of approaching the same situation. Once Darcy and Elizabeth can overcome their limitations, an opportunity arises to accept each other, and a new relationship is born. Are you ready now to simply allow it to blossom," Phoenix said, kissing my cheek lightly. He then walked away without waiting for any response.

There was nothing else that needed to be said.

Chapter Thirty-Eight

I cannot fix on the hour, or the spot, or the look, or the words, which laid the foundation. It is too long ago. I was in the middle before I knew that I had begun.

Jane Austen, Pride and Prejudice

Imani and Phoenix
West Chester, Ohio
October 2017

When Bran entered the church parking lot I noticed that Phoenix's car was the only one already here. For some reason I expected more cars.

"Pastor said to meet him in the sanctuary, so let's get this show going," Bran said, opening the door for Faith and me.

The lights shining outside through the stained glass windows were quite inviting. When we entered the narthex, Bran proudly pointed out the blueprints still taped to the wall.

"This church has added so many members that there was barely enough room even with three services. Now we can continue expanding without feeling crowded. Since no one is here, Liam must already be inside," Bran said, looking through a glass window into the sanctuary.

"Yes, I see them in the first pew in front of the altar. Phoenix must have gotten here some time ahead of us. Let's join them before I get the blame for making you late," Bran said, leading the way down the center aisle.

"Greetings, everyone. Take a seat. I know that we have not all formally met before, but I have been waiting for this day for a long time. Probably from the time Bran arrived here from St. Augustine, nineteen years ago. Can you believe how the time has just passed us by?" Liam asked, Bran.

"Every day has been a great adventure Liam. I am so pleased to have witnessed how everything we planned has finally been fulfilled," Bran said proudly.

"It has definitely been a remarkable transformation. But, before we move into the newest addition of our building I want to alert you on what is soon to happen. There have only been a very few people throughout history to ever behold what you are about to see. I have no idea what to expect. To be able to share this blessed event with you, regardless of the result, will always be a memorable moment I will cherish," Liam said.

"I am not quite sure I understand. Isn't tomorrow to be the official viewing of *The Agape?*" I asked.

"It will be a celebration, you are correct. But I predict we will all watch tonight is a very private and personal showing of The Agape. It would help if you appreciated that *The Agape* is always in control, not us. I am sure of only one truth; whatever happens, tonight is a message from God, and I am only his messenger," Liam said.

The Pastor then told Bran and Faith that located in the fellowship hall; they would find a delicious assortment of desserts prepared by the church ladies for tomorrow's festivities.

"I have asked them to provide a few samplers for you and Faith to critique. I can't wait to hear which ones are your favorites," Liam said as Bran and Faith exited the sanctuary leaving the three of us alone.

I wasn't sure what the Pastor had in mind, but it didn't take long for Phoenix to move closer to me on the pew.

"Now that we have a few moments of privacy I want to address the fate of *The Agape.* As I told Phoenix, before you arrived, Imani, only a few of the church council are fully aware of the desire to exploit this carpet. I would like to claim that I am the guardian of *The Agape, but* that would be inaccurate. *The Agape* needs no champion to protect it. For over two thousand years, it has traveled wherever it is needed. Sometimes with human assistance, but many other times with its power. On this occasion it was brought to me for the sole purpose of uniting lost souls. Once those souls are healed, its mission will continue through them," Pastor Liam paused, allowing us to understand the importance of his message.

"Are you suggesting Pastor that while we were searching throughout the world for *The Agape,* it was really leading us here for some spiritual purpose? Because, as unique as you make us sound, I certainly am not worthy of being chosen by any God to make changes in this world. However, I am prepared to assist you in your outreach programs. I have the authority to offer you a tremendous amount of money for the carpet. Indeed, enough for that new wing I noticed is still incomplete on the blueprint out front. There is little doubt that your congregation would reject, let's say three million dollars? You must realize how that amount of money can contribute to improving the lives of the homeless," Phoenix said, like the politician he always denied he wanted to be.

I could not believe that he actually made this proposition while sitting in the church. But, then again Phoenix never denied what he was here to achieve.

"My dear friend. You know that there is no value that can ever be placed on *The Agape*. But, it will not be my decision it will be yours once you see it. There is a story that I want you to hear before we view the carpet. After that, I will let you decide on where *The Agape* belongs."

At that moment, Pastor Liam stood up. I sensed that what was about to happen next would be quite enlightening, but I had no idea to what extent.

"When you were in St. Augustine, Imani, did you ever consider that the beggar you met, *The Professor,* may have actually been in disguise?" I could feel the color draining from my face.

How was it possible that Pastor Liam knew anything about my strange encounter with this man, unless Phoenix had told him. But why? Why would Phoenix share that with Liam?

I turned to Phoenix just about to ask him that question. But he must have expected this because he immediately took a very defensive stand.

"I assure you Imani I never shared that story with anyone," Phoenix stated adamantly.

"It was not Phoenix, Imani," Liam intervened.

"Then how could you have known about this?" I asked, perplexed.

"It was God. God told me. Yes, I have many dialogues with God. You see Imani, what God wants you to know is that he does not only appear to believers. Also there are many times he appears where we least expect it. Like on a corner dressed as a beggar.

Today He will be in the form of a carpet. You, Phoenix, Bran, and even Faith have all been chosen to experience the power of *Agape* in this form. Remember Imani, that I am only a messenger. You are all the receivers. Consider me God's conduit. After this revelation the time will come to make some very difficult decisions, ones that will alter the course of your lives forever. Do not be afraid to make the right choice," Liam said, with great passion in his voice.

When I heard this, it was the first moment in my life that I could not logically explain why I was here.

"If you are both ready for this last leg of your journey, I will send Bran and Faith a text to meet us in the Annex," Liam said, waiting for us to follow him.

We all stood up together. Then Phoenix leaned over toward me and whispered,

"We can still walk out the door. I am sure that I can convince Liam to change his mind. He is an intelligent man. He knows how much my offer can help his cause."

"I don't think that any of this has to do with logic, Phoenix. It has everything to do with facing our demons," I said, prepared to move forward, even if it meant independently.

Bran and Faith were already waiting for us as we approached the front door. Everyone was quietly waiting for instructions as if we were about to enter a solemn shrine. Maybe we were, but Liam was finished with all of his sermons. He turned the key, and we all walked in unified.

Although it was pitch black, there was a vague outline of some beds, separated by colorful wall dividers. I presumed that these cubicles were where the homeless families were to be housed during their visit. In the center was a large open area. We were all waiting for the lights to illuminate the remainder of this room.

Just as I was about to turn around and ask if anyone knew where I could find the light switch, an abundant stream of colors that I had never seen before in my life moved in a circular motion. It resembled a rainbow halo, with dazzling sparklers turning kinetically in ring shaped movements. The invisible maestro was now unifying each independent flashing explosion into a perfectly orchestrated cascade of golden moonbeams. The entire light show was a magnificent collection of electricity, resembling shooting stars, converting into thousands of shattered fireflies and illuminated starfish.

Then at last we could all see the large carpet lying in front of us. *The Agape* was ablaze with living colors so vibrant that we could feel it drawing us closer to its center until, at last, we all became a part of its tapestry.

Only Pastor Liam stood on the outer limits.

"Each of you will leave here tonight with a piece of *The Agape*. It will not be visible, but it will be felt every day. *The Agape* will now reside within your soul forever. Go forth, and discover your mission," Pastor Liam said, blessing us with the sign of the cross.

When the light show stopped we moved away from the carpet. Bran was the first to speak.

"How are we to know exactly what we are called to do Liam? Is there anything that you can tell us that will help us achieve our mission?"

"What you have experienced today is all that you need. When this room is opened to the public tomorrow morning whatever spirit we witnessed tonight will continue with our Family Promise obligations. I do not expect that there will be any light show, fireworks, or rainbows, as we have encountered. *The Agape* will do its work like it always has for over two thousand years, and you will do yours," Liam said, walking us out of the room and locking the door behind him.

When we walked to our cars everyone was still trying to comprehend what we just witnessed. I gave Bran a kiss goodnight and embraced Faith.

"If you don't mind, Phoenix and I have a few items to discuss tonight. I will give you a call tomorrow morning," I addressed Bran but looking at Phoenix for his reaction. He said nothing.

It was Bran that responded.

"Absolutely, sweetheart. This has been a very emotional evening. I hope the two of you will be able to resolve what to do next. I know that Faith and I are going to be doing some soul searching tonight as well."

Once we were alone in the car I wasn't sure what to say next. Phoenix was silent during the entire spectacular event. I had no idea what to expect.

"What do we do now?" That was all I could say.

"Well Imani, I suppose we follow the plan. I am not quite sure yet about all the details but, I am now confident that there is a plan," he said with confidence.

"Does this plan happen to include me?" I asked.

"Include you? Of course it includes you. It is your plan. I will need to take care of some financial arrangements at home before we return back to St. Augustine. I predict by the holidays? What do you think?" Phoenix asked, smiling.

"Are you inviting me to go with you to London and then move to St. Augustine, Phoenix?" I asked, amazed.

"Naturally. You will need to meet my mother before we marry. And, once we get all the finances arranged we can start by opening our local nonprofit restaurant near Lincolnville. I already have the perfect location in downtown St. Augustine. What do you say about naming it, *El Agape?*"

"Have you totally lost your mind? Whatever gave you the idea that I wanted to marry you, Phoenix?" I said, a little angry but primarily disgusted.

For the past four months, with maybe the exception of the Lighthouse incident at Santander, we were rivals. Phoenix was determined to locate *The Agape*, make a fortune, and return to his extravagant playboy lifestyle. Not even the impressive spiritual awakening that we experienced tonight could convince me that this man was ready for any lifetime commitment.

"Alright, you might be correct about the marriage proposal, but you have to admit that the restaurant idea at St. Augustine is a great idea," Phoenix said, still wheeling and dealing.

I did have to admit that I liked the idea of opening a restaurant in St. Augustine that would support the homeless community. But, the only way that this would ever work is if we agreed to become equal partners.

"If you are really serious about a partnership, you should understand that my move to St. Augustine will be to complete the programs that my dad started. I have saved enough money to at least try to make this work for a while," I said, thinking out loud.

"Well then we have an agreement. Equal partners. You can even have an attorney draw up a contract. Make it as professional as you like," Phoenix said, extending his hand for me to shake to confirm our agreement.

I am not sure exactly why, but I did it. The very worst that could happen is that our endeavor would be a fiasco. Phoenix and I could always go back to our old lifestyle if that occurred.

The image that I could not erase in my mind was this carpet with all its splendor, renewing my enthusiasm for human nature. This was a new stimulating awareness that I now had about the universe, allowing me for the very first time to appreciate the ebb and flow between polar bodies.

The time was now to let go of all my insecurities. It was time now to accept that this cosmos is a beautiful creation of God.

Epilogue

> The future belongs to those who believe in the beauty of their dreams.
> — Eleanor Roosevelt

Two years later
October 2019
St. Augustine, Florida

When Phoenix Baldwin left Cincinnati, Ohio, to return to London; I had no expectations that he would ever return. We were both free souls, that somehow for a short time, discovered that within us is a spirit that recognizes our true authenticity. But, would that be enough to bring him back?

Maybe. At least, when I visited Cassadaga, the psyche resort near St. Augustine, my spiritual advisor suggested that I be patient. This was enough for me at the moment.

Soon after that metaphysical experience, I located a deserted building in Lincolnville that needed to be completely refurbished. It was originally a neighborhood market located on Bridge and Cordova Street near the park, where various civic and religious groups distribute food to the homeless.

When I hired a building contractor to convert the market to a restaurant, I soon learned that it would require more funds than I expected. If *El Agape* was ever going to happen, I would need to make some serious decisions as soon as possible.

Just as I was about to admit that this project would never be completed, Phoenix Baldwin resurfaced from nowhere.

"Were you ever going to call me, Lady Bud?" Phoenix said, walking into the front of a skeleton building.

Immediately I recognized his voice. When I turned around, there he was, looking exactly the same as when he left sixth months earlier.

"Are you here as a tourist Mr. Baldwin," I asked, trying not to show my excitement.

"What do you think, smart ass?"

That was all he said. Eight months later, *El Agape* opened its doors with a grand celebration. It was the only restaurant downtown that offered meals with no set prices. Anyone wanting to eat was always fed. Those who could afford to pay, did.

Since we are a nonprofit business many companies donate money, or food. Local ranches provide beef that we can freeze. Once a month there is a fishing tournament. All the fish caught is either donated to our restaurant, or the fish is sold. All profits go to our local pantries, including mine.

At first, many of the homeless were skeptical about eating here. But, once they realized it was safe with no restrictions, *El Agape* became their favorite location. We even hired some of the homeless people to help us with the daily undertakings.

In the back of the restaurant there was a community garden. Phoenix taught those who were curious, how to plant and care for the vegetables. A skill I had no idea that he even possessed.

Twice a year *El Agape* sold tickets to our major fundraiser event, known as *The El Agape Bounty Festival.* We reserve The Colonial Oak Music Park, invite food trucks, and musicians to feed the guests. Community volunteers serve, and clean up afterward. On a large screen we showcase our program. The highlight of this event is when former homeless people mingle with the guests. It establishes how effective our program has become.

All the money collected during these fundraisers is enough to purchase land in deserted areas for the homeless camps. Phoenix arranged for tents, wood structures, trailers, and portable bathrooms. Also included are hen houses and vegetable gardens.

These residents are taught how to maintain their villages. They also must practice proper hygiene, avoid physical conflicts, and mental abuse. Some refer to this camp as a halfway house, although there are no restrictions on how long the residents can stay. All community members are expected to contribute in some way to the commune.

Not everyone is allowed in the village. Those who are selected qualify for medical and dental care, and many other social benefits. With the assistance of the Sheriff's community service unit, a majority of the homeless are no longer roaming the streets or panhandling.

Did we solve the homeless dilemma in St. Augustine? Unfortunately not. There are still many souls that refuse assistance. Yet, there are many success stories as well.

After two years, I agreed to marry Phoenix. By this time, we both knew that it was impossible to ever live without each other. I suggested that we travel to West Chester where Pastor Liam could officiate our vows, with *The Agape* under our feet for good luck.

"Congratulations! This is an excellent idea, Imani. Just pick a date," Liam said.

"Is next month too soon? This will only be our immediate family, no need for much preparation," I said.

"No, of course it is enough time. I am looking forward to this blessed event, Imani," Liam said, before hanging up.

On February 19, 2019, at the *Lord of Grace Lutheran Church*, Phoenix Baldwin and I became man and wife. Under our feet was the ancient *Agape* carpet. There was beauty surrounding us with the majestic darkness of night, lit by celestial torches as the roaming planets returned once again to the heavens where secret infusions remain a contradiction.

It was the following morning, before the 8:00 am service, when Pastor Liam entered the sanctuary early to move *The Agape* back to its original location. But, when he approached the same altar where Phoenix and Imani exchanged their vows, twelve hours earlier, there was no carpet.

Where has The Agape gone?

Agape Appendix

Villa Zorayda St. Augustine
Sultan Room

2,000 Ancient Egypt Cat Rug

Library Room

Original Memorial Lutheran Church of the Martyrs,
St. Augustine, Florida

Interior of original Memorial Lutheran Church of the Martyrs

Current Memorial Lutheran Church of the Martyrs

Current Memorial Lutheran Church of the Martyrs

Mission de Los Nombres
St. Augustine, Florida

Cross Honoring Pedro Menendez Landing

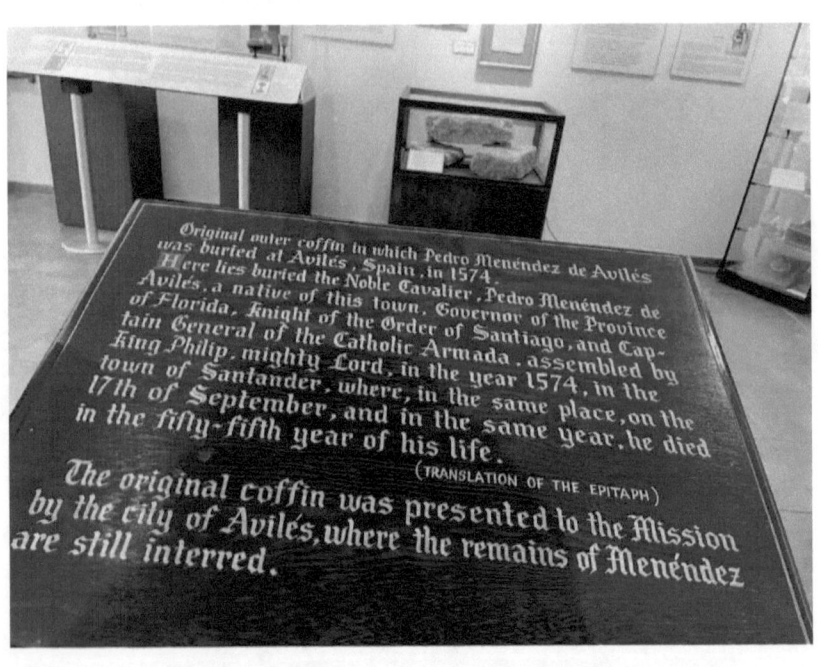

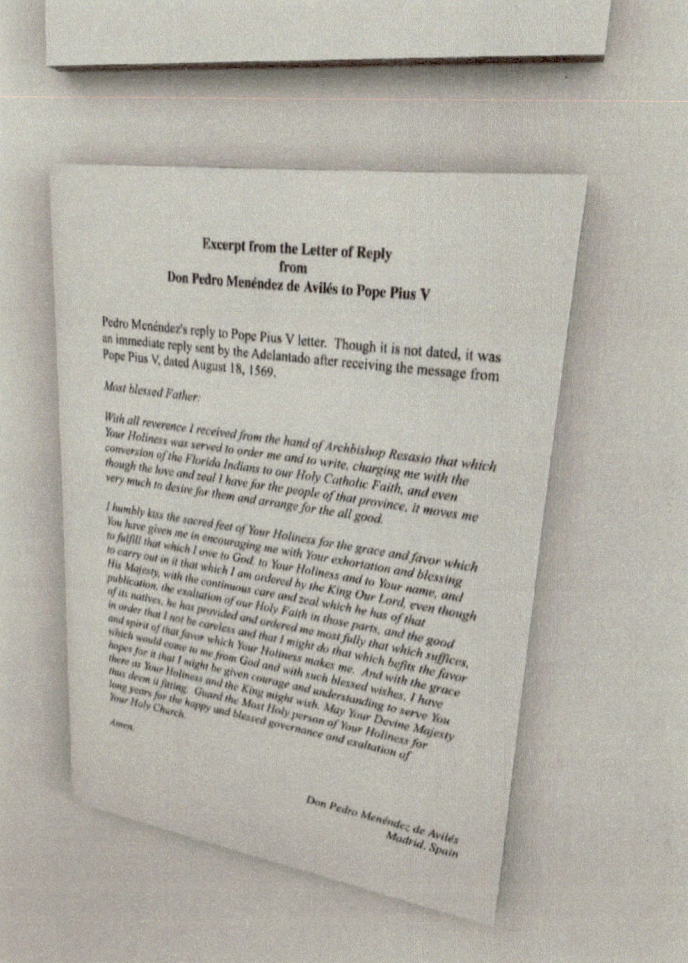

Excerpt from the Letter of Reply from Don Pedro Menéndez de Avilés to Pope Pius V

Pedro Menéndez's reply to Pope Pius V letter. Though it is not dated, it was an immediate reply sent by the Adelantado after receiving the message from Pope Pius V, dated August 18, 1569.

Most blessed Father:

With all reverence I received from the hand of Archbishop Resasio that which Your Holiness was served to order me and to write, charging me with the conversion of the Florida Indians to our Holy Catholic Faith, and even though the love and zeal I have for the people of that province, it moves me very much to desire for them and arrange for the all good.

I humbly kiss the sacred feet of Your Holiness for the grace and favor which You have given me in encouraging me with Your exhortation and blessing to fulfill that which I owe to God; to Your Holiness and to Your name, and to carry out in it that which I am ordered by the King Our Lord, even though His Majesty, with the continuous care and zeal which he has of that publication, the exaltation of our Holy Faith in those parts, and the good of its natives, he has provided and ordered me most fully that which suffices, in order that I not be careless and that I might do that which befits the favor and spirit of that favor which Your Holiness makes me. And with the grace which would come to me from God and with such blessed wishes, I have hopes for it that I might be given courage and understanding to serve You there as Your Holiness and the King might wish. May Your Devine Majesty thus deem it fitting. Guard the Most Holy person of Your Holiness for long years for the happy and blessed governance and exaltation of Your Holy Church.

Amen.

Don Pedro Menéndez de Avilés
Madrid, Spain

Original Cordova Hotel

Casa Monica

Historical Mural Casa Brava

Casa Brava Inside of Casa Monica

Alcazar Restaurant inside Lightner Museum

Columbia Restaurant

Lightner Museum

Crystal Room Lightner Museum

Stoggies Cigar Bar

Flagler College

Raintree Restaurant

Outside Patio Raintree

Lightner Inside Pool

Bibliography

Anand, Margo. *The World's Leading Expert on Tantra*. July 9, 2021

Bryant, Calvin. Explorer and Conquistador. I*ntroducing Pedro Menendez de Aviles of Spain. Florida History*, French Huguenots.

Clark, James C. *What was Flagler's Wives*. Orlando Sentinel. June 7, 1987.

Cooper, Melinda Eye. *How Would Jesus Respond to Beggars?* Crosswalk.com. July 1, 2021.

Dotson, Sarah. *Untangling the Symbolism of Art History's Most Famous Redheads*. Artsys. May 24, 2019.

Faulks, Claire. *The Amsterdam Miracl*e. 2021.

Harvey, Karen. *Meet Flagler's Three Wives*. St. Augustine Record. May 9, 2010.

Hurst, Barbara. *Thoughts on the Menendez Coffin in St. Augustine, Florida*. February 13, 2019.

Lane, Marcia. *Menendez Coffin Moved*. The St. Augustine Record. September 5, 2010.

Martinez-Diaz Rodriguez. Coleccion Canonica Hispania. 1992.

Meyendorff, John. Imperial Unity and Christian Divisions: The Church 459-680AD.1989.

Phillips, Andrew. Orthodox Christianity and the English Tradition. Farthgarth, UK. 1995.

Regan, Sarah. *The Seven Hermetic Principals & How to Use Them to Improve Your Life*, Spirituality & Relationships. February 22, 2021.

Reynolds, Tiffanie. *Menorca in our Hearts Brings Little Known Saint Augustine History to Light*. The Florida Times Union, Jacksonville, Florida.

Singer, Isidore. *The Jewish Encyclopedia*. New York, Funk and Wagnalls, 1901.

Turner, Sam. *Pedro Menendez de Aviles Judged Harshly for Mantanzas.* St. Augustine Record. October 18, 2015.

Turner, Sam. Pedro Menendez de Aviles, the end of an Alliance. St. Augustine Record. May 17, 2015.

Willits, Peter. *Where History Lives: Villa Zorayda in St. Augustine.* St. Augustine Record. March 22, 2021.

Dr. Bronson's St. Augustine History. www.drbronsontours.com. August 6, 2020.

About Us the Andean Shamans and Shipibo Shamans. Perushamans.com

America's Oldest Shrine Received National Recognition. Faithfigital.org. December 5, 2019.

Andeandiscovery.com. "Classic Inca Trail to Machu Picchu".

Baldwin Name Meaning. Houseofnames.com

Culture Sights of Santander. What to Visit. Museums, Temples, Castles, and Palaces. Orangesmile.com

Christian Symbols and Their Meaning. Ancientsymbols.com

How Egypt was Christian Before the Birth of Christ. Alarbiya News. May 20, 2020.

Inca Trail Trek. Alpaca expeditions.com

Florida Traveler. *A Religious Massacre Haunts This Tiny Florida Island.*

Machu Picchu. Sacredland.org

Machu Picchu History. Machupicchu.org

Mission of Nombres de Dios/Shrine of our Lady of La Leche. Florida Historic Coast. September 2015.

Prince of Peace Church. Mission and Shrine organization.

Queen's Gambit. The Chess Website.

Sanctuary Lodge Machu Picchu. www.jacadatravel.com

The Grave Girl Cemetery. Cemetery Blogger. February 12, 2019.

"The Main Characters". Anne Frank Website, September 25, 2018.

The Past and Present of Historic Tolomato Cemetery, St. Augustine, Florida. Tolomato Cemetery Times. June 7, 2015.

The Great Cross. Mission shrine.org. August 6, 2015.

The Hauntings of Casa de Suenos. Ghostcitytours.com

The World's Oldest Rug. Villazorayada.com.

Visions, Fades and History of Saint Augustine, One Fade at a Time. Floridapast.com.

Welcome to Criccieth in Wales. www.criccieth.org

About the Author

Eleanor Tremayne is the author of five award winning novels, Destiny Revisited, Destiny Revealed, Seven Days in Lebanon, The Mermaids Grandson, and High Tea with Ophelia. All have been recognized for innovative character development, striking settings, historical insight and elegant prose by Literary Titan Book Awards. In 2019, at The Dayton Book Expo, Seven Days in Lebanon was awarded the Best Selling Historical Novel Award.

Moving to St. Augustine, Florida in July 2019, with her husband, Mark, and her beloved Weimaraner, Enya inspires Eleanor every day to continue with her passion to write. Surrounded by all the history, creative vibes, and natural environment is the perfect setting for any artist.

Currently Mrs Tremayne is working on a play script for *High Tea with Ophelia,* and her next novel, *The St. Augustine Sisterhood.*

Eleanor continues to promote all of her novels through, speaking events, book festivals, book clubs, and creative workshops. Mrs. Tremayne is a member of The Florida Writers Association, The Amelia Island Book Festival, and Authors for Authors. You are invited to visit her website at eleanortremayne.org to view video book trailers of all her novels, upcoming events, book reviews, and newsletters.

www.ingramcontent.com/pod-product-compliance
Lightning Source LLC
LaVergne TN
LVHW091531060526
838200LV00036B/569